Praise for *Gwen & Art Are Not in Love*

"In this frivolous medieval romp of a queer rom-com, Lex Croucher toys with Arthurian legend to delightful effect."

—*Entertainment Weekly*

"Croucher's simultaneously sharp and subtle prose boasts delicious banter and a propulsive story populated by intersectionally diverse characters whose interactions feel fresh and vital through the novel's climactic conclusion."

—*Publishers Weekly* (starred review)

"Lex Croucher offers readers a quirky, queer Arthurian remix in which lighthearted, entertaining banter alternates with political machinations and intense battlefield scenes."

—*BookPage* (starred review)

"A wonderful expansion of the YA romance genre . . . Frankly a delight."

—*Kirkus Reviews*

"A high-spirited medieval adventure with a modern heart."

—*Booklist*

"A total, rollicking delight. *Gwen & Art* gave me the same cheeky, swoony, giddy, irresistible high of the first time I saw *A Knight's Tale.* Lex Croucher is one of my favorite rom-com authors, and they should be yours, too."

—Casey McQuiston, #1 *New York Times* bestselling author of *I Kissed Shara Wheeler*

"Fun and genuinely funny, with lovely friendships and first-rate dialogue. Gwen and Art may not be in love, but I fell for both of them."

—Rainbow Rowell, #1 *New York Times* bestselling author of the Simon Snow trilogy

"*Gwen & Art Are Not in Love* was exactly what I needed right now—a delightful, heartwarming, hilarious historical romp overflowing with queer panic and terrible jokes. I loved it."

—Alice Oseman, *New York Times* bestselling author of the Heartstopper series

"Congrats to Gwen and Arthur on their permanent acquisition of my *entire* heart. Suffice it to say that I loved this book to a degree that's slightly ridiculous."

—Becky Albertalli, *New York Times* bestselling author of *Kate in Waiting* and *Simon vs. the Homo Sapiens Agenda*

"An utter delight . . . This is the gay Camelot I always wanted!"

—C. S. Pacat, *New York Times* bestselling author of *Dark Rise*

"A work of hilarious and heart-mending genius. I read it in a joyous rush and I can't wait to buy it for literally everyone I know."

—Freya Marske, national bestselling author of *A Marvellous Light*

"This is the queer YA take on *A Knight's Tale* I've always dreamed of! A charming, witty, and completely unputdownable adventure."

—Ava Reid, *New York Times* bestselling author of *A Study in Drowning*

NOT FOR THE FAINT OF HEART

Books by Lex Croucher

Gwen and Art Are Not in Love
Not for the Faint of Heart

Reputation
Infamous
Trouble

NOT FOR THE FAINT OF HEART

LEX CROUCHER

WEDNESDAY BOOKS
NEW YORK

This is a work of fiction. All of the characters, organizations, and events portrayed in this novel are either products of the author's imagination or are used fictitiously.

First published in the United States by Wednesday Books,
an imprint of St. Martin's Publishing Group

www.wednesdaybooks.com

The Library of Congress Cataloging-in-Publication Data is available upon request.

ISBN 978-1-250-84723-2 (hardcover)
ISBN 978-1-250-84724-9 (ebook)

Our books may be purchased in bulk for promotional, educational, or business use. Please contact your local bookseller or the Macmillan Corporate and Premium Sales Department at 1-800-221-7945, extension 5442, or by email at MacmillanSpecialMarkets@macmillan.com.

Originally published in the United Kingdom by Bloomsbury YA
First published in the United States by Wednesday Books

First U.S. Edition: 2024

10 9 8 7 6 5 4 3 2 1

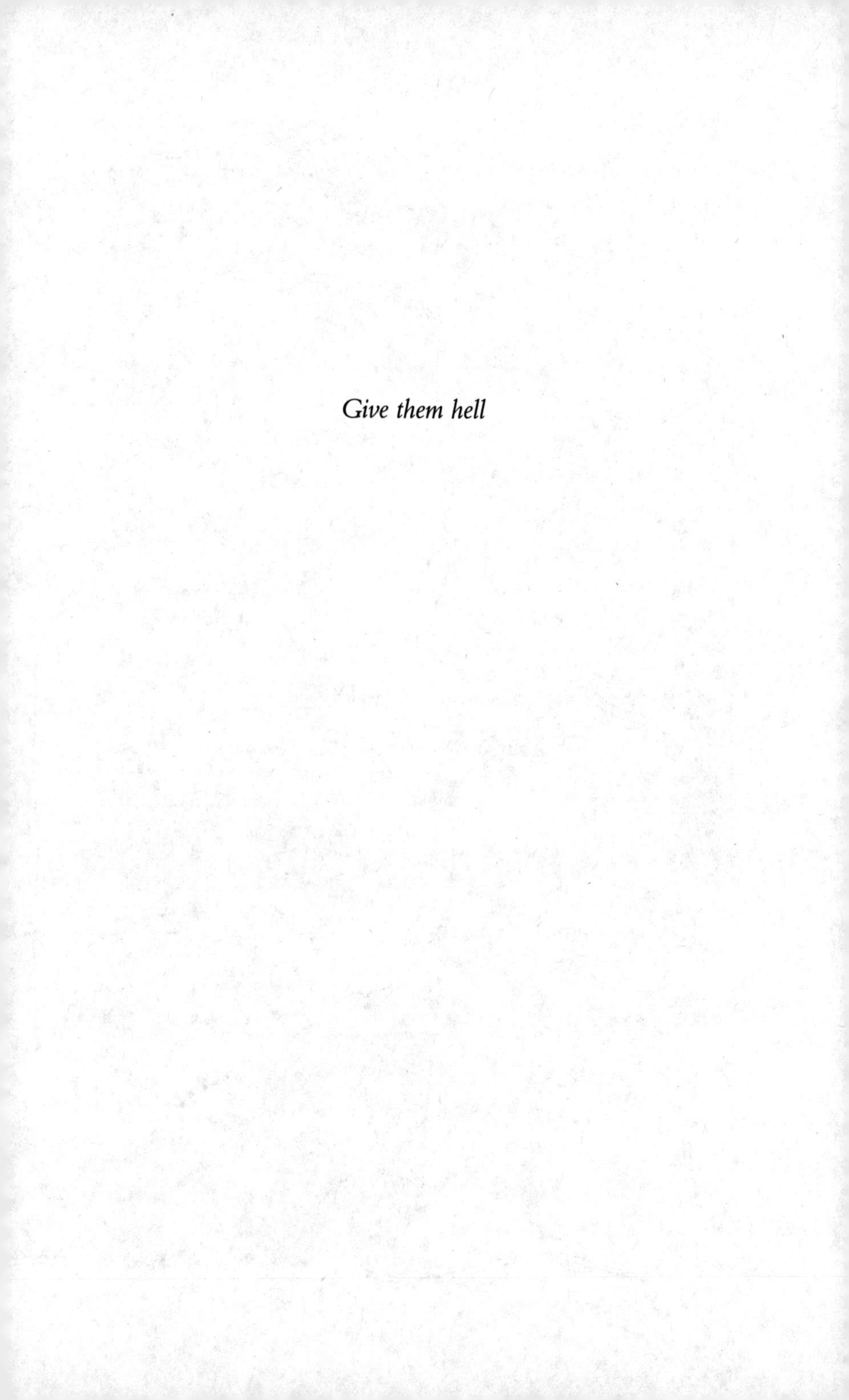

Give them hell

UNDERWOOD

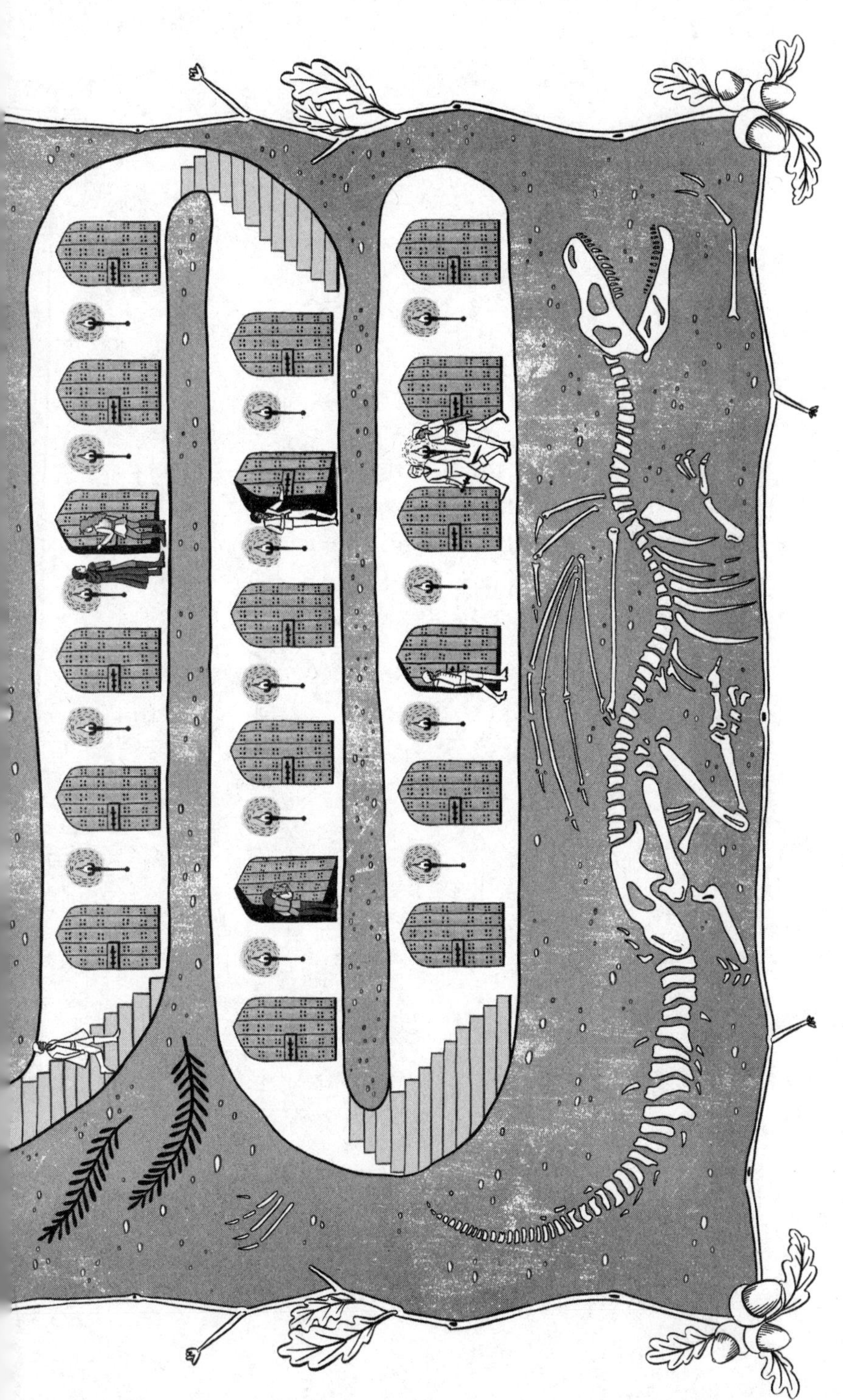

Author's Note

This book takes place in an alternative fantasy timeline, so please don't be alarmed by potatoes and other less delicious inaccuracies, as they are entirely intentional. Also, a word of warning: the journey our characters are about to embark on will, at times, be *very* perilous.

1

The morning the Merry Men came for Old Rosie, Clem was trying to put a hat on a fox.

She felt quite bad about this later.

At the time it had seemed important; the fox had become tame enough to take scraps of meat and twists of hide directly from her hand, and putting a hat on him was the next logical step.

The construction of said hat had somewhat consumed her morning. She had visited the seamstress over by the river and come away with some soiled felt, unfit for trade; she'd swapped a little sage tea with Jon, who had a chronic sore throat, for a single turkey feather, just the right size to accessorize a small vulpine head.

She had been waylaid for a while by the miller's boy, Alfred, who was seven and had scraped both his knees raw but was being very, very brave about it. His elder sister Loos squeezed his hand while Clem blotted his wounds with thinned honey, and then wasted a narrow strip of bandage on him, sending him home a proud, wounded warrior. Rosie always grumbled that Clem was too free with both her compassion and her supplies, but she could hardly argue that they were in dire need right now. Clem's penchant for *experimenting* was earning her quite the reputation, and had been attracting the sort of customers who paid in actual coin rather than stray bits of ham and pats on the head. They weren't well-off by any stretch of the imagination, but tying linen bows on Alfred's bloody knees wasn't going to tip them over into destitution.

Shaping the offcut of felt into something hat-shaped had taken a sweet half hour, sitting with her boots off in a stretch of buttery sunlight in the far reaches of the garden, among Rosie's ramshackle beds of mint, soft lavender and elder. The fox had made a few appearances, poking his head out of the woods to snuffle for treats and glare accusingly at her when none were to be found. He'd chosen the right garden to frequent; anyone with livestock would have made it their life's mission to see him turned into cloak-lining, but Clem and Rosie had been told very firmly by Jon that their temperaments were "ill-suited to the needs of chickens," so Rosie's beds remained eggless and the fox was free to come and go as he pleased.

When Clem had finally reached a hattish conclusion, she fetched a soup bone, still stringy with meat, and offered it up with an enticing wiggle.

"Good little lads get hats," she said, not bothering to talk soft or low; this fox was used to her by now, and would only have been suspicious of a gentle cajole. "Bad little lads too, I suppose. A hat for every little lad, regardless of temperament—that's my guarantee."

The fox seemed indifferent to the concept of hats, but

very interested in bone meat. He approached. Clem readied the hat. The fox dithered, sensing a trap.

This continued for quite some time. Clem was so engrossed in her task that she didn't notice a knock at the front door, or hoofs on the path.

It was only when she heard something shatter inside the little house, ruining her best hatting attempt so far, that she realized something was amiss.

Her body's reaction to danger at her door was immediate.

Her chest contracted. Her breath caught. She was suddenly sweaty in strange and unexpected locations, like the insides of her elbows and the backs of her ears. For one terrible moment, she was nine again, and the world was ending.

She shook it off.

By the time she had barreled through the back door, there were two cloaked and hooded figures standing by the hearth. They were armed to the teeth and comically ominous among all the charming clutter, some of which now lay broken and smashed underfoot. One of them had Old Rosie—who wasn't really that old, but had lived long enough to wrinkle around the edges, like she'd soaked for too long in the bath of life—with both hands pinned behind her back.

From the color of their cloaks, it was immediately apparent that these were Merry Men. Merry Men! Standing in Clem's house! Threatening Clem's Rosie!

She would have asked for autographs if she weren't prioritizing finding a weapon.

"Hullo, Clemmie," Rosie said, perky as ever. "Is it my birthday?"

"No," said Clem, groping around on the table next to her for something sharp. "At least . . . I don't think so. Is it?"

"It's not," said the enormous man who had Rosie pinned. "Well . . . it might be. I don't know when your birthday is. But to be clear, that's not why we're here."

"It's just, you're awfully handsome," Rosie said, trying to twist in the young man's grip to get a better look at him. "And *strong*. I don't go in much for Merry Men, but if they all looked like *you* . . ."

Clem snorted. "He's not *handsome*, Rosie, he's kidnapping you."

"When you've been around for as long as I have, Clemence, you'll begin to understand that these things are not mutually exclusive."

Clem's fingers had closed around a heavy stone pestle, still dusty with crushed fennel.

"If you came to woo her, then be my guest," she said to the large man, "but it's a little presumptuous to grab first, and it's *very* telling that you had to bring a friend along for moral support."

The other hooded figure, who was approximately a third of the size of the first, made a brief, choked noise that Clem thought might have been a laugh. This held promise.

"Now, why don't I make some tea?" Clem said brightly, with a smile. That sounded nice. Tea. Tea with actual Merry Men. A bit of a misunderstanding, followed by laughs and bonding over biscuits. "Then we can all sit down for a moment and talk about why you're here, before anybody does anything—"

The door flew open, smacking against the wall and

then coming to an undignified stop, and a third person—also anonymized by a long, mossy Lincoln green cloak—entered. Their associates straightened up slightly; the tall one tightened his grip on Rosie, who said "Goodness!" not sounding nearly as upset as she should have been.

"What's this?" said the newcomer. She had a low, no-nonsense voice with a little rasp to it. "Stop dicking around."

"Not dicking," the tall man protested. "What part of this says *dicking*? Just didn't expect there to be two."

There was a brief pause, during which Clem felt the unseen eyes of this new authority upon her.

"Who is she to you?" she said to Old Rosie.

"Not sure that's really any of your business," Clem said, still friendly as ever, at the exact same time that Old Rosie said, "Well—that's my *Clem*."

The newcomer did not seem particularly moved. "We don't have time for this. Let's go."

It finally dawned on Clem that they really were going to take Rosie with them; Rosie, who never left the village of Oak Vale if she could help it, and had a bad knee, and drank her nettle tea at the same time every morning standing with her hand on her hip surveying her garden. She'd hate that. It wasn't very Merry of them at all.

"Take *me*," she said quickly. "If you need a healer. I'm good . . . ish. Young too. Sprightly, even."

"Could do, Captain," said the tall man, addressing the hood in charge. "If she's offering."

"Leverage," said the smaller person, speaking for the first time. "Right?"

"Yes," said the captain. "That's what I was about to suggest. Knock her out. Bring some of . . . this. Whatever looks useful."

"Now hang on a minute," Rosie said, struggling against her captor, finally having the good sense to sound concerned. "You can't just be *taking* people. That's not on."

"I don't like being knocked out," added Clem. "That's just a personal hang-up of mine, you understand."

She raised her pestle, readying for a fight she had no chance of winning; before she could take a single step forward, someone new grabbed her from behind, squeezing her wrist until she was forced to release her weapon. Clem hadn't even heard the back door creak. She felt a heavy blow to the back of her knees and immediately crumpled to the floor.

The only advantage of this was that she could see her pestle where it had rolled away and become wedged in the dust under the nuts, seeds and berries cabinet. She reached for it, but was stopped by a foot, which landed firmly on her forearm and pressed her gently into the floor.

"What are you even going to do with that?" said her unseen assailant, irritatingly wry. "Ask me to lie still and grind me into a fine powder?"

"Enough," snapped the kidnapper-in-chief. "Let's go. And you"—Clem could only assume that Rosie was being addressed now, as she was at entirely the wrong angle to see for herself—"you know why we're here. We must all act in the best interests of the people of the wood."

"That's funny," Clem said into the packed dirt of the floor. "Because I sort of thought I was one of *the people of the wood*, and I'm over here being pummeled."

Her attacker removed her foot, and then hauled Clem to her feet. “This wasn’t a pummeling,” she said in a low, amused voice. “It was closer to a massage.”

Clem glimpsed the young woman under the hood—umber skin, a black braid and a flash of a smile—before a blindfold was slipped neatly over her eyes.

“No offense, but I wouldn’t like to be the receiving end of—”

“Bye now.”

Clem’s mouth was prized open with firm precision; she tasted the sharp, vinegary tang of dwale on her tongue before the world blinked out.

2

There was something wrong with one of the front wheels of the wagon, and Mariel had already lost half a fingernail trying to fix it. She was regretting removing her leather gloves, which had been necessary to get a proper feel under the hub; she was having second thoughts about jamming her fingers in there again at all, now that she was lightly bleeding.

Unfortunately, she had declared that it would be an easy fix and shoved Morgan aside to do the thing properly; anything less than perfect future rotations from the wheel in question would be unacceptable.

"It's probably because this is more of a potato wagon," said Morgan, who was now kicking sullenly around the back wheels, "and not a potatoes-and-dead-bodies wagon."

They were parked in the trees, out of sight of the village; Mariel was grateful for the small mercy of not having to try to fix a wagon in full view of local urchins, farmers and lollygaggers, who would have been suitably intimidated by their green cloaks at first, but might have been less so as they watched her trying to jam a wheel back onto the axle with a bleeding hand and a hood that kept falling over her eyes as she worked. The horses were standing about looking politely bemused, but they were disciplined enough not to wander away or start grazing the shrubs. If only her people were quite so well-behaved.

"She's not dead," said Josey, leaning over to check their cargo. "She's just resting her eyes." One of Josey's older sisters had spent hours meticulously combing and braiding her hair back at camp, and she had taken those hundreds of tiny braids and pulled them into one tight, single plait that started at the top of her crown and brushed her shoulder blades as she straightened up.

Morgan's hair was a self-shorn shag of dark feathers, and they liked to glare sullenly out from underneath their fringe like a wildcat sizing you up from under a bush, as they were doing now; the effect was ruined slightly by the fact that they were a foot shorter than Josey, who was lithe and rangy and made no effort to look threatening at all. This made it all the more satisfying when somebody underestimated her so thoroughly that they were unconscious before they realized she had stopped smiling.

If Mariel had been allowed to pick her own company, Josey Abara was one of the only names that she would have written willingly on her list.

Morgan, on the other hand, had been assigned to Mariel's company because absolutely nobody else was willing to take on a green fourteen-year-old who had managed to pack enough rage and apathy for a lifetime into just a decade and a half. Mariel was constantly weighing up how incompetent she'd look if she "accidentally" left Morgan behind one day on a patrol—or let them fall into a fast-running river, or sent them on an errand and then instructed everybody else to run away very fast—against how peaceful and orderly she might find a Morganless existence.

Alas, Baxter would never stand for it.

He came to crouch next to Mariel by the wheel now, his bulk so substantial that it was like a big, blond hillock had taken up residence at her shoulder. Despite her previous insistence that she could fix a goddamned wheel by herself, he wedged his enormous hands under the bed and lifted the entire front half of the wagon from the ground.

"Reckon there's a stone jammed in there," Baxter said, his voice as even as always and barely strained. "You might want to poke it with a knobby stick, Captain."

Mariel was not going to do anything as undignified as *poking it with a knobby stick*; she poked it with her finger instead, despite the risk of further violent de-nailing, and when it came loose, Baxter gently lowered the wagon back down onto the ground. He at least had the good grace to look slightly embarrassed by this latest in a long line of Herculean feats.

He leaned in, darting a glance at their cargo and then aiming soft concern in her direction. "She *isn't* dead, is she?"

"No," Mariel said, not bothering to lower her own voice. She'd checked that herself, when they'd loaded the oddly cheerful girl up next to the supplies. The healer's companion was shorter than she'd looked in the cottage, but she was by no means small. She had spring-curled hair the color of milled flax, ropy pink-and-white scars on her palms, and legs that looked so capable of kicking that Mariel had been glad that she was unconscious, even if knocking her out had been a little overzealous on Josey's part. She had definitely been breathing.

"Good. 'Cause it was good of her to offer to come."

"Good of her?" said Mariel, wiping her finger impatiently on her tunic, the blood mostly vanishing among the dark, mottled green. "She's not on a summer jaunt, Scarlet. This was a tactical decision. We're killing two birds with one stone: healer for us, and it sends a message."

"Right," said Baxter, frowning. "And the message says . . ."

It said: pick your side, and then stay on it. Remember what's being fought for. Remember who the good guys are. Don't fuck with the good guys.

The message was for Mariel's father too. If he thought she couldn't handle anything more than a company of dull-witted children and easy retrieval missions, she'd show him that she could think like a leader; that she could be bold, and enterprising, and ruthless. He'd have no choice but to respect her, when all her victories were laid at his feet.

Ultimately, it was a very good thing that it wasn't the sort of message that needed to be written down, because it was too bloody long.

"People often demonstrate a troubling lack of self-preservation," was all Mariel said in reply. "Threaten somebody they love, and suddenly they're all ears. She offered herself instead—that means they care for each other. We can use that. Do you think the old woman is going to step out of line again, knowing we have her ward?"

"I do love it when you talk like that," said Josey, from where she was strapping some of the non-human cargo down. "Brutal. Bloodthirsty. It makes me feel so warm and fuzzy inside."

Such insubordination from anybody less useful would have pushed Mariel from generally perturbed to very pissed off. Josey had earned a generous helping of leniency.

Mariel glared at her anyway. "I'm just being practical."

The wheel was fixed, the cargo secured. They were expected to rendezvous with other companies shortly to trade off supplies with those traveling elsewhere in the wood, and then it'd be back to camp to deliver the miniature healer and receive further instruction. "Where the hell is Chisaka? I told him not to go far."

The last member of her small troop appeared instantly. Apparently he'd returned from the wood while she'd been elbow-deep in wheel, and had since been talking to the horse harnessed to the wagon.

"Was she like this when you took her?" he said, leaning over the wagon to look at their captive; she watched him extend a hand as if he might be about to touch her neck to check for her heartbeat, and then stop before he made contact. "Or was she more . . . you know. Upright? Conscious?"

"She's fine," Mariel said, taut with impatience. "*Leave her.* We need to go." Kit had a haphazard bouquet of weedy-looking yellow flowers in the other hand. When he saw Mariel looking, he smiled.

"The St. John's is out," he said, waving it at her. "First blooms."

Mariel sighed, because it stopped her from shouting. She'd been told that *shouting* was not conducive to a healthy working environment.

Whatever. She needed a tightly knit unit of trained, disciplined fighters; what she had were infants, gentle giants, aspiring florists. She would very begrudgingly admit that most of them could fight well enough, but at what cost?

For example: instead of hopping to it and taking charge of the wagon so that they could depart, Kit was now showing Morgan the flowers and repeating excitedly, "St. John's wort."

Morgan said, "St. John's what?"

And Kit said, "Exactly!"

This was the sort of thing that, quite frankly, made Mariel want to kill them all.

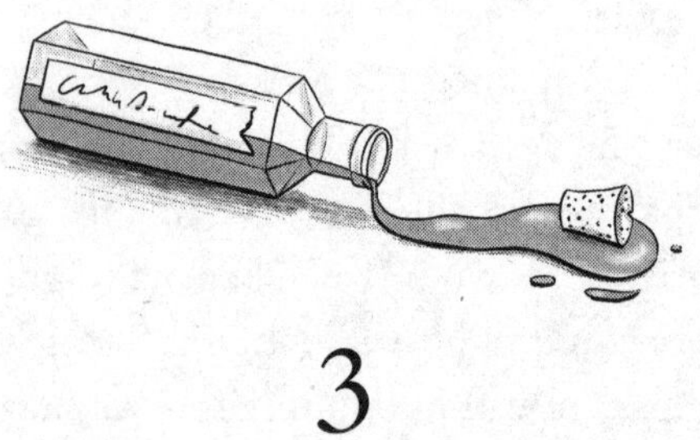

3

Clem came back into her body slowly. She could see something bright and green overhead (most likely trees). She could feel the trundle of wheels below her, smell the sweet hay-and-earth of horses (all signs pointed to a wagon). Her hands were tied, and she was lying on her back, which was so medically irresponsible she would have screamed if it weren't for the fact that something had been shoved into her mouth. The blindfold had at least slipped, so she could squint out of one eye. Never skimp on blindfolds! What kind of kidnappers were these?

"Squirrel," said someone to her left. "That's fifty-seven to forty-nine. You're screwed."

"Could have been a pigeon," someone grunted. Clem knew *that* voice. It was Rosie's tall, handsome birthday present.

"*You* could have been a pigeon," said the first voice sulkily.

"You can't just say words in any order like they're an insult. You have to make it personal. Like, what are my insecurities? My hang-ups? Start there."

"Morgan. Baxter. Enough."

Clem rolled over very slightly onto her side. The enormous young man was riding on her right, astride what must have been a draft horse. His hood was down, revealing a generous quantity of floppy blond hair, which bounced cheerfully as he rode. His nose had been broken and badly set, or likely not set at all, and he was lightly tanned. There was a long, thick scar running from his temple and tapering out just under his right eye, where he'd clearly had a near miss. *Baxter,* Clem decided. Baxter was a good name for a very large man.

This meant that the short, scowling, fair-skinned brunette person on the much more reasonably sized horse next to him was Morgan.

Morgan made direct eye contact with Clem and jumped. "Ugh! Is she meant to be awake?"

There were general noises of interest; the cart slowed slightly and curved to the left, as if the driver had turned their whole body to look and confused the horses.

"Nah. I dwaled her." This was clearly Clem's wry assailant.

"*Dwaled* her?" said a new voice. "Was she threatening you?"

"She was trying to pestle me."

"To *what* you?"

"I could tell she wouldn't have gone quietly. And I was told in no uncertain terms to bring her quickly and quietly. No fuss."

"All right. Take the reins, will you? I'm going back."

A young Nihonjin man with blue-black, closely cropped hair and freckled fawn skin dropped into Clem's field of vision. His movements were controlled and precise despite the fact that the cart was moving; even in her half-addled state, there was something about the way he used his hands that scratched pleasantly at the back of Clem's brain.

"Hello," he said, peering at her, a frown wrinkling his forehead. He pulled her blindfold down so that it was resting around her neck. "Are you experiencing any stomach cramps, nausea, or violent hallucinations?"

Clem shook her head. She was feeling a little gently poisoned and woozy, but it was nothing to write home about.

"Are you thirsty?"

Clem nodded an emphatic yes. He helped her up into a sitting position, back against a sack of something lumpy, and then paused.

"There's no point in screaming, all right? No dramatics. We're miles from anywhere. You'll just get me into trouble, so . . . you know. Don't."

He eased the rag out of her mouth and then smoothly lifted his waterskin to her lips. She took a few awkward gulps, water streaming down her neck and beading in her curls, before leaning back and frowning at him.

"Dwale isn't for knocking people out on a whim, you know. It's for *surgery*. And only to be used in the most dire of circumstances. It's hemlock soup!"

"Yeah, well. You don't have to tell *me* that," said the young man affably, with a quick glance upward. "The captain likes efficiency. Josey's sorry."

"Kit, you idiot. Don't tell her names," said Morgan.

Clem catalogued this away. The captain gave the orders. Josey was her efficient right-hand woman. This guy was

Kit. Despite herself, she was intrigued. It was like being invited to join the best circle with the most popular kids at a dance—if the popular kids knocked you out first and then trussed you up with rope (which, for all Clem knew, they did). The Merry Men had always been folklore, myth, and legend; they were a flash of green in the wood that you hoped might be a cloak, and the distant sound of hoofbeats at night as you lay in bed dreaming of brave deeds and wildwood adventures.

Over the years, the reality of the Merry Men—silent figures who barely seemed to exist to the people of a small village like Oak Vale, distant players in a war for Nottinghamshire that had been going on for decades—had somewhat dampened her dreams of donning a green cloak of her own, but they hadn't quite been extinguished.

It was all just a *little* bit exciting.

"You haven't asked if I have muscle pain, an increased heart rate, or excess salivation."

Kit sat back on his heels. "Well, you aren't screaming in pain, your breathing seems fine, and you aren't drooling. Plus, you're a regional healer—"

"Assistant to a regional healer."

"Fine, *assistant* healer, so I imagine you'd be sounding the alarm if you suspected you were dying of hemlock poisoning."

"If I were dying of hemlock poisoning there'd be no cure."

Kit reached for a large, dented chest and pulled it toward him. When he flipped the latch and opened it, Clem recognized a jumble of her and Rosie's supplies. Some of it made sense; bandages, bottles of tincture, the little bag Clem took with her for on-the-go emergencies. Some of it was leftovers from yesterday's lunch. "What do you prescribe for yourself then? Ginger?"

"You know about ginger?"

"The concept of ginger? I'm familiar," said Kit. "I know a fair bit about plants. Mostly the ones you eat for fun, but I can do practical, if pushed."

"There should be a bottle of barley water in there, if it's not already broken. And . . . give me some peppermint."

"Kit," said Baxter, putting one enormous hand over the edge of the cart and tapping the wood. "Coming up to the rendez-point."

"Just a second," Kit said, picking through the contents for Clem's barley water.

Baxter tapped again, harder. "Captain is coming back, Kit."

The wagon pulled off the road and into the trees, still going slightly too fast for comfortable forest-maneuvering. It was not doing Clem's roiling stomach any favors. The wheel hit something hefty and they bounced, the bottle in Kit's hand making a bid for freedom. He snatched it out of the air with impressive dexterity, then uncorked it with a flick of his thumb and began the undignified process of pouring more liquid into her mouth. The wagon rolled to a bumpy stop. It was while Clem was in this position, mouth agape, barley water flying, that the aforementioned captain returned.

"What are you doing, Chisaka?"

She was riding a dignified black horse, and was the

only one still hooded; her cloak had looked the same as the others back at Rosie's, dyed the verdant, dappled greens of the wood, but now Clem noticed that it was slightly darker, more pine than pasture, and fastened at the throat with a dull bronze pin in the shape of an oak leaf. Underneath, a glimpse of dark boiled leather armor and yet more green. They were all *very* committed to the theme.

Kit didn't remove the barley water, but he did shift uncomfortably in his squat.

"She didn't need to be knocked out."

"Josey was following my orders."

"I gathered that. To be clear: I was questioning your initiative, not hers. Anyway, she's a healer, so she—"

"I don't care, Chisaka. You shouldn't be back here having a juice picnic. And if she's conscious, she needs to be blindfolded."

"It's barley water," said Clem, knowing she had some dripping down her chin. "It's good for dehydration." Nobody seemed interested, but Clem pressed on, even attempting a smile. "When you poison somebody, sometimes they get a bit thirsty. Other times they die, horribly, writhing in a pile of their own shit. That's what makes it so fun! It's the luck of the draw!" She would have added a little flourish with her hands to really drive the point home, but they were tied.

Both Kit and the captain stared mutely at her for a moment, and then the latter abruptly turned her horse to leave.

"She was gagged for a reason."

Kit re-corked the empty bottle with care and then gave her an apologetic shrug, reaching for the gag.

Clem weaved to avoid him like a baby ducking a spoon. "Can you tell me why I've been taken?"

"Er . . ." Kit glanced over his shoulder. "I'll let the captain tell you."

Clem had been trying to puzzle it out and had decided that there was no way the Merry Men had carried out a cold-blooded kidnapping for no reason, even if Rosie *was* right that they were not the cheerful bandits of yore (for some reason Rosie didn't like it when Clem referred to her childhood years as "yore"). There must have been a plan; a higher purpose that had not yet made itself known.

"Do you need a healer for an important mission? Have you heard tell of my excellent innovations and experiments? People misattribute those to Rosie—maybe they think I'm too young for genius, I don't know . . . She does help a bit, but the ideas are mine. I don't have my things here with me, but if you'll get me something to write with, I can—"

"I wouldn't worry about that," said Kit. "But, uh . . . for now, you're our captive."

"Your captive?" said Clem, her brow furrowed. "I have to be honest. That doesn't sound merry. And you aren't all men. So there's been a bit of marketing confusion at some point down the line."

Kit treated her to a very small smile.

"It's easier to write on the pamphlets than *A collection of people experiencing a full range of emotions.*"

Clem just had time to say, "Yes, but think of the wanted posters," before he carefully replaced the gag. He also rejigged the blindfold back into place, but it had clearly been tied too loosely in the first place; Clem immediately discovered that she was able to shift one eye slightly free again via vigorous blinking. She watched him dust off his hands and glance around, reorienting himself, before bending to pick up a sack of something almost the same size as him. He managed it—he must have been packing some serious lean muscle under that cloak—but it was obviously a bit of a strain; Baxter the friendly giant stopped him with a gentle hand to his shoulder and then easily hauled it out of the cart one-armed. Kit looked slightly wrong-footed and ducked his head, grabbing a smaller bag at random and then hopping lightly off the end of the wagon and carrying it out of Clem's sight.

Clem tested the rope at her wrists. Annoyingly tight. She wasn't actually attached to anything, but none of her kidnappers seemed particularly worried. Perhaps they thought she was still too woozy. Maybe they imagined she'd be too afraid of the fathomless, creeping reaches of the greenwood to try.

If so, they were idiots. Clem and the greenwood were old friends.

4

It hadn't always been that way. Clem couldn't remember the first time she'd been lost in the wood, but she remembered the worst time.

Nine years old, eyes swollen mostly shut, and barely breathing, pushing onward through snagging brambles and a constant stream of tears. Her hands had been a mess of blood, her lungs screaming. It had grown dark around her until every groan was a ghoul, every rustle a wolf. She and her mother had walked the wood near their house a hundred times with their homemade woven baskets, following the same well-worn route until Clem knew it by heart, her ma humming an old walking song and pointing out the plants that would help stanch bleeding or calm the mind as she gathered them—but Clem had never ventured farther than a few hundred feet away, even when she started taking walks alone; had always eventually found the route back to the storm-blackened stump and curve in the stream that marked the way home. That terrible day when the world had turned upside down she'd sat frozen all night in the teeth of a tree and been near-delirious by morning—but that hadn't been the worst of it.

Kneeling on a bed of foul-smelling mulch two days later, staring down at the puny mushrooms in her red-raw hand, trying to recall what exactly her ma had told her about the signs of poison, unable to dredge up a single word or even the sound of her mother's voice as her stomach devoured itself. *That* had been the worst.

She'd eaten the mushrooms. She hadn't died immediately. Unbelievably, she hadn't died at all. Later, she'd decided this was due to a fortitude of spirit that had impressed the wood. Rosie had called it a perverse inclination toward optimism and had implied that it would have been a better lesson if the mushrooms had poisoned her, just a little bit.

She had never told Rosie this, but it felt like from the moment those mushrooms touched her lips, the greenwood had opened up for her. Like it *wanted* her to live. She found more mushrooms, soft ears sprouting on the elder. Fat, ripe blackberries. A stream that became a river; a river that led her to Oak Vale, and Rosie, who had found Clem starving and filthy, eating apple after apple in her garden and immediately held the back door open with a roll of her eyes and told her to come inside.

The wood was so big that even though many had tried to map it, they never seemed to be able to confine it to a piece of parchment; it sprawled and wended, crammed itself into valleys and spilled out into meadows, turning up where you didn't expect it and coming to a sudden end when you were counting on it carrying on for miles. It was ridiculous to think that something so vast cared about the fate of one nine-year-old Clem, weeping and useless, vomit in her hair and a scream trapped in her throat.

Luckily, Clem *was* ridiculous. She prided herself on her commitment to the absurd.

The wood wasn't giving her any clues right now, but it didn't matter; it would be there when she needed it. The clearing they had pulled into had no identifying features, no memorably weird trees, no helpful wooden signs telling her exactly how many miles away she was from Oak Vale. It was a wonder that the Merry Men had found it at all—but then, they had their own relationship with the greenwood, on terms that weren't for Clem to know.

The mysterious captain reappeared, still on horseback and properly hooded, unlike the rest of her company. Perhaps, Clem reasoned, she had a face complex. Or a particularly complex face.

"Wheels east and west. They'll be here in a moment."

"Yeah," muttered Morgan. "We know, Mariel. Because they said they'd be at the rendez-point at noon, and we're at the rendez-point, and it's noon."

"What was that, Parry?"

Morgan straightened up. "Nothing, Captain."

"Put your hood back up and be quiet."

Everybody re-hooded. It was fascinating to Clem; the rest of the Merry Men seemed to believe that they were taking part in a jolly forest jape, while their leader—Mariel—was clearly convinced she was running a serious military operation.

There was a loud, swooping bird call from somewhere just out of sight. Clem was trying to place it—a larger-than-usual robin? A very horny blackbird?—when Josey came striding into view. She was delightfully tall, with deep brown skin and intricate braids pulled back into a practical plait, and her cloak was cut differently from the others—shorter, curved to points, like the wings of a bat. Maybe it was better for maneuverability. Maybe she had a note from the captain, allowing her to alter her uniform. She had the sort of smile—slow-burning, warm with more than a little edge—that you might want to invent special rules to accommodate. She caught Clem looking, winked, then lifted her fingers to her mouth and answered the bird with an identical whistle of her own. A third call came a second later, and then two parties thundered around opposite corners, their wagons surrounded by hooded horsemen, and converged.

Clem felt as if she were witnessing some kind of majestic fish-spawning event or rare goose migration; she had spent her entire life in the wood, knowing that the Merry Men must be all around her, wondering if they were passing her on just the other side of a thicket of trees or the opposite bank of a stream, never able to glimpse more than one or two cloaked figures who came through the village, allowing themselves to be seen.

This was beyond anything she'd ever dreamed she'd witness firsthand. It felt like there must have been at least sixty or seventy of them, a fast-moving swarm of leather-booted feet and billowing cloaks, moving with purpose as they dismounted from horses and jumped down from wagons. They looked competent and practiced; they looked like they could take down an army or organize a wedding feast for two hundred at the last minute with ruthless efficiency.

Clem, on the other hand, looked like a trussed chicken with hair. It wasn't the sort of first impression one liked to make on childhood heroes. Especially when it was so easy to imagine that underneath their hoods, they might all be *extremely* handsome.

Everybody was in motion, loading and unloading so that they could swap supplies, a coordinated dance featuring flying vegetables and chests that clinked suspiciously, likely full of shinier plunder.

Baxter leaned over and pulled Clem's half-arsed blindfold fully off, then tapped on the chest full of her and Rosie's medical supplies.

"Anything valuable in here?"

Clem tried to say, "Well, I'm hardly going to say yes if there is, am I?" but it came out as muffled nonsense.

"Gotcha," said Baxter. He paused. "How valuable are *you*, personally?"

Clem shrugged.

"Aw, don't be so down on yourself." Clem almost jumped out of her skin; Josey had somehow appeared on the wagon behind her and was rummaging for something in a bag. "You might be worth as much as a goat, at least. Little one. With mange."

"*Famks,*" Clem enunciated into her gag.

She watched Josey saunter down the length of the wagon and then land noiselessly on the ground.

Why was everybody here so *good* at things? It was extremely distracting.

There were more hoofs on the road; heads snapped up everywhere, but relaxed slightly once the riders came into view.

Three men thundered into the clearing on horseback. Their backs were straight, and their cloaks were dark; the man in the middle was dressed head to toe in black.

Black didn't seem particularly practical for the wood, but Clem didn't suppose he was going for practicality. Menace, more like. And he was succeeding in being a tad menacing.

"Uh-oh," Morgan muttered from next to the wagon. "Daddy Hartley."

Kit made a strangled sound in response; through the gaps in the wooden boards to her left, Clem saw him give Morgan a little shove of warning.

"No '*Daddy Hartley*,'" he hissed back.

Finally, a name that meant something. Not the Daddy part, good Lord, but the rest. It stood to reason that the man in the middle—the pale, dark-haired one in black who dismounted abruptly and was immediately met by the frosty Mariel and two other captainly figures from the newly arrived parties—was Jack Hartley.

Old Rosie might have been willing to forgive the handsome for all manner of crimes, but Jack Hartley's free pass had been emphatically revoked long ago.

She was always telling Clem that back in *her* day—Clem often tried to leave when these stories began, but Rosie had a knack for catching her when she was doing something delicate to a sock or was elbows-deep in plums, so she couldn't escape—back in *her* day, the Merry Men had been kindhearted, scrappy thieves who stole from the rich, gave to the poor, and looked good doing it. There had been no *captains*, no formal companies, no yearslong warfare over territories; their politics had been simple, and their presence sent a thrill through every village and town. Whenever they'd slowed down for long enough to receive a hero's welcome, they'd had the local children tugging at their cloaks and begging to join up.

Not so much now. They were hardly ever seen in the villages, and there was something more private and closed off about them. They weren't just fellow citizens of the wood; they were almost a cult with their own divine purpose, too important to concern themselves with the lives of ordinary people.

Rosie placed the blame for all of this squarely at Jack Hartley's feet. The way she told it, Jack Hartley had seen an opportunity when the founder had retired, and grabbed it, proclaiming himself their new overlord and turning an unofficial position of leadership into one so official it required an impractical uniform. Looking at him now, Clem wasn't surprised; she liked to think she was relatively open-minded, but the man was almost entirely frown, and he had a *goatee*, for Christ's sake. The calling card of cads and villains!

Mariel had dismounted and was listening to him speak, her posture unnaturally upright; as Clem watched, they both turned and looked directly at her.

Optimistic as she was, even to Clem this did not seem a good sign.

5

Mariel wasn't entirely sure how to be a daughter.

She thought she knew how to be a fighter, an archer, a captain. She knew to stand to attention when her father approached and listen closely, watching him for cues, nodding in all the right places. She knew what impressed him when he evaluated his Men: physical prowess, a mind for strategy. An arrow that hit its mark and could do so again and again. A steady hand. A steady mind. A quiet heart.

She knew that she could be a good soldier. Perhaps that was the same as being a good daughter.

Everything had been different when her mother was around, but she was mostly gone, and her father was mostly here, so it didn't matter what kind of daughter Regan might have wanted. She clearly didn't know how to be a parent, so who cared?

Not Mariel. That was for sure.

She knew that her father wasn't universally beloved by the Merry Men, but he had taught her a long time ago that being *loved* wasn't the most important thing. It was hardly an important thing at all. He wanted the Merry Men to become something better, something bigger. He wanted to be more than a jovial presence in the shadows; more than a band of happy fellows who dropped off a few bags of food at every village and toyed with the Sheriff's men when the opportunity struck. The wood belonged to them, and they would take it back piece by piece, no matter how hard they had to fight for it.

He gave variations of this speech a lot. Mariel had parts of it memorized, and had to stop herself from mouthing along when he got to the really rousing bits. She was proud to be a Hartley as well as a Hood—two powerful legacies, so entangled with the Merry Men that it was unthinkable that she would ever do anything but try to live up to them.

She just wasn't good enough yet. Her father didn't exactly say so outright, but he didn't have to. At eighteen, she was the youngest captain the Merry Men had ever seen, and she'd worked bloody hard to get there, but there had been too many mistakes along the way for her father to trust her with more responsibility yet. She couldn't relax just because her father was leading the Merry Men—if anything, it meant she had to be *better* than everybody else, to prove that she had earned her place in the ranks and not simply been handed it.

That was why it mattered so much when Morgan slipped up and made too much noise on patrol, breaching one of the principal rules of the Merry Men, not to be seen; why it had been unforgivable a few months ago when Mariel herself had allowed her frustration with the Sheriff's son and heir, Frederic de Rainault, to distract her from a simple fetch-and-carry mission, resulting in a tussle that had been needlessly risky on all sides.

Mariel and Frederic had history. He'd humiliated her the first time they met in a fight, left her sprawling in the mud and even *apologized* to her for it, like she was a little girl he took no pleasure in defeating. It had mostly been luck, but her father had seen, and Mariel knew that he was thinking of it every time he looked at her for months afterward.

She'd managed to deal Frederic an arrow to the knee during that recent fetching mission though, so it had almost been worth it. She often thought fondly of the expression on his smug blond face as he'd toppled over, bleeding profusely, white with shock. The memory was very cheering.

Her father didn't see it that way.

"You're letting your personal feelings get in the way of being a leader," he'd said, during the dressing-down that had taken place after the Frederic incident. He didn't understand how much Mariel hated that boy; that he perfectly encapsulated all the worst things about Nottinghamshire, a rich kid with a corrupt father and the world at his feet. "A good captain doesn't let petty vendettas—or friendships, for that matter—get in the way of following orders. I can't believe I even have to say this to you."

"You don't," Mariel had said quickly. It came out a little slurred, thanks to her enormous fat lip, a parting gift from one of Frederic's men. "It won't happen again."

He'd looked at her with something that was half disappointment and half pity, an absolute shit sandwich of a look that always made Mariel feel lower than a grub.

"See that it doesn't," he'd said, giving her a dismissive, businesslike pat on the shoulder, the closest he ever came to fatherly affection. Mariel had treasured those little pats, until she saw him doing exactly the same to another young captain and realized that they weren't reserved for her at all. "I'm counting on you, Mariel."

A lot of people were counting on her. Mariel wished she could trust her own judgment absolutely, but as she approached her father in that clearing with the wrong healer tied up on her cart, she felt a sickening lurch of worry that she'd made a bad call. It was always like this—she'd feel confident in the moment, right up to the part where she had to face her father and explain the logic behind her decisions, and then suddenly she'd be sure she'd ruined everything instead.

Jack was talking to his deputies; Deputy Commander Neill, more commonly known as *Big John*, a gruff man of nearly sixty who had probably never even heard of the concept of retirement, and Deputy Commander Payne, her father's best friend and second cousin, who could have been his twin in certain lights and certainly seemed to agree with Jack on every matter brought before him. Mariel was fond of the first and wary of the latter. It probably should have been the other way around.

There were sixteen captains underneath them, distinguished by the pins at their throats, each responsible for their own company of Men. Most of them—even the ones almost as young as Mariel—commanded upward of fifteen fighters, the most experienced thirty or forty. Mariel had been allowed four, and her father had chosen them for her. The humiliation still smarted, although she was well-practiced in pretending she hadn't even noticed that her father did not yet trust her with any real power.

Big John clapped Deputy Commander Payne on the

back—he wasn't a particularly tall man, but he packed a lot of power into the little stature he did have, and Captain Payne almost stumbled—and then the two of them separated to deal with other business.

"All well?" Jack said, finally turning to his lower-ranked captains.

"Fine," said Captain Morris, who'd been leading one of the other wagons. She had leathery brown skin and graying hair, in perfect twin braids, and she never laughed at anybody's jokes. "Copped a bit of noise down nearer town, but nothing to write home about."

"Good," said Mariel's father. He turned to the other captain, a steady and comfortingly boring man, Captain James Hughes. "And you?"

"All well."

Last and very much least, he looked to Mariel. "Anything to report?"

"No," said Mariel. She glanced behind her at the wagon, caught herself, refocused. "Well. Yes. The healer you sent us for—she had an apprentice. A ward. We took her instead. It seemed the better option, and I thought it might provide . . ."

She trailed off, because her father had raised a hand, frowning. He seemed tired but, as always, he didn't have a hair out of place or a stray smear of mud on his Commander's cloak. Sometimes she looked at him and couldn't believe he was her father. Not because they didn't look alike—they did; fair skin, lean build, dark hair, although her father's was graying at the temples and his eyebrows were even more impressive than her own. He just felt like a stranger to her some days. A man who existed entirely apart from her, half his life a mystery, with so much going on below the surface that she couldn't even begin to guess at.

"You took . . . her ward?"

"Yes," Mariel said. She realized that she was fidgeting with the knife at her hip, and abruptly stopped. "She seemed more suited. And . . . she offered."

Jack didn't quite *sigh*, but he exhaled quietly through his nose, and Mariel clenched her fists hard enough that she could feel the dull pressure of her blunt fingernails against the creases of her palm.

"Captain Hartley-Hood, you were given a very simple order."

Mariel was the first person to tell the members of her company to call her *Captain*, but it was fucking weird when her own father did it. She supposed that was proper procedure in front of the other captains, both of whom were looking fixedly at the ground.

"I know," said Mariel. "But I believe I carried out that order effectively, with some changes to a few small . . . details."

"Details like retrieving the correct person," said Jack.

There wasn't really anything Mariel could say in response to that, so she looked back over her shoulder at Clem, instead, and discovered that she had somehow wriggled free of her blindfold and was blinking right back in a brainless, watchful way, akin to a large pigeon.

"All right," said her father, already on the move. "Let's do this now."

Mariel had to rush to catch up with him.

She hated it when he left her behind.

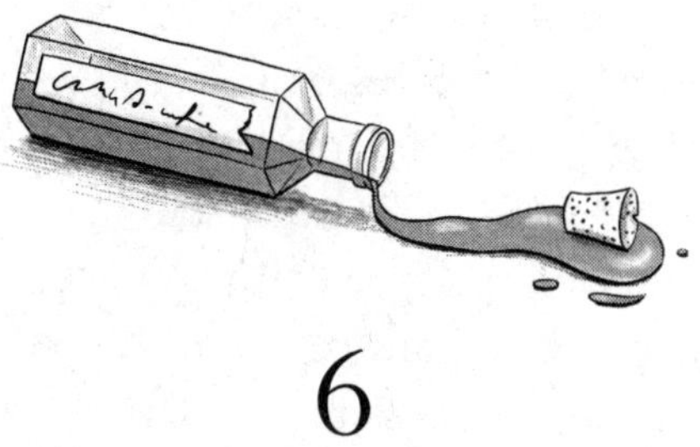

6

Mariel and Commander Hartley were definitely discussing Clem.

She attempted to look as much like a sack of potatoes as possible, but they walked toward her anyway, the rest of the Men moving apart in twin waves to let them pass. Despite circumstances, there was something quite exciting about meeting *the* Jack Hartley; if he didn't order her to be summarily drowned, it might make quite a gripping story to tell the others back at the village.

"Name?" said Commander Hartley. He also had an oak leaf pin fastened at his throat, but his was thin, delicate gold. Old Rosie would have had several conniptions at the very idea of it. Gold jewelry! On the Merry Men! Unironically!

Clem just frowned at him, giving him a chance to realize that she was gagged and therefore unable to reply. She looked down at the wad of fabric and then back up at him, to see if that helped. His mouth twitched and then he gave Mariel a pointed look; she immediately climbed up into the wagon and crouched in front of Clem to ungag her.

Up close, Clem could finally make out Mariel's features. She had very dark hair under that hood, almost true black, with high cheekbones and a surprisingly full, soft-looking mouth split by a small scar at her Cupid's bow. Her eyes were hazel, that peculiar starburst of amber in a muddle of muted forest green. When the gag was untied she glanced sharply upward and met Clem's gaze, her face twisting into a hint of a sneer.

"Don't say anything stupid," she hissed, before climbing back down.

"*Name?*" Jack Hartley said again.

"Clemence Causey," said Clem. "Of Oak Vale."

"Clemence Causey of Oak Vale, do you know why you're here?"

"I imagine you might have heard about my experiments," said Clem, already feeling that things were going to start looking up now that the boss had arrived. "Those aren't Rosie's, they're mine—Rosie's an excellent healer, of course, but she leaves the chemistry to me."

"Experiments," Jack Hartley repeated. From his tone of voice, it seemed he had *not* heard about them and perhaps didn't really grasp what an experiment was.

"I've been testing out new combinations of plants and suspensions to investigate their healing properties," Clem explained. "Trying all sorts—heating them, cooling them, grinding them, making pastes and powders. I mostly test them on myself, first, to see how much I vomit. Of course, sometimes you *want* to vomit, but that's—"

"Please," Jack Hartley said. "Stop."

Clem stopped . . . for approximately three seconds.

"I suppose you need me for something important," she said. "Is somebody unwell? Or do you perhaps need an expert on plant healing to consult for a top secret mission?"

Jack and Mariel exchanged a look. It did not fill Clem with hope.

"Clemence," Jack said, his tone reasonable and gently confidential despite the fact that he looked like he had a bit of a headache. "Oak Vale is under the protection of the Merry Men."

"Yes?" said Clem, unable to stop it from coming out like a question. That fact would probably be news to the citizens of Oak Vale, who had barely seen a Merry Man for years.

"If somebody from the village is collaborating with the Sheriff, we must take swift action to protect the people of the wood."

"Right," said Clem. It was dawning on her that they really hadn't brought her here because of her healing prowess, which was a significant disappointment. "I see."

"Clemence—your guardian, Rosalind Sweetland. Does she treat people from outside the village?"

Clem nodded.

"Have you witnessed her liaising with somebody who might work for the Sheriff? Well dressed? Town accent? Moneyed?"

"No, I haven't seen her *liaising*," Clem said honestly. "We don't ask for the names of the people we treat or where they're from, and even if we did, we keep everything confidential. It's only polite."

Jack Hartley's cool veneer was beginning to crack. His

fingers were tapping agitatedly against the belt at his hip. "I want to know what's been said to your healer, Clemence, what she might have been offered—and what she's said about the Merry Men in return. And I want to make it clear to everybody—not just in your village—that fraternizing with the Sheriff's men harms us *all*."

"Er—hang on," said Clem. "I don't know about *fraternizing*."

"You will be in our custody for as long as we deem necessary to send a clear message to Rosalind Sweetland that this will not be tolerated. Some of our men will pay her another visit—"

"It was me," Clem said immediately, without forethought, or any kind of thought at all. "Actually. So you don't need to go bothering Rosie."

"It was . . . you?" said Jack. Clem was finding him quite annoying, so she chanced a look at Mariel instead and saw that she was frowning so intensely that it looked like her face might split in half.

"Yeah," Clem said breezily. "I'm the one you're looking for. I treat everyone—washerwomen, serfs, sheriffs, kings. I don't ask for job titles either. I'm old-fashioned like that. Tie the limbs back on first, chitchat later. It was definitely me. So you can leave Rosie out of this."

Mariel twitched, like she was shaking off an irritating fly. "She's lying."

Commander Hartley's annoyance intensified. "Explain."

"She's got some kind of martyr complex," Mariel said, which was so rude and uncalled for that Clem let out an indignant little *huff* sound before she could stop herself.

"She volunteered to be taken instead of the old healer. I think she'd say anything to protect her."

"I'm not lying, actually," Clem said hotly. "I don't lie. It was me! I betrayed you, I'm a criminal mastermind. Clap me in irons, I treated a boo-boo for the other side."

Mariel rolled her eyes.

"I don't think you're taking this very seriously," said Commander Hartley.

"Well, to be honest, I don't think it's actually any of your business," said Clem. "And I'd be quite interested to know who came running to you to tell tales, because as I said, that sort of information is private."

"We're everywhere, Clemence Causey," said Jack. Clem supposed he thought that using her full name gave him a bit more gravitas. It just made him seem like he saw himself as the main guy in a play. "This is our wood. Oak Vale belongs to the Merry Men."

"Can I just get something straight?" Clem said, ignoring him. "You've actually just kidnapped me? You don't need me for my healing skills? There's no . . . greater purpose to all this? You're annoyed because you think Rosie talked to the wrong sort, and you've taken me as a hostage to teach her a lesson?"

"You will certainly be put to use as a healer while you are our guest," said Commander Hartley.

Something very rare happened then: Clem was lost for words.

It was just too big a letdown. She'd held on to her childhood notions about the Merry Men long after Rosie had tried to disavow her of them; she'd truly believed that if the green cloaks had come knocking, it must have been part of some grand, clever scheme that would bring her into the fold and perhaps even lead to a cloak of her own someday. Head Healer to the Merry Men was a job she could do. It sounded *good.* Clem had made it up, of course, but even if such a role didn't exist, she had been sure she could persuade them to invent it.

Now she was experiencing such deep-seated, guttural disappointment that it was actually making her chest hurt. Rosie had been right about the Merry Men. They really weren't heroes in jaunty stockings stealing from the rich and giving to the poor anymore. They'd become something murkier, uglier—more complicated. Robin Hood wouldn't have kidnapped somebody just to send a message about *allegiances*, she was sure of it.

"Are you sure *you* don't need a healer?" she said eventually, when she found her tongue. "You do look a bit peaky around the edges. Fluxy. Have you had any unusual bowel movements in the past day or two?"

Commander Hartley didn't seem to know what to do with such obvious belligerence dressed up with a smile. Behind him, Mariel's eyes narrowed.

"I hope you don't mean to make a nuisance of yourself," he said, benign with a hint of threat.

"Why not just kill me?" she shot back. "That would send a pretty clear message to Rosie. And then you wouldn't have to feed me or use all your rope allowance on tying me up."

Jack Hartley sighed, obviously done with her and itching to move on. All that intense, keyed-up tension had gone from him. Now he just looked tired. "We're the Merry Men, Clemence. We don't kill children."

"I'm seventeen," Clem said, with immediate regret. A not-killing-children policy was all well and good as long as you hadn't aged out of the scheme.

"Exactly," said Jack Hartley. "A child."

Mariel twitched again next to him, the only evidence a brief flutter of her cloak.

"Right," said the man in question, addressing his daughter but not looking at her. "We have business to discuss."

They departed. Clem leaned back against her potato plinth, feeling bereft of bright sides and silver linings. Her disappointment was transforming rapidly to indignation: what business was it of Jack Hartley's who they did and didn't treat? Nobody should run through a checklist of moral beliefs and failings before they whipped out their bandages. Yes, it was possible for Clem to tell the difference between a fancy man and an ordinary citizen of the wood when they came knocking with very different ideas about remuneration in their pockets and/or purses, but who cared? Clem would never turn away someone in pain. Besides, they all looked the same without their skin on.

Clem was miffed. Miffed enough, in fact, that she resolved to escape.

Not right now. Right now she was completely surrounded. A group of Men was fixing the wheel of one of the other carts, working in practiced harmony, talking in hushed voices. Farther afield, tucked beneath the trailing fronds of a willow tree, she could see a small group of younger Men—Baxter and Josey included—standing in a tight circle, arms crossed, heads together. Everybody kept darting looks at Jack Hartley and his companions, as if they were all on their very best behavior.

This, Clem supposed, was what happened when a group went from a fun, ballsy, anarchist autonomous collective to an organized militia, with an official leader instead of an honorary one. People got delusions of grandeur. They put their silly gold pins on and believed that they were better than everybody else.

It was easy to see why the Merry Men had followed Robin Hood; the man had a dream, the gumption to pull it off, the charm to win people over, and a great little hat to boot. He was a legend in the greenwood. Old Rosie had certainly talked about him with a hand to her heart and a twinkle in her eye.

People followed Jack Hartley because . . . hmm. That was a thinker. Because he was so self-assured? Because he told them to, and nobody had any better ideas? It wasn't like the wood was replete with options. There weren't any other gangs of outlaws doing quite as well as the Merry Men, and they were the only ones still upholding basic codes about common decency. A not-killing-children policy was relatively progressive, as bandits went.

Clem had clung to her belief that they were untouchable gods of the forest, good to the core. It was depressing to discover that they were just . . . people. Ordinary, flawed people. Definitely not untouchable.

One of them currently *was* touching her. Kit was

tapping her on the shoulder; when she glanced up at him, she saw that he was holding out a wad of peppermint leaf.

"For your stomach," he said, trying to repress a smile. "In case you're feeling . . . fluxy."

7

One moment everybody was mid-task, and the next they were packed up, mounting their horses, and on the move. The party divided into two, setting off in different directions; Clem's kidnappers were part of a much larger company now, following an enormous wagon up ahead.

In a moment of either kindness or oversight (and Clem suspected the former), Kit had left her ungagged, and still only blindfolded in the loosest sense of the word. Hard as it was to stay quiet—especially when she spotted a squirrel and considered announcing her count of one versus Morgan and Baxter's fifty-seven to forty-nine—she slumped back and pretended to fall asleep. She was almost entirely sure that she'd spotted an old, stubby knife in among Rosie's things, and while it wouldn't be particularly useful in a fight, it would do for sawing through wrist-rope, at a pinch. Clem was just tilting over, trying to give the impression that she was unconsciously lost to gravity rather than falling with intent, when Josey dropped down into the wagon and gave her a little pat on the head.

"Nice try," she said, slipping a length of rope over Clem's ankles and knotting it expertly. Her teeth caught on her lower lip as she did it, and Clem wondered if that always happened when she concentrated. It was a curse, being so damned observant—so tuned in to the habits and tells of people's bodies. Some of these Merry Men were just so *attractive.*

"Morgan, did you tie this blindfold? It's terrible."

"Leave me alone. And if you're not driving, swap," Morgan called from ahorse.

"Your horse doesn't like me," Josey answered evenly.

"Um, nobody likes you?"

"Is this how we win favors, Morgan?"

Morgan sighed. "Swap, *please.*"

Josey gave a little sarcastic bow of thanks and then swung her leg over the side of the wagon and neatly mounted the horse; Morgan's scramble to do the same journey in reverse was distinctly less graceful, and by the time they sat down on the chest of Rosie's things, they were scowling.

"I saw a squirrel," Clem said, giving up on silence. "So. That's one for me."

"Why would you think I'd give a shit?" said Morgan, producing a perfect, vermilion apple from somewhere inside their cloak and taking a bite.

Clem didn't really have an answer for that. She watched Morgan crunching away, her own stomach growling and mutinous; Morgan definitely noticed, and only reacted by turning away from her slightly. An hour later Clem's wrists were starting to smart; her back hurt from sitting in such an odd position, and what with all the irritated *sighing* Morgan kept doing, she was starting to feel fed up.

Kit, she knew, would have offered her some apple. An

entire gang of teen highwaymen, and she was stuck with the only one of them who insisted on actually acting like a teen.

The wood grew dark around them, glimpses of hazy summer sky giving way to a violet dusk. Clem listened to the familiar warbles of owls and grumbles of natterjack toads, the creaking of the trees like door hinges on endlessly opened and closed cupboards as they trundled quietly along the narrow road. It was no track that she knew; all of the common, well-traveled routes through the wood ended up at villages and towns sooner rather than later, and were often populated, even as the light faded. They hadn't encountered another soul for hours, and conversations had lapsed, leaving only the soft clopping of hoofs and the turn of the wheels.

She knew the Merry Men had secret routes through the forest. She wished she were in a better mood to enjoy her first proper peek at one.

"Aren't we stopping?" Morgan called to Baxter, who had been humming a quiet, soothing melody as he rode. Clem had been rather enjoying it.

"Hmm?"

"I'm starving."

"You can have my bread, if you like."

"No, don't give me *your* . . . I just thought we might stop for the night."

"Somebody didn't like the recent troop movements. No stops, for safety," Baxter said, shrugging his broad shoulders. "Sorry, Morg. No sleep till camp."

"Ugh," said Morgan. "I don't see why—"

There was a quiet whistling sound, followed by a muted

thud. It was so faint that it would have seemed of no consequence, but for the weird little gasp Morgan had let out. Clem wriggled upward, shaking her blindfold fully loose, and found herself staring at a large, ugly arrow, stuck fast in Morgan's shoulder. Over thc side of the wagon, Baxter was staring at it too.

There was a brief pause, and then Baxter's expression went from twisted-up shock to ashen comprehension.

"Fuck! *Ambush!*"

There was an explosion of noise; shouts of warning, breaking undergrowth, and battle cries. At first the cart sped up, but then Clem heard the indignant bray of a horse and they came to an abrupt stop that knocked her sideways. Morgan was still sitting mostly upright, staring down at the arrow, chest heaving and eyes unfocused. Baxter was reaching over the cart, trying to get to Morgan with fumbling urgency, but then a man in shades of scarlet and blue—one of the Sheriff's men, evident from the polish of his boots to the gilt on his sword—came at him on horseback, blade first, and he had to break away to engage, blocking him with his own hastily raised knife and dislodging him from his horse with a forceful shove. It felt like there were hundreds of them streaming out of the wood, manicured and expensive-looking danger descending from all directions, but Clem only had eyes for the recently skewered.

"Morgan!" Clem shouted over the chaos. "Hey! Morgan?"

Morgan lifted a hand and touched the brown-feathered fletching, as if they weren't entirely sure it was real.

"Don't touch it, Morgan. *Don't* pull it out."

Somebody was approaching on horseback; Clem glanced

up, hoping for help, and instead saw another of the Sheriff's men riding free from the cover of the trees with his bow pulled taut and his arrow aimed right at Morgan, who hadn't even noticed. For a terrible, nauseating moment, all Clem could do was watch as he drew back and aimed, one eye squeezing shut—but then he jolted backward in the saddle, his bow going slack in his hands, and Clem realized that there was now an arrow shot cleanly through his neck. A second later, Mariel passed them on horseback, her face white and furious under her hood, just a brief thunder of hoofs and a whip of wind as she drew another arrow from her quiver and disappeared into the fray.

Morgan moaned, and Clem refocused. She had to thrash like a pecked worm to move herself down the bed of the wagon, but she didn't stop until she hit her head on the heavy trunk. This maneuver had flopped quite a lot of her own curls into her mouth; she had to spit them out to speak.

"Okay, Morgan, are you listening to me? You need to apply pressure to the wound. Use your good arm."

Someone made a horrible gurgling noise close to the cart, and the air was suddenly thick with the smell of blood and shit. Clem swallowed, hard. She was used to blood and shit—that was practically her entire job, master of bodily fluids, king of questionable stains and smells—but it had never been like *this* before. Cruel. Violent.

Dazed, Morgan lifted their hand and pressed it to their shoulder, the shaft sticking out grotesquely from between their fingers. They were crying silently, tears leaking without effort, their face screwed up in pain and misery.

"That's good," lied Clem. Morgan was doing a pretty

subpar job. Plus, they were a sitting duck. In fact, they both were. Clem couldn't use her hands, she couldn't run—she couldn't rummage through the trunk to locate some clean cloth and make a proper compress, or assess the bleeding. The amount streaming down Morgan's fingers didn't indicate a mortal wound, but it was always hard to tell, even under the best of circumstances.

These were not the best of circumstances.

"*Morgan.*" Josey had appeared at the end of the cart, bloodied and enraged, holding a very well-used knife. "Damn it. We have to move."

"You shouldn't," Clem said. "You need to keep the arrow still, you can't—"

"We have to," Josey repeated, her eyes constantly scanning the action beyond Clem's field of vision. "Healer. What do I do?"

"Hold it still. Cut the length off, quick as you can. There are bandages in the trunk. You need to keep pressure on it to stem the flow."

Josey nodded. She assessed, glancing from Morgan to Clem, and then leaned down and sliced through the ropes at Clem's wrists and ankles in two short, easy movements.

Clem was stiff and sore beyond belief, but she willed her limbs into action and opened the trunk, finding some of the scraps of cloth she used for bandages still clean-ish and folding them into a wad. She applied pressure and steadied the arrow as Josey sawed through it with quick, precise cuts that jostled Morgan as little as possible. It was gratifying, even in the grip of panic, that Josey hadn't questioned her methods. In Oak Vale it was always *Don't be stupid, pull it out right away, people shouldn't have objects inside them*, and *Have you tried putting egg whites or leeches on that?* Always, *always* with the leeches. Most people would go to Rosie instead, even when the older healer reassured them that, despite her newfangled ideas, Clem was more than competent. Josey hadn't even frowned. She'd just wielded her knife and started cutting.

"Ow," Morgan said, slumping forward until their forehead was resting against Josey's shoulder.

"Sorry, kid," Josey said, grasping the arrow firmly by the shorter section and then snapping the rest of it clean away as Morgan swore profusely into her shoulder. "That'll have to do. Come on."

She helped Morgan up into a crouch, their good arm slung over her shoulder.

"Don't pull it out until you're somewhere safe and with someone who knows what they're doing."

Josey nodded. "Thanks, healer."

She helped Morgan off the end of the wagon and away, and Clem sat paralyzed, staring down at the chest of supplies. Leaving it would be foolish; taking it all was impossible. There was no time to think. The fight seemed to have moved away, farther along the road, but it could come back to claim her at any moment. Her hands were clammy, her breathing shallow; it seemed silly that she could have felt perfectly calm as the battle raged around her but be left a clumsy, shaking mess in the aftermath. Her vision narrowed until she was just looking at her hands—her freckled, quivering, useless hands—and then she took a deep breath in, pushing down the nausea that had bubbled up into her throat, and told herself *no.* She couldn't fall apart now. She had things to do.

She grabbed bandages, stuffed them clumsily into the soft leather satchel, and then threw the strap over her shoulder. At the last second she snatched up a skin of wine too, and then exited the wagon with as much haste as her protesting legs could muster.

There was a dead man on the ground, face down, bleeding from the back of the head. Clem only looked for long enough to ascertain that he had definitely expired, and then kept moving.

She was used to the aftermath of violence—injuries sustained from working with heavy equipment or cantankerous goats, the victims of inn scuffles or unfortunate hunting accidents—but it was very different to be confronted with the kind of pain that had been intentionally and brutally inflicted.

Morgan hadn't looked a day over fourteen. They should live, as long as nobody decided to yank the arrow out at a questionable angle or leave the wound to fester. She tried to tell herself that it wasn't her responsibility anymore, even as she pictured the arrow's entry wound in her mind, deciding it had been shallow enough that she'd pull it out the way it had come in.

She didn't even know where Morgan had gone. Their fate was somebody else's problem now.

Clem's only job was to run.

8

Mariel had never particularly wanted a nemesis.

Her grandfather's tussles with the previous Sheriff were the stuff of legend; chapters in a long and very personal feud that had only ended when that de Rainault died a timely death. Robin had even attended the funeral, albeit from a distance, to make sure they'd really put the old bastard in the ground.

Unfortunately, his legacy hadn't died with him. The de Rainaults had their fingers in a lot of rotten pies—connections to almost every bit of bad business that Nottinghamshire had managed to cook up. They'd amassed a lot of power that way, and they had absolutely no plans to let go of it. The county was infested with a small but powerful clutch of them—the Sheriff, his brother, an uncle and a handful of cousins—either with estates of their own or permanent lodgings in the guest wings of important people, and it often seemed that the magistrate worked for them, rather than the other way around.

Roland de Rainault was the sitting Sheriff, and despite the fact that they were supposedly at war with him, Mariel had only caught a glimpse of him once. He was a hands-off man, happy to send his guards to do his bidding, fonder of fine things and posturing than he was of actually doing his job. Her father found this endlessly infuriating and dreamed of the day he'd be able to meet Roland in actual combat.

His only son, Frederic, was another story entirely.

Frederic had spent his childhood cosseted in the family estates and had only recently been let loose in the wood to chase glory. Having crossed swords with him a few times, she could not imagine anybody with a more punchable face or hateful demeanor.

Of *course* he was here, at this ambush that should have been impossible. And of course he'd waited until the first wave of fighting had passed to come cantering out of the treeline and play the hero.

If she'd still had her bow, she could have put an end to him right then and there. The rush of battle sharpened her focus to a fine point; it was almost too easy to line up, draw, loose, and watch her latest target go tumbling to the ground. The movement of her horse was nothing. It was like breathing. Air in, arrows out. She hadn't missed a single shot.

She had, however, been involved with a small collision with one of the Sheriff's soldiers, and he'd managed to relieve her of her primary weapon, leaving her to scramble for her blades instead.

She was engaged in combat near the middle of their convoy, where those least able to fight for themselves usually traveled, trying to push the Sheriff's men back into the trees, somehow still atop her horse. She'd lost track of the others—Josey, her father, her prisoner. When she saw Frederic riding toward her with his nonexistent chin raised and his ridiculous blond hair bouncing, her quiver was empty, and her horse was deeply unhappy. The Merry Men trained their steeds well, but even the finest horse had its limits, and could be excused a small tantrum when people kept trying to stab it.

The last straw came when a man riding a frankly unhinged stallion tried to barrel straight into Mariel and her mount, his sword swinging wildly. Mariel ducked, knifed him neatly in the side where the Sheriff's shiny but corner-cutting armor had left him exposed to cuts on his corners, and then pushed away from him very hard; her horse stumbled, bucked, and a moment later she found herself on the ground with all of the wind knocked out of her and pain rattling up her spine.

This was the moment Frederic chose to make his grand entrance, sword gleaming, scarlet cloak billowing in some sort of prearranged breeze. He dismounted and then walked slowly toward her with the confidence of someone either very talented or very stupid.

He was not a man of talent.

"You just got off your horse *willingly*," Mariel said, once she'd heaved herself to her feet and unsheathed her sword. "Tactics Lesson One for Idiots and Babies: don't."

"I do not need lessons from you," Frederic said, all the smarm wiped from his face. He was so easy to goad, it was embarrassing. "I have come to meet you on even footing, to best you in combat, so that we might finish this with dignity . . ."

Mariel rushed him. He managed to raise his sword in time, but he didn't realize that she was also going for his foot, and she succeeded in unbalancing him. She watched him wince as he braced against that bad knee she'd given him, and frowned. She was *so* sure she'd managed to sever something important with that arrow, and yet here he was, back on the battlefield and ready to shout inanities at her.

"Fight with honor!" he sputtered on cue, as he righted himself to meet Mariel's next blow.

The problem with Frederic—one of the many problems, actually, enough to fill a large leather-bound volume—was that he was convinced he was a knight of daring and valor instead of his father's lackey, sent to subjugate the common folk of the wood. He liked to deliver these little speeches, and imply that he'd graciously spare her life when he eventually bested her, while Mariel tried very seriously to cut his throat.

He was the youngest de Rainault by a long shot, and as far as she was aware, the only one under forty with any legitimacy. The Sheriff liked to keep things in the family and hadn't managed to produce any more heirs; ending that bloodline would be quite the coup.

Unfortunately, they'd trained him well up at Sherwood House. He wasn't an inventive fighter, and he wasn't particularly brave, but he did have about five inches on Mariel in height, and he'd learned the sword like a man with a sword instruction manual and literally nothing else going on in his life.

Mariel hated him to the point of obsession.

"Mariel," he said now, red-faced, with a textbook parry

that made Mariel want to scream through her clenched teeth. "I do not wish to hurt you. It is unbecoming of a lady—"

"I'm going to kill you," Mariel gritted out. "I'm going to stab you in many and varied locations, and I'm going to let you bleed out *slowly*, and then—and then I'm going to send your head to your father in a box."

"I find this sort of language very disappointing."

He feinted and then advanced faster than she'd anticipated, and she only just managed to catch him against her guard. "Then I'm going to kill your father, and I'm going to put his head in the box too. The box will be very full of heads, but . . . I'll make it work."

"You demean yourself," said Frederic, "and you demean your cause. Do you see me talking like this? Discussing the base removal of heads?"

"I see you and your father—sending your men—to starve and harass and—beat people," Mariel said, punctuated by the sound of steel on steel, "and tax them halfway to death, and then make them come—*begging* to you for scraps."

"If you understood economics . . ." Frederic began, but Mariel's wordless howl of a reply was drowned out by the fact that two people locked in combat practically fell into them, pushing them apart.

Mariel had killed quite a few people before. She wasn't exactly *proud* of it, but she wasn't ashamed either. She did not kill without cause.

Most of those deaths had come at the point of one of her arrows, many feet away, the actual moment of extinction lost in the whirlwind of a fight.

She hoped she got to see the exact moment Frederic de Rainault drew his last breath, stuck through with her knife, probably with a half-finished sentence about how she'd *never win anybody over by being so discourteous* on his lips.

That, she'd be very proud of.

He'd managed to recover faster than her. She was still getting up when their swords met again.

"The wood is *ours*," Mariel said, trying to stand, unable to push past the full weight of him bearing down on her.

"No, Hartley-Hood, it's not," he said, with a touch of feigned sympathy. "The great men of this country own these lands. The yields are for the lords, the deer are for the king. It's not *our* fault that you simply can't afford it."

Mariel tried to push him away and duck under his guard, thinking only of her blade sunk deep into some soft part of him that no amount of money could stitch back together, but it was useless. With her free hand, she went for her knife—and Frederic's sword slipped, with a teeth-gritting screech, and embedded itself in her side.

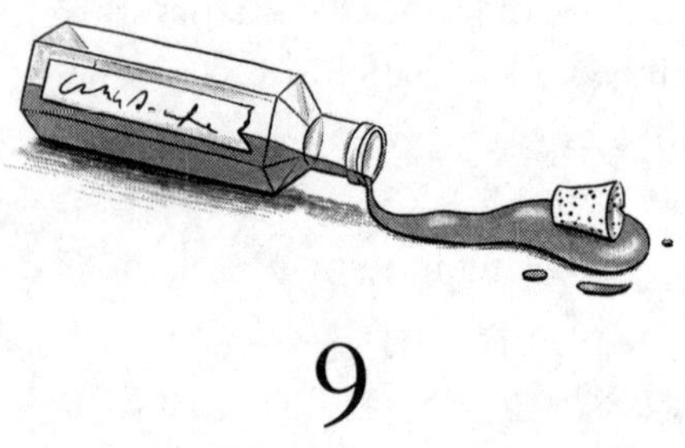

9

Clem wasn't exactly sure where she was running to. She couldn't scarper at full tilt or she'd risk losing an ankle to a tree root, so she settled for little bursts of energy that quickly brought her to the limit of her physical prowess, her lungs burning and her breath ragged. The fighters seemed to have scattered themselves through the wood, the noise distant but coming from all directions; there was absolutely no way to tell which way she should be going, and so she found herself moving in a very confused fashion, turning on her heel anytime she felt too close to a scuffle. She was recovering from one such sprint when she staggered between two trees and suddenly found herself standing on a narrow road.

Momentarily baffled into uselessness, she decided that trees were safer than road and turned herself right back around. She'd been walking two seconds when somebody reached out and grabbed her by the ankle.

She didn't scream, but it wasn't because she was being brave; she didn't have enough air in her lungs to do anything more than squeak with genuine terror as she was unceremoniously toppled to the ground.

"Shut up, *shut up*," somebody hissed, clawing for Clem's mouth and only managing to grab a handful of hair.

Even with so few words spoken between them, she'd have recognized that haughty, imperious voice anywhere.

It shouldn't have been a relief, but a familiar asshole was better than an unknown one.

"Evening, Captain," Clem wheezed, when her heart had slowed its hammering. "I can't help but notice that you're lying in a puddle."

Mariel made a furious little grunting noise and then let her head fall back against the trunk of the tree she was sheltering against. She was pallid and waxen, a sheen of sweat on her skin, strands of her hair curling and clinging to her forehead. Something about the way she was holding herself forced Clem's exhausted brain to engage.

"You're hurt."

Mariel didn't say anything, but she had given up on trying to do any more strategic grabbing. Clem glanced around, looking for any signs of danger: none. Chances that Mariel would be able to stop her from getting back up and sprinting away? Also none. Any minute now, probably, the wood was going to show Clem the way. Her escape was imminent. Freedom just around the next corner.

It would have been easier if Mariel had just begged for help. Clem couldn't have refused that. But she wasn't even asking. She knew Clem was a healer, knew she was her best chance at getting out of here alive, and she was just lounging there palely like a picked mushroom instead, looking half dead and fully furious in the failing light.

Clem glanced longingly at the tree cover beyond and

then reached for Mariel's side instead, ignoring her look of seething indignation.

It was impossible to see the problem without proper light, so Clem had to *feel* for it instead. She brushed the fingertips of one hand as lightly as possible over the side of Mariel's abdomen and felt her muscles tense as she jolted away from Clem's touch. Her fingers came away dark and wet.

Mariel was breathing hard through clenched teeth.

"*Don't.*"

"I'm actually doing you a favor—"

"I'm fine."

"Yeah. You're fine," Clem agreed, lying cheerfully. She resumed her probing, questing under the hem of Mariel's shirt until the captain let out a brief, sharp exhalation of pain. She was already using her other hand to rummage through her bag, and when her fingers closed around one of the bandages, she folded it and then pressed down hard where it seemed to hurt the most.

There wasn't even a hint of a tremor in her hands, but that made sense: she always felt better when she could be useful. It helped to focus on a task, a next step, and healing was often so urgent that it pushed everything else to the recesses of her mind and then kept it going right out the back door. Later, in the quiet after the storm, it would be a different story.

Mariel bowed her head, her eyes scrunched tightly shut, and then let out a long, shaky breath. Clem was squinting at the bandage, trying to see how long it took to be soaked through with blood. It was slow going. That was a good sign.

"Why are you still here?" Mariel said tightly. It sounded more like an accusation than a question.

"Got lost," said Clem, "about halfway through my escape."

"No, I mean—" Mariel broke off to swear up at the canopy of branches above them, gathering herself before she spoke again. "Nobody's coming. Go *away*."

"Thanks," said Clem. "How's this? If I decide you're going to die, I'll just give you a pat on the head and leave you to it."

She pushed a little harder into what she hoped was a small but enthusiastic wound, and took Mariel's answering grunt of pain as a sign of success.

Clem thought of Rosie, always calling her *soft*, intimating that one day it would be her downfall. Tutting when Clem was gone for hours listening to Widow Redgate from the next village list endless nervous complaints; shaking her head when Clem used up good supplies tending to a stray dog that some of the local children had discovered miserable in a ditch. She had been right, in the end, because this was where Clem's *softness* had landed her: sitting arse-deep in a cold, muddy puddle, trying very hard to save the life of somebody who had not only kidnapped her, but was being a real dick about it.

"Who skewered you?" Clem asked quietly, just to keep Mariel talking.

"I don't . . ."

Mariel looked down at the bandage, which was now almost fully black with her blood, and trailed off. There was an odd, detached look in her eyes that Clem had seen before when people realized the extent of their injuries and their minds decided to abruptly nope out of consciousness.

"Well," Clem said. "Don't look at that. That's nothing."

She removed the bandage and replaced it with a fresh one, and then wiped her bloodied hand on her breeches and felt in the darkness for Mariel's wrist. When her fingers closed around it, Mariel seemed to jerk back into full awareness, indignant as a watered cat.

"I *told* you to go away."

"Believe me, I'm not getting anything out of this either," Clem said, pressing down to find the fluttering of her pulse. Mariel was doing plenty of *breathing*, at least. Furious little huffs that kept ruffling Clem's curls.

"Are you *holding my hand*?"

This was so ridiculous that Clem laughed; she abruptly stopped and dropped back into the hushed, half-whispered register they'd been using.

"Yes," Clem said. "I'm holding your hand. I'm making my move. I understand that you have trouble expressing your feelings and that my violent kidnapping was just your way of telling me you *like*-like me."

Mariel's heart was still beating steadily away, so that was something. She tried to shove Clem off, but raising her arm was all she had the strength for, and the final blow was distinctly lackluster.

"Keep it in your trousers, there'll be time for lusty fistfights later."

Mariel was about to respond, no doubt with something cutting, but they both heard what sounded like a twig cracking underfoot, and froze; injured as she was, Mariel immediately straightened up, her eyes roving methodically through the dark.

"Clear this way," she said quietly, as if they were suddenly comrades-in-arms. "Your end?"

Clem peered around the tree trunk apprehensively. She couldn't see anybody, but then, she wasn't entirely sure what she was looking for. A skilled attacker wouldn't just be standing there in plain sight, waving and waiting to be spotted.

"Er . . . clear?"

"Reassuring," Mariel sneered. Apparently their brief fellowship had ended.

They both lapsed into silence, still on high alert. After ten or twenty seconds nothing had changed, and Clem felt Mariel relax slightly under her hands.

"It wasn't meant to be violent," Mariel said reluctantly.

"What?"

"The *kidnapping*," Mariel snapped. "I may have been overzealous with my instructions. It was just meant to be . . . fast."

"Ah, yes. A nice clean abduction, with proper attention paid to the procedures."

"Stop being so dramatic. You're just on loan."

"You shouldn't kidnap innocent people, Captain," Clem said sharply. "People might start to get the wrong idea about you and your merry mates."

"You don't know anything about us," said Mariel, slow and self-assured. "Everything we do is for the greater good."

This was very annoying. Clem had a long fuse, but she'd had enough disappointments today for a lifetime.

"Well," she said, forcing lightness. "Seeing as you're *not* about to die—you're welcome, by the way—and that you're currently about as menacing as a wet glove and have no chance of stopping me, I suppose I'll be going."

Mariel shrugged, then winced. "Do as you please."

Her attempt at nonchalance was ruined when she abruptly leaned to the side and vomited. Clem almost reached to pull her hair back for her as she spat froth into the dirt, and then decided she was going to make a point of *not* doing it.

"God," Mariel muttered brokenly, dragging her sleeve across her mouth with considerable effort. "My father . . ."

"What? Is he going to ground you for playing around with the wrong end of a sword?"

"*No*," Mariel gritted out. "He was riding at the front, but we got separated. And then—Frederic de *bloody* Rainault . . ."

"Is that the guy who skewered you?" Clem said, just to keep her talking. She eased up on Mariel's side, then took a fresh strip of linen and used her teeth to tear off a thin length of it. She had it wrapped around Mariel's abdomen to keep the wad of bandage in place and tied off with a neat knot before Mariel could draw breath to complain.

"Yes," Mariel said, closing her eyes. "He's mine. We have a score to settle. I nearly *had* him, but then he . . . And then Baxter found us, and I was somewhat incapacitated, and . . . suddenly we were besieged. Baxter let him get *away*."

"That's nice," Clem said mildly, gathering her things. She staggered to her feet and stretched, the muscles of her calves screaming. She was basically just one giant tendon, ready to snap. "Take care of that wound," she said. "Clean it with wine and honey. Don't let it fester."

Mariel didn't respond at all.

Clem rolled her eyes. She hadn't exactly been expecting effusive thanks, but this commitment to sullen belligerence even in the face of life-saving first aid was rude. Still, the captain owed her now. Mariel could hardly send the Merry Men back in to recapture Clem after her *life* had been saved. It was actually all quite convenient. Clem could go home to Oak Vale, and to Rosie, without threat of reprisal. Back to patching everyday wounds and experimenting by candlelight, dances once a month at the inn, pranks on foxes. A dull life, perhaps, but a good one. It looked even more appealing now Clem knew that the Merry Men she had once dreamed of joining didn't seem to exist at all.

"See you around, Mariel," she said, with a small salute. "Or, you know. Hopefully not. Good luck with your vengeance."

She started back into the wood, plastered with mud and blood, discomforted by a lingering sense of unfinished business and trying instead to be glad to be on the move.

She had only made it a few steps when, without warning or fanfare, she was suddenly surrounded by Merry Men. Some of them were scuffed, bruised, and bleeding, none of them were smiling, and every one of them was pointing a weapon straight at her. Clem stopped. She held up her hands and turned to face the captain with an expression she hoped was winningly imploring.

"*Finally*," said Mariel, all signs of humanity wiped from her face. Clem clutched her supplies to her side, looking half-heartedly for openings in the circle, as if she might suddenly do something terribly athletic to get herself out of this mess.

"I just did you a massive favor," she muttered out of the corner of her mouth. "In case you need reminding."

Mariel waved in her direction with a bloodied hand, annoyed, as if she were already an afterthought.

"Seize her."

10

Mariel was still bleeding.

The pain wasn't an issue anymore; she had isolated it, assessed it, and catalogued it alongside her myriad other problems. Yes, it hurt to breathe, and there had been a horrifying moment while Baxter was hauling her upright when she'd dangled precariously at the edge of consciousness, but now that she was sitting on a horse the pain was predictable and almost commonplace. She'd had worse.

The bleeding, though. That was potentially cause for concern.

"You're not about to lose your biscuits, are you?" said Josey, who was alternating between riding next to her and circling around to the back of their bedraggled caravan of survivors and walking wounded, checking on their makeshift rearguard, keeping an eye out for stragglers.

They had new horses, allocated by convenience. Mariel had learned early on in life not to get attached to any particular pony. Not because they died—the Merry Men took very good care of their animals—but because they were swapped out constantly, traded at rendezvous points and at camp, with never enough time in between to form a lasting relationship. She had made the mistake of becoming enamored with her first full-sized horse, Percy, and it had felt like being cheated on, watching someone else ride away on him a few weeks later.

Not that she had ever actually been cheated on. You had to bother with love first to be able to lose it.

"Mariel?" Josey prompted.

Mariel didn't say anything. This was her usual response to inane questions.

"Are you ignoring me because you're in pain, or are you ignoring me because you don't know what I'm talking about, vis-à-vis biscuits?"

"I know what you mean," Mariel said, reinforcing her voice with steel to get her through to the end of the sentence. "Please do not concern yourself with my . . . biscuits."

Behind them, Mariel heard what sounded like Kit laughing weakly. Morgan—who had been loaded into the only cart that still had all four wheels—groaned in pain, and Kit's laughter ceased.

"You're all right," she heard Kit say, his voice thready. "Nearly there, Morg."

Now that the rush of battle was ebbing, the horror was sinking in. This ambush just shouldn't have been possible. *Nobody* knew the exact routes they took through the greenwood. The Great Road and the other main arteries had been etched into the dirt by hundreds of years of hoofs and wheels, and were well-used by anybody passing through; the paths the Merry Men traveled, the backways, were barely paths at all. They were the silty beds of slow-running streams. Unremarkable gaps in the branches of trees. Tracks that barely looked wide enough for a horse, but were passable with a cart, if the driver knew exactly where to put their wheels. New paths were forged whenever they were needed, and old ones abandoned entirely. Anybody who was not initiated was supposed to travel blindfolded, just in case.

Sitting around the big fire at camp—the beating heart of the Merry Men, the place where plans were discussed and routes agreed—her father had once suggested that young children should travel blindfolded too, before they could be trusted to keep the secrets.

Big John had been the only one brave enough to break the silence, scratching the back of his neck as he did. "Don't you think that might come across as a bit . . . fucked up?"

He was able to say such things with relative impunity, while the rest of her father's captains aggressively side-eyed and shuffled their feet without a gorm between them.

The young children had remained un-blindfolded. The backways had stayed secret.

Somehow, Mariel doubted that the babbling of a toddler could have given the Sheriff of Nottingham enough information to coordinate an ambush of this magnitude.

They had been attacked on their own road. They had lost people—good people, old and young, born fighters and those whose talents were quieter—more Men than Mariel could ever remember losing in one go in a lifetime of skirmishes. She had seen them die, ridden past them as they lay on the ground breathing their last, and only thought about how to stop the next sword from falling.

She had no idea where her father was. The last she'd seen, he'd been fighting four of the Sheriff's men at once, with discipline in his form and violence in his eyes. At least he hadn't been there to see Frederic landing his blow. That had stung in more ways than one.

Somebody had betrayed them. It was unthinkable, but it was the only thing that made sense.

Mariel's side throbbed. Her head pounded. Her posture on the horse never faltered.

"Morgan's looking very green," Baxter said. *He* still had his own horse, thank God; he'd have turned a smaller steed to grease and kindling. "Are we stopping?"

"Not yet," Mariel said curtly. There was a protocol, in times like this. Another of her father's inventions: emergency meeting points scattered throughout the greenwood for when it wasn't safe to return home. She ached for camp, even if they'd only set up a few weeks before. She always arranged her tent in the exact same way, paying meticulous attention to detail; everything had its place, and once it was settled, she was home. She felt naked without her bow, but there was another with the rest of her supplies, and her mind rushed ahead of her body and imagined the heft of it in her hands, testing the limbs, rewrapping the grip. If she could just retreat into her own tent, to spend a few hours alone where nobody could see her—where nobody would *ask* her for anything . . .

Except, of course, there would be no retreat. No quiet. There were emergency meetings to convene; strategies to discuss. As a captain, she needed to have answers.

Perhaps, if this bleeding continued, she might be dead by then. The thought was almost restful.

She was the only captain leading a group of maybe twenty, the exact numbers hard to gauge. Every one of them knew the greenwood down to their bones, but only Mariel knew where they were supposed to be stopping, and her thoughts kept sliding sideways, battle-drunk and weary. Blood loss was so inconvenient. She was counting trees, and then she was wondering if she could hear an owl, and then she thought for a moment that she was supposed to have been counting owls—but there had only been one, hadn't there? Or was she failing in her solemn duty at owl-counting? . . . And then Josey was back, an instant relief, frowning at her in the starlight.

"Respectfully," she said, "your face is all wrong."

Mariel tried to put her features back in proper order and then, mercifully, spotted a familiar oak. She raised a hand, halting the procession behind her.

"This is it. Get everyone well-hidden. Have Kit see to the casualties."

"Kit *is* a casualty," said Baxter, as they dismounted and proceeded into the trees. There was a small clearing in the embrace of the oak tree's wizened branches, surrounded by thicket, providing cover from the path. If Mariel had the strength to check the trunk, she'd find a knife-slash vaguely resembling a bird carved into the bark, right at the fork of the lowest branches. It matched the tattoo on her inner bicep, hand-poked on her fourteenth birthday when she'd sworn the oath. "He's bruised all up one side. Horses bolted."

"He's walking, isn't he?" said Mariel. Sliding from her horse hadn't been the most pleasant of experiences, but she had gritted her teeth and prevented herself from groaning all the way down. "Get everyone settled. No fires."

They tucked the cart as far into the undergrowth as possible until it was almost invisible, and the horses followed. Their encampment made for a miserable lot, huddled beneath the tree, muttering to each other in low, fearful voices.

It set Mariel's teeth on edge. Being afraid wasn't going to help. What were the practical applications, unless you were facing down a lackey or running from a wolf?

"What's happening?" said a boy with dark hair, holding his arm at an odd angle but clearly trying to play it off as casual. William. He was a year or two younger than Mariel. She knew his father. She noted his father's absence. "We need light. Food."

"No," said Josey, glancing at Mariel. "No fires. Not yet."

"Is somebody going to pull that splinter out of that child, or is it going to be a permanent feature?" said an older woman, probably called Joan, nodding over to where Morgan was being laid out on a makeshift litter by Baxter and Kit. Even in the gloom, Mariel could see that Morgan looked distinctly undercooked.

"The healer said not to," said Josey, shrugging.

Mariel blinked. She had momentarily forgotten that she had a captive, and a very useful one at that.

When she went with Josey to cut the healer's bindings and remove the new and very securely tied gag and blindfold, Clemence looked unimpressed, but for entirely the wrong reasons.

"You shouldn't be walking around with a wound like that."

"Would it kill you to react appropriately to *anything*?" Mariel said, as Josey helped Clemence upright.

"How's that? You want me to act *kidnapped*?" said Clemence, wiping a smear of either dirt or blood from her freckled cheekbone and stretching. Her tightly curled hair, which seemed to defy gravity by routine, was struggling. "Sort of . . . screaming and crying? I could piss myself, if you like. Actually I might anyway, if you don't give me a sec to sort myself out . . ."

"Watch her," Mariel said to Josey, nodding toward the bushes.

"Hard luck," Clemence said to Josey, all sympathy. "Best fighter I've ever seen, and they have you on piss duty."

Josey smirked. Mariel was less amused.

"Come on then," said Clemence. "I'm not afraid of an audience. It won't make me shy. If anything, I'll piss harder, just to try to impress you . . ."

Clemence's insistence on being cheerful to the point of madness was already *extremely* wearing.

She snapped out of it once she had returned from the bushes and approached Morgan. Mariel noticed an innate shift in her, a rearranging of herself to meet the task at hand; she squared her shoulders, rolled up her sleeves, even had the audacity to ask Josey for a little twine to tie back her hair.

Josey obliged, of course. Mariel went to walk the perimeter of their makeshift camp, to make the rounds and speak a few quick words of meager reassurance to anyone who asked for news, but every time she passed the place where Morgan had been laid out on a bed of cloaks she slowed to watch Clemence at work.

She was bloodied up to her wrists, her brow knitted in concentration. By Mariel's third pass, Baxter had come to help. He was holding Morgan down by the shoulders and looking unhappy.

"You," Clemence said suddenly. Mariel hadn't realized that she'd been spotted. "*Captain.* If you're not going to rest, make yourself useful. I need you."

Mariel bristled, both at the sarcastic *Captain* and the indignity of being ordered around by one's own captive—but Morgan was currently under her command, and therefore her protection, and was clearly in agony. Mariel knew all too well how much pain a single arrow could inflict, even if it missed your important organs.

Clemence crooked a finger, and Mariel sighed through her nose before going to help.

She'd restore the proper order of things once Morgan was back to counting squirrels.

11

"I need more light," said Clem, not bothering to look up as the captain approached.

"No campfires," Mariel said, as if repeating by rote.

Clem paused briefly in her ministrations. "Then you'd better come up with a magical new way to conjure light in the next ten seconds."

Tears were leaking silently out of Morgan's eyes, cutting tracks through the mud on their cheeks. Mariel glanced up at muscly Baxter, who shrugged. He'd been surprisingly agreeable when Clem had flagged him down, obeying her without question.

With a put-upon sigh, Mariel disappeared. Clem didn't look to see if she was, indeed, fetching fire; she was too busy focusing on the unpleasant bulge of Morgan's skin around the wound she'd been cleaning as best she could with wine. The impact of the arrow had been partially absorbed by the thick, boiled leather of Morgan's armor. Leather was good at being lightweight and silent, but at the end of the day, it was just skin—arrows had one job, and they tended to do it well. If it had gone all the way through Morgan's shoulder, Clem could have yanked it out from the back. As it was, it would have to come out the same way it had come in, which was going to be unpleasant for everybody.

Well, mostly for Morgan.

At home, Clem had been trying to map the common veins and arteries, keeping a diagram nailed to the wall above her workbench; from what she'd discovered so far, she could reasonably guess that this arrow hadn't interfered with anything too vital, but she wasn't entirely sure. The key to keeping people calm was to not let them know your margins for error.

When Mariel returned, she was carrying a makeshift wooden torch. She placed it on the ground in front of her and then did a series of odd things in such quick succession that Clem couldn't quite follow. It *looked* as if she only flicked her thumb across her palm and then brushed her hands together forcefully; somehow this produced sparks, and a second later she was holding the lit torch aloft, completely expressionless as she met Clem's baffled squint.

"What?"

"Er . . . I was joking about magically conjuring light."

"It's not magic," Mariel said disdainfully. "Unless you think *rocks* are magic."

Clem caught a glimpse of a roughly hewn stone ring on Mariel's finger, a matching one in dull silver on her other hand, and craned her neck trying to get a better look.

Some sort of flint contraption. Fascinating.

"I thought you were in a hurry," Mariel snapped back.

"Yes," said Clem, remembering herself. "I am. I need your knife."

"No," said Mariel, from under furious eyebrows.

Clem was getting a little tired of that word. "Well, it's either you give me your knife and I can get this done right now, or I use my teeth, and I'll have chewed the arrow out in about half an hour but we'll all be *very* upset."

"Give her . . . the knife," Morgan rasped on an outward breath. Mariel relented and handed it over, the torch dipping as she did.

"Great. Hold that steady for me. Baxter—you're doing an excellent job, no notes for you."

Clem could see where the dark barbs of the arrowhead were now, just below the surface of Morgan's skin. The easiest way to get them out without lots of painful wiggling was to cut them free.

"Morgan," she said, as breezily as she could manage as she heated the knife in the torch flame. "I'm just going to ask you to bite down on this bit of leather, all right? Fun fact: it's actually some of your armor. Waste not, want not. All right—hard as you can now. Three, two . . ."

Morgan screamed so loudly, even through the leather, that in the silence that followed Clem distinctly heard a small child on the other side of the camp say "Oh dear."

When the wound was cleaned and bandaged as best as Clem could manage and she'd applied a small amount of a pungent, experimental salve to the parts she dared to touch, she patted Morgan on the head and moved automatically to a boy lurking nearby with a very dislocated shoulder. She already had her hands on him when she realized that her little circle of light hadn't followed her; she glanced back over her shoulder at Mariel, who was talking to Morgan in a low voice, and then cleared her throat.

"*Light*. Captain."

Mariel gave her a look that could have shredded steel and then thrust the torch into Baxter's hand instead. To his credit, he dutifully followed Clem from patient to patient as people started coming forward, offering up sliced arms, skinned elbows, broken teeth and fingers. It was like being escorted by a friendly blond bear; his presence next to her seemed to legitimize her, so they didn't ask the usual questions about her methods, or perhaps they were simply too tired to care. She was halfway through extracting a broken canine with just her fingernails and sheer force of will when the light dipped; when she turned around, she saw that Baxter was vomiting politely behind her.

"Don't like teeth stuff," he said grimly, wiping his mouth and immediately resuming torch duties.

Kit appeared at his elbow and silently handed him a flask of something, which he drank from deeply before offering to Clem.

"Drink."

"I'm busy," Clem said, midway through splinting a hand. "Anyway, I'm a prisoner. Expendable. You're supposed to make me lap rainwater from a leaf while you chug honey wine and laugh at me."

"*Drink*," Baxter insisted. "It's been hours."

This was a genuine surprise to Clem. Time always did pass strangely when she was focused. She finished tying off the splint and then accepted the flask and upended it, only realizing how thirsty she was when it hit her tongue. Now that she wasn't staring at a wound, she realized that her vision was patchy around the edges, her limbs tingly and distant, like they were somebody else's problem; she sat down on the ground, hitting it so hard that the world went black for a moment, and when her eyes were back in business she saw Baxter exchange a look with Kit that she was too exhausted to parse.

Kit disappeared and came back with bread, hard as a rock and twice as tasteless, but she wolfed it down. Baxter extinguished the torch, stretched his arms until they cracked, and then he and Kit went to speak to Josey and the captain. The four of them stood over Morgan like a violent, murderous gang of parents, some of them doing a better job of pretending that they weren't concerned than others. Mariel was the one doing most of the serious talking, but she kept glancing down at Morgan out of the corner of her eye, despite the fact that Morgan wasn't doing anything more interesting than breathing.

It was sort of touching.

Meager supplies were being passed around as people settled in around the clearing, bedding down for an uncomfortable night under the stars. Clem sat leaning against a mossy tree, exhausted to her bones, and waited for somebody to come and tie her up again, or to carry her unceremoniously back over to the wagon, but nobody did.

Josey seemed genuinely preoccupied. *This* was her chance to escape. With a bit of luck, she might be back in Oak Vale by tomorrow dinnertime. Rosie had been planning to make her famous chicken-with-nothing-else. There were patients to visit, hypotheses to confirm. The Merry Men could splint their own fingers and clean up their messes.

She immediately fell asleep.

*

Someone was saying the word "simultaneously" in a hushed voice. It was repeated back in incredulous tones, and then confirmed with grim finality.

Clem groaned awake. Her neck was aching where it had been cricked uncomfortably against the tree, and her stomach felt clawed out and hollow. She couldn't believe she'd fallen asleep half upright on the ground when sleep usually evaded her even in her soft cot by the hearth in Old Rosie's kitchen. She always found herself jumping back up, returning to some idea that had been forming during the day, scooching closer to the fire so she could work as Rosie snored. She must have been so tired that her body simply said *no*.

"Someone tipped them off." It was a clipped, harsh voice, hardly softened by the whisper. Clem imagined angry, wet cats and then placed it as Mariel. "This has *never happened*. We've been compromised."

"Congratulations on your excellent deduction skills," said an unfamiliar man dryly. "Yes, there's been a leak."

"Don't be a dick, Richard," said Josey. Clem had cracked open an eye and could see them now, Mariel and Josey and two newly arrived strangers with captains' pins, gathered by a tree ten feet from where she'd been sleeping.

"You haven't made captain, Abara. You shouldn't even be listening to this conversation."

"Shut up, Flores. I need a map," Mariel said. Flores was of medium height and looked very deliberately muscly under his clothes, which might have been slightly too tight for the express purpose of making people notice. Mariel rubbed a hand across her eyes and then shook her head impatiently, as if she were fighting exhaustion and losing. "I need—I need supplies, and a map, and Parry."

"Morgan needs rest," said Josey.

"I'm not asking them to ride with the vanguard, I just need—"

"Hang on, you don't get to decide next steps," said one of the men. "We'll convene with the council of captains back at camp. We didn't come here to make plans, we were just sent to find you—this is a *rescue* mission. Besides, you have no seniority."

"If they have my father *and* Deputy Commander Payne *and* Big John, then we need to act—"

"I can assure you that *nobody* thinks of you as next in line for command just because of the convenience of your name."

There was a short, ugly silence, during which Clem ruminated on the meaning of *my father* and *next in line* and, after joining a few more dots, *Daddy Hartley.*

Ah. Well. That probably explained Mariel's terminal case of uptightness, and how simultaneously straight-backed and shriveled she had looked in front of Jack Hartley, like a tall, desperate prune. Commander Hartley was her father.

What must it be like to have a father like that? Not good, was her guess. Her own father had loved insects and birds and telling terrible jokes. He'd cheered Clem on in anything she set her mind to, and on the rare occasions they seriously argued, he'd always been the one wiping away a tear. He'd hated conflict; loved Clem.

Clem wondered, fleetingly, if Commander Hartley had ever told Mariel he loved her.

★

"Your orders are to return to camp now, with us."

"So we're urgently convening the captains? To decide on a course of action?"

"We have yet to decide."

"So you want me to run back to camp right now and then sit around on my arse and wait for the rest of you to—"

"Your *orders*—"

"Orders from *who*?" Mariel hissed. "As you have so helpfully pointed out, we have no clear chain of command."

"From me. And others. We agreed. And also . . . your mother was there."

Nobody actually *said* "Ooooh" in the mocking tones of childhood bullies, but it was implied.

"As you well know, Regan is in no position to be giving orders," Mariel said, all bile and ice.

"She didn't. But she's there to see you, and you ought to return."

A very awkward silence.

"We'll inform reinforcements of your location, and they will be here in an hour or two to escort everyone to the new site. Camp wasn't compromised in the attack, but we relocated anyway as a precaution."

Mariel snorted. "I suppose you decided this as a group project too. I'm amazed you managed to pull together something as complex as 'We should probably move' without five days of rigorous debate."

"We *debate* so that we can decide, democratically, on the right course of—"

"You *debate* because you're all trying to prove you've got

the loudest voice, even if you have no idea what you want to say."

Richard Flores was almost shouting now. "We all know that if your father *were* here, he wouldn't be asking *you*. You're on probation, and you'd do well to remember that."

"I don't answer to you," Mariel said, each word like the cut of a knife. "And I'll be staying until dawn to help escort these people myself, as any decent captain would."

The next silence was so uncomfortable that apparently it signaled an end to the conversation altogether.

The two men departed. Clem watched Mariel stand there, perfectly still, and then explode into life, striding into the trees so that she could kick something that sounded soft and hollow. She put her hands on her hips and glared up into the leaves, taking deep breaths, before she returned to Josey.

"Feel better?"

"I feel fine."

"Well. They took your father. You're allowed to be freaked."

"My father can handle himself."

Clem couldn't see the expression on Josey's face, but she sounded like she was being more careful with her words than usual. "If he's been imprisoned by the de Rainaults, I don't imagine he still has free use of his hands."

A pause. "It was Frederic," said Mariel. "I just know it was. He's the one behind this. Don't tell me I always say that, because I don't, and—I'm right."

"With respect," said Josey. "Why does it matter whose idea it was?"

"Because," Mariel said heatedly, seeming baffled that Josey even needed this explaining, "it means I will be perfectly justified in seeking revenge. He was out to prove himself. I'll *kill* him."

"Well," said Josey. "You know what it's like. Young, bloodthirsty. Desperate to impress his daddy."

"*Excuse me?*"

Josey coughed. "Yeah . . . I did hear that coming out of my mouth in error."

"I need to think. I'm not leaving my father's fate up to committee."

"Well, it wouldn't be a meeting of the lower captains without a six-hour debate about seniority and procedure before we crack on with the first item on the agenda."

"Perhaps by the time we arrive, they'll have finished their pre-squabbles and moved on to the discussions of real importance."

"A girl can dream."

"Go back to sleep. I'll wait for the cavalry."

"Yes, Captain."

Josey strode away, definitely not looking like a person about to go to sleep, and Clem watched Mariel sit heavily down on a tree trunk and check twice that nobody was looking before she put her head in her hands and allowed herself one small, world-weary sigh.

12

When Mariel was five, her father had handed her a bow and looped the strap of a quiver over her tiny shoulder and told her to shoot and shoot until she hit her target. There had been no tolerance for slack posture or a too-short draw, even though her chubby fingers couldn't quite fit around the grip. When her mother had found them in the clearing just outside the latest iteration of the main camp—Mariel red-faced and stubborn as arrow after arrow clattered to the ground or made a half-hearted attempt at flight before falling short, her father watching dispassionately with his arms crossed—she had been absolutely furious.

It was a surprise, because she really wasn't the furious type. She had always been what people might generously call a *free spirit*, committed to following the impulses of her own heart. She didn't like logistics or warfare; she liked playing with the children, going for long walks and swimming in icy lakes and streams regardless of the weather. She was idealistic in a way that Mariel would come to think of as naive, and chased her own whims even when they took her away from her only daughter. As far as Mariel remembered, her mother had never really cared enough about her to be angry on her behalf until that morning.

The shouting had drawn an audience.

Her grandfather had intervened and scooped her up, hefted her easily onto his shoulders and carried her away. He'd been on his way to a campfire meeting; she remembered sitting in his lap as they gathered around the fire, mythic giants all around her, feeling safe and awed and important with Robin's hand on her shoulder. It always felt that way when he sought her out; even at five, she knew that all heads turned his way wherever he went, and that the other children were endlessly impressed by the stories of her grandfather's daring adventures. It took a few years to realize that he wasn't just special to her, or to the other children of the Merry Men.

She'd thought that he was *her* hero. It turned out that he belonged to everybody.

He couldn't always be there to pick her up and take her somewhere distracting when her mother and father were arguing—and they argued a lot. It only got worse as Mariel grew older. Worse because the fights were more frequent, and worse because Mariel began to understand that on some fundamental level, her parents were deeply unhappy. It meant perpetual unease, danger gnawing in her gut, and people acted as if it were contagious.

Baxter had remained her friend, even as the other children drifted away. He was the only one who didn't mind when she got quiet and cold, withdrawing into herself, wary of everybody. He was so damned happy-go-lucky that it genuinely didn't seem to affect him, at first. She threw herself into training, worked her fingers bloody until night fell, reluctant to return to her own fireside, where her long days of fighting, her black eyes and shredded hands only caused more arguments.

Eventually, as the years passed and training became her entire life, even Baxter had given up trying and stopped coming to her fireside. It would have hurt if she'd allowed herself to notice. Thank God for Josey. She'd been aware of the Abara sisters—it was impossible not to be—but the youngest hadn't been of particular interest until her father sent Mariel to train in a group with the other children, an initiative of his own design, and she and Josey sparred for the first time; Mariel had taken one look at the tall Black girl with the long braids and the grazes on her knuckles who'd already mastered the knife, the sword, and the bow, and was now focusing on fighting without any weapons at all, and had decided she wanted either to befriend Josey or to *be* Josey. They had trained together side by side, not really needing to speak at all, and Mariel had learned that Josey saved her words for when she had something particularly witty to say, and Josey learned . . . well, Mariel didn't know what Josey had learned. Hopefully that Mariel was a worthy adversary in combat and an even better comrade.

Her grandfather was often away, lending his men and his name to other causes around the country. She never stopped being Robin Hood's granddaughter, of course—it was indelible, unshakeable—but on a day-to-day basis she became *Jack and Regan's girl*, often appended with "poor thing" and shaken heads.

She couldn't remember exactly when Regan had started to pull away. In some ways it felt that she had been putting distance between them for Mariel's entire life. All she knew for certain was that one day her father had sat her down and told her that her mother was going to live in a town, of the sort they passed through sometimes on supply runs. That she would live in a house, not a tent. And that of course they weren't going with her.

Mariel hadn't understood why anybody would want to leave. Whenever she spent too much time away from wood and trees she was filled with a terrible sense of loss, and a bone-deep longing for mud and mulch, furry moss on stone, the smell of trampled grass and clear streams. It created a stillness in her heart, completely at odds with the fact that the greenwood was always moving.

When Regan came to say goodbye, Mariel wouldn't even look at her. She ran to her father's side and pressed her face into his tunic, hoping that the moment allowed for a little weakness, and willed her mother to be gone when she next turned around.

She was.

From that day onward there was nobody around to take the bow or sword or knives out of her hands and say that she was too young, or to tell her father that he was working her too hard, that the Merry Men had never been about training children to be killers. She liked it that way. She'd sneak away from camp to practice shooting for hours in the evenings, chalking targets on the trees and retrieving her arrows from them again and again. Friendly contests and bets had been rife at camp back then; the first time she'd won a game, shooting at empty bottles from a cargo of stolen wine, the clap on the shoulder it had earned from her father had been sweeter than all the pooled spoils she collected as her winnings.

The next time Robin returned from his roving tour of England, he'd watched her hit a moving target from forty paces, and the glow of his approval had almost canceled out the muttered argument she'd heard him having with her father a few hours later when all the lanterns had been put out.

Her father had pulled her aside when she was fourteen to tell her that Robin was retiring to an undisclosed, overseas location—"You can just say France," Josey had said, when Mariel told her in confidence that evening—and that once he'd departed, Jack would be taking charge of the Merry Men.

"We can be *more* than this," he'd said, gesturing toward the rest of camp in general. Mariel hadn't understood yet; she'd loved the Merry Men just as they were, chaotic and ramshackle and good. "And I'm the one who can get us there."

If there had been grumblings about Robin Hood's son-in-law being the one to lead them, Jack had silenced them all by proving himself to be ruthless, efficient; more than up to the job. It wasn't like he had been a *Hood* anyway.

If they'd been as nepotistic as the de Rainaults, her mother would have been the one left in charge—but Regan was living in a house somewhere, enjoying a life of privilege and leisure. Her father was the one who'd been willing to put in the work, to take up that mantle and pledge to make the Merry Men a force to be reckoned with. He'd taught Mariel how to fight, and he'd taught all of Nottinghamshire to take them seriously. That was something to believe in.

Now he was gone. Captured. Imprisoned. Potentially on his way to the noose.

And the other captains wanted to take their sweet time making a plan of action—to move to a new campsite first and then waste a lot of time talking. Mariel knew how *that* meeting would go. Democratic process was all well and good, but the only people half these hot-blooded captains wanted to represent was themselves. They all wanted to be the next Jack Hartley. She was getting a headache preemptively, just thinking about it.

Oh, and her mother was going to meet them there. The joys never ceased.

Now Mariel took a few laps of the camp and came to a stop back where she'd started. She was so tired that the edges of her vision were beginning to swim alarmingly, but she was kept upright by the leftover exhilaration flooding her veins, and her mind forming and re-forming scraps of plans until they tied into indecipherable knots. She knew what *she'd* do with important captives, but what would an imbecile like Frederic do? She closed her eyes briefly, wondering if it might count toward offsetting her sleep deficit just to be in blessed darkness for a second or two.

"Don't kick me."

Mariel opened her eyes. Clemence the healer was standing there, her hair a complete disaster, squinting sleepily at her.

"Only, I saw you kick that tree," she continued ill-advisedly. "And I thought you might lash out at me. Like a—you know. A defense mechanism. Automatic. Octopus ink."

"You talk too much," said Mariel, her voice hoarse.

"Yeah, well, I know you like to be mysteriously taciturn, but you overlook the benefits of loquaciousness. Firstly, it lulls people into a false sense of security . . . or a *stupor,* I suppose, if I'm in particularly good form . . . and secondly, it provides a distraction so that I can do things like *this.*"

Suddenly Clemence's hands were on her. Mariel reached instinctively for the knife at her hip, and realized it wasn't there.

Of course. Clemence had it. She had left her captive in possession of a knife and sent Josey off to get some rest, like the world's most comprehensive fool, and now she was going to be stabbed by the human equivalent of a perky Labrador with verbal diarrhea. The sheer indignity of it spurred her into action.

She tried to raise her hands to defend herself, as if fists stood a chance against the press of steel from somebody who knew exactly where her most important organs were, and found them pinned with a surprisingly strong grip. She was too far past the point of exhaustion to do anything flashy in response. She just jerked in Clemence's hands, useless as a grounded moth, and reconciled herself to the killing blow.

"What the fuck are you doing?" Clemence said conversationally.

"I'll shout," Mariel rasped. "You won't make it two paces."

"You won't shout, you'll be a very brave girl," Clemence said. She released Mariel's hands and reached for something in the bag slung over her shoulder; Mariel took her chance and grabbed the healer by the shoulders, reversing their positions and slamming Clemence into the tree so hard her bones rattled. She put a hand to Clemence's throat, pressing just hard enough to provide adequate warning.

They stayed frozen like that, Clemence's eyes wide and disbelieving as she looked up at Mariel from behind a few loose curls, breathing hard.

"There's been some sort of a miscommunication here," she said, with a certain degree of difficulty. "Because you've just shoved me into a tree."

Mariel began to pat her down with the hand that wasn't clenched at her throat, ignoring the slightly choked sound Clemence made as she did. She felt something hard just to the left of Clemence's waist and rucked up her tunic to get to it, pulling it free and taking a step back with the knife raised.

"Cool," said Clemence, still sounding strangled even without Mariel's hand on her neck. "So for the avoidance of any further quirky misunderstandings between us . . . I was coming to look at your sword wound."

Mariel frowned. This didn't seem right.

"You were armed."

"As you just so intimately discovered, the weapon wasn't exactly close to hand."

"Right," Mariel said, the knife wavering slightly and then drooping. She almost felt embarrassed, but cut it off at the pass. Better embarrassed than dead. "Fine. Do it."

Clemence rolled her eyes and took a moment to pull her hair back from her face and smooth down her tunic, which was so covered in mud and blood that it had gone from natural linen to quite effective forest camouflage. Her fingers lingered briefly at her own throat, hovering over the faint red marks Mariel had left there, before she became brusque and businesslike.

"I'm going to touch you now," she said. "So, you know. Don't go off like a guard dog and strangle me."

She put both hands on Mariel's hips and turned her slightly, bringing her out of the shadow and into a patch of bluish moonlight, and then gently lifted her tunic until the wound was exposed. It was excruciating, being touched so casually and gently, but at least Clemence was making it quick.

Mariel didn't look. She didn't need to know how bad it was. It didn't seem important.

"Oh, for God's sake," said Clemence, which didn't seem like a good sign. "You haven't cleaned this, you haven't kept it still, you've just been riding about doing whatever the hell you want. You have essentially shimmied your hips at death and told it to come hither."

Mariel grimaced. "At what point during our rapid escape from armed loyalists would I have had the time to take a scented bath?"

"Jesus, not a *scented bath*, that'd be even worse than packing it with dirt and sticking your finger in it—which is basically on a par with what you've done, for the record. You should have been lying down in a wagon."

"And how would that have looked?"

"Like you'd . . . been recently stabbed?"

"No," Mariel said, trying not to flinch as Clemence trickled wine onto the wound and started dabbing deftly at it with a wad of cloth. "It would have looked weak."

"Well, you'll certainly look very formidable and impressive when you start rotting from the inside out and spewing from both ends until you die. Or—not *formidable*, but people won't want to come anywhere near you, which I suppose is taking different routes to the same results."

"Can you just—*stop talking*?" Mariel's head was pounding.

Her skin was prickling like ants were eating her alive. Now that Clemence was prodding at it, her wound was making itself very known. "You are so incredibly irritating."

"Thanks," said Clemence. She was mercifully quiet as she finished up, daubing Mariel with medicinal-smelling salve. "I could sew this shut for you, if you'd like. I think I have a needle . . . somewhere."

"No."

"Great. Fine. Well, you know where I am if you need me. Still kidnapped." Clemence took a few steps away and then hesitated. "If you want to heal that, you really ought to get some sleep."

When Mariel didn't say anything, the healer finally walked away and sat down in the roots of a tree, pulling her knees up to her chin and closing her eyes as if she intended to sleep hunched like a gargoyle. She shivered slightly, and Mariel noticed for the first time that the breeze was cold against her face.

On her next lap of the camp, she bumped into Josey, who had her hood pulled up over her head and one eye open.

"I was just accosted at knifepoint, Abara," Mariel said flatly. "And you were clearly awake. That didn't seem like any of your concern?"

"Uhh . . . she's got the temperament of a dandelion tuft, I wasn't worried," said Josey. "And besides. I didn't want to cramp your style."

"What?"

Josey smirked, pulling her hood lower. "You know. All the flirting."

Mariel was so incensed she just walked away.

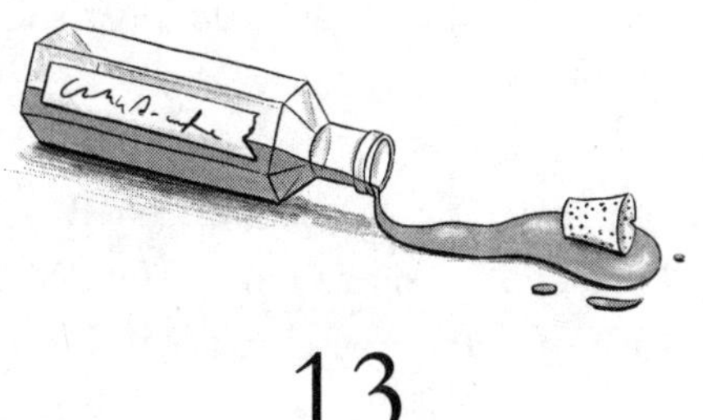

13

Clem dreamed of her parents.

It was very annoying that no matter how hard you tried not to think about something during the daylight hours, at night, memories had carte blanche to run riot over your brain, feeling fresh and raw even if they'd long been left behind.

In the dream, Clem's father was sitting by the fire in their house, whittling something. Her mother was at the table, stewing honey and lavender, humming. Both of them had their backs to Clem, who was everywhere and nowhere at once. She could smell delicate, floral musk and the smoky sweetness of burning applewood.

Later, she knew, her ma would let her eat the crusty end of the bread before dinner, and her pa would present her with whatever he'd whittled and insist it was a carrot, despite Clem's outraged corrections (it would be a rabbit, a doe, a dog—anything but a carrot, but his little joke persisted). Both of them would be bone-weary after a long day's work, but it wouldn't stop them from telling Clem a story or insisting that she tell one herself while they listened, fighting sleep until Clem reached her happy ending.

In the dream, she desperately wanted her parents to turn around, but they didn't, and suddenly she was afraid. She was afraid she wouldn't know their faces; that they'd be strangers to her now.

That jolt of panic woke her up. It ebbed as she got her bearings and realized she'd been dreaming, then was overtaken by a wave of sadness so overwhelming that she had to breathe through it until it was under control.

Dreams. Ugh.

Somebody had draped a cloak over her in the night. It wasn't the lush, mottled green of the Merry Men's cloaks. It was thick, gray and scratchy, with suspicious stains around the hem, but she clutched it to her as if it were silk bedsheets and immediately began to dread the moment someone would take it away. It was a misty summer morning, the cold clinging to the ground as the pink of the sunrise started to filter through the trees. The air was wet with the smell of earth and mulch and moss, and the doves were warbling soft good mornings to each other from the canopy above. Old Rosie would be walking the wood soon, looking for the offerings it had provided in the night—fresh crops of mushrooms, sprouting berries, spiderwebs bejeweled with dew—before returning to her hearth.

Clem ached for it. She just ached, full stop. She was bruised, battered, and covered in everybody else's blood; her dream had shaken her, and her hunger was needle-sharp in her gut. She was dangerously close to feeling sorry for herself, but it was easy to shake off; better her here than Rosie, who'd come far too close to being dragged into this mess. Rosie's hip was getting bad, and sometimes the joints of her fingers swelled until she couldn't cut or mix or grind. She still combed Clem's hair when she was feeling friendly, and darned her woolens when they started to fray, but Clem tried to get to these tasks before Rosie could even think of them. She prepared ingredients too, stripping leaves and cracking nuts, waiting until Rosie was out of the house and speeding through the day's tasks. Rosie would tut and sigh on her return, and tell Clem that she could manage it all perfectly well, and Clem would agree that she certainly could, and then sneak her socks outside for darning before starting on her own day's work.

Clem would sleep on the ground every night for the rest of her life to stop Rosie from ending up trussed in the back of a wagon or shivering through the dawn on a mattress of rocks and twigs.

Rosie would have to see to Clem's patients while she was gone. She wondered what her guardian would do with the strange mushrooms Clem had been drying on the rack in the hope that this batch might calm the nerves, or the solution that had been left to ferment so that she could see if it helped ailments of the stomach. There was a child from the next village over with a gruesome thigh wound whose mother had permitted Clem to see him weekly, to remove the dead tissue and clean the insides, in direct opposition to the advice from a traveling healer who had said that excess pus and a green tint to the skin was *good*, actually.

It would all have to wait until this brush with adventure was over.

The Merry Men were on the move. Fresh fighters unencumbered by injuries came rolling in to escort them as the sky lightened, and after a sleepy, confused interlude as people were shaken awake, the makeshift camp prepared to depart with surprising haste. Morgan was still moving very slowly, but hadn't succumbed to a fever overnight, which was promising. Mariel was already on horseback directing operations; Clem caught a glimpse of her face, which was drained and hollow-eyed, and sighed.

Clem was *not* a good sleeper, but Mariel seemed worse, and her sad, vampiric tendencies were not conducive to wound healing. It was amazing, really, that she'd had the strength to push Clem so hard into that tree trunk—to keep her pinned with one rough hand while she retrieved her knife.

Nobody had ever pinned Clem to a tree before. New experiences were good for the soul.

Kit came to fetch Clem and then very politely helped her up onto the wagon and back into her restraints, like he was easing her into a fine gown. The only sign that he was bruised under his armor was a slight wince when he raised his arm. These people were a bunch of masochists and martyrs.

"I don't know why you bother," said Clem, as he tied a careful knot to secure her hands. "Nothing gets past Josey. She notices every time I blink."

"Ah, well," said Kit. "It's nice to give her a break, every now and then. Cataloguing blinks is labor-intensive."

"Yeah," Clem said, her stomach cramping uncomfortably. "Hey . . . your name is Kit, right?"

"Yes," said Kit. "Akito, if you're fancy. Which . . . we're not. It's ridiculous—I spent so long trying to think of a new name when I was ready, and then it turned out I'm not really a three syllables sort of guy."

"Got you. I'm only Clemence to Rosie. To everyone else, it's just Clem."

"Right," said Kit, nodding as he checked the restraints

at her feet. "Clem. That's you all tucked in. Just need your blindfold."

"My real question is . . . I'm hungry?"

"Not a question," said Kit. "But yeah, I know. Me too. We'll be home soon. I mean—not *your* home. But there'll be food that isn't raw potatoes. How's your stomach?"

"Empty," said Clem.

"I keep thinking about my mother's nishime. She says you can't make it properly here, not like it was for her back home, but I think I'm getting close." He sighed, clearly savoring the taste of phantom food. "It's mostly batch cooking anything we can get our hands on back at camp. No time for finesse. Big steaming cauldrons of anonymous meat stew."

"You're a good cook?"

"I'm an excellent cook."

"But you're also a healer."

Kit shrugged. "I dabble. There's quite a bit of crossover."

"Right," said Clem, thinking she understood. "Because food is healing."

"Oh. Well. I actually just meant that both involve chopping and plants. But yeah, sure. Your thing too."

"I didn't know the Merry Men were refined enough to have dedicated cooks traveling with each company."

Kit laughed. "We absolutely aren't. I'm also *very* good with swords."

"Stop talking to the cargo," griped Morgan, as Baxter helped them up into the wagon.

"Her name is Clem," said Kit.

"Oh, yeah?" said Baxter. "I've just been calling you Giblets."

Clem frowned. "Giblets? Like . . ."

"Like the inside parts of a chicken, yeah. I dunno. You just love rummaging around in people's innards."

"That is true," Clem said, as Kit slipped the blindfold over her head, tied properly this time. "I do love that."

Clem was beginning to feel like her entire life had been reduced to being put in and taken out of the back of this wagon. At least she didn't have to watch Morgan scowling at her for the entire journey; she could pretend, in the dark, that Morgan was actually being perfectly pleasant with their face. In this wildly ambitious daydream, they were also doing some careful and fastidious wound care so as not to undo all of Clem's hard work.

They traveled for what felt like hours. Clem had always known the wood was huge, stretching for a hundred thousand acres at least, but she really *felt* it now as they went for so long without seeming to encounter another soul. The greenwood wasn't really just a wood; it was copses and glades, rivers and waterfalls, lakes, hills, valleys. It swallowed you whole. You could enter at one end of it intending to follow the Great Road straight on through to the south and find yourself still there a few months later with a promising career in lumber, a wife, and a baby on the way.

She might have had no idea where they were, but she sensed when they were close to their destination. Conversations flared into life around her, light and easy despite the circumstances. The cart seemed to pick up speed, as if even the horses felt that magnetic pull home. Once they had come to a stop, she could hear activity all around her, footsteps and fires and shouts of reunion, set against the background hubbub of habitation. It smelled like woodsmoke and freshly turned earth, and when the wind changed, Clem's nose was suddenly full of roasting meat.

It took a while for somebody to remember and unload her, along with the potatoes.

It was Baxter. She could tell by how easily he lifted her. *He* smelled sweet, like fresh hay, and his hands were rough with calluses. He carried her for quite a while, without any audible effort, and then placed her very gently on the ground.

"Gonna tie you to this," he said. "And then Kit told me to tell you that he'll bring you something to eat."

"This is a five-star abduction," Clem said, noticing that her voice was a little ragged. "I'll think of you next time I'm in the market."

"We aim to please," said Baxter. "Do you want the blindfold off?"

"I think you can safely assume that any blindfolded person would prefer it if you removed the blindfold."

"Right. I'll remember that. Always looking for ways to improve our service."

It was such a relief to be able to orient herself when the blindfold had been removed that Clem just sat there, blinking, taking it all in.

She had imagined tents set up in a large clearing, a miniature village crammed into a small space with narrow walkways and side alleys dividing the rows, but this was something far more organic. It wasn't one clearing, but lots of interconnecting ones, stretching farther than she could see through the trees. Tents were arranged in clusters around fires; some were more like makeshift shacks, somehow built into the trunks and lower boughs of trees. It looked as if the camp had been there forever, grown up with the wood, but Clem could see new tents being put up in all directions, people unloading and unpacking with the weariness of a long day in the sag of their shoulders.

"Am I allowed to be seeing all of this?" she said to Baxter. He was stoking the fire a few feet from her, coaxing it into life. She seemed to have been tied to the entrance of somebody's tent; there was a small pile of belongings to her left, well out of her reach, sacks and small trunks and a very imposing stash of weaponry.

"Yeah," Baxter said, with a shrug. "It wasn't even here last night, and it'll be gone by the time you are. You could bring people back ten minutes after we let you go and all they'd find is mud and ashes."

He left, and Clem watched him cross the camp, people shouting out to him in greeting as he went. He seemed popular, but it might just have been that he was tall.

A large covered wagon came rolling in through the trees, and Clem noticed the change in the atmosphere at once. People stopped talking, pulled their children close and shushed them, got up from their fires and removed their hats. The biggest and broadest came forward without any kind of signal—Clem could see Baxter turning with the tide, head and shoulders above them all—and began the slow, solemn job of unloading. Clem didn't really understand until the first body came into view, wrapped lovingly in a cloak, placed on a bed of woven willow.

They were bringing home their dead.

The solemn procession went on and on as people came forward in pairs and then carried the casualties away through the camp. Clem counted fifteen, and then stopped counting. Sometimes family members and friends came forward to take the burden, or to walk alongside the bier with hands resting on the bodies, as if trying to offer them comfort. Sometimes the quiet was interrupted by a wail breaking free, a scrap of somebody's raw and unfettered grief.

By the end, the entire camp was following the procession. There seemed to be hundreds of them, appearing out of trees and tents, different from each other in every way possible but moving as one, united under their cloaks. Clem watched them go, feeling light-headed and insubstantial, hunger gnawing at her, nursing a vague fear that she had been forgotten. She pushed it down. It didn't matter that she was hungry. She could wait. She wasn't going to start whining for a snack at a funeral. She closed her eyes and let her mind drift instead, weaving close to sleep but never quite touching it.

"Here."

Clem opened her eyes and beheld a miracle. Kit was standing there, holding a dented tin bowl full of steaming beef stew. He put it on the ground so that he could untie her wrists, leaving her still restrained by the ankles. The second her hands were freed, she snatched up the bowl and started tipping the contents into her mouth, ignoring the burn as it went down. It was fragrant and salty, rich with gamey meat, and in that moment it was the most *food* food Clem had ever tasted.

"I actually had a spoon for you," Kit said, waving it at her. "But this works too."

He sat down heavily next to her and waited in silence,

so that embarrassingly eager slurping was the only sound aside from the crackling of the fire. When she'd finished and deposited the bowl on the ground, she held out her hands to be re-tied. Kit didn't even notice until she gave him a gentle nudge, and then he shook his head slightly as if his mind had been somewhere very far away before he got to work securing her.

"Did you make that?"

"Hmm?"

Clem nodded toward the empty bowl.

"Oh. Yes."

"It was incredible," Clem said, with almost tearful reverence.

"It was fine," said Kit. "You were just starving. Plus . . . a brush with death makes everything taste better."

"Did you know them?" she said as he knotted. "The people who died."

"Yeah," Kit said, frowning. "I mean, everybody knows everybody here. Sometimes it's more like, *That's Gregory's grandad's daughter's husband, name probably begins with a T,* rather than knowing all their particulars. But . . . yes, I knew most of them."

"I'm sorry," Clem said, knowing how useless it was as a sentiment but meaning it anyway.

"Me too," said Kit. He sat back on his heels, scrubbed a hand through his hair and then got to his feet. "Me too."

He left again, and Clem waited. Waiting grew too boring after an hour or so, and so she once again tried to sleep. At some point she must have succeeded, because when her eyes next opened, it was dusk, and Mariel was standing in front of her.

Her hair was falling out of its plait and she had taken off her cloak and slung it over her arm, her movements slow and weary. She didn't seem to notice or care that Clem was awake, or there at all—she removed her leather vambraces and undid the top button of the soiled shirt underneath, which Clem supposed was her idea of letting loose, and then rummaged in her things until she found a bottle of something and unstopped it with a minute sigh. It was weird seeing her looking like a real person. Clem almost felt sorry for her.

She watched through half-closed eyes as Mariel sat down next to the fire, which was crackling heartily as if recently stoked, and took a swig from her bottle. She jolted fully upright when Mariel held out the bottle in her direction.

"Thanks," Clem said, her voice thin and scratchy, as if to demonstrate the point.

Mariel leaned over and untied one of her hands, pulling the rope slowly loose, and then shoved the bottle roughly into it, like she was desperate to ensure this didn't come across as a genuine act of kindness.

Clem took a sip and found it surprisingly sweet.

"Elder tea?"

Mariel nodded. "Kit makes it."

They sat in an almost companionable silence for a while, until Josey appeared. She too looked tired, and she had a smudge of soot on her cheekbone.

"Gimme," she said, sitting down next to Clem and holding her hand out for the bottle.

"It's elderflower," Clem said, giving it to her.

"Oh good," said Josey. "The hard stuff."

"I don't recall inviting you to my fireside," Mariel griped.

"You didn't have to say it. I'm intuitive. I pick up on social and behavioral cues," Josey said, leaning back on her elbows and crossing one leg lazily over the other. "When are you meeting the rest?"

"Soon. I wanted to go straight away, but Captain Morris had a . . . cousin. On the pyre."

"Well, that was depressing as shit." Morgan limped from out of the darkness and into the glow, and sat down gingerly next to Mariel.

"You were shot in the shoulder," Josey said, passing them the bottle. "Why are you limping?"

"I'd prefer it if you were resting," Clem said to Morgan, who glared back at her. "Not that you should pay any mind to me, obviously. I'm just the one who saved you from an untimely and deeply embarrassing death."

Morgan muttered something inaudible into the lip of the bottle. Clem decided to interpret it as groveling thanks.

It seemed inevitable that Baxter and Kit would join them, and they did a few minutes later, each bloodshot and sooty, Baxter patting Kit on the back and then giving him a gentle push away as they sat down. Mariel rolled her eyes but didn't bother protesting further. It was clear they all found some comfort around her fire, and even though Clem doubted that Mariel would ever admit to it, she noticed a further loosening of the captain's posture as her Men filed in. Baxter had a bottle of something stronger than flower juice tucked into his jacket, and he passed it around for everybody to take small sips, Mariel neatly tossing it behind Morgan's back to Kit when the former wasn't looking.

"I'm just going to put it out there," Josey said, wiping drops of amber from her mouth with her sleeve. "I don't want to go to any more fucking funerals."

"Sarah Atterbury was on that pyre," Baxter said grimly. "We used to do night watches together. She's got two daughters."

They all contemplated this.

Kit sighed. "Feels like it's only getting worse."

Tension followed, evident in Morgan's sidelong glance at Kit and the stiffening of Mariel's spine. It didn't take a genius to figure out why.

If things were getting worse, they were doing so under Jack Hartley's command. Clem had known that people thought like this in Oak Vale, but to hear it spoken aloud at this camp felt tantamount to treason.

Mariel was both Commander Hartley's daughter and one of his captains. Entrenched in every way possible: blood *and* rank.

Clem caught her eye, searching for a sign of offense or remorse, but Mariel abruptly looked away and then got to her feet.

"Go to bed," she ordered, rebuttoning her shirt as she went and swinging her cloak back over her shoulders. "I've got business to attend to."

14

Mariel's mother was waiting for her under an oak tree, the funeral pyres still smoldering beyond. Her hair was long and had turned silvery-gray, knotted at the nape of her neck with the kind of glamorous formality that always seemed out of place when she visited camp. One of the up-and-comers vying for captaincy had escorted her, and was now waiting a short distance away, definitely eavesdropping.

She didn't seem to notice Mariel approaching, which was odd. Usually she was smiling anxiously, waiting for her daughter with open eagerness, so intense in her attempt to display affection that it made Mariel wince.

"Regan."

"Oh—hello, Mariel." Her mother had a hand pressed to her collarbone, clearly still deep in thought as she watched the fires burning low. "It wasn't . . . I didn't . . . How many?"

Mariel scuffed her boot against a gnarled tree root and tried not to sigh.

"Twenty-two," she said.

Her mother sounded aghast. "*Twenty-two?*"

"And there are still a few wounded who might not make it."

"Twenty-two," Regan repeated. Mariel couldn't tell if there were tears in her eyes or if she was just a bit blinky from the smoke. Regan had no right to be sad about their casualties. She had no right to any of this anymore.

"You could have come and paid your respects."

"No," Regan said, distracted. "No, I . . . I'm not really permitted. Club members only, you know."

Mariel didn't want to let her off that easy. "Probably the worst we've had since the early days."

"Listen to you," Regan said, finally turning to look at her with a sad, lopsided smile. "*The early days.* As if you were there. Goodness, you sound positively ancient."

"Right, well. I'm here *now*, aren't I?" said Mariel, not attempting to hide how pointed this was. "I don't have much time. I don't know if they told you—the Commander has been taken. Big John and Deputy Commander Payne too. I'm meeting the captains, and then I imagine I won't be back until it's done."

"Yes," Regan said, rubbing her hands together absentmindedly in a way that always annoyed Mariel. "They told me. Your father always loved running headlong into fights."

"He didn't run headlong," Mariel snapped. "He was *ambushed*. He didn't want this. None of us wanted . . ." She gestured toward the pyres and then let her hand drop.

Regan took a deep breath in and then let it out in a long, extravagant sigh.

"I know you think a lot of your father, Mariel, but you

must admit that he does have an unnatural taste for blood. Something I'd hoped you wouldn't inherit, although . . . by the look of you, you've been scrapping."

"Scrapping," Mariel said. "Yes. I've been *scrapping*, Regan. How silly of me, to get into scraps."

"Oh, don't get upset," said Regan, her hands fluttering toward Mariel, even though there was no way she was foolish enough to believe she'd ever be allowed to touch her. "Look . . . People need a strong leader in a time like this. Let all the captains with their funny pins run off to play soldiers. You should stay here. Reassure people. Take care of them. That's what I was always good at."

Mariel didn't dignify this with an answer, but she did snort disbelievingly as she crossed her arms.

"I know you don't like to listen to silly old Mummy, but think about it, won't you?"

"My father has been *captured*, and you want me to stay home and keep the fires burning? Some of us aren't shameless cowards."

"It's not cowardly, Mariel," Regan said, her voice suddenly sharper than usual. "In fact . . . I imagine it's exactly what your father would want you to do. If you won't think of what *I* want, think of him."

Mariel hated that she was probably right. Jack wouldn't think her ready for something like this: a serious retrieval mission, important lives in her hands. He'd probably send her to kidnap another healer, or stick her on guard duty. It was exactly why she couldn't just wait around for everyone else to decide how they were going to play this. They'd order her to stay put. She needed to act. If she wasn't ready . . . she'd just have to *get* ready, and fast.

And now she was doubting herself. A classic move from the absentee mother.

Mariel closed the shutters. "This is Merry Men business, Regan, and therefore none of your concern."

"I wish you'd call me *Mother.*"

"Mother," Mariel said, the word feeling odd and lumpy in her mouth. "I have to go. We can meet at a later date, once this is over."

"This isn't a meeting, Mariel. I just want to sit with you. To talk to you."

"Another time," said Mariel, desperate for this conversation to be over. She hated her mother's visits. Hated how infrequent they were, and yet simultaneously found every moment of them excruciating. Sometimes she thought she only missed the *idea* of a mother, a vague concept not at all rooted in her actual experience of being Regan's daughter. She'd find herself longing for something, thinking perhaps she was even looking forward to seeing her, and then Regan would usually arrive and spend a few uncomfortable hours making small talk by a fire, glancing around as if she couldn't wait for an excuse to leave, and Mariel would be struck with disappointment all over again. *Ah. Not you.*

In fact, this was the longest Mariel could remember her sticking around for years.

"Do think about it," Regan said again, reaching for Mariel's arm and actually managing to grab hold of it when Mariel didn't move quickly enough. "You might not think much of me, but I don't want to see you captured or . . . or hurt."

Mariel thought of the bandages under her tunic, and

resisted the urge to touch them. "I don't take orders from you, Regan."

"Then take advice instead. You don't have to go running off with your bow and your knives, full of fire and vengeance. That's not how you prove yourself! When they order you to remain here, make the most of it. Show them that a leader nurtures trust. A leader stays."

"A lecture on the value of *staying*? From *you*?" Mariel snarled, unable to keep herself in check a moment longer, secretly glad for an excuse to yank her arm violently out of her mother's grip, sending sharp pain lancing across her abdomen. "Plumbing new depths of irony, Regan. If you'll excuse me."

She ignored Regan calling after her, even sped up a little, knowing it was childish and not really caring. Let her stand there, watched by her guard and unable to follow, shouting Mariel's name until she was hoarse.

They had agreed to convene after a brief recess, so to fill the time she did what she always did: laps. She lapped the camp, mentally mapping out the borders and boundaries, the places where people who liked seclusion had set up their homes a little farther out into the trees. She took note of all the guard posts, invisible to anybody who didn't know where to look, natural platforms high up in the forks of trees with a dark, greenish-gray shadow standing watch. Every time she passed her own fire, flickering in the distance, she counted the figures sitting around it. Tonight there were five. Even from this far away, she could tell that somebody had untied the damned healer's other hand.

They were all too soft. Even Baxter, who looked as if he

could crush a walnut between thumb and forefinger if the mood took him. Even Josey, who could cut a throat and be gone before the first drop of blood fell. It was ridiculous to have a captive in the middle of all this, but Mariel had made her decision, and now she had to see it through.

Night fell in a hush over the camp, and Mariel made her way to the agreed meeting place.

She always had to gird her loins for these meetings. Normally her father or one of his deputies would be there to lead the proceedings, which at least kept tempers at a low simmer, but they were always an ego fistfight, and without anybody in command, Mariel knew this might become more of a proverbial mud-wrestle.

She nodded at a few of her more reasonable comrades assembled there—Captain Morris, Captain Hughes—and tried, without success, to unclench her jaw.

Richard Flores was watching her. He was a good eight years older than Mariel, who considered him a posturing, sycophantic fool. He liked to do push-ups in the middle of camp when he wasn't on watch; he liked to follow Commanders Hartley and Payne around, nodding at absolutely everything they said before they'd even finished their sentences. It felt so obvious to Mariel that all he cared about was aggrandizing himself, but any attempts to point this out to her father would have been pointless. Richard Flores obviously thought himself next in line for Deputy Command. Perhaps even Commander, one day. Over Mariel's dead body.

Flores cleared his throat.

"Now that we're *all* assembled—"

"I'm not late," Mariel said, before she could stop herself. He always irritated her, but the fact that he'd been acting as if he had jurisdiction over her all day was still grating. If her father had been here, she would have held her tongue, but as it was . . .

"You refused an order to return with us this morning, Hartley-Hood."

"What good would that have done? I was two hours behind you. You may have noticed that it's not morning anymore, Flores. We should have convened immediately upon my return. We've wasted the day."

"We agreed to wait until we had paid our respects to the fallen."

"The fallen are already fallen," Mariel snapped. "What about those who might still be living? And when you say 'we,' Richard, who exactly do you mean? Did you poll everybody here, or did you confer with your little mates and then do as you pleased?"

He'd probably only demanded that she return to camp because he delighted in giving her orders. He was always pulling shit like this; finding ways to ensure he was the one passing on directives from her father or Deputy Commander Payne, so he could see the look on her face when she was told to pick up some dull duty or stay put at camp while the others rode out together. God, she loathed him.

Flores shared a glance with some of his aforementioned little mates—Captains Bennet and Howard, fellow like-minded, pigheaded soldiers who stuck together in a pack—and then sighed, sounding put-upon.

"I understand that your emotions must be running

high, Mariel. We'll get your father back. If you wish to go and rest instead—"

"Oh get *fucked*, Flores."

"Please," said Captain Morris. "That's enough. Captain Flores, please catch those of us who weren't here this morning up to speed."

Richard narrowed his eyes at Mariel, but then cleared his throat and straightened up. "We have a good idea of potential holding locations, thanks to scouts—"

"You sent out scouts?" said Captain Hughes, his voice as slow and even as usual. "Before we had convened?"

"If I had waited for us to convene, I wouldn't have any information to present . . ."

A raucous argument broke out immediately. Mariel didn't debase herself further by joining in. They shouldn't—and couldn't—completely break down simply because her father wasn't there to guide them and they were left to the whims of Richard Flores. Some of these captains were far too newly blooded. Two of them she had barely ever spoken to before . . . which, Mariel realized with a jolt, meant that either of them could be the source of the leak.

Who did she trust, really, standing in this circle? Captain Morris. Captain Hughes. Flores sucked, but—she grudgingly had to admit—he wouldn't be the one to betray them. Harry Hassan wasn't there, but she knew her father had personally sent him away on some urgent mission. Elias and Sarika were newer to their posts, but Mariel had worked with them, knew them to be practical and no-nonsense, and she had faith in those instincts. The others she knew well enough, but she couldn't truly vouch for at least half of them. Her father had, and perhaps once that would have been enough . . . but now that they had been betrayed, all bets were off.

"I think," Mariel said, having to raise her voice to be heard, "we need to consider the possibility that Frederic de Rainault . . ."

There was a general groan, which Mariel resented deeply.

"We're not doing this again," said Captain Bennet, one of Richard's bosom buddies. "It can't be Frederic de bloody Rainault *every time*, Hartley-Hood."

They were wrong, Mariel was sure of it. But laboring the point was futile; she clearly wasn't going to win over anybody here. She shut up and listened to them argue instead, talking over each other, each insisting that their plan was a masterpiece and the others were madness.

"We can't make a move until we know exactly who the mole is," said Captain Morris, finally cutting through the chaos. "Anything we do from this point onward will be compromised if the wrong person is privy to our plans."

There were a lot of sidelong glances and shuffling feet after this. Mariel wondered how many people were being weighed up as potential traitors. She felt relatively confident that she would not be among them.

"Nobody at this fireside would betray the cause for whatever meager reward the Sheriff would promise," Richard Flores scoffed. "We should draw up a list of newcomers to camp. Anybody we suspect could be spying—anyone with links to the Sheriff's world. Then we can begin the interviews—"

"You mean interrogations," said Captain Hughes, frowning.

"*Interviews.*"

"And what of the scouts?" said Captain Morris. "What use is it sending out scouting parties if we cannot trust the intel they return with?"

"Perhaps we should interview the scouts too, to ensure . . ."

Mariel stopped listening. She'd heard enough. Endless hours would be lost to this, perhaps even days, all while her father's fate—and Big John's, and Captain Payne's—hung in the balance. Members of her own company might be called in for questioning. The indignity of it was unthinkable.

What would her father do?

Not sit around and wait, that was for certain. He cared about order and procedure, yes, but he'd always told her that a leader needed to make difficult decisions and be steadfast in their convictions. He'd been talking about himself then—he expected Mariel to be the one on the receiving end of those decisions, not making them—but things had changed.

Her grandfather wouldn't have even bothered attending the campfire muster; he'd have already been out there on the road, action before words, loyalty to his Men above anything else.

Nobody even noticed when Mariel slipped away.

Back at her fire, the healer still had both hands untied. She was tending to Morgan, who looked as if they'd rather be shot again than have somebody do something as mortifying as *fuss* over them.

"Good," they said, as Mariel approached. "You're back. Tell her to stop poking me."

"Count yourself lucky that she doesn't have you by the scruff, as would be appropriate," Mariel said. She glanced at Clemence, who was cleaning Morgan's wound with a very intense expression of concentration, the tip of her tongue visible from between her lips as she worked. "Be quick. We have something to discuss."

Clemence didn't look up. "We? As in, *you and I*, we? Because I've been meaning to lodge a complaint about my accommodation. Beds are too hard, management are inflexible, and I seem to be receiving somebody else's paid-for extras in the form of rope restraints."

Mariel grimaced. "Is everything a joke to you?"

"Is *anything* a joke to you?"

"No," said Mariel, hoping she was coming across as authoritative, feeling one stiff breeze away from total physical collapse. She sat down to minimize the risk of falling over, glanced around to ensure that they weren't going to be overheard, and then rummaged in her things until she found a dirty but unused piece of parchment.

She retrieved a thin, hot scrap of charcoal from the fire, waited barely a moment for it to cool, and began to write.

Josey leaned over to take a look and grasped the significance immediately.

"That's a lot of estates."

Baxter had been listening to Kit with a frown on his face, the two of them ensconced over by the entrance to Mariel's tent, but he snapped to attention now. "Estates?"

"Places they might be holding Commander Hartley and the others. Morgan?"

"Hmm," said Morgan, who had broken free of the healer's grip and was now squinting down at Mariel's smudged writing. "Yep. I can narrow this down a bit. Someone draw me a map?"

Kit held out a hand for the parchment and then nudged some more charcoal out of the fire with his boot and waited a few seconds before picking it up. He snapped it in two, turned over the paper, and started to draw.

The healer had stopped trying to paw at Morgan and now looked completely mesmerized, watching with cat-like intensity as Kit mapped the wood in sure, thin strokes. He added the Great Road and its colleagues, the four largest ancient oaks, little squares to denote the larger villages, and then handed both charcoal and map to Morgan, who winced as they leaned down to draw on it.

"Oh, for God's sake," said Clemence. "No leaning! It's like you're just *looking* for opportunities to hurt yourselves. Why not roll in shit while you're at it?"

"I thought shit was good for wounds," said Baxter.

"I think that's for sore throats," said Kit. "And it's powdered *dog* shit, specifically."

"No," said Clemence, aghast. "Absolutely not."

"I only *bent down*," Morgan whined. They considered the map and then started drawing crosses, accidentally smudging some of Kit's carefully drawn lines as they did. "Some of these, maybe. I can tell you straight away that they won't be using the hunting lodge out to the west, because there's a bear in it."

"Nice," said Josey. "Live-in protest. Bears for the cause."

"It won't be this one either. Way too close to the village—you can see the inn from the courtyard. They'd worry that people would talk. But it might be . . ." They kept drawing crosses. Too many crosses.

"Stop," said Mariel.

"I can stop drawing them if it makes you feel better," said Morgan, "but they won't stop being possible prisons."

"This isn't going to work," said Mariel. "Parry, I need to call in the favor."

Morgan's face shut down, just as Mariel had known it would. "No."

"Parry."

"*Mariel.*"

"What favor?" said Kit, retrieving the map from under Morgan's blackened fingers.

"The secret favor," Josey said helpfully.

Baxter had the audacity to look a little hurt. "You've been keeping secrets? About favors?"

Mariel's patience was reaching breaking point. "Parry, there's no point sulking. It's happening. Now more than ever I need everybody to listen to me, follow my orders, and stay in line."

"Sounds fun," said Clemence.

Mariel ignored her. She looked around at their weary, confused faces. They certainly weren't the company she would have chosen—too young, too green, too inclined to make everything into a joke—but they'd do. She could trust them with this. She had to; even though Morgan was currently wiping their charcoal-stained fingers pointedly on one of Mariel's blankets, and Baxter had his cloak on inside out.

"Let's go tonight," she said quietly. "Just us. I'll signal you when the time comes. Until then, play dumb. You don't know anything."

"Absolutely will not be a problem," said Baxter. "Don't know why you don't ask us to do that all the time."

"We're defying the council?" Josey said, with the sort of fire in her eyes that usually meant somebody was about to find themselves with their elbows on backward.

"We're doing what my father would want us to," Mariel said firmly.

"So that's a yes," said Kit. He didn't look quite as ferociously excited about this as Josey, but it was hard to deny that the energy around her fire had shifted from defeated exhaustion to an infectious anticipation.

Josey gently nudged Mariel's elbow and flicked her gaze toward Clemence. Mariel gave a terse nod in return. The healer was her captive. Her responsibility. Annoying as she was, she had already proved just how useful she could be after a skirmish. She'd had plenty of opportunities to try to run, but had obviously seen just how fast Josey could move and had thought better of it. Those were good instincts. The healer was coming with them.

"Great," said Clemence, who wasn't supposed to have seen any of this wordless exchange take place. "But if you're going to make me use a potato for a pillow again, I'd prefer it if you just smothered me now."

Josey raised her eyebrows at Mariel and shrugged, as if to say that this wasn't such a bad idea.

"Just be ready," Mariel said. She picked up the map and folded it very carefully, so that it wouldn't smudge further. She was considering her route across the camp, the best way to pick up supplies without raising suspicion, when Richard Flores stepped out of the shadows, fully armed, flanked by Captains Bennet and Howard.

"Morgan Parry. I think you need to come with us."

Four swords were drawn simultaneously as Mariel's Men rose to their feet.

15

From her vantage point on the ground, all Clem could see, now that Mariel and her Men had closed ranks around Morgan, was a forest of legs.

"Like hell," Mariel said, her voice hard. "On what grounds?"

"Stand down, Mariel."

"*Captain Hartley-Hood.*"

"Stand down, *Captain.*"

"I vouch for Parry," said Mariel. "As you know. So I'd advise you to step off, with haste."

"We will not be 'stepping off,'" said the leader of their current opposition. "Think, Mariel. Don't pollute yourself with blind loyalty. It's *Parry.* There's nobody more likely to be the mole, even if it was done by accident or due to old sentiments and attachments—"

"If you're sentimental about your head staying attached to your body," Morgan said, teeth gritted, "then you should shut up. I'm no fucking mole."

"They've given us good information," said Mariel. "They're on our side. *I vouch for Morgan.*"

"How do you *know*? They might be leading you into a trap. They're a waste of your vouch."

"You know," said Josey. "There's only so many times you can say the word 'vouch' before it starts to sound weird."

"*Vouch*," said Baxter, lowering his sword slightly to look over at Josey. "Yeah. You're right."

Kit, who was standing the closest to Clem at the back of the group, suddenly took a few steps forward; this caused a minor ruckus, and somebody on the other side gave him a hard shove that left him sprawling on the ground beside her.

"Smooth," whispered Clem. Kit turned his head and winked. Unnoticed by everybody else due to the argument now taking place at full volume, he cut through the bonds at Clem's feet and let his eyes flick toward the trees behind Mariel's tent. As he scrambled up, he brushed a finger over his lips to indicate that Clem should ignore all her natural instincts and keep quiet.

Untied, it was easy to start shuffling in very small increments toward Mariel's unattended things.

"We need no more violence after the events of the past few days," said Morgan's would-be abductor. "Surely you aren't going to see the blood of good Men spilled over this? Parry will be held for questioning, and once we have recovered Commander Hartley and the other men . . ."

Mariel sounded well past impatient and was fast approaching piqued. "Parry was questioned extensively when they joined us. Twice by the council and once by Commander Hartley. I'll give you one last chance to change your mind about this, Flores."

Clem's fingers closed around the hilt of a dagger, which

she carefully extracted and then slipped into the bag of supplies still strapped firmly across her chest. She hoped it was a good one. Mariel probably only had good ones.

"My mind is made up."

"Fine," said Mariel. "Then . . . *now*!"

This last exclamation was not aimed at Richard Flores, but at her Men, who immediately jumped into action. Kit grabbed Clem, Baxter grabbed Morgan, and Clem couldn't tell who or what Mariel and Josey had grabbed, because she and Kit were already sprinting for the trees.

Somebody shouted "Cut them off!" from back by the fire, but their sentence ended in an almighty, wheezy *oomph*, as if they'd just been suddenly and violently relieved of all the air in their lungs.

"You can try to escape," Kit panted, as they sprinted into the dark, "but you don't know the roads. They'll catch you. Or you can . . . stick with us. We're nice."

"You're not *that* nice," Clem gasped back at him. She was beginning to realize that for all her hikes in the wood, the hours spent slicing and crushing ingredients, and the few occasions when she'd had to hold a person down to attend to their wounds, she wasn't anywhere near as fit as any one of the Merry Men. Not even Morgan.

They found the horses by almost running into them, and Kit untied them, shoving a dark mare's reins into Clem's hands. She mounted clumsily and then gave her a cautious, experimental squeeze with her legs; luckily, the other three were steering their steeds with more direction and enthusiasm, and all she had to do was hold on as hers took off in pursuit, surprisingly fast considering the treacherous ground. Even if she'd wanted to launch a daring escape, this horse didn't seem likely to abandon its fellows right now. Clem ducked, pressing herself almost flat against the horse's neck to avoid the genuine risk of a sudden arboreal decapitation.

Clem didn't realize that they were looping back on themselves until they burst out into a clearing at the edge of the camp, Mariel's campfire just visible in the distance. Mariel and Josey were no longer standing by it. They had somehow managed to fight their way through, leaving the Men who hadn't taken off in pursuit of the runners bent double or groaning in the mud in their wake. Nobody seemed to be seriously wounded, although one of the Men on the ground was experiencing an overzealous nosebleed.

Mariel's bow was slung over her back, the quiver full of arrows at her hip untouched. She was fighting with her sword and her fists, on occasion her feet, clearly reluctant to cause any real harm even as the others came at her with what looked like murderous intent. You wouldn't have been able to tell that she was wounded and under strict instructions not to do anything to make that wound worse. In fact, you wouldn't think she'd ever received any kind of medical advice from a consummate professional at all.

Josey wasn't bothering with a weapon. As Clem watched, she managed to use a hulking man's own weight against him, sending him stumbling; she applied some specific and focused pressure to his neck and his eyes rolled back into his head.

Josey was a marvel, but Clem's gaze couldn't stray too far from Mariel for long. She was fighting the very haughty

Richard Flores, and he was relentless. Her dark hair flew as she parried, dodged out of his reach, then attacked with an unbelievable amount of force considering the fact that Clem *knew* she had basically been awake for two days straight and had an extra hole in her, to boot. Richard was good—taller, packing more meat on his bones—and in the end he'd probably best her, but for now he was being pushed back, away from where the rest of them waited on horseback. Josey had run out of people to humiliate and was sprinting toward the horses; she leaped up behind Kit, leaning back to keep an eye on Mariel.

"Shouldn't someone be helping her?" Clem said, watching as Richard rallied. He managed to press into Mariel's guard, so that she had to give ground and duck to get out of his reach, catching an elbow to the mouth as she did.

"Doesn't want our help," said Baxter, as Mariel spat blood into the dirt. "If anything, she'd be offended."

Clem caught the expression on Mariel's face.

Her eyes were narrowed in focus, her lips slightly parted, blood on her chin and color high in her cheeks. In combat, she was an avenging demon; a wronged queen of the Celts. All the muscle Clem had felt under her hands was being put to use, her movements strong and precise.

Clem didn't want to be impressed, but her rational mind had closed for business.

The next time Richard attempted to strike, Mariel did something fiddly that knocked his sword completely aside, and then raised hers and slammed the pommel into his nose. There was a hideous crunching noise audible even from the horses—*broken*, Clem thought automatically, and would need to be set properly, lest it inhibit his breathing—and Richard staggered sideways as Mariel came running for the horses.

"*Drop the reins*," she shouted at Clem, scarlet in her teeth. Clem did, and the next moment Mariel was swinging herself up onto the dark horse, taking charge, relegating Clem to passenger.

"*Mariel*," Richard choked, shaking his head and sending blood flying as he took a few steps toward them. "You broke my *fucking* nose. You won't get away with this, you—"

"Let's go," Mariel said, kicking the horse into gear.

They went.

Clem had to throw her arms around Mariel so that she wouldn't be hurled unceremoniously into a bush; at first she felt Mariel stiffen, as if she'd been attacked for fun rather than embraced out of necessity, but after a while of riding through the dark with Clem's hands clutching her waist and her cheek pressed to her back, she seemed to either relax or forget it was happening at all. At one point the other captains seemed to be catching up with them; Clem heard the distant sound of many hoofbeats, a soft roll of thunder that went on and on, but Mariel immediately led the group in evasive maneuvers, taking sharp turns and wild leaps over fallen trees until Clem felt a little bit sick, and eventually their pursuers fell behind.

"Think that's it?" Josey called from behind, when it felt like they'd been running forever.

Mariel seemed reluctant to stop, but she threw up her hand to halt them, and they came to a skidding, bucking halt.

She pulled herself out of Clem's weakening grip and dismounted. Clem followed her, feeling (and probably also looking) like a low-budget scarecrow. The others joined them, stretching tired legs, popping joints, and sighing, leading the horses to a gently trickling stream.

"He knows as well as I do that Parry is not the mole," Mariel said to Josey, who shrugged. "He's not going to waste more time chasing us around the wood when he could be back at camp giving orders *and* slandering me as a traitor."

"It might have been me," Morgan said, inexplicably offended. "I could be a criminal genius."

Baxter laughed breathlessly. "Is that really the angle you want to push right now, Morglet?"

"He just wants to humiliate me and call my leadership into question," said Mariel. She scrubbed a hand over her face. "So, look, we're just . . . we're going to . . . it'll be a couple of days' ride, and if we . . ."

"No," said Kit.

"What do you mean, *no*?"

"I mean *no*," said Kit. "We aren't going anywhere. Most of us have barely slept since Oak Vale. You've got a hole in your side, Morgan has half a shoulder missing. We're useless. I reckon a medium-sized crab could wander over and finish us all off right now in a few snips. We need *rest*."

"But . . ." Mariel seemed a bit lost. "But there's no *time*."

Kit was immoveable. "Better to get a proper night's sleep and start fresh in the morning than to stumble into a fight and get a face full of knife because you took too long to open your eyes after a blink."

"Yeah," said Baxter. "Slow and steady keeps your limbs on."

Morgan didn't say anything, but was clearly only staying upright by sheer force of will. Mariel looked at Josey, who shrugged. "I slept," she said, flashing a grin. "But I can't fight on behalf of four people who are dead on their feet. Two, sure. But four?"

"For what it's worth," Clem said, "I agree with Kit."

"It's worth nothing, thanks," said Mariel. She tried to pace, but seemed to realize that she could only make it a few steps in either direction, and she stopped, her gaze stuck on Morgan.

Morgan, who was currently dropping off and then jolting awake again with sleepy determination, like a milk-fed kitten.

"Fine," Mariel said. "We'll rest."

She said it like "rest" was the worst swear word she could imagine.

There wasn't an *actual* collective sigh of relief, but the tension went out of everybody at once. Clem sat down so forcefully that it was almost a collapse. Baxter immediately rolled his shoulders and went off to do something industrious—probably uprooting trees with one hand and then snapping them in half over one knee—and the others saw to the horses, built a fire, took stock of what they'd managed to bring with them as they fled. It wasn't much.

"If you're wounded and you need seeing to, you'll have to come to me," Clem said. "My legs don't seem to be working." Nobody came to her. Typical. Baxter returned and deposited an armful of firewood, and Morgan drew their knees up to their pointy chin and glowered. "Seriously, what's the point of forcing me to come with you if you aren't going to *utilize* me? If you don't let me heal, I'll get terribly bored, and then I might start hatching a plan to escape."

Kit poked at Morgan until they reluctantly shuffled over and offered up their shoulder. The wound was pink but not swollen, healing as best as could be expected under the circumstances. There wasn't much Clem could do without hot water, and nobody seemed in the mood to whip up a burn bowl for boiling. If it began to fester, she might need to start removing flesh, something she was sure Morgan wouldn't accept gracefully. She risked a light daubing of elder balm for the swelling and then gestured Mariel over with a finger.

"Later," Mariel said dismissively.

When the fire had been coaxed to a roar, they formed a circle around it, Morgan making a cocoon of their cloak and falling almost immediately asleep. Their head was dangerously close to a sticky patch of mud; Baxter took hold of them by the ankles and gently pulled them to drier ground.

"I'll take first watch," Mariel said, her voice dry as chalk.

"Don't be ridiculous," said Kit. "I will."

"First is best," Mariel said. "It'll be a waste if I go down now. I won't be able to . . ." She didn't finish this sentence, but Kit just sighed.

"I'll take second," he said. "Wake me up *soon*, Mariel."

"Captain."

"*Mariel*," Kit said, defiant until the moment he closed his eyes.

All was quiet except for the soft whickers of tired horses and the crackle of the fire when Mariel eventually came to sit by Clem.

"We must stop meeting like this," Clem said quietly, so as not to disturb the others. "Can you take off some of your clothes?"

Mariel gave her a weak attempt at a stern look, but then did as she was told. Clem watched her tunic ride up as she removed her cloak, revealing an expanse of scarred and lightly muscled torso. The amount of scars wasn't unusual, even in somebody so young; plenty of the children back at the village had been scarred by disease or injury by the time they could walk. What made Clem shudder was the fact that these had all been inflicted intentionally, shot or hacked into Mariel's skin.

The sword wound was a narrow, ragged hole and a purple stain of a bruise, and it looked unhappy. Clem did what she could, careful to touch Mariel as little as possible as she applied her salve, and then gestured for her to turn. She slowly reached for the captain's face and wasn't the least bit surprised when she flinched away.

"What *now*?"

"You caught a stray elbow," said Clem. "Just wanted to check on your teeth. Don't bite."

Mariel seemed as if she might be about to say something, but it died on her lips as Clem took hold of her chin.

"Turn," Clem said, and Mariel did, looking slightly dazed, tilting her head toward the fire so that Clem could get a better look. There was a cut on her bottom lip, the soft skin split and raw-meat red; Clem used a gentle thumb to ease Mariel's mouth open and found a matching lesion on her gum. Apart from that, she had a surprisingly healthy-looking mouth for somebody who didn't seem to care for her body except to use it as a weapon.

"I recommend that you don't eat any sour fruits or salted meat for the next few days," said Clem, releasing Mariel from her grip. "But you'll live."

"Devastating," said Mariel, blinking at her. "What with all the gift baskets of provisions we're expecting to receive."

Clem grinned. "You *really* need some sleep," she said, rummaging in her bag. "You were just almost pleasant. Or . . . not *pleasant*, but you cracked half a joke. Hang on, don't run away yet."

She pulled out a tiny pot of balm and then held it up to Mariel, as you'd first show a halter to a horse to stop it from panicking. Mariel narrowed her eyes, but didn't bolt. Clem used her little finger to scoop some out and then carefully daubed it onto Mariel's lip.

Mariel frowned, her tongue probing just as Clem had been about to tell her *not* to eat it.

"Taste good?" she said instead.

"Like blood," said Mariel, brow still furrowed. "And lavender."

"Great name for a musical troupe," said Clem, carefully re-corking her balm. "Blood and Lavender. How the hell have any of you survived this long when you act like I'm threatening to skin you slowly with a fork every time I try to patch you up?"

"We have healers," Mariel said. "But they're more . . .

splints and amputations. Church for a cold, dunk in an icy stream for a fever."

"Ah. Yeah. I know the sort."

"And we have Kit. He knows plants and herbs. He tries to . . ."

"Take care of you," said Clem.

"Cook for us."

"Same thing."

This made Mariel look slightly uncomfortable, as if it hadn't occurred to her that a meal could be anything other than a loveless exchange of fuel.

"Why did your delightful colleagues want Morgan?" Clem said, pushing her luck. Mariel rubbed at her temples, not speaking for so long that Clem was sure she was about to get the brush-off.

"Morgan is . . . cousin to the bailiff's wife," she said eventually. "A family very close to the Sheriff. They only joined us recently."

"Ah," said Clem, glancing over at Morgan, who was fast asleep. She knew that those who weren't born into the Merry Men tended to be runaways; people who had nowhere else to go and went into the greenwood desperately seeking a new place to put down roots. She *had* heard of people with perfectly nice lives setting off to join, chasing mystery and prestige as she'd once dreamed. Having seen how they ran operations, she imagined the glamor probably wore off quite quickly when it became clear that it was more about procedural kidnappings, moving sacks of potatoes, and building fires than opportunities for heroics and private seminars with legendary outlaws.

"Won't they find us here? I thought you were all excellent trackers."

"We are excellent trackers," said Mariel. "And we can always find each other—when we want to be found."

She was getting very blinky, like she was losing the battle to keep her eyes open.

"You can sleep," Clem said. "*I'll* take first watch."

"You're not qualified," said Mariel, although she had slumped back on her elbows, her whole body sagging hopefully toward the ground.

"I am extremely qualified," said Clem. "Twitchy as a ferret and terrible at sleeping."

"No," said Mariel, her voice cottony around the edges. "*I'm* terrible at sleeping."

"Oh, sorry, didn't realize you had the monopoly on stress-induced sleep disorders."

"Shut up," Mariel said. "You're a hostage. You're in my . . . custody. You'll run."

"I'm not going to run," Clem said, trying not to smile, watching Mariel fight sleep like an angry baby. "Josey will wake up and garrotte me with a big leaf. Besides . . . I don't know where I am."

What she *didn't* say was that, right now, she felt rather invested in keeping these fools breathing. Once patients came under her care, she liked to see them healed. Mariel and Morgan excluded, they weren't a bad bunch, and even Mariel had shown a surprising amount of backbone when it came to defending her own. Since it had all gone so wrong for Clem early in life, she'd been pretty good at going with the flow, because she knew better than anyone that there was no point fighting it. Things would happen to you, both great and very terrible. You might as well make the most of them, when you could.

Clem would escape eventually—find an opening by a familiar crossroads, wait until Mariel's back was turned and Josey was busy gently maiming somebody else—and make her way home.

Until then, she really would keep watch; and it was a good thing too, because Mariel had fallen asleep, her head cushioned on her arm, one hand unconsciously curled around the wound in her side, her only concession so far to the fact that she was in any sort of pain.

16

Mariel was horrified to discover that she had slept, and even more perturbed by the fact that it had actually helped. Her head felt clear, her pain slightly more manageable, the constant low-level buzz of nausea in her stomach had somewhat abated. Kit had trapped a large hare, apologized to it profusely and then roasted it, so they had hot, lean meat for breakfast. Mariel ate in silence, watching Kit and Clemence take everything out of the healer's bag and line it up carefully on the ground, taking stock. It was surprising how much she'd managed to fit into such a small satchel.

"Marigold for the skin. Feverfew for headaches," said Kit, handling each of them gently. "You should talk to my mother. She's the queen of kampo. She even has some herbs you can't get here—she saves them for special occasions."

"Really?" Clemence said, sounding frankly breathless with interest. Mariel rolled her eyes. "She sounds like my kind of woman."

"Oh, yeah. You should apprentice under her for a while, when you . . . Well, another time, maybe. What do you use yarrow for?"

"Wounds," said Clemence. "Inflammation."

"And these mushrooms?"

"Er, that was an . . . early experiment in pain management," said Clemence, looking slightly shifty. "But the side effects were . . . interesting, to say the least."

"You're a weird kind of healer," Morgan griped. "You haven't put leeches on us even once. I've got too much blood, I can tell. I feel all . . . heavy with it."

"You have the exact right quantity of blood," said Clemence. "I'll let you know when you don't, but with the amount of new and exciting holes you all like to procure, I wouldn't be concerned about a surplus."

"Ha," said Baxter. "Holes *are* exciting."

"Scarlet," Mariel said warningly, intervening before this could get any more out of hand. Baxter didn't look particularly cowed. "Look, we need to move fast. We don't know who the mole is, but I'm not willing to trust anybody else right now. We can't squander our head start."

"The Sheriff's people will know we're coming," said Baxter. "We're hardly going to let them capture our Commanders without retaliation."

"Yes," Mariel said, her patience already waning. She wasn't a fan of audience participation. "But they're used to my father's way of doing things. Shows of force. All-out battles. They won't be expecting there to only be six of us, gaining access by stealth."

Because it's foolish, her mind added stubbornly.

"Because it's foolish," said Josey happily. "*That's* why it'll work."

"We're going to Stoke Hanham?" Morgan asked grimly.

"Stoke Hanham?" Kit said, brow furrowing. "But I thought—"

"Yes," said Mariel. "And I'm not interested in arguing the point, Chisaka."

On the edge of Stoke Hanham perched the bailiff's grand estate, Hanham Hall, which also happened to be the house where Morgan had reluctantly spent their childhood years. They were running blind right now, and they didn't have the luxury of scouts to scatter across the wood, scoping out every possible target. If they were going to find Mariel's father, they needed real intel. Morgan had left their previous life behind them, but for one fraying thread of contact—and it was that thread Mariel needed to pull on now.

It would hurt Morgan, but it would be foolish not to use this advantage when so much was at stake. And besides, Mariel had put herself on the line for Morgan more than once. It was time to demand something in return.

"We took Morgan with us to protect them," Kit said slowly. "Right? And not just because you wanted to call in this . . . favor, away from the other captains."

"What exactly are you suggesting?" Mariel said, knowing that the edge to her voice could cut glass.

"That it's not worth taking unnecessary risks just to try to prove—"

"*Chisaka.*"

Kit finally had the good sense to be quiet.

"Parry," Mariel said. "Stoke Hanham."

"Fine," Morgan said. "But don't ask me for any more favors after this. The favors stall is closed."

"Fine," Mariel repeated.

Kit wasn't making much effort to conceal the fact that he thought this was decidedly *not* fine—probably some concern about the reopening of metaphorical old wounds and literal new ones—but he was too sentimental, and Morgan was old enough to make their own decisions. "It's at least a day's ride. Let's go. Morgan, ride with me, we need to talk."

Morgan talked—or, more accurately, listened to Mariel talk and gave short, insolent answers—as they all packed up their meager belongings, mounted two to a horse, and started picking their way through the trees. It was a strange feature of living her entire life in the greenwood; Mariel never had to think about exactly where they were, but she could position herself within the boundaries of the wood, righting their course without even noticing she was doing it, and the others did the same, picking up the slack whenever her inner compass went quiet.

They rode for hours, Mariel's head already filled with Stoke Hanham and what they'd find there, repeating the finer points, with Morgan sulking in the saddle behind her getting increasingly frustrated at the mundane repetition of her questions.

It probably wasn't just the questions. It was the pain. It seemed to barb everything; make even the smallest of tasks feel mammoth.

Not that she'd know, of course. Pain didn't bother her.

The first sign that there was something amiss was that Josey abruptly stopped talking to Kit and went still in the saddle, listening; she glanced over at Mariel and raised her eyebrows very slightly, then put a finger to her lips and cantered away into the trees, Kit clinging on for dear life.

"That's encouraging," said Clemence. She at least had the presence of mind to say it quietly.

"Shut up," said Mariel. They kept riding in silence, Mariel straining to listen for whatever had alarmed Josey.

Baxter frowned. "I can smell . . ."

"Smoke," said Clemence. Mariel noticed that she looked a bit odd; drained of some of her usual color. "Something's on fire."

The horses didn't seem particularly keen to trot directly toward certain danger, but they had been trained well and were practically bulletproof, so despite their flared nostrils and rolling eyes they picked up speed. Soon the smoke was unavoidable; the air was dirty with it, thick and cloying. Baxter started coughing, his eyes streaming, and Morgan let out half a strangled sneeze.

"Shallow breaths," Mariel said, blinking rapidly to clear her vision. "Cover your mouths."

When the trees thinned, they saw the fire: three squat wooden houses burning like torches, columns of flame grasping for the sky and spitting sparks into the neighboring trees where they smoldered ominously. There was a sparse line of villagers passing buckets up from the well, but the inferno did not seem particularly intimidated by the occasional splash of water.

Mariel and the others dismounted and sprinted the rest of the way toward the village as one.

"Healer, Parry—help at the well. Scarlet, with me."

Morgan and Baxter did as they were told. Clemence did

not. She looked dazed, smoke-drunk, her eyes fixed on the flames as her hands clenched uselessly at her sides.

"*Healer,*" Mariel said again, but she didn't have time to wait and see if Clemence was going to snap out of it; she and Baxter approached the nearest house, Baxter wincing as something within gave an ominous crack.

"There are people inside," a woman said tremulously as they approached, her hand clutched to her heart. "Children. And a girl just went in . . ."

"Green cloak?"

"Yes," said the woman. She was trying to say something else, but Mariel was already on the move, Baxter at her heels. The door at the front of the house was a lost cause, the lintel half collapsed and already burned deep black, but around the back there was another way in, smoke billowing from within. Mariel exchanged a grimace with Baxter, and then they both moved toward the entrance, pulling their cloaks up over their faces. An insistent hand on her arm forced Mariel to stop, and when she turned she saw Clemence standing there, her expression fierce now, holding two sodden strips of gray cloth.

"Wrap them around your mouths and noses," she said, raising her voice to be heard over the clamor of the fire. "It helps with the—with the smoke."

They did so without hesitation, and Clemence fell back as they stepped cautiously inside, Baxter looming over Mariel like a human scaffold, bracing for falling debris.

It was hell. Fire on all sides. Even through the cloth, Mariel knew she was breathing in death. The house was simple, just a pair of modest rooms, but their path through it was blocked by smoldering beams and blazing thatch, and they made excruciatingly slow progress as Baxter heaved things out of the way, every movement increasing the risk of total collapse.

As soon as he cleared the doorway into the second room, Josey appeared, a silent toddler in her arms and a child of about six or seven with their arms wrapped around her leg.

"Took you long enough," she shouted, her voice ragged.

"That's it?" Baxter replied, scooping up the biggest. "Just two?"

"Hope so," said Josey, pushing him. "Move. It's coming down."

They were barely out of the doorway when there was a sound like the last groan of a falling tree, and the roof caved in completely, raising a collective gasp of horror from the watching villagers. When they were out of range, Mariel sat heavily down on the grass and wrenched the wet cloth from her face, watching as Josey gently eased the half-conscious toddler onto the ground, the older child still completely unwilling to let go of Baxter. They were quickly surrounded by people offering water to drink, words of thanks, soothing hands for the children; the crowd parted to let a panting, red-faced man through, and when he saw them he let out a strangled, wordless cry and dropped to his knees, gathering the youngest child up into his arms as the other finally released Baxter's leg and went to cling to him instead.

"Where's Kit?" Mariel said to Josey, who was taking in deep, serrated lungfuls of air.

"Not inside," she choked out.

Good enough. Mariel closed her eyes and took a few deep breaths. Her own throat felt scorched, prickly, and hot when she swallowed. When she opened her eyes again, Clemence was crouched over the children, her ear to the smaller one's chest.

"They just need rest," she said to the gently weeping man Mariel presumed was their guardian. "And fresh air. Steam once they can tolerate it, from hot water with thyme. Here."

Clemence rummaged in her bag and then pressed something into his hands, and he accepted it with a nod, pulled the child close, and gazed tearfully at the healer like she was a celestial being. Beyond, she could see Kit applying one of Clemence's salves to a painfully pink arm.

Mariel hauled herself upright and went to take stock of the rest of the damage. It seemed that the people of the village had given up on any firefighting efforts, and were now simply watching the houses burn. She thought of the funeral pyres back at camp, all those faces awash with incongruous sunset gold, their expressions grim with grief.

An older woman stood at the center of a circle by the well, the people leaning toward her like plants to the light, a dead giveaway that she was in charge. Mariel approached, and the villagers moved aside to let her through, a few muttering about the color of her cloak and giving her once- and twice-overs as they did so.

"Captain Mariel Hartley-Hood," Mariel said, by way of introduction, and she saw the way the older woman stood up a little straighter. "What happened here?"

"Sheriff's men," said the woman. "Punitive. They think we were light on our taxes."

"Of course," said Mariel. She was already moving away, on to the next thing, when she realized that this was probably a moment that required more tact and subtlety than was usually in her arsenal. "I'm sorry."

"Don't be sorry," said the woman. "Just give them hell, would you?"

Mariel nodded seriously. "We will."

Clemence and Kit had run out of villagers to treat for burns and were insisting on slathering Mariel, Josey, and Baxter with musky, sweet-smelling salve from Clemence's seemingly bottomless bag of tricks. Mariel flinched when Clemence first touched her, still not used to this near-constant physical contact that she insisted on, and then determinedly focused on watching Kit and Baxter. Baxter's eyes were closed as Kit rubbed salve over his pink knuckles, using his other hand to inexpertly smoke something from a borrowed pipe that Clemence had insisted would help clear his airways. When his eyes opened, heavy and bloodshot, he smiled at Kit, and Kit smiled back, before reddening and bending over Baxter's hand again. Something about the intimacy of the moment made Mariel feel even more out of sorts.

There had been far too much *touching* around here lately. Sure, it was medicinal, but it was also very *weird.* Next thing they'd all be holding hands and talking about their feelings.

"That feels nice," Baxter said to Kit in a low, wheezy

voice as the latter made slow circles over his knuckles; Kit's ears flooded scarlet.

"Enough of this," said Mariel, pushing Clemence away. "We're fine. Abara? You're . . . fine?"

"I am not currently on fire," said Josey, which was adequate for now. Clemence sighed in a very put-upon way, but nevertheless packed up her supplies.

Mariel tried to get them ahorse and on their way without any further unnecessary pleasantries, but the man who had received the rescued children so gratefully came to grasp Josey by the hand and offer gifts of trinkets and a few fresh vegetables, which she refused. He took Baxter's uninjured hand too, and seemed on the verge of doing the same to Mariel when she gave him a brusque nod and then called for them to move out.

She didn't have the strength to talk to Morgan about the particulars anymore. In fact, they were all silent and weary as the horses trudged on through the trees. They had been traveling an hour or so when Mariel heard something in the distance, caught a flicker of color; she raised a hand for everybody to pull their horses to a stop.

"Somebody's made camp," she said quietly. "Maybe . . . thirty feet west?"

"Good for them," said Morgan, not quietly enough. "Let's go and ask them if they have any sausages."

"Fuck," sighed Baxter. "*Sausages.*"

"Kit, Josey. Let's take a look," said Mariel. She decided she must have imagined the five sighs of disappointment as she dismounted her horse.

Josey took the lead by silent agreement, and they followed

her, crouching low and then almost flattening themselves completely to the ground as they approached the camp; they were situated on a little rocky hillock, with a view down into the hollow where pink, gamey meat was being roasted over a fire by a large encampment of men.

Most of them were unrecognizable to Mariel. A handful were Sheriff's men she'd encountered before, although she couldn't have put names to faces. She only had eyes for Frederic de Rainault.

He was sitting by the fire with one leg elevated in front of him, presumably to ease the pain in his knee (*ha!*), but even so there was a relaxed elegance about him—a carelessness that belonged only to the rich. He was completely apart from the others, letting his father's men deal with things like fires and provisions, here to playact the role of dutiful knight on a noble quest.

If he ever did anything interesting enough to warrant someone writing his story, would Mariel be the villain? The bandit in the wood who terrorized him, despite his attempts to civilize and spare her? The hand that raised the knife and brought his tale to an end?

Robin Hood was a hero in the stories told around campfires and hearths in the villages, but Mariel could only imagine what they said about him in the cold stone halls of grand houses. Delinquent. Rabble-rouser. Thief. Perhaps unpalatable even to those more sympathetic to the cause: of course *something* must be done about the poor, but to take from those more fortunate to do so? It just wasn't the right way to go about it . . .

Mariel didn't care. Frederic was hers. He represented

the next generation of the Sheriff's line, poisoned by his father, groomed to take over and bring more corruption and misery to the greenwood, part of a cycle that never seemed to end. It was a future without hope, and Mariel would not allow him to bring it to into being.

She scanned the group again for captives, knowing it was futile but daring to hope for half a second anyway. Of course, her father wasn't there. It wouldn't have made sense for Frederic to cart his precious cargo around the woods, but you never knew with these people. They weren't always the best and brightest.

They weren't quite close enough to hear what was being said around the fire; the occasional word was borne aloft with the smoke, but otherwise it was just overlapping man-chatter. If they could just get closer—if Mariel could eavesdrop properly, allow Frederic to let slip all manner of vital information before she pulled out her knife and silenced him forever . . . But they'd chosen their campsite well. To get closer would be to declare war.

The numbers weren't on Mariel's side, it had to be admitted. Frederic had many more men. They'd probably had hearty meals and plenty of sleep, somehow untroubled by the thought of torched villages and burned children. There were, what? Twenty of them? Thirty? How many could she take?

The wound in Mariel's side throbbed. She could give him one to match, to start.

"No," Kit said quietly in Mariel's ear.

She hadn't even realized that she'd moved. She unclenched her hand from the hilt of her knife and shot him a sideways glare.

"I know we're good, but we're not *that* good."

He was right. It would have to wait for another day. Mariel wasn't going to allow herself to be killed at the hands of a *de Rainault*. She'd never forgive herself.

As they retreated from their vantage point, Frederic's dog glanced sharply up in their direction. Frederic himself didn't notice at first, but it was only a matter of time before somebody followed that dog's nose . . .

They hastened back toward the horses, then mounted and rode away in swift silence, a bitter and potent hatred powering Mariel's pounding heart.

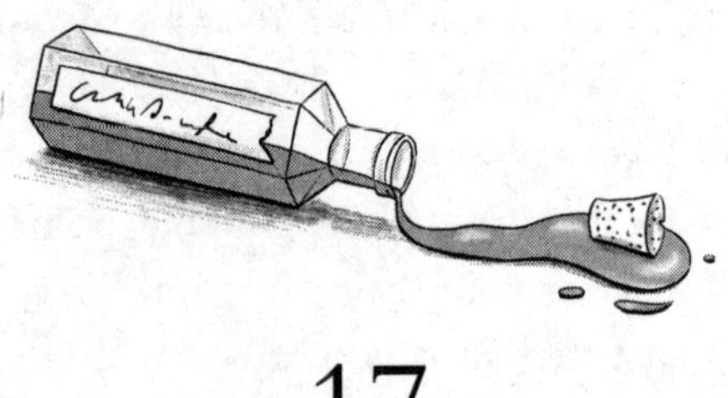

17

Sharing a horse with Baxter was a logistical challenge.

He was just so *enormous*. Clem's options were to cling to him and risk being bumped backward over the horse's hindquarters, or sit in front of him and feel roughly the size of a toddler in his crushing embrace.

She chose the latter, and they fell into a slightly ridiculous pattern during which Baxter would apologize—for taking up too much space, for crowding her, for some other crime Clem wasn't even aware of—and she'd tell him it was fine, and then a few minutes later they'd start the whole exchange again.

It was around the fifth or six apology that Clem's teeth started chattering, and she realized she was going to be sick.

"I'm gonna puke," she told Baxter. He reined in the horse and put two fingers to his mouth so that he could whistle for the others before they came to a stop.

He hefted himself down and then helped her out of the saddle with one arm. Clem would have thanked him, but she was already sprinting for the bushes.

It had been a while since breakfast, which meant there

wasn't much to come up, but her stomach did its best regardless, and she stood doubled over and choking bile into the grass, accompanied by the pleasant sounds of nature all around her. Babbling brook, birdsong, girl loudly heaving up nothing and muttering "*Shit, ugh, Christ!*" in between.

She'd watched Mariel and Baxter run straight into that inferno with barely a moment's pause, and been completely certain that they wouldn't be coming out again. It seemed impossible—the fire was everywhere—and when they'd emerged, sooty and gasping and *alive*, she'd felt her whole life lurch sideways, from the reality that had seemed inevitable to the one actually playing out in front of her.

It was silly. She didn't even really know these people. Still, the surety of their impending deaths had rattled her, and she hadn't been able to shake that feeling.

Somebody put a gentle hand on her elbow, which made her jump violently. When she looked up, Kit was sheepishly offering her a waterskin.

"Thanks," Clem croaked, wiping her mouth with her sleeve and then taking a deep drink.

"Are you ill?" he said, frowning at her as water trickled down her chin.

"No," Clem said. "I'm fine."

"Oh, yeah," Kit said. "*Fine*. There's a lot of that about."

"I just need a moment," Clem said, waving him away. He went, and she sat down hard on the ground, taking another drink of water and pressing the fingertips of her free hand into the earth to ground herself. The air smelled *green*—mossy and lush with a hint of rain—which helped to slow her breathing and her racing heart.

When the wind shifted, the smell of smoke lifted from her tangled hair, undoing all of that progress.

"Are you finished?"

Mariel was standing with her arms folded, scowling. There was a scattering of burn marks across her forehead, angry dots where she must have run into a shower of sparks. Clem had attempted to apply calendula, but Mariel had pushed her away.

If she wanted to be sore and crispy, that was her prerogative.

"Give me a break," Clem said, breathing in through her nose and out slowly through her mouth.

Not again. She hadn't felt this out of control since she was a child. She'd mapped routes around this feeling, careful to avoid reminders and pitfalls, but years of carefully maintaining those paths had been no match for a few days with the Merry Men. Why did it feel like the danger was still ahead, even though it had passed? And . . . what was it she usually told people when their breathing got too fast? In for seven, out for eleven. Listen to the sounds around you. Take a second to . . .

"We don't have time for this," Mariel said shortly. "We need to move."

"You move," Clem said, closing her eyes. "I promise I won't take it personally if you leave me behind to hasten your departure."

Mariel let out a cantankerous huff, but Clem was trying to count along with her breathing again.

When she eventually opened her eyes, Mariel was standing right in front of her.

"If I leave you behind," she said, with no attempt at patience, "the Sheriff's men will catch up to you."

"Lucky them."

"What's wrong with you? Are you . . . *upset*?"

The disgust with which she delivered this was almost enough to make Clem laugh. "Yeah. Yes. I'm upset. It happens."

"It was just a fire. Everybody lived. Pull yourself together."

"Mmm," said Clem, trying to inject some normality into her voice. "Tough love. I *do* like it, but if you could try being nice, then I can compare the two and see which is better."

"Enough," Mariel said. "You're fine."

"Hey, that was my diagnosis too."

Mariel grabbed Clem by the arm, and Clem didn't even bother feigning outrage.

"I am not putting everybody at risk because you needed your little moment of weakness."

This was so hilariously telling that Clem considered about ten things to say that would *really* piss Mariel off, but in the end decided against them, mostly because she had sharp, pinchy fingers.

"You've got soot in your eyelashes."

Mariel frowned, and then blinked a couple of times. It didn't help.

"Shut up," she said eventually, before storming back toward the horses, pulling Clem along in her wake.

Riding for long periods of time was both dull and difficult. The added incentive of potential enemies at their heels did add a little frisson of excitement to the first hour or so, but they saw neither hide nor hair of them, and Clem began to suspect that they had never been in pursuit in the first place.

She had imagined that they would arrive on the outskirts of a grand house and that she'd be left tied to a tree while the others jumped into action with some sort of far-fetched rescue plan, but instead they all clattered into the central, packed-dirt square of a tiny village. It was early evening, fires lit in every house, but nobody came to greet them or to ask them their business.

"We'll stop here for the night," Mariel said, obviously a begrudging concession to the fact that they were all dead on their feet. Clem looked around at the little houses and translated this to mean *real beds*, which immediately lifted her spirits. The others seemed to feel the same. The relief was so palpable Clem almost laughed.

There was a face at one of the windows, but it quickly whipped out of sight.

"They're . . . friendly, right?" Kit said, gingerly dismounting, and then stretching out his limbs with a wince. "Where's the welcome wagon?"

Yes. "This is New Pigot," said Mariel. "They took up arms with my father last year to chase away the Sheriff's forces."

"Oh, yeah," said Josey, nodding over at the nearest doorway; a few more concerned faces had appeared to stare at them, but the door was quickly slammed shut again. "Super-friendly energy."

"I don't . . . understand," Mariel said, which was probably a testament to how exhausted they all were; Clem didn't think she'd ever heard Mariel admit to any kind of deficit of knowledge before.

On further inspection, the square wasn't actually empty. There were children watching from corners and between houses, half-hidden in deep shadows. Some harried-looking mothers came out to glance sternly over at the newcomers and then usher them back inside.

"I'm too tired to work this out," Kit said sadly. "Let's just go and find a nice ditch to lie down in and we can solve this mystery tomorrow."

The door to the largest building opened, and a graying, middle-aged woman with three children following like solemn ducklings came out, wiping her hands on a stained apron.

"Hello," she said, appraising them all frankly, a hint of wariness behind her eyes. "Merry Men?"

"Captain Hartley-Hood," Mariel said, her tone military and hostile. Morgan rolled their eyes, just out of Mariel's sight.

"Right," the woman said. "Captain. I'm Ula. What is it I can help you with?"

"Food. Baths."

"Lodgings?"

"If you can stretch to it. We won't stop long. Away before first light."

It was somehow like watching an argument, although Clem hadn't the faintest what had set it off. Ula turned abruptly and started talking quietly to her children as she walked back inside, sending them scurrying ahead of her, executing orders.

"That was like . . . a *master class* in diplomacy," said

Morgan. Baxter tried to ruffle their hair, but they stepped out of the way and scowled. "Don't jiggle me, Scarlet, I'm *injured*."

"Are you in pain?" Clem said automatically, her hand reaching for her bag. "I can—"

"Stand down, weirdo," said Morgan. "I swear you're *obsessed* with me."

"Morgan," said Kit. "She saved your life."

"Whatever."

Josey snorted. "If you keep being so nice about it, shrimp, maybe she won't do it next time."

This wasn't true, but there was no need for Morgan to know that.

"Coming?" Ula said, from the doorway of what Clem deduced was probably the closest thing they had here to an inn.

Inside, there was a large room with a long table flanked by benches, blotched and scarred from years of use. There was a fire in the hearth, a man's hat and cloak on a hook by the door, some straw on the floor, and little else. Clem sat down next to Morgan, who sighed and made a point of shifting down a few spaces.

They were served some sort of stew by the children—who stared openly at them the entire time and said nothing at all—along with heels of hard, pale bread and watery ale. It was mostly silent except for the mildly disgusting sounds of six very hungry people rapidly vanishing stew, until Josey, her chin somehow free of broth, nudged Mariel and directed her attention out of the window. Clem followed their gazes and saw a small group of women gathered in the square, talking furtively, not a smile to be seen among them. They were vastly outnumbered by their children.

"Not that I'm complaining," Josey said quietly, "but where are all the big, strapping men?"

Clem wiped stew from her cheek and watched as one of the women outside threw up her arms in exasperation and stormed away. The rest of them seemed to notice that they were being observed, and disbanded, throwing dirty looks over at the inn as they went.

"Maybe the rest of them are off . . . hunting?" Kit offered. "Fighting?"

"Fighting where?" said Mariel.

"You don't know about every skirmish that may or may not be taking place at this exact moment in time," said Morgan, rather soupily; eating with one hand was clearly not coming easy to them.

"I do," said Mariel. "Actually."

She looked troubled though.

Clem didn't know why they were all so confused. It seemed like exactly the sort of welcome they should have expected; the people of Oak Vale certainly would have been wary if green cloaks had arrived and asked to stay for supper. From the look on Mariel's face, she'd never thrown herself at the mercies of villagers, and now that she had, she was shocked to find them not-so-tender.

Clem ate her bread and watched as Kit offered the rest of his to Baxter, who accepted it with such reverence he looked as if he might be close to tears. Clem wondered if they were perhaps in love, or if it was just that bread tended to bring out those sorts of emotions in people.

Mariel had somehow pushed her bowl away while it was still around one-third full, and in the end that went to Baxter too.

Ula reappeared, and Mariel immediately got up from the bench.

"We'd like to—"

"Won't be baths for all of you," Ula interrupted, twisting a rag between her hands as she did. "Haven't got the wood to spare for burning."

"Fine. I—"

"Don't have the beds either. Normally we'd find places to put you up in the houses, but as it is . . ."

"How is it, exactly?" Mariel snapped. "Because there's clearly something you're not saying. I'd appreciate it if you spoke plainly."

Various expressions that ranged from mild horror to shocked amusement were exchanged between her Men.

"Fine," said Ula, throwing the rag down on the table and squaring her shoulders. "If you want plain, I'll say it plain: you are not welcome here."

"Why?"

"*Why?*"

"It's a simple question. Last year you stood shoulder-to-shoulder with us when the Sheriff came after nearby land and holdings. What possibly could have changed in a year?"

"What could have . . . ?" Ula stared at her, thunderstruck, and then swept from the room, letting the door slam quietly behind her.

Mariel stared after her, grim-mouthed and almost vibrating with frustration, and then followed.

"What was that about?" Morgan said, leaning back in their chair to try to peep through the window.

"Uh," said Kit. "I suppose you could say that we are not always . . . universally beloved."

"Nobody's ever done anything like *that* in front of me before. She acted like we'd eaten all her food, shat on the floor, and then asked for seconds."

"I wish," said Baxter, wistfully glancing toward the kitchen.

"Baxter," Kit said, pained. "Don't agree with that. There was a whole first half of that sentence."

"We're Merry Men," said Morgan. "What's she so mad about? Did we fight a little *too hard* for people's rights? Did we save *too many* people from fires?"

Clem had been biting her lip throughout this entire exchange, but she must have let slip An Expression, because Morgan zeroed in on it. "What's so funny?"

"Well," said Clem. "Just . . . you know. It's a *little* bit funny, from the perspective of the recently kidnapped. Imagine that you don't have a green cloak, you've never even *seen* a green cloak unless you were being ordered to pick up your pitchforks and go and fight the Sheriff, but you are expected to magic up room and board for anyone who strolls in wearing one."

"We're nice," Morgan said defensively. "We've been nice to you."

"Actually almost everybody's been nice to me except you, but I do accept your point."

"Hey," Morgan said, abruptly forgetting that they were trying to clear the group's name. "Josey knocked you out! And dragged you out of your house!"

"Yes," said Clem. "But she was *polite* about it."

Kit grimaced. "I can't help but worry that the captain might be talking us out of a place to sleep tonight."

Clem stood. "I'll go and see. I'm friendly. *Too* friendly, apparently, and I'm also not a Merry . . . Man? A member of the . . . a Merry-Men-member?"

"A Merry Men-ber," said Josey.

"Exactly. Not tarred with that brush. So that'll probably help."

"Is this an escape attempt?" said Josey, not looking particularly concerned. "You have to tell me, if it is. It's only fair."

"No," said Clem. "Probably not."

"Good," said Josey, slumping down on to the table with her head resting on her arms. "Because frankly, I cannot be arsed to chase you."

This was not the sort of thing you were meant to say to somebody you *didn't* want to escape, but Clem supposed they were a little bit past all that by now. It wasn't like they were friends, exactly, but they were currently all being boiled in the same pot, which inspired a certain amount of camaraderie.

Her problem was that she allowed herself to get attached too easily. Patients, ideological enemies, garden foxes. Three days with these people and Clem was *involved*.

Outside, most people seemed to have returned to their houses, although a few were carrying baskets of clothes away into the wood to wash them in the creek. The comforting quiet of sleepy, window-glow domesticity had been draped over the village like a blanket. Those children who were too young to be delegated tasks of their own were playing at hopscotch and shoving. Clem walked the circumference of the houses, then followed the last dregs of the setting sun west, on a well-trodden path that hugged the trees and sloped gently upward to the crest of a small hill.

Mariel was standing at the top, looking down at a slab of stone with a slightly wonky cross carved down its center, followed by numbers, and what seemed like an endless list of names. There were wildflowers everywhere, knee-high, although somebody had carefully pruned them away from the monument. It looked as if it was visited often; the ground under Mariel's boots was muddy, and the slab was scattered with offerings: pretty stones and cakes, casks of mead, pieces of wood whittled into rings and crosses and boats.

"Oh," said Clem, coming to an abrupt stop and a just as sudden realization. "Oh, shit."

"They fought with my father," said Mariel, sounding a million miles away. "He mustered them to defend territory to the south. And . . . they all died. I didn't—nobody told me, I hadn't . . ."

"You didn't know," said Clem.

Still. Mariel might have guessed that when you sent ordinary people off to fight, lots of them died. It would have been one thing if the Merry Men had fought side by side with the people here in defense of their village—they'd be heroes still, welcomed with open arms and as many vats of broth as they fancied—but it was something else entirely for the villagers to be called to fight to defend an abstract line on a map. Clem couldn't blame them for their wariness, their standoffishness. They'd lost so much, in service to a cause that had been so thoroughly muddied that it was hard to see where *good* started to bleed into *bad*.

In Robin's days, fights like these had been few and far between; the Merry Men had only taken up arms when absolutely necessary. Mostly they had come to the villages bearing supplies. Food when it was scarce, seed potatoes and milk cows, extra pairs of hands to pick up the slack ahead of winter. They had left every village they visited in higher spirits and better stead than they found it.

Now they left beds half empty, and helped fill the graveyards instead.

"What do they say about us?" Mariel said, her voice tight, as if she'd been reading Clem's mind. "In your village? What do they say about the Merry Men?"

"Er . . . I don't know if that information would be particularly helpful to you right now."

"Right," Mariel said, nodding, still looking vacant. "Of course."

"They say worse about the Sheriff's men," Clem offered. "Always."

"And . . . whose side are you on?"

Clem was taken aback. She watched the wind lift loose strands of Mariel's hair from her shoulders and then set them back down again.

"I suppose I'm on your side, if these are my options."

"And you're not a liar." It wasn't phrased as a question.

"No," said Clem, thinking of Oak Vale and Rosie and the money hidden under her bed, the gold she'd accepted from well-dressed folk that she was sure Mariel wouldn't approve of. "Not a liar."

Mariel crouched down in front of the monument and reached toward a crudely carved wooden horse that had fallen on its side. At the last minute she seemed to change her mind, her hand skimming up and away, and she left it where it was, one shallow nick of an eye gazing up at the darkening sky.

Knowing it didn't matter to Mariel if she stayed or went, Clem stayed anyway until the captain was ready to go.

18

"I wanted to say that we're—that *I'm*—sorry."

Ula didn't look particularly impressed, but then, Mariel wasn't particularly good at apologies. She took a breath and tried again.

"I wasn't aware—I was not kept apprised—of the situation. Obviously I wouldn't have . . . made demands of you, and your hospitality, had I known. And I'm sorry. As I said."

"As you said," Ula repeated. They were standing in the small garden behind the inn, gently lit through the open doorway by the flickering fire. Ula straightened up slightly, winced, put a hand to her lower back, and then sighed. "Fine. You have to understand—it's been very difficult. It's not that we didn't want to fight the Sheriff—that bastard's name is mud around here, same as the rest of the wood—but . . . he took them all, your father. As good as said that any man or woman able to fight who didn't come was a coward, and that anyone who stayed behind would only regret it. And in the end, the Sheriff lost that fight, but he took the land back again not six weeks later. All those people, dead. For six weeks when you could say you'd won something."

Mariel winced. It wasn't quite as simple as Ula had made it out to be; there were things she didn't understand, things that even Mariel herself wasn't privy to, about the inner workings of the Merry Men. Everything her father did had purpose. The Sheriff had to be taught a lesson. The borders had to stay strong. They *had* to fight for what was theirs.

"Was it worth it?" Ula pressed.

"I—I don't know. I wasn't there, I don't know the details of the—"

"Captain Hood," Ula said. "Was it worth it?"

"Captain . . . *Hartley*-Hood," Mariel said faintly. "No. No, I don't suppose it was."

Ula let out a long sigh that seemed to come from the depths of her. "You know, when I was a girl, the Merry Men brought hope. Our doors were always open to you. Now . . . we find ourselves wishing we'd closed the shutters and turned the locks, before it was too late. The harder you hit, the harder the Sheriff strikes back, and then we all suffer."

"But we're still fighting for the people of the wood," Mariel said, hearing how ineffectual and childish this sounded in the face of so much grief. There was still soot under her fingernails and in the creases of her palms, and she almost wanted to hold up her hands, to show Ula proof of her virtue. Pulling children from that fire had been uncomplicated and without motive. She had been right. She had been good.

"You're just fighting," said Ula. "I don't think even you know what for anymore."

Painful as it had been to have this conversation, it helped to clear the air. Mariel's company was obviously hoping to be packed off to bed, but Mariel was determined that they would make themselves useful. After some of the village women convened for a discussion, it was decided that they would divide and conquer. Clemence and Kit saw all those with health complaints; Baxter helped with the last tricky bits of a roof repair; Josey went out to help retrieve a lost sheep. Mariel and Morgan sat with Ula and prepared food, plucking and gutting scrawny game birds, Morgan looking as horrified as if the birds had been their close personal friends the entire time.

Signs of those who had been lost to battle were everywhere. Cloaks growing dusty on hooks, children in boots that wouldn't fit them for a decade, dark shadows under the eyes of those left behind. Mariel looked down at the rust-colored blood mixing with the soot on her hands and tried to remember what her father had told her about the villages who joined the Merry Men in their cause. They had always come willingly, she'd thought; eager to defend the land. Who wouldn't be driven to vengeance and violence by the Sheriff and his men?

The way Ula had told it, there'd been some pressure from her father, some gentle threat in his words—but that wasn't right. The story must have warped over time, changed by tragedy. Fighting was painful but necessary. Any death was to be regretted, of course, but sometimes sacrifices had to be made for the future of the greenwood. And . . . if *Clemence* claimed that the people of her village had plenty of bad things to say about the Merry Men, her opinion was hardly to be trusted. She was just an irritant. A thorn. She was probably enjoying trying to rile Mariel into a snit.

But Mariel would not be riled. She could see the series of deeply unfortunate events that had left this village in ruins and know that they were misplacing their anger, desperate for somebody to blame. The gnawing in her gut that persisted was irrelevant.

When it was getting quite late, a child came stumbling into the inn with a black eye and a split lip, and Ula came out to receive him, checking his face over with a tut and telling him to go and visit the healer.

"I didn't do anything!" he protested, wrenching away from her. "There's some lord on the west road with all these carriages, mountains and mountains of stuff. All I did was ask if he had coin to spare . . . He told his guard to box my ears, but he only got one ear boxed before I ran away."

"Mountains of stuff," Morgan repeated, catching Mariel's eye over the top of a chicken.

"No," Mariel said. "No unnecessary risks. It's late, we're tired. We'll finish up here and go to sleep." She went back to her work, expecting Morgan to do the same.

Instead, Morgan scraped back the bench and stormed off outside. When they eventually came back, they had the entire company in tow, plus the healer.

"Lord on the road?" Josey said. "*Mountains of stuff?* Captain. Come on."

"You have to," added Clemence, sounding far too happy. "This sort of thing is exactly what I was promised."

"You weren't promised anything," said Mariel. "Abara, we haven't done anything like this for—"

"*Ages*," said Josey. "Come on. We can be a band of anonymous highwaymen. Let's throw these people a party."

Mariel looked at Ula, who was listening with great interest.

The older woman put her hands up in protest. "Nothing to do with me," she said. "I'm not even listening to this. And if our stores and coffers should happen to be full tomorrow morning, I certainly won't have any idea where it came from."

Mariel's grandfather would say yes.

Her father might say no, if Mariel was the one asking. But her father also believed in following his instincts—writing the letter of the law as he went, scrawling additions in the margins, steadfast in his belief in himself and his decisions.

They needed a win so badly in this village. Looking around at the hopeful eyes of her Men, despite all reason, Mariel suddenly wanted to be the person to give it to them.

She put down her half-plucked chicken. "It *is* a dangerous road after dark."

Morgan's answering attempt at an actual fist-pump of victory was only interrupted by their damaged shoulder.

This was how Mariel found herself an hour later, wedged between two rocks, with her company crouched at her side. They'd found the lord in question—he really was traveling with an *extravagant* amount of things, so very robbable it was like he had painted an enormous banner that said *Traveling Wealth Redistribution Center Here*—and then ridden on ahead until they discovered a craggy outcrop perfect for an ambush.

Having ascertained that this man would not particularly care about a lost child in the road, using Morgan as bait was out, so they were taking their chances with Josey instead, who, when asked about her angle, had simply said "sexy."

It was not the angle Mariel would have chosen, but she had never been given any reason to doubt Josey in the past. She watched now as Josey approached from the other direction on horseback, wrapped in an old gray cloak, feigning distress.

They were close enough to hear when the carriages stopped and a door opened; unfortunately, this meant they also had to listen to every detail as his lordship himself came to the rescue.

"Good lady, be not alarmed! Are you lost?"

"I am," Josey called out. Mariel rolled her eyes. The breathy falsetto was a little much. "Thank God I have found you, sir, I was almost ready to give up!"

"A lady such as yourself should not be wandering these cruel, barren lands alone. The villages are full of ruffians and reprobates! Come and sit in my carriage. You will like it very much—there are lanterns on the ceiling, and I have installed a tap that produces a flow of wine."

"Might I sit on the seat with you, my lord? I am terribly frightened and shaken, and while I do not wish to be untoward, your presence will surely calm my nerves."

"Uh-oh," said Baxter, grinning like a tomcat. Mariel was torn between horror and awe.

"Well . . . I never would have suggested such a thing myself," said the lord, as Josey dismounted and approached.

"But actually, you do get the best view of the lanterns if you lie directly on your . . . Oh. I see."

Josey had obviously revealed what she was hiding in her bodice, and it was not as he had hoped.

"Go," said Mariel.

There was a guard riding with every vehicle and two additional men at the front and the rear—they leaped into action once they realized what had happened, but Josey had their lord at knifepoint, and when Mariel let loose an arrow that struck the ground a carefully calculated half an inch away from the foot of the bravest, they started backing up with their hands in the air.

All it took was Baxter looming out of the shadows to seal the deal with battle-axe in hand, and it was done.

Mariel wouldn't ever have admitted it, but she took pure pleasure in watching Josey direct the lord and his men to load some of their finest wine and provisions onto the smallest of their own carts, one hand applying gentle pressure with her knife and the other pointing the way. She almost felt like smiling. They tied his lordship to a horse, instructed his convoy to wait until he returned to them or else ensure his instant death, and then rode away with both lord and cart in the opposite direction of the village. Once they had reached a safe distance, they sent the horse back with a gentle slap to the rump, and then pulled off the road and into the trees so that they could wend their way safely back to Ula.

Clemence was so happy she was practically bouncing in the saddle. It was unnerving, from somebody who claimed to want to help absolutely everyone; like watching a previously angelic toddler killing their very first ant.

Their welcome back into the village this time was nothing short of jubilant. Mariel had her hand shaken so many times she thought it in danger of falling off. Eventually she started pretending that she'd injured it, just so that people would leave her alone. The spoils were hidden away in cellars—except for some of the wine, which was immediately drunk by those old enough to do so and a few who certainly weren't—and by the time they reconvened at Ula's table it was the early hours of the morning, and they were all completely exhausted. When Mariel tried to engage Morgan in another conversation about the contact they'd be meeting in Stoke Hanham, Baxter very gently reached over and flicked Mariel on the forehead.

"That's . . . that's gross insubordination," Mariel said, clinging to the last vestiges of her authority.

"*Gross?*" said Morgan.

"Yucky," said Josey. "Disgusting."

"Plans in the morning," Baxter said. "*Sleep* now."

They were all granted the luxury of warm, shallow baths to scrub off their many layers of dirt, and Ula had even gone so far as to procure some very well-worn men's shirts to replace the tunics that had already been torn and bloodied *before* they absconded from camp.

"You'll have to double up on beds," she said over her shoulder, as she left to fetch blankets. She looked so different when she smiled. "Can lodge four of you here, but two will have to go next door."

"Oh," said Kit, who'd been tying up the sleeves of his too-large shirt to maintain dexterity. "Well. I don't . . . Morgan, who do you want to bunk with?"

"I'll sleep standing up," Morgan said dryly. "Like a horse."

"You'll sleep lying down," Josey said. "Also like a horse. Come on, you can have the bed, I'll kip on the floor."

Morgan shrugged and followed Josey out of the room.

"Right," said Kit. "So—I'll just—I can sleep on the floor too, I don't mind, or actually I could just set up somewhere outside, I'm—"

"Akito," said Baxter, "'s'fine. Come on. I'll bunk with you."

He touched Kit very softly on the shoulder, and Kit looked like he might be about to swallow his own face, but he recovered himself and nodded good night to Mariel and Clemence before exiting.

"Josey did that on purpose," Clemence said into the uncomfortable silence they left behind. "Smart. Very smart."

"What—Scarlet and Chisaka?" said Mariel, momentarily startled.

"Big time," said Clemence. "You're very committed to the last names, aren't you? Chisaka, Parry, Abara. Very uptight. Very military."

"We're commanding an independent militia."

"Nobody's going to want to be in your secret club if you make it sound so terminally unfun."

"It's not supposed to be fun."

"Obviously," said Clemence. "Why don't you last-name me?"

Mariel sighed through her nose. This was a pointless conversation, but when it ended, they were going to have to go and find this one bed they were supposed to be sharing. "I don't recall your last name."

"It's Causey," said Clemence. "Hey—Baxter's last name is Scarlet? As in, *the* Scarlets?"

"Yes," said Mariel.

"I really lucked into the all-star lineup," said Clemence. "Robin Hood and Will Scarlet's descendants. I *should* get autographs."

Mariel gave this as much response as it warranted by immediately walking out of the room. She found Ula standing by the stairs, blankets over her arms, and said nothing except to offer curt thanks when they were walked to the house next door, greeted by a silent old man with prodigious eyebrows and ushered up into a tiny cupboard of a room which offered absolutely nowhere to exist but on the narrow pallet bed.

"Well," said Clemence. "I would be gallant and offer to take the floor, but the bed has eaten it."

There was no candle and only a very small window, which made it a little easier for Mariel to wearily shuck off her weapons, cloak, and boots, putting them in a neatly folded pile on the warped floorboards by the door. Her bow went last, placed atop her cloak with the reverence it deserved, ignoring what might have been a huff of mockery from the healer as she ensured it was properly nestled in its bed of green wool. She sat down at one end of the pallet and stared at what she hoped was an innocuous stretch of wall as Clemence undressed clumsily next to her. At one point she almost toppled over, grasping Mariel by the shoulder to keep her balance. Mariel hissed slightly and shook her off.

"Sorry," said Clemence. "Tired. Thought you were furniture."

Eventually she sat down next to Mariel, who was alarmed to discover that her eyes were adjusting so well to the darkness that she could see her. Clemence had for some inexplicable reason taken her breeches off and was now only wearing the very oversized men's shirt that trailed at the wrists and skimmed her knees. She was tying up her curls, combing them through with her fingers and twisting them up on top of her head, which made the shirt lift just enough that Mariel could see her thighs. Her legs looked strong, sturdy, the hair light and downy where the faint moonlight was picking out her edges.

"You know that if you can see me, I can see you," Clemence said around the strip of twine in her mouth. She removed it and finished tying up her hair. "Starey."

"I'm not staring," said Mariel. "I can hardly see you."

"I can see *you,*" said Clemence. "I've got eyes like an owl. And legs like one too. Have you seen an owl's legs? They go on for much longer than you'd expect."

"No," Mariel said, closing her eyes. "I haven't seen an owl's legs."

"I see you're still pretending to find me annoying."

"Yes," said Mariel. "*Pretending.*"

"Shove over."

Mariel did, just to put some distance between them, and Clemence lay down, turning onto her side so that when Mariel reluctantly joined her, they were back to back. The bed really was unreasonably small; it was impossible not to be somehow touching, even when Mariel tried to cringe away from the contact.

"Are you one of those people at sleepovers who talks

and talks all night and doesn't let anybody get a moment's rest?" Clemence said, and Mariel snorted derisively. "Oh good. Me too."

"This might be the only chance we have to sleep in a bed for weeks," Mariel said wearily. "And we only have a few hours to spare. Please let me make the most of it and *shut up*."

Clemence laughed, but it was weak, and they lapsed into silence. Mariel was extremely discomforted by the overly familiar feeling of somebody else breathing next to her in the dark. She had slept next to plenty of people before, both friends and relative strangers, used to bedding down wherever was necessary when they were traveling through the wood, but sharing a bed with *just* Clemence felt too . . . specific. It felt *extra* specific when Clemence shifted slightly, and Mariel felt their shoulders brush together before she twitched away.

"Hey. Mariel. What's the tattoo on your arm?" Clem said, and Mariel instinctively touched a hand to her biceps, where the scarred lines of ink were slightly raised. "You all have the same one. And I've seen it carved into the trees."

"Yes," said Mariel. "It's a bird."

"It doesn't look like a bird. It kind of looks like an *R*."

"Engage your brain for a few seconds before you speak and you might make sense of that."

A pause.

"Oh," said Clem. "It's meant to be a bird *and* an *R*. Clever."

"Imbecile."

"The way you delight in being rude to me says more about you than it does about me, Captain."

"Well, it hardly seems to bother you. Nothing seems to bother you," Mariel said, pulling the blanket tighter around her just to see if Clemence would try to tug it back. She didn't.

"Loads of stuff bothers me," Clemence said, her voice thick and sleepy. "You're insufferable, for one."

"But you're so relentlessly fucking *cheerful*."

"Well, look," Clemence said, turning onto her back. "We all cope with life differently, all right? You . . . pretend to be a world-weary veteran soldier, and do a lot of frowning, and I keep light spirits and bring joy to the lives of all I encounter. Who's to say which is right?" She paused. "It's my way though. Obviously."

Mariel rolled her eyes, which was entirely wasted on Clemence, who was still considering the ceiling.

"You aren't always in light spirits."

"Pretty much."

"What about the fire?"

"Hmm?"

Mariel shrugged. "You were . . . rattled."

"Well, everything was on fire. It didn't seem the right time for . . . wisecracks and pithy one-liners."

"You were rattled," Mariel said again. She felt Clemence turning over again, her face to the wall.

"Congratulations," she said eventually. "I was rattled."

Her voice was dull and hard, and Mariel found herself experiencing a squeeze of discomfort, of the sort that had dogged her all evening since arriving at the village. Everything felt a little bit wrong, somehow, or like *she* was doing something wrong. Though she'd experienced it before—

she knew she disappointed her father on a regular basis—it was not a feeling she had ever learned to live with.

She didn't respond to Clemence, and eventually the healer's breathing became slow and steady, the sound of it now surprisingly soothing—or at least less irritating than the sort of sounds she made while awake.

I thought you were terrible at sleeping, Mariel thought as she too drifted off.

19

There were no two ways about it: Clem and Mariel were spooning.

It had happened entirely unconsciously, a genuine accident, but regardless of how they'd ended up there, the result was the same; Clem woke up with her face tucked into the back of Mariel's shoulder, under a curtain of dark hair. It was slippery-soft and still smelled faintly of smoke, although underneath was the pervasive scent of the greenwood. Trees. Moss. Mud. Flowers, probably. Clem was distracted by the very strange feeling of Mariel pressed against her, all long limbs and lean muscle, her body in a state of total relaxation almost unrecognizable. She curled in on herself when she slept, like a dandelion putting itself to bed.

Clem had apparently thrown an arm carelessly across Mariel's waist at some point in the night, and she set about carefully removing it by degrees, knowing that if Mariel awoke and discovered that she was essentially being *cuddled* she might resort to violence, or at least some very hurtful verbal bitchery. She had just managed to retract her arm when Mariel made a little sound of discomfort in her sleep, turning slightly toward Clem so that they were somehow even closer together.

It was such a novelty to see Mariel like this that Clem wanted to put off the moment things became awkward and brittle and horrible, but she wasn't entirely clear on the ethics of letting this continue with one party conscious and the other very much not, so she took a breath, shoved Mariel away, then immediately turned toward the wall in a stunning display of horizontal gymnastics. She had been a little bit too forceful; Mariel fell out of the bed entirely, pulling the blanket with her, and started swearing almost before she'd hit the ground.

"What the hell is wrong with you?" she said finally, squinting up at Clem with her hair disheveled and her cheeks slightly pink.

"Uh," said Clem. "There was a bee?"

"There was a bee," Mariel repeated disbelievingly. "Jesus *Christ*."

In daylight, it was doubly apparent how small the room was, and Clem was suddenly very conscious of the fact that Mariel was trying and failing not to frown at her bare legs.

Clem pulled on her trousers for decency and then sat back down on the pallet and watched, without even attempting subtlety, as Mariel pulled on her boots and then picked up her knives and slid them back into place; one at her wrist, one at her ankle. It was soothing. Fascinating, even. There was already a knife in her belt along with her sword, which made Clem realize that she had *slept* in said belt, indicating new and uncomfortable realms of paranoia.

"I thought you just carried the one knife?"

"It was recently made very clear to me that it would be prudent to carry backups."

"Not this again. *I wasn't trying to murder you.* In fact—let me look at that wound again."

Mariel didn't move for a second, but then she wrenched her shirt up and stood facing the wall, silently fuming, as Clem inspected her. All was as it should be; there was no discoloration or excessive swelling, and her healing was making nice progress already. Clem only wished she had her notes, so that she could write this down. Her healing salve *worked.* Perhaps she could find a way to make it thinner, to let more air in? Perhaps she could use the ingredients in a hot poultice, for instant relief?

"I'm a genius," she said to herself fondly.

Mariel ignored her and set to braiding her hair back, just as Clem took her own curls down and shook them out, wincing as she ran a hand through them. She needed a comb and an hour bathing in a cool stream, followed by a hearty breakfast and a slow morning pottering around Old Rosie's garden.

Instead, Mariel didn't even give them ten minutes to eat breakfast before she was marching them all out of Ula's, past the hilltop graveyard and into a small outbuilding that might have once held livestock. It definitely had a certain goaty *je ne sais quoi.*

"Stoke Hanham," she said. "We'll be there by this afternoon."

"Did we have to be in a shed to do this?" said Baxter, still eating sharp cheese sandwiched between dense, grainy bread. He must have grabbed as much as he could carry on his way out of the door.

"Yes," said Mariel.

"Don't trust them?" Josey asked, nodding toward the village.

"Don't want to implicate them," said Mariel. "The less they know, the better."

"Do you want me to wait outside?" Clem asked hopefully. "The less *I* know the better too. Find me somewhere to sleep, and you can just wake me up when you're finished."

"Yes," said Mariel—but Baxter had shaken his head, and Kit had actually said "No" out loud.

Mariel was obviously thrown off. "What do you mean, no?"

"She's in this now," said Kit. "Don't you think?"

"She's still our prisoner."

"She's right here," said Clem, irritated but vamping through it. "She's listening. She's gorgeous!"

"The thing is, she's not been much of a prisoner since we split from camp," said Baxter. "And I was never wild about the idea of having prisoners in the first place."

"We don't know that we can trust her," said Mariel, which actually hurt quite a bit. Clem had been keeping her alive, tending to her wounds; they'd shared a *bed*, even if it had been out of necessity. Why was it so hard for Mariel to see the good in her, when the others had been trading jokes and comforts with her from the very beginning?

It was a Mariel problem, Clem knew. But still. Ouch.

"She's in," said Josey. "Aren't you, Giblets?"

Clem crossed her arms, still feeling a little injured. "And if I refuse, on account of not actually being in your gang?"

"We'll . . . stab you?" Josey offered half-heartedly.

"You'll hurt our feelings," said Baxter.

"Quiet," said Mariel. She exchanged a long look with Josey, and Clem saw the exact moment that she gave up. "In that case . . . all of you, listen. This is the favor. Parry needs to make contact with a servant who works at the house, but Stoke Hanham will be crawling with the type of upstanding citizens who'd be more than happy to hand us over to the nearest guard. Most of them will know Parry on sight. The Sheriff's men might recognize some of the rest of us too, if we've had dealings with them in the past." Morgan shifted uncomfortably, clearly hating every second of this plan. "Clemence—if you're really in this—you're the only one of us who can't be identified."

"Oh," said Clem. She hadn't been expecting the plan to involve her in any other capacity than cleanup crew. "Right. So you want me to . . ."

"Be Parry's mother."

Morgan let out a choked sound, and Baxter thwacked them gently on the back.

"There's nowhere to hide in town," Mariel continued, unperturbed. "The guards are relentless busybodies, they'll spot Morgan from a mile off."

"Morg can just pretend to be a little street urchin," Baxter said. "No offense, Morg."

"There aren't any bloody street urchins," Morgan said gruffly. "They have this whole thing about . . . keeping the town clean. No poor, no beggars. They get moved on."

Mariel had clearly already run out of patience. "This isn't up for debate. This is the plan. Morgan has told me everything I need to know. The healer will escort them into town, where this servant . . ."

"Colin," Morgan said glumly.

". . . *Colin* should be at the market, as long as his routine hasn't changed."

Morgan laughed dully. "It won't have. Nothing ever changes in Stoke Hanham."

"Good," said Mariel. "Causey—a word."

Everybody else got up and filed out of the little shack, and Clem watched them go, knowing she wasn't doing a good job of disguising the confusion on her face.

"If you betray us," Mariel said matter-of-factly, "I'll kill you."

"Yep," said Clem. "Makes sense."

"I mean it. This isn't a joke. This is too important. Whatever your guardian has been getting up to back at Oak Vale—"

"Giving the village chickens names," Clem said. "And inventing large-scale dramas between them. Bethel is divorcing Eric."

"Enough. You seem a little confused about our purpose here, but I think I can trust you not to make stupid decisions that will get Morgan hurt or killed, with you soon to follow."

Clem gave her a tight-lipped smile. "Coming from you, I know this is a grand and magnanimous gesture."

Mariel fiddled with her knife, looking past Clem instead of at her. "If you . . . if you make yourself useful, I might put in a good word with my father. Ask him to release you as soon as we're done."

Clem sort of wanted to point out that Mariel's father wasn't in a position to be filling out kidnappee release forms, but didn't.

"Does this mean I *am* part of the crew now?" she said instead.

"No," Mariel said, quickly and with a finality that made Clem's heart do an unpleasant little flip. Whatever. She didn't really want to be in Mariel's gang anyway.

Mariel took half a step backward and looked Clem up and down with alarming interest, which was a weird change of pace—Clem almost wanted to cover herself up with her arms, even though she was fully clothed. "All right. We just need to find you a dress."

Of all the things Clem had imagined the Merry Men might get up to in the deep of the wood, *makeovers* had not been one of them.

Ula had seemed very amused by Mariel's request, and had immediately sent a gaggle of children on a mission from house to house until they emerged carrying a carefully wrapped dress that had apparently once belonged to a bride. Mariel had insisted on handing over some extra coin, protesting that it might be the last they ever saw of that particular dress, and then Clem went into Ula's own room to put it on. Her daughters clamored at the door, and eventually Clem let them in to comb and braid her hair back with ribbons and straighten up the bodice. The gown was a sweet thing, obviously well-loved, faded periwinkle with improvised embroidery at neckline and sleeves. The matching coif she had to wear was less sweet, and made her look a bit like a blue penis. She took it off immediately, with plans to only return it to her head when it was absolutely necessary.

There was something strange about her reflection in the glass, and as she scrunched the hat between her hands, she realized what it was: she looked like her mother.

She'd never had that thought before, and it swelled bittersweet in her chest before she put it aside.

Ula's daughters seemed very proud of their handiwork. Clem knew that Morgan was in the neighboring house being dressed up as an adorable little boy. The less said about that, the better.

When Clem emerged into the courtyard, Kit and Baxter cheered, and Josey gave her a long wolf whistle that made Clem go a bit pink.

"Leave me alone," she said. "It's all for the cause."

A door slammed, and Morgan stomped jerkily out in neat breeches and doublet and walked past her toward the horses. "Let's get this over with."

Mariel was standing by the horses, and when Clem approached she turned from packing saddlebags and paused. They both just stood there looking at each other, Clem fidgeting nervously with her skirts, and then Mariel cleared her throat and started giving Clem a very thorough looking-over, frowning all the while, making Clem turn so that she could examine her from all angles.

"You're going to give me a complex," Clem said, and Mariel stopped and nodded awkwardly.

"It's fine."

"Just what a girl likes to hear."

Mariel leaned forward suddenly to adjust one of Clem's sleeves, the leather of her gloves smooth against Clem's skin, and Clem froze like a deer in a dress and didn't dare move again until Mariel had pulled away. She didn't think she'd ever seen Mariel touch someone on purpose unless she was about to do violence to them.

"It looks . . . good," she said stiffly. When Clem broke out into a smile—a smile that she did actually know to be relatively devastating when aimed directly at people, based on prior experience—Mariel immediately turned away to unbuckle and rebuckle the bag she'd just finished closing.

Ha. Good. Let her be confused.

"Let's go."

Ula sent them away with plentiful food and fresh water, and the faces that watched them leave were more curious and hopeful than openly hostile, which was a vast improvement on their first welcome.

Clem and Morgan shared a horse, something Clem was already becoming accustomed to, along with all manner of oddities that were usual for life on the road, and when they drew closer to Stoke Hanham, the others melted away into the wood to allow for their performance to begin.

The town didn't look particularly special at first glance—it was certainly larger and more built up than Clem's village, the houses neater, actual streets clearly defined and filled with people on their way to and from the market—but as they dismounted and entered on foot, Clem realized that everything was unnaturally clean. The people were well-dressed, the children quiet; even the dirt of the road looked like somebody had recently raked it.

"This is weird," Clem muttered to Morgan.

Morgan, who had been instructed to look sweet and winsome, glowered from beneath their hat. "It's hell."

They followed the flow of people toward the market, and once they were there, Clem rather forgot that she was supposed to be Morgan's mother. She was much more interested in visiting the stand of a herbalist, who was selling bogus protection charms and bundles of mildly poisonous herbs that would supposedly help to balance the humors. She asked a few well-aimed questions, the stallholder growing increasingly stammery and defensive, until Morgan dragged her away.

Next she used some of the coins Mariel had given her to purchase sweet buns, stuffed with pale lemon cream and glazed with honey; she tried to give one to Morgan and was ignored, so ate both of them, one after the other, like a snake chugging eggs. She missed Rosie's cooking. Questionable as it usually was, she could make a flapjack like nobody's business.

"We're not here to eat cake," Morgan muttered scathingly.

"If I were your mum, I'd need something to take the edge off," Clem said back, patting Morgan on the head fondly, knowing that they couldn't do anything to fight back. "Cake . . . wine . . . unspeakable acts of violence."

"Shut up," said Morgan, coming to a standstill and tugging urgently at her arm. "That's him."

They nodded toward a short, slender Black man dressed

entirely unremarkably except for a feathered bycocket hat and the gold ring on his right hand. He was talking to the wine merchant and didn't seem to be in a hurry to get away. Clem tried to be as nonchalant as possible as she sidled up next to him, Morgan practically tucked under her arm.

Someone else came to actually purchase some wine, engaging the merchant's attention, and Morgan took their chance.

"Colin," they muttered.

Colin jumped about a foot in the air, pressed his hand to his chest, and let out a breathy laugh.

"Jesus Christ, little M! Where the hell have you been? Hiding under this table?"

"No," said Morgan. Clem was shocked to discover that they were fighting a *smile*.

Colin's expression dropped, and he darted a glance over his shoulder before drawing closer.

"At the house they reckon you're dead. I knew you'd just gone rogue. Blew it all up and scarpered, like you said you would, and now you're running with the wolves. Is this—are you . . . ?" He was looking at Clem with wonder, and Clem found herself standing a little taller and speaking with borrowed authority.

"Yep. I am. Can we find somewhere more private to have this conversation?"

They walked right past a clutch of privately hired guards at the entrance to the market and ducked down an alleyway, where Colin insisted on taking Morgan's hat off and ruffling their hair.

Incredibly, Morgan didn't bite him. Clem was beginning to suspect that they had a *crush.* Colin was very nice to look at; closely cropped hair with fastidiously straight edges, a softly architectured face, and enormous, expressive eyes that were currently taking in Morgan in all their glory.

"You're good? They're feeding you? You're kicking all their scrawny little arses?"

"I'm fine," said Morgan. "Look, I need a favor." They took a deep breath, clearly trying to remember exactly what Mariel had told them so that they could regurgitate it. "I need information, and you know everybody. Have you heard about any . . . any high-profile prisoners? Anything about the Sheriff's movements? Has *he* said anything? Hinted at anything?"

"Oh, shit, okay. They have you running serious espionage," said Colin, glancing up at Clem like she was a schoolmaster giving too much homework and this was somehow her fault. "I did hear something. The Sheriff's away in London for the next few days, but he's planning something big for when he comes back. The boss was hoping he might get an invite."

"At Sherwood House?" Morgan said, sounding excited. "Good. That's good."

"Right, but M . . ." He checked the entrance and exit again. Clem realized she probably should have been doing that instead of leaning against the wall listening to them. Mariel would have a conniption if she realized how inept she was being. "They've also got someone *here.* At Hanham."

"*What?*"

"In the old buttery. You didn't hear this from me, obviously, but . . . two guards at the door, the usual everywhere else."

"In the old buttery," Morgan repeated.

"Look, I have to go. Big dinner thing tonight—bards, dancers, the works. They're all in high spirits . . . which I guess makes sense now, if they've snagged some of yours. Sorry, M. Good luck. I miss your happy little face."

Clem snorted, and Morgan shot her a dirty look before being enveloped in a brief hug. Colin gave them a gentle shake, nodded at Clem, and then turned and strode down the alley and away.

"Sherwood House. And the buttery at Hanham. Two guards. A party tonight," Morgan repeated under their breath, as they started walking in the opposite direction.

This was very exciting. Their little reconnaissance meeting had turned up something huge. A captive, here in town! Mariel was going to be happy. Or, as happy as she was capable of being. And Clem had been integral to executing the mission.

Well, she'd been standing very close to the mission, which felt like the same thing.

"He was handsome," Clem said, giving Morgan a friendly nudge to their uninjured shoulder.

Morgan just gave her the finger.

20

The first thing Morgan said when they rejoined the others was: "Clem pretended she was one of us and ate two cakes."

"Traitor," Clem said, taking off the stupid coif and folding it with care it didn't deserve. They were standing in a small clearing, Baxter up to his knees in a pebbly stream to cool his feet, and Clem suddenly felt too hot and very overdressed.

Mariel didn't seem to care about the cakes. "And what else?"

Morgan told her.

"The Sheriff is away," she repeated. "That gives us some time, at least. They're not going to put anyone on trial until he's back in Nottinghamshire."

Kit went to say something, but Mariel raised a hand for silence, then abruptly walked off to stare into the middle distance and think.

By the time she was done, everyone had wet feet.

"All right," she said firmly. "We're going to Hanham Hall. Tonight."

Everybody who wasn't Clem looked at Morgan.

"You don't have to come," Kit said quickly. "Right,

Mariel?" There was a hint of warning in his tone, which was definitely new.

"Well . . ."

"I want to come," Morgan said quickly. They had removed their hat and dipped their head into the stream, slicking back their dark hair. It made them look a little older than usual. Then again, they usually looked about ten. "And I *should* be there anyway. I know stuff. I can't explain it all to you beforehand."

"Good," said Mariel.

Kit looked unimpressed. "Morgan, you don't have to—"

"If Morgan wants to come, they're coming," Mariel said sharply. She took a breath, and Clem noticed that there was a dangerous little spark of something in her eyes, superseding her exhaustion. "*This* is the plan."

It was actually far simpler than Clem had imagined. "Extracting a target," as Mariel insisted on calling it, conjured up images of carefully timed break-ins, elaborate ruses, crawling down chimneys, etc. In actual fact, what she was suggesting was that they split into two teams—"Distraction" and "Extraction"—and that the former create a diversion while the latter entered the house just before dinner on the pretense of being traveling bards, and removed the prisoner before the guards had stopped finding the diversion diverting.

"They won't expect us to know someone's being held there, and they *also* won't expect us to be intimately familiar with the layout of the house. They think Morgan is dead."

Morgan's face twisted. "Thinking I'm dead would require them to think about me at all. I'm sure they *hope* I'm dead, if guests ever bring me up at dinner."

There was a slightly awkward pause, and Baxter gave Morgan a squeeze on the shoulder with a river-damp hand.

"Well," said Mariel, once again demonstrating her aptitude for managing human emotions. "Good. Abara, Chisaka, and I will be on extraction. Scarlet, Parry, and Causey—you'll be responsible for drawing the guests and guards away."

"I want to go inside," said Morgan.

"You might be recognized."

"What good am I *outside* if it all goes tits up *inside* and you need a different escape route?"

"It will not," said Mariel, "go *tits up*."

"I want to extract!"

"No," said Mariel. "That's an order, Parry. I mean it. You can stay out here and make sure the healer doesn't eat any more cakes."

With the sun still high in the sky, Clem dared to hope that this might leave the day open for leisure activities, namely sitting down and thinking no thoughts whatsoever; her hopes were dashed when Mariel announced that they would be going to acquire new clothes and some important props immediately, followed by a recce of the house. Of all the long days Clem had experienced recently, somehow this one felt the longest. By the time dusk was approaching, she had added five squirrels to her count (Morgan was up to sixty-three, Baxter fifty-five), been sent back to the market to barter with Mariel's coin, then spent what felt like an eternity traipsing back and forth through the rows of stalls to try to glean snatches of information that might be useful when gaining entry to the house.

By the time they all reconvened in the cover of the wood, the horses were twitchy and Morgan looked about ready to fight God.

"That's the last fucking time you're leaving me with busywork," they said. "Next time, make the healer mind the horses."

"Morgan," said Josey. "You do realize why we didn't leave all of our transportation in the hands of a flight risk?"

"Not a flight risk," said Clem. "I consider myself to be an honored guest. An apprentice, even."

"You're gaining work experience," said Baxter, flashing Clem a grin.

"Exactly."

Mariel made them all listen to the plan again twice over before they parted.

"Remember the signal," she said. "Once we find them—"

"You'll use the horn," Morgan said impatiently. "Yeah. We know."

"What if somebody else plays the horn?" said Baxter.

"We have purchased a particularly horrible horn," said Kit. "You'll know it when you hear it."

"Fine," said Mariel, at the same time as Baxter said, "All horns are horrible."

Clem was glad that the distraction team got to stick around to watch the bardification of the others; seeing Mariel take her hair out of its customary single plait, put on a jaunty little maroon outfit and then swing a lute over her shoulder like it was a bow, grimacing chronically all the while, was an image she planned to treasure forever.

★

Hanham Hall was pretty standard, as manors went: imposing stone walls, elaborate gates at either end, servants' buildings clustered at the north end of the courtyard while the great hall and other more pompous rooms favored the south.

"They don't usually bring the undesirables up to the house," Morgan said bitterly. "They cram them into the tiny old prison on the outskirts of town."

"How many prisoners can they possibly have?" asked Clem.

"When you start rounding up anybody from the holdings who can't pay their taxes, or spits in front of a *lady*, or looks at a member of the household wrong . . . loads."

The plan was that the distraction team were to cause a ruckus near the south gate in an attempt to draw out trigger-happy members of household security, while the others made for the buttery.

"They'll be expecting us to attack like an army," Baxter said, as they made their way slowly around the perimeter, leading the horses, sticking to the trees. "Big wave of fighters, lots of drama. That's Da—That's *Commander* Hartley's style."

"Were you going to say *Daddy Hartley*?" said Morgan.

"Uh," said Baxter. "No."

Morgan grinned. It was once again both alarming and unexpected, like seeing a fish do a facial expression. "See, it *is* funny. I'm telling Kit."

"It's only because you keep bloody saying it, Morg, it's got into my head."

"Isn't Jack Hartley basically your uncle?" asked Clem,

as Baxter used his unnatural strength to bend about half a tree out of their path.

"Step-uncle," said Baxter. "Wait. No. He's my . . . We're not blood related. Mariel and I basically grew up as cousins, when we were tiny. We're . . . Is it once removed? Or—"

"No," said Morgan. "You were never removed. Your grandfathers are married. So . . . you're . . . Wait, is there such thing as a step-grandfather?"

"This is a treat to watch," said Clem. "I can almost see the wheels turning. Please, do go on."

"Okay, wait, it's—Robin and Marian had Regan. Regan and Jack had Mariel . . ."

"Wrong," said Morgan. "Mariel was hatched from an egg, soft-boiled in the fires of hell."

"Robin and Will—that's my grandfather—got together before I was born. So we're like . . . step-cousins? Related by marriage."

"Does she ask you to call her *Captain* at family gatherings?" asked Clem.

"Ah, give over. She's a good captain. I trust her. She wasn't always the friendliest, but she's always been good at this."

Morgan made a noise of derision but, perhaps out of some reluctant deference to Mariel, kept it short and to the point.

"*You're* very friendly, for a hardened warrior," Clem observed, and Baxter laughed.

"Don't know if I've ever been *hardened*. I don't really like it—the violence. Should have been a farmer or something. Raised lambs. But when you're already six feet tall by the time you're fifteen, and it's in your blood, people sort of expect you to start throwing things about." He smiled. "Plus, it makes people *very* happy when I do it. And I like making people happy."

They had reached the south gate. From their position in the cover of the wood, Clem could see a guard standing either side; as they watched, a couple of well-dressed guests arrived and were admitted into the courtyard.

Clem looked up at Baxter; he'd gone silent and still. "What's the plan?"

"The plan is that I'm going to be ten guys," said Baxter. This made no sense whatsoever, but he didn't offer any further explanation.

"You're going to be . . . ?"

"Maybe eight," Baxter conceded. "I don't know if I have it in me right now to be ten."

Morgan nodded. "That's nine then, with me."

"You have a rotten shoulder and are meant to be resting."

"Oh, right, I'll just lie on the ground humming a little song while everybody else saves the day."

"Fine," Baxter said. "Nine."

"I can be your tenth guy," said Clem. "I mean, I don't know what that entails or really understand anything about what's going on, but I'm a quick study and I've not got anything else on at the moment. Just give me a second to change out of this dress."

"Good," said Baxter. "Okay. Ten. Are you any good with a bow and arrow?"

21

Mariel's father would never debase himself by putting on a little hat and pretending to be what amounted to a musical *jester* to try to retrieve a captured comrade—but then, he was the one sitting in a cell or a dungeon or a converted buttery somewhere, and Mariel was the one who was going to set him free, even if her methods *were* deeply embarrassing.

"We have numbers on our side," he'd once said to Mariel. "We're no longer a fringe group, we're a force to be reckoned with. Pretending otherwise just makes us seem weak. We don't tiptoe. We don't *sneak.* We announce our coming with trumpets, and when they hear us, they should be deathly afraid."

She supposed she should be grateful that he'd given the Sheriff's men such clear and consistent expectations; it meant they'd never see her coming, at least this first time. If it felt like she was letting her father down and giving him even more reasons to doubt her abilities as a captain (and it did—of course it did), then that was a problem for another day.

It was easy enough to enter the courtyard of the house,

thanks to a fatal flaw in the wealthy of Sherwood: they were all too willing to believe that bards they had never seen before would travel for miles just for the *honor* of entertaining Lord Hanham and his guests. They simply couldn't imagine anything more thrilling for the average layperson than to be in the presence of a member of the landed gentry and his litter of spoiled, trussed-up whelps.

"You'll have to wait here," said a snooty member of staff, giving them a quick once-over as they stood with their instruments in hand and their friendliest smiles (Kit and Josey could manage them easily enough; Mariel was convinced that her face must look uncanny, like a child's badly painted doll). "And we'll see if they want you for the feast."

"Thanks ever so," said Kit. The man rolled his eyes and disappeared off toward the southerly buildings.

There were servants crisscrossing the yard, hurrying to bring food and drink, seeing to horses. It was relatively easy for them to shuffle toward the buttery, which was exactly where Morgan had said it would be. The only problem was that the one small window had been thoroughly boarded over with wooden planks several layers deep, and the walls were far too thick to hear who might or might not be trapped inside.

"Abara," Mariel muttered out of the corner of her mouth. "Can you . . . ?"

"*Can I?*" Josey scoffed. "Rude."

Mariel glanced over at the guards by the gates, who had their backs to the courtyard. When she looked back, Josey was gone.

"How does she *do* that?" Kit whispered. "I was looking right at her. Or, I thought I was."

"You blinked," Mariel said. "The trick is . . . don't blink."

A serving woman tripped, and the platter she was holding crashed spectacularly to the cobblestones. While people clamored to help her, Josey reappeared by Mariel's side.

"Only one guard at the door. The other must have wandered off for a snack break."

"Good," said Mariel. "Okay, go. Horn."

"You horn," said Josey.

"What?"

"I can't play the horn. I've got the pipes."

"You can't play the pipes either," Mariel said disbelievingly.

"Yes I can. Better than I can play the horn. I've got small lungs."

"I'll play the horn," Kit said resignedly.

It was genuinely mortifying to launch into a musical number with an audience. A few people glanced over at them, but it was only when Kit gave a truly impressive blast of the horn that the member of staff who had showed them in came rushing across the courtyard looking apoplectic.

"Shut *up*," he hissed. "Good God, I told you to *wait*. You're certainly not bringing that horrible thing into the hall."

"Sorry," said Kit. "Was just . . . trying something new."

"Well, don't."

"Feedback noted. Now I know. No horn."

The man shook his head, and then scurried away to admonish the woman with the dropped platter.

They only had to wait a minute or two before chaos erupted.

The first sign was a shout of surprise from somebody over at the party end of the courtyard. This quickly turned into calls for reinforcements; Mariel had the pleasure of watching the badly paid servants turn and run, not toward the apparent violence in defense of the house, but for safety. A couple of guards were sprinting in the opposite direction. Mariel and the others ran for the entrance near the buttery, pretending to be taking cover.

"Help!" Kit shouted down the dark corridor. "We're under attack!"

Momentarily, it didn't seem as if this was going to work, but after a beat of silence they heard the guard moving toward them.

"You there . . . what's happening?"

"God, it's just so easy," Josey said, cracking her knuckles. "It's almost not even fun."

He was unconscious in an instant, not a mark on him.

"We're not here to have fun," said Mariel, as he slumped to the floor.

"Speak for yourself," said Josey. She smacked on the end of her pipes and then gave them a shake; three carefully sharpened lockpicks and an even sharper, very thin knife slipped out.

The door to the buttery, unguarded, only took a minute of jimmying and quiet swearing to unlock. It was stiff and heavy; both Mariel and Kit had to shoulder it hard to get it to shift. The air inside was stale, and it was so dark with the window boarded that, at first, Mariel just blinked into the gloom.

"Mariel fockin' Hartley-Hood, is that you?"

Big Jon was sitting on a roughly hewn bench of stone cut into the wall. He slapped his knees and then got to his feet, grinning despite the fact that his tanned face was bloodied and his graying hair was matted with dirt.

"What kind of a rescue party is this? Where's the cavalry?"

"Busy," said Mariel. Big John tried to go for a friendly clap on the shoulder, but Mariel shook her head and handed him a spare cloak and the larger of her two lutes. "No time. Hood up. Got to go."

"Fair do's. Lead the way."

They dragged the unconscious guard inside and locked the door behind them, leaving no evidence that they'd been there at all.

Leaving was the tricky part, but they'd been so quick that everybody was still caught up in whatever mayhem Baxter was inflicting on the other side of the house. It was almost too good to be true—the gate guarded by only two very distracted men, whose eyes barely skimmed over the top of them as they pretended to be fleeing in terror.

Then they were home free, the greenwood ahead of them, Big John limping along, almost keeping pace despite the fact that his leg was obviously paining him.

"Shit."

Mariel glanced sharply over at Josey, who had slowed to a stop and was looking back over her shoulder at the house, and immediately ascertained the problem.

"Go," Mariel said. "I'll deal with this."

"I'm coming."

"One is less suspicious than two. *Go.* That's an—"

"Order," said Josey. "Yeah, yeah. Okay." She looked back over at the house again once more before taking off after Kit and Big John.

Mariel secured her lute a little tighter over her shoulder as she ran toward the house, and the doorway that she'd just seen Morgan Parry disappearing through.

Inside, it was almost as if nothing out of the ordinary was happening at all. The wood-paneled hallway was empty, the noise of the rest of the house distant. Mariel walked quickly, her footsteps muffled by lush rugs, checking each open door and trying to look as if she were a lost lute player in distress. Baxter's distraction wouldn't hold out for much longer; he and the others were likely beating a hasty retreat, their ruse already disintegrating.

The corridor led to an entrance hall with thick tapestries on the walls and an embarrassment of candles burning on every surface. Mariel paused, listening, loath to make herself so vulnerable in a room with far too many entrances and exits and nowhere to hide, but then she heard light footsteps on the stairs above her and narrowed her eyes. It sounded suspiciously like a teen about to be in a lot of trouble.

She darted up the staircase and discovered that it was indeed Morgan, and that for absolutely no reason Mariel could have ascertained in a thousand years, they were currently trying to remove an extremely heavy ceramic vase from a pedestal on the landing.

"What the *shit*, Parry," Mariel hissed. Morgan startled,

fumbling the vase for one heart-stopping moment before adjusting their clawlike grip. "Put that *down*. Let's go."

"Just a sec," Morgan panted, unbelievably still trying to heft the vase. "I need to—"

"*Now*," Mariel said, in a tone that she thought conclusively invited no argument. Morgan didn't seem to have factored a wounded shoulder into whatever disastrous vase-stealing scheme they had planned, and Mariel certainly wasn't going to help.

"It's his fucking *Crambeck* ware," Morgan said, as if this explained this sudden bout of madness. "Roman pottery. Never stopped going on about it. Made every guest go and pay their respects, gave endless lectures about it, and I just—"

"What the devil is going on here?"

There was a short, scowly-looking middle-aged man with a very pink face staring at them from down the hall. He was dressed in heavy velvet and furs despite the pleasant weather, and was holding a bejeweled dagger that had obviously never been used in combat. He squinted at Morgan, and his expression turned from outrage to confusion.

"*Morgan?* Is that you? What the hell have you done to your hair?"

Morgan darted a panicked glance at Mariel and then turned very reluctantly to look at him, their expression warping as they did.

"I've been missing for a *year*," they said, although their usual murderous rancor was somewhat dampened, "and you want to know what I've done with my *hair*? I could have been dead!"

"Well, you're not dead," said the man Mariel could only assume was Lord Hanham, as if Morgan were being very unreasonable. "And you set fire to some very expensive furniture before you left!" He frowned over at Mariel. "Who's this?"

Mariel took a breath. "Just a bard, m'lord, I was in the yard when the fighting started—"

"I'm here for your fucking Crambeck ware!" Morgan shouted, suddenly seeming to find their voice. "Don't take another step, or I'll—I'll smash it!"

"You wouldn't *dare*," shouted Lord Hanham, suddenly furious, spittle flying. "I don't know what you're after coming back here, but that vase is worth more than your life. Unhand it at once, and come here."

"No," said Morgan, a slight shake in their voice. "I don't think I will."

"Morgan Parry, you will do as I say, or I will call the guard. You always were the most meddlesome, abnormal little—"

The vase hit the ground with a satisfying and very final crack, shattering into dusty pieces on the polished floorboards. Lord Hanham made a noise halfway between a gasp and a squeak, and Mariel watched with mounting horror as Morgan stood defiantly, shoulders heaving, staring him down. Mariel's hand moved very slowly and carefully toward the knife at her hip; she couldn't imagine that this gammon joint of a man was likely to launch a physical attack, but you could never be sure when it came to posh people and their antiques.

"*Guards!*" he screamed, at a register best suited for the

calling of dogs; Mariel grabbed Morgan by the arm, the time for trying to pull rank long past, and started moving.

"Ow," Morgan grunted. "I'm coming, I'm *coming*."

The hallway downstairs, which had seemed of reasonable length when Mariel had entered the building, now seemed to go on forever. They sprinted along it, rooms which had previously appeared to be empty now sounding as if they were packed with people, all of whom were intent on investigating the source of the commotion. Doors flew open as they rushed past. Mariel tensed for somebody to block their only means of escape, but they exploded out into the courtyard and made for the gate with what sounded like half the household behind them.

Morgan glanced over their shoulder and then gave Mariel a running shove. "Get down!"

Mariel ducked, just as a volley of arrows flew over the top of her head.

The household guard had obviously given up on any chance of apprehending Baxter and returned. Excellent, excellent, excellent.

If everything had gone to plan, they would have simply left the courtyard looking like terrified, jobless entertainers, and then they'd have practically skipped to the treeline and mounted their horses at their leisure. In all the commotion, it could have been hours before they realized who was now locked up inside the buttery. Instead, when Mariel chanced a glance over her shoulder, she saw at least twenty well-dressed people spilling from the house into the yard, and the guards advancing at a very convincing pace, some of them hanging back to nock fresh arrows to their bows.

"Come on," Mariel said through gritted teeth as they ran across the open grass, bracing for another volley. "Any second now . . ."

Her heart lifted as she heard the thundering of hoofs; a moment later, Kit was reaching down to pull Morgan onto the horse as Mariel grabbed the saddle and launched herself up in front of him.

"Never been so happy to see you, Kit," Mariel said, as the horse cantered messily toward the wood.

"You've never called me Kit either. But, you know—first times for everything all around."

22

Mariel had been ripping Morgan various new orifices for at least ten minutes, and wasn't showing any signs of letting up. Her victim was sitting grim-faced and stoic, just taking it, clutching what looked like a bit of broken pottery in their hand. The rest of them were all trying very hard to pretend they weren't there; Clem was standing so close to a tree that she'd almost become one with it. There was a knobbly little branch sticking into her lower back, but she didn't dare move.

She had tried to check on Morgan's wound as soon as they'd escaped from imminent danger, to see if all of their cavorting around against Mariel's wishes had broken it open again, but had backed away when Mariel wouldn't stop standing over them both and glowering.

"Risking everything because of a petty personal vendetta! Disregarding direct orders! Disregarding them *again*, in the middle of a covert operation, blowing the entire thing—someone will have joined the dots by now, Parry. They'll know you're with the Merry Men, they'll know what we plan to do next—"

"Hold on," Baxter interjected, his voice level. "I don't know if that's fair."

Mariel's glare briefly redirected itself toward him; Clem thought she detected a small depletion of Baxter's life force in the sag of his shoulders.

"We weren't supposed to be seen," Mariel continued. "You put us all at risk, Big John included."

Clem glanced over at the man in question. He was short of build and had a weather-beaten face, salt-and-pepper hair swept back from his temples, and was currently using the clear trickle of the stream to wash blood out of his beard. Clem couldn't help but think that some of Mariel's overblown performance might be for him.

"You're no longer a member of this company," she said now, eliciting a short, sharp gasp from Morgan that they had clearly tried to repress. "You need some time to think. We'll drop you somewhere safe and come back when the job is done."

There was a horrible silence, and then Morgan lifted their head.

"You said you vouched for me. Back at camp. And you might think I was being stupid, or reckless, or whatever . . . and I am sorry, I didn't *mean* to . . . but Mariel—I mean—Captain, sorry, sorry, shit—you don't know what it was like there. It was hell. And when I left, they didn't even care. They were dicks to me every minute I spent in that house because they thought I didn't fit in, and then I left and somehow they didn't even *notice.* I hate that—I hate that they were the worst thing about my life, the biggest and worst thing, and to them it was . . . tiny. Nothing." Morgan stopped to take a breath, determinedly blinking back tears. "I just wanted them to remember that I was there, and that they hurt me, and that it wasn't *nothing.*"

Baxter stepped toward Morgan and slung an arm around their shoulders. To Clem's surprise, Morgan didn't shrug him off; they just leaned very slightly into Baxter's chest, a tear finally escaping down their cheek.

"We'll discuss this tomorrow," Mariel said finally, which was at least better than continuing to shout.

Big John, perhaps sensing that it was safe to re-enter the conversation, straightened up from where he had been washing himself and pulled his wet shirt back on over a very bruised and hairy chest.

"Don't know where they took Hartley and Payne," he said to Mariel, immediately getting down to business. His voice was deep and hoarse, and he had a slight Lancashire accent, as if he'd spent some time away from the wood. "Split us up on purpose, I reckon, so we couldn't get into any mischief, and probably sent Jack off to somewhere with better security."

"Do you think—"

"He was hale and whole last I saw of him. Payne . . . I'm not sure. Saw him get a nasty blow to the head when they took him."

"Was it Frederic? Who took my father?" Mariel asked, as if she'd been dying to get the words out. She really seemed to have a hang-up about this guy. Clem supposed they were sort of each other's equals in rank and standing—son of the Sheriff, daughter of the Commander. It made sense. But Big John was shaking his head.

"Not personally, no, but might have been his orders, I suppose. I don't reckon it matters too much. Sheriff, Sheriff's son. You're right that they won't make big moves until the big boss is back in town. But I've got no idea where the Commanders might be. Guards put me in a wagon with a bunch of terrifying criminals—you know, starving elderly folk, sobbing mothers behind on tax—but I had a sack on my head. Then they brought me to his lordship's."

"Ha," scoffed Mariel, with a bit of bravado. "Shows exactly how foolish they are. Of course we'd check the estates. Morgan said they keep their regular prisoners on the outskirts of town—if they'd left you there, it could have taken us months to find you."

Clem knew it was absolutely not the time or place to speak, but that had never stopped her before. "Why?" she said.

Mariel looked startled, as if she'd forgotten Clem existed. "What do you mean?"

"I mean—hi, I'm Clemence, by the way, I've been kidnapped—why would it have taken months to find him? Isn't freeing people from the Sheriff's oppressive regime basically your whole thing?"

There was a very pregnant pause and then some awkward foot-shuffling.

"Well," Mariel said, as the others looked everywhere but at her. "Yes. But there are a lot of prisons, and we're . . . very busy."

"Oh," said Clem. "Right. I suppose I get that you can't pop in and rescue every single person thrown in prison without cause. But . . . while we're here?"

"They wouldn't expect us," Josey said to Mariel, looking thoughtful. "It doesn't make sense for us to go back to Stoke Hanham. We could just rush them."

Mariel looked at Big John.

"Don't look at me," he said, holding his hands up. "This is your show."

"But . . . you're our highest-ranking captain, with Commanders Hartley and Payne out of action."

"These are your Men," said Big John, shrugging. "And the guards gave me a pretty enthusiastic beating at that house, so I'm about as useful as a knitted fish right now. It's your call. But . . ."

"But?"

"But . . ." He looked around at them all, then crossed his arms. "You're right, they wouldn't be expecting us. They'd assume you'd grab me and run for the hills. And maybe that's exactly why we should be doing it. Because I'm not worth any more than any other poor sod in those cells. Me and your dad have butted heads over this too many times to count—one of many reasons I think he prefers having Payne around—and I won't be having it get back to him that I filled your head with this noble guff and ordered you to play the hero, so . . . it's up to you."

Clem raised a hand. "I don't mind it going on the record that *I* filled your head with this noble guff. I think it makes me sound very go-getting and valiant."

"You don't seem very kidnapped," said Big John, rubbing at his beardy chin.

"Yeah," said Kit. "We've all noticed that, actually."

"We'll vote," said Mariel. "That's . . . I think that's the only fair way to do this."

"This has never been a democracy," said Morgan. They had shifted away from Baxter, apparently no longer requiring his support. "I thought you gave the orders and we followed them, no exceptions."

"Morgan," said Josey. "Yikes."

"Quit while you're ahead, kid," Baxter said, and Morgan's mouth slammed shut.

"All those in favor of going back, raise your hands."

Clem raised her hand, pretty sure that her vote wouldn't count, but wanting to make it clear that she supported her own plan regardless. It took a second or two, but then every other hand in their little circle went up. Big John laughed and clapped Mariel quite hard on the back.

"Look at that. There's hope for the next generation after all, eh?"

"Don't celebrate yet," Mariel said gruffly. "We can be pleased with ourselves when it's done."

"I'm going to be pleased with myself now," Clem said, "if that's all right. I think it's important to take the positives where you can get them."

"Be quiet," said Mariel, fingering the knife at her hip, her brows knitted. "All right, let's run this through. What do we know?"

"Two prison breaks in one day," Clem heard Baxter say to Kit. "This is like *Christmas*."

If Big John's rescue hadn't seemed particularly taxing, this was child's play.

Clem had seen Baxter in action up close as part of their distraction team—had watched as he fired off three arrows at a time, went crashing through the trees like an entire battalion was on the move, threw rocks so far and so hard that the people of Hanham Hall must have assumed that somebody had rolled a trebuchet up to the house and then slipped away silently once the job was done—and knew he was a force to be reckoned with. By comparison, Clem had fumbled the job, and had hardly been any help at all. She had managed to fire a few arrows off into the sky, and then had immediately started worrying that they might hit somebody on the way down (which Morgan informed her was "the whole damn point") before they'd slipped away from Team Distraction to cause trouble elsewhere. Clem had no doubt that Baxter could have rescued these prisoners entirely by himself: once you added the others into the mix, anybody who tried to stand in their way was doomed.

Morgan and Clem hung back with the horses, and the other five went to storm the building, which was really not much more than a shed with a big lock on the front door and two skinny-legged guards half asleep outside it. Even with one of their assailants only recently freed and hobbling along on an injured leg, apparently nobody was paying those guards enough to risk being knifed by Josey or have their bones crunched into dust by Baxter, because they barely put up a fight before scrambling out of the way.

Big John, who had an enormous, alarming grin on his face the entire time like he was hungry for violence and he'd just stumbled upon a vigilante justice buffet, shouted for the prisoners to stand back from the door and then broke the rusted lock with ease. At least forty people came running, loping, or limping out, some leaning on each other, some wounded, all shouting their thanks, and then scattered before the guards could return with reinforcements and start rounding them back up.

When Mariel remounted the horse Clem was waiting on, Big John cackled with delight, and Mariel let slip an unlikely but unmistakeable skitter of answering laughter.

They were all giddy with triumph as they put as much distance between them and the village as possible, Baxter whooping as Kit fondly told him to be quiet. Even Morgan was smiling, which seemed extremely improbable, seeing as they were bumping along sharing a horse with both Josey *and* Big John.

"Where are we going?" Josey called over to Mariel, ducking to avoid a branch.

Clem was clinging to Mariel's back as she tried very hard not to fall off the horse, so she couldn't see Mariel's face, and it was actually sort of annoying. That tiny laugh had been bizarrely out of character. Clem wanted to study this development, like it was an interesting disease.

"Underwood," Mariel said, and Josey threw back her head and crowed with pure glee.

"Underwood!" she shouted, the others joining her. Their joy was contagious; Clem found herself grinning, thrilled to be going to *Underwood*, a place she'd never heard of before and that could easily just be their favorite patch of wood dirt.

They rode hard, spurred on by excitement and relief, but it was fully dark when they finally stopped; to Clem, it seemed as if they *had* just pulled up to another patch of dirt. There were no buildings, no torches, no sounds other than the usual rustle and hoot of the wood—not the slightest hint that anybody might be alive in the vicinity.

"Are we lost?" she said eventually, and Mariel laughed *again.* This time it was low and quiet, like she was enjoying knowing something Clem didn't, but not to hold it over her; like she was glad she got to be the one letting Clem in on a closely held secret.

"No," she said, dismounting from the horse. Josey landed next to her and immediately stretched so widely that Clem heard her joints crack in at least four different places. "Josey, do you want to do it?"

"Nah," said Josey. "Morgan can." Mariel sighed, but didn't disagree. "Oi, Morgan—do the thing."

"Me?" Morgan said, dismounting much more slowly than the others had.

"Yeah. You. You've been practicing, haven't you?"

"Okay," they said. There was a pause, and then Clem almost did fall off the horse; Morgan had somehow produced an extremely loud, trilly sort of bird call, relatively close to the cry of a robin. Baxter cheered, and then something completely inexplicable happened: there was a muffled answering call, and then one of the trees *opened.* Clem could only see it because there was a faint glow of light spilling out from the gap—no, the *doorway*—that had just appeared in what had seemed, in the dark, to be a completely bog-standard tree trunk.

"Okay," she said, sliding off the horse. "*Now* this is finally getting good."

"Finally," Mariel repeated, shifting half a step so that Clem could lean briefly on her shoulder on her way down to the ground. "All the adventure so far hasn't been thrilling enough for you? Sword fights? Escapes? Running from the law?"

"Nobody opened a tree," Clem said, grinning at her. Mariel's mouth twitched in response.

A figure appeared in the doorway, silhouetted against the light, and Mariel went to talk to them in a low voice. More people came out—from where, Clem still didn't understand—and took charge of the horses.

"What is this?" she said to Kit, who was patting down his clothes, trying to get rid of some of the horse dust.

"This is Underwood," he said. "You'll see."

"Are we not on the run from your perturbed colleagues anymore?"

"Nah," Kit said, smiling through his exhaustion. "We've got Big John! Nobody can be mad at us if we've got Big John. And Morgan can't be the mole, because they're the reason we pulled it off. They won't be happy, but the captain's been proven right. We can reconvene with some of our people here, check what's what. Sheriff's not even in town, which buys us some time. So. Victory lap."

"Victory lap," Clem said, nodding.

Big John was already disappearing through the doorway with a quick rap on the bark with his knuckles for good luck, and in single file, they followed him. Baxter came in last behind Clem, and she heard him saying "Oof" and "Ungh" and "Oh no" a lot as he tried to contort himself into a smaller shape to fit.

Inside, there was a very narrow staircase, winding down into the depths of the earth. It was dark and a little damp at first; it looked like the ground had been carefully dug out and then shored up with wooden timbers. The lower they traveled, the more organic it seemed—in place of beams, there were twisty roots, until Clem couldn't tell if they'd been placed there on purpose or if they were naturally holding the ceiling aloft. There were lanterns every twenty or so steps, and when Clem looked up, she could see that there was some complicated system of ventilation: small openings where she could somehow feel the night breeze on her, even so far underground.

Eventually the steps became less steep, and the corridor wider. Clem could hear voices now—not the serious, strained muttering of people conducting official business, but easy chatter and laughter. It sounded almost like a busy inn, of the type you found at the sunset edges of large villages or sprouting out of the foliage at crossroads, full of weary workers and travelers eager to have their spirits lifted.

When they turned the last corner, Clem discovered that it essentially *was* an inn; there was a bar at the back of the room carved from one long length of wood, and an assortment of mismatched chairs, tables, and benches spread across the rest of the space, half full of people. The ceiling above them was a web of thick, pale roots, following a gentle curve down to the walls. Lit only by lamplight, the entire room glowed, and Clem could still feel that gentle breeze coming from somewhere mysterious. It felt like they were *inside* a tree somehow, cradled beneath it like soft bunny-kits, safe from harm.

"Underwood!" said Josey, smiling. A few people had stopped talking when they walked in, and Clem wondered if Mariel and her Men had been put on some sort of Do Not Interact list after the stunt they'd pulled getting Morgan away. Had Richard Flores's broken nose ever been properly set?

If Mariel sensed any of this, she pretended not to. The slightly stooped, bearded man behind the bar looked up, and when he spotted Big John his eyes crinkled.

"John!" he said, coming out to shake him by the hand. "Heard they'd jumped you. Out already, eh? Must be a record."

"Ah, yeah. Just annoyed them so much they had to let me go."

"Hey," Clem said to Josey, sotto voce. "That's what *I've* been trying to do."

"Nah," Big John continued, gesturing at Mariel. "It was Captain Hartley-Hood who got me out. And her top-notch company. Brazen little fuckers, even if they've barely got hair on their chests."

"Stop," Mariel said awkwardly. "We were just doing our jobs. Ralph—we're starving."

"One of everything for the heroes of the hour," Ralph said, with a wink that certainly didn't make Mariel look any less uncomfortable.

They sat down at a very old table that was carved all over with missives, initials, broken hearts, arrows, runes, and sigils. Some of the artists seemed to have been having conversations with each other, most of them conducted in elaborate code. In some corners, people had simply drawn genitalia. The symbol Mariel and her company had tattooed on their arms was everywhere, etched by hundreds of hands, each iteration slightly different. Clem absent-mindedly ran her fingers over them as the others talked among themselves. A couple of grizzled Men entered, and when they spotted Mariel, she immediately got to her feet and went to talk to them. They ensconced themselves in a corner for a short while, and Clem found herself watching, able to enjoy this captainly Mariel much more now that she'd been allowed a peek at the other side of her.

It was obvious that these people respected her, even though they had at least ten years on her. They leaned in to listen when she addressed them, nodding seriously as she spoke, and something about it made Clem feel . . . proud? Confused? Restless?

She sort of wanted to pick a fight with the captain, but maybe just so Mariel would lay hands on her in reply.

When the drinks arrived—huge pitchers of light ale, wine, and honey water—Mariel came back to the table, and her eyes softened when Kit poured her a cup. It was probably the closest Clem had ever seen her to being at ease while still conscious. Everybody was loose-collared and tired, light with hunger and relief, and happy to be there. When they all had full cups, Big John cleared his throat and lifted his drink, and Mariel pressed a long-fingered hand to her brow as if she sensed imminent humiliation.

"Listen, listen—Mariel, you can pretend I don't exist all you want, but I'm speech-making all the same. You did a good thing today. Not just coming for me, although obviously, much obliged. It's not always easy to see the wood for the trees when you do what we do—pun intended, pun intended, leave me alone—but there'll be parents reuniting with their children right about now, and lovers back in each other's arms, and probably a few pickpockets back fiddling rich folk on the streets where they belong . . ."

"Hear, hear," said Josey, solemnly dipping her cup.

". . . and that's thanks to you. You did it for the good of the wood."

"For the good of the wood," the others repeated. They knocked their cups together, Baxter being a little too enthusiastic and spilling half of Morgan's drink onto the table—and then Ralph interrupted the solemnity of the moment by appearing with two enormous golden loaves of still-steaming bread and a slab of butter that elicited a unanimous sigh of joy.

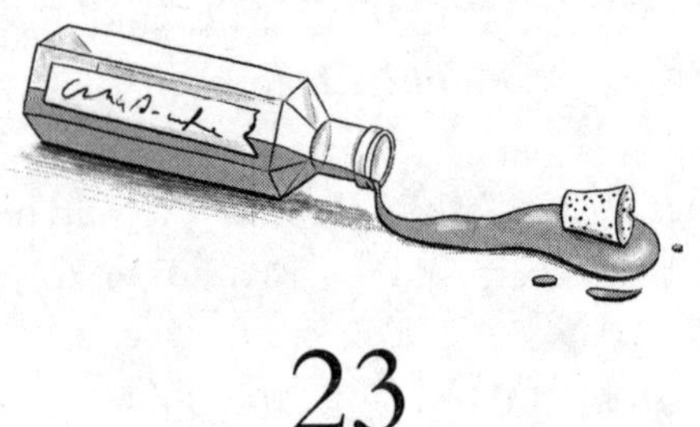

23

Clem was feeling very content.

Thick, creamy soup crowded with golden potatoes had followed the bread, and crispy roast chicken and rabbit, and every time a new dish was placed on the table she felt slightly tearful with gratitude. There was more than enough to go around, enough that Baxter didn't have to pilfer from anybody else's plate, and they were all quiet as they ate without ceremony or even basic manners.

More people entered, not from down the staircase but from a different door entirely, and Clem's brain emerged from its soup haze to wonder if there were other entrances elsewhere in the wood—more seemingly magical doors carved into trees that made no logical sense but were not to be questioned when going through them led to roast chicken. The room was getting steadily louder as people ate and drank, calling out to friends and jumping tables to continue old quarrels and jokes, shaking hands and shoulders, laughing heartily and spilling drinks. All of them went to pay their respects to Big John, and Clem wondered if word had spread, and they had been drawn here to toast him specifically.

Over in one corner somebody brought out a lute; his companion produced a fiddle, and they started to play little snatches of country dances while they talked, the music dropping out every time they laughed too hard to play and then picking up again when they'd finished wiping their eyes and slapping their knees.

Mariel was talking to Josey. Her hair was down now, falling in gentle waves, and Clem wondered how she'd missed the moment she'd released it from its braid. She was still wearing the funny little maroon jacket with puffy sleeves that she had donned for the bard ruse, although it was now unbuttoned and her hands were gloveless. She was nursing a half-empty cup as she leaned back in her chair, listening to something Josey was saying, focused but for once not *frowning* about it. Her eyes flicked briefly over to meet Clem's, revealing nothing, and Clem took an abrupt sip of her drink, and then looked at Kit instead, who was currently laughing with a hand pressed to his mouth as Baxter said something in his ear. Baxter's arm was draped lazily over the back of Kit's chair, potentially because he was just so large that it was necessary for him to find places to rest his limbs, but more likely because it was almost the same as putting his arm actually *around* Kit.

Big John had been telling a story about the time he'd accidentally set sail for France in a ship he'd only boarded to hand over a message to someone on deck, but he broke off and nudged Morgan in the ribs.

"Ow," said Morgan.

He lowered his voice, looking dastardly and conspiratorial. "The Scarlet boy and Chisaka?"

"That's exactly what I've been saying!" said Clem, and Big John grinned at her. She liked him. He was easy to like. Clem wondered how he'd managed to cling on to Deputy Commander, when he seemed so different from Commander Hartley in every conceivable way.

"They're being very . . . touchy," Morgan said, sounding pained. "I bumped into them coming out of the room when they bunked together in that village, and they seemed . . . *happy*. I don't know what happened, and I don't *want* to know what happened."

"Amazing," said Clem. "Incredible. I love love."

"No offense," said Big John, pointing his tankard at her, "but I still don't understand why you're here. Couldn't you have run off back home when this lot were distracted?"

Clem squinted at him and then shrugged. "I have patients here, unfortunately."

"Clemence has a saving-people complex," said Morgan. "It's really embarrassing."

"Er, excuse me, I'm a healer. I heal. It's not a complex, it's a job. Speaking of which, John—Mr. Big—I can take a look at that leg later, if you like."

"You should have killed us all in our sleep!" Morgan said, throwing their hands up in the air and then wincing slightly. Full range of movement definitely wasn't coming back anytime soon then. "Half of us should probably be dead by now already without you even needing to lift a knife! And yet you keep *patching us up* instead."

"Would it make you feel better if I started actively trying to hurt you?"

"Yeah, actually, it would. It'd be normal anyway."

"All right—shall we play a game of knucklebones? Winner gets to stab the loser. Or the loser has to get the winner a drink. Either will do."

"All our drinks are free tonight," Morgan said witheringly. "But—fine."

What Morgan didn't know was that Old Rosie was a terrible trickster who liked drinking for free, and that she and Clem had played a lot of tavern games together when Clem had first stumbled into Oak Vale and been unable to speak for the better part of three months. You didn't have to talk to play games with bones and dice.

Having clearly expected to be playing with a pushover, Morgan was stunned into crafting some very creative combinations of swear words that Clem had never heard before. When Morgan eventually demanded an arm-wrestle instead, and Clem had to remind them that they were still recovering from a shoulder wound, Big John offered to act as Morgan's second.

"I'd rather have Baxter," they said, but they allowed the arm-wrestle to proceed, and Clem won by virtue of *not* being covered in deep, black bruises from a recent beating, and then immediately lost to Josey, who had seen what was happening and come to take a turn. The whole thing was over so fast that Clem had barely blinked before her hand hit the table. Clem and Kit were almost evenly matched in the arms department and called it a polite draw after a minute or two of straining, and then Baxter offered an arm and Clem immediately forfeited, to general cheers.

"I'd like to keep my bones in the same sort of arrangement they're in now," she said, as Baxter shrugged and smiled affably. "It's really been working for me so far."

"Captain," Josey called to Mariel, who was talking to the barman. "You're needed!"

Mariel had her let's-get-down-to-business face on when she approached the table, even though she was holding a drink and her face was slightly flushed. "What's the problem?"

"No problem," said Josey. "Just needed somebody to arm-wrestle Clem. Tiebreaker."

Mariel frowned at her. "Er. No. You arm-wrestle her."

"I have. Destroyed her. Kit could have won but bowed out like a gentleman, and she wouldn't wrestle Baxter on account of . . . bone concerns."

"Bone concerns," Mariel repeated. She was trying to sound scathing, but her voice was honey-slow.

"You don't have to arm-wrestle me," Clem offered, her hand flexing in anticipation even as she did. "I know I'm very intimidating."

"That's reverse-braining," Baxter said, snapping his fingers and pointing. "I know what you're doing. Tricksy."

"I'm not intimidated," Mariel said, tilting her head so that her hair swung forward over her shoulder. "I just don't see the point."

"It's fun!" said Baxter.

Morgan snorted. "Mariel doesn't put any stock in fun."

Mariel sighed, looked from Baxter's smile to Morgan's scathing eyebrows, then rucked up her sleeve to the elbow and sat down opposite Clem. "Fine. Let's make this quick."

"The words that always come before absolute oodles of fun," said Morgan.

Clem had left her sleeves where they were, but seeing the ceremonial rolling-up of Mariel's, she decided to do hers to match. She didn't stop at the elbow; she pulled it up until there was a lot of biceps on display. She was rarely the strongest person in the room, but she was proud of those biceps nonetheless. Mariel just looked at Clem's arm, her face unreadable, and then cleared her throat.

"When you're finished preening," she said, and Clem grinned.

Clasping hands was weird. It felt intimate, even with everybody watching. Mariel's fingers were long and slender, only slightly calloused, probably because she was fastidious about glove-wear when it came to riding and archery. She was fastidious about everything, even arm-wrestling. She asked Josey for a countdown, her grip on Clem's hand tightening the moment Josey told them to begin and not a second before.

Clem knew straight away that she was going to lose, but she wasn't going to do it without making Mariel sweat a little.

"Oh shit," said Kit, looking from Clem to Mariel as the table jolted. "Should we . . . We should move the drinks."

The drinks were whisked away to safety and Clem settled in, adjusting her grip slightly and raising her eyebrows when Mariel twitched.

Clem started easy, lulling Mariel into a false sense of security. She knew Mariel would only use the exact amount of strength she deemed necessary to win—no more and no less. She let Mariel press her down, her hand inching toward the table at a snail's pace.

"Boring," said Morgan. "Give up, healer."

Clem just smiled serenely, although she was under considerable strain. Mariel was *strong.* It was probably from hefting that enormous chip on her shoulder, or dragging kidnapping victims around the wood by the hair. Her eyes were narrowed in concentration, her cheeks pink, lips pressed together as her victory neared. There was the slightest suggestion of a satisfied smirk beginning to form when Clem sighed, stretched with her free arm, and then exerted so much force on Mariel's hand that it jerked backward.

Mariel let out a thin hiss through her teeth. "What the hell was that?"

Clem laughed breathlessly, already beginning to lose the ground she'd gained.

"*That* was the element of surprise," said Clem. "My favorite element, after water."

Mariel was beginning to look dewy around the temples. She was very red now, her whole faced screwed up in concentration, her palm hot. Clem was enjoying this an unreasonable amount; she let Mariel push her almost to the point of losing, and then rallied again.

"What are you *doing*?" Mariel said through gritted teeth. "Just—play *properly.*"

"Do it, Clem," Morgan said, banging their fists on the table, apparently experiencing an abrupt and unexpected change of heart. "Finish her!"

Clem only had one last burst of energy in her, and she

delighted in watching Mariel's eyes widen with fury as she employed it.

"Worried?" Clem asked in a low voice. Mariel almost *snarled* in response, a wild, animal sort of noise that should have been very funny. It mostly made Clem feel a little warm under her shirt. Best not to think too hard about the implications of that, lest it awaken something in her.

"*No.*"

"Why is it so hard for you to lose, do you think? Just a quirky little personality flaw? Deeply broken brain?"

Mariel bit down on her lip, the muscles of her arm shifting as she pushed, her strength never wavering. "Why won't you just give . . . *up*?"

Clem's knuckles finally hit the wood, hard. Baxter whooped; Morgan slumped back in their chair, arms crossed, clearly mortified to have shown even a crumb of support for Clem's lost cause.

"There," Mariel said, her breathing unsteady. "Happy?"

"Yeah," said Clem, still smiling. "And you can let go of my hand now."

Mariel dropped it like a hot pan and blinked confusedly at Clem before scraping her chair back and going to fetch another drink.

Clem kept watching her though, tracking her progress across the room. She lingered with the barman, leaning against the bar as he talked, nodding seriously. Some of her hair was tucked behind her ear, but the rest spilled forward, tumbling around her face. She was waylaid by Josey halfway across the room, and when Josey said something to her, she laughed. Not a full-bellied laugh, but still, it was beautiful to watch—unexpected, like a stubborn shock of wildflowers in a barren field.

Jesus. *Wildflowers?* Clem shook her head. Clearly, she needed another drink.

Morgan was drunk. Nobody knew how it had happened. Josey had been challenging fellow patrons to knife-throwing fights and winning outrageous amounts of coin in the process, Kit and Baxter had been holed up in a corner having a quiet conversation while the physical space between them gradually narrowed to a sliver, and Mariel had been talking shop with those grizzled military-looking types again at a table in the corner.

Clem suspected Morgan's drunkenness might have been something to do with Big John's lackadaisical attitude toward age-appropriate beverages. She requested fresh water at the bar, and when she was met with blank looks and suggestions that she go to find a river herself, she settled on a cordial of honey and sat down next to Morgan with a large pitcher of the stuff and an iron will.

"You're to drink it all," she said, filling a cup and nudging it toward Morgan across the table. "And then eat some bread, have a very big piss, and go to sleep."

"I'm allowed to be drunk," Morgan said, looking squinty and slightly off-balance.

"Yeah, well, duh. Lack of appropriate supervision and questionable decision-making are apparently two key pillars of the Merry Men ethos. But you've already nearly been thrown out of this company once in the past day—I can't imagine that waking up tomorrow with a pounding headache, puking your guts up, and begging for mercy will do much to improve matters."

Morgan scowled at her, but picked up the cup and took a swig.

"This is horrible. You're horrible."

"I'm your guardian angel, you ungrateful little goblin. Drink up."

Morgan steadily drank their way through half the pitcher before saying that they were "all juiced out." Clem grabbed Baxter by the elbow when he was on his way to the bar and asked about sleeping arrangements.

"We'll have rooms," he said, gesturing vaguely toward one of the doorways. "I don't know. Ask Mariel."

"Where is she?"

"Dunno. In meetings, I think. People have heard we're here by now, so they want to talk strategy."

Strategy meetings! After this many drinks? It was inconceivable.

Clem hadn't even considered the possibility of this subterranean rabbit warren having bedrooms. She looked around for Mariel but couldn't see her anymore, and decided to haul Morgan up and hope that she ran into somebody helpful on the way.

"I can *walk*," Morgan said bitingly. With spectacular comedic timing, a second later they had tripped on a chair leg and fallen very loudly to the floor, sending miscellaneous furniture flying. There was a brief pause in music and conversation, before people laughed and whooped and started up again.

"What's going on?" Mariel said, appearing as if from

nowhere and taking Morgan's other arm as Clem struggled to right them.

"Morgan has been partaking of the wine," said Clem.

"And the mead. And the strong ale," Morgan added, not sounding the least bit sorry. "I partook of them all."

"Come on," Mariel said. "Bed."

"Yeah, yeah," slurred Morgan. "You're all singing the same song tonight."

Between Clem and Mariel they managed to get Morgan mostly upright and moving in a forwardly direction. The open entryway into the tunnel beyond was a bit cramped, but Clem was surprised to discover that the tunnel itself was actually rather roomy, and not the least bit claustrophobic.

"This is bizarre," she said, as they made slow progress past lit sconces. "I don't even feel like we're underground."

"Well," Mariel said, grunting slightly as Morgan's weight shifted in her direction. "We are."

"How did they dig all this?"

"They didn't. It's an old wyrm den," Mariel said. Clem just stared at her over the top of Morgan's head. "That was a joke."

"Wow," said Clem. "It sure was."

They passed a series of doors with numbers carved carefully into them; when they reached number sixteen, Mariel kicked it open and together they maneuvered Morgan onto the narrow bed.

"Do you need us to take off your boots?" Clem asked, as Morgan lay face down and unmoving on the blanket. They made a small sound of assent, more a grunt than anything else. "I'll take that as a yes."

Clem knelt to untie said boots, dropping them unceremoniously on the floor. Mariel surreptitiously picked them up and arranged them neatly at the end of the bed as Clem tried to get Morgan to roll over.

"Sleep like a normal person," she said, when Morgan surfaced. "You look dead."

"Maybe I am dead," Morgan said. "Wouldn't that be nice."

"Not particularly," said Mariel. "I'd have to write it in the book back at camp. Arrange the funeral."

"Right," Morgan said despondently. "Admin."

"Let me look at that shoulder, please, drunkard." Morgan sighed extravagantly, but turned over enough to let Clem poke medicinally at them until she was satisfied. "Get some sleep. You'll feel better in the morning."

She and Mariel had just made it to the doorway when Morgan spoke again.

"Mariel," they said, in a very small voice. "Have I fucked it all up?"

Mariel exchanged a brief look with Clem, who wrinkled her nose back, feeling quite sorry for Morgan and knowing that Morgan would kill her if she ever expressed such an emotion out loud.

"No," Mariel said eventually. "You made a . . . mistake. It was a moment of poor judgment. It only ruined that one thing."

"Yeah," Clem said slowly, thinking this wasn't quite the angle she'd have gone for. "Plus, everybody makes mistakes."

"No they don't," said Morgan. "Mariel doesn't. Sorry, I mean—*Captain*. Captain Mariel . . . does not."

Clem looked expectantly at Mariel, waiting for her to sigh and shake her head and tell Morgan that even *she* had made errors in judgment in the past, and that it was all part of growing up and didn't mean she was terrible and irredeemable.

"I . . . can't afford to make mistakes," said Mariel. "It's different for me."

"Er," said Clem. "Sorry, but that's horseshit."

Morgan snickered from the bed, and Mariel glanced sharply at Clem, looking none too pleased.

"Let's continue this conversation elsewhere," she said. "Morgan needs rest."

Clem heard Morgan mutter, "G'luck, Giblets," as she followed Mariel out of the door.

"Don't undermine me in front of my Men," Mariel said, walking quickly. Clem matched her speed, not paying the slightest bit of attention to where they were going.

"Don't lie then!" said Clem. "Obviously you've made mistakes! You're a person! Not a divine being! You've made mistakes, I've made mistakes, your *father* has made mistakes—"

"You don't know anything about my father."

"Oh," said Clem. "Right, I see. So it's intergenerational, is it? This little obsession with never being wrong. Honestly, I think your head got a bit messed up somewhere down the line. And you're passing it on to Morgan, so that the cycle continues forever, breakdown after breakdown stretching hundreds of years into the future . . ."

"Nobody is having a breakdown," Mariel scoffed. They had reached another door, number twenty-seven, and

Mariel shoved it open without breaking stride. Clem followed her in, still arguing.

"Has it ever occurred to you that it's a sign of *strength* of character to admit to being wrong? Beat yourself up over everything all the time, whatever, that's your prerogative, but don't do the same to Morgan. Not when they've obviously had such a shitty go of it. I don't know what happened in that house, but—wait, what are you doing?"

"Changing," Mariel said. She had taken off the maroon jacket and was now carefully hanging it off the back of a chair.

"But I'm standing here."

"You followed me into my room," Mariel said, now making a start on the fiddly little ties on the sleeves of her shirt.

"I didn't know it was your room," Clem said stupidly. She probably could have figured that one out using context clues, if she'd been looking for them, instead of focusing on berating Mariel—who was still trying, without luck, to undo the tight little bows at her wrists. "Oh for Christ's sake, come here."

Mariel hesitated and then held out her arms, wrists up, her expression expectant. It was very un-Mariel-like. Almost . . . sweet.

"Have you been drinking all night?" Clem said, piecing together this inability to untie a knot and the slight loosening of everything else.

"I had a drink with David," said Mariel. "He's not ranked, he's . . . sort of a mercenary. Goes his own way. *He* approved of what we did back at camp, at least. But he's . . . well, he's different. Everybody thinks he's very handsome." She stopped and grimaced, as if listening back to her own words and finding them lacking. "It . . . might have been two drinks."

Clem snorted, then finally finished unpicking the first knot and started on the second.

"Kit said you're not on the run anymore, now that you've got Big John back."

Mariel sighed and closed her eyes briefly, as if taking a very short nap. "No. The others can hardly argue with my approach, now that I've . . . but it *was* very rash. I've been telling myself that my father would have done the same thing, but . . . I know it's not what he would want *me* to do. When he hears about it . . . Well, I don't know what I was thinking."

"You were protecting Morgan."

"And *then* look what they turned around and did. My fault. Should have known they weren't ready for something like that, something so . . . so *personal.* I wish I could be sure I've done the right thing. That I'm *doing* the right thing. We need to go after my father next. Tomorrow. The other captains are coming. John won't even give me orders."

"Maybe he doesn't think you need orders," said Clem. "Maybe he trusts you."

"My father has never had any problem giving me orders."

The implications of this lingered in the air between them.

"Well, from where I'm standing . . . you've done a pretty good job. Dangerous levels of perfectionism aside."

"Causey . . ."

"Clem, thanks."

"We were ambushed," Mariel said. "I betrayed my fellow captains; absconded with my team and key intel about our target; almost ended up captured or killed back at Hanham. And don't even get me started on you."

Clem waved an obliging hand. "No, please. Go ahead. Start on me."

"You've seen far too much, you *know* too much, not to mention the ridiculous amount of unprofessional familiarity . . . You're in *Underwood*, for God's sake, without so much as a blindfold—"

"I'd never be able to make it back here in a thousand years, if it helps," said Clem. This knot was tricky; she was having to get her very short nails involved. "I still don't understand how we walked through a tree and ended up in a pub."

"Everybody's acting like you're part of the team," said Mariel. "Including you."

"Would that be so bad?"

Mariel let out a huff of a breath. "You aren't trained in sword or bow, you can barely ride a horse—and you *still* think your guardian was right to heal one of the Sheriff's men, don't you?"

"I disagree with you on some of the finer points of that, but yes."

Mariel rolled her eyes. "See? And . . . and you make no sense. Your entire job is blood and guts, but half the time you can't handle violence. A bit of smoke and danger made you sick, but you keep looking for fires to throw yourself on anyway."

"Fires?" Clem said, her hands dropping from Mariel's wrist. What the hell did Mariel know about *fires*?

"What I mean is," Mariel said slowly, "I think you'd risk your life for a perfect stranger in the first three seconds of knowing them if they had a hole that needed patching, even if it killed you."

"Well, who wouldn't?" said Clem, the feeling of tight dread that had overtaken her beginning to drain away.

"Most people."

Clem yanked Mariel toward her again by the wrists, and it seemed to shock all of the air out of her, which was extremely gratifying. The knot was nearly freed. "Look. I like you. You and your band of Merry Men. Putting aside all that military nonsense, I think you're decent people, whether or not you screw up from time to time—which obviously you *do*, because if you didn't I wouldn't be here. Kidnapped. But that's okay."

"That's . . . *okay*?"

"Yeah. It is. Look, I know it's hard for you, I can tell you're in a . . . difficult position. But I think you care about people and you want to do good, even if you have a crap way of showing it. I always hoped the Merry Men would be . . . I don't know, pure paragons of goodness, even if that was a bit naive. You're not that. Maybe nobody is. But you are trying, and I think you're doing a pretty good job. And also . . . I don't have a *complex*, but I like helping people. It's not always easy for me, as you've noticed, but it's what I'm doing with my life. You needed my help. So here I am."

Mariel looked almost horrified, as if there were nothing

in the world more embarrassing than being honest about your feelings. But it was true. All of it. Clem was having fun. She liked Baxter's easy laughs and candor, Kit's open heart and keen mind, Josey's considerable prowess and sharp wit, even Morgan's constant low-level antagonism.

She liked Mariel. It was almost unfathomable, but it was true.

"I don't need you," Mariel said. It was delivered with such a foolishly stubborn tilt of her chin that it made Clem feel a bit giddy. Why were they standing so close to each other? It had seemed vaguely necessary for knot-untying, but now Clem realized it was ridiculous. *Mariel* was ridiculous. She was stubborn and handsome and a lost cause, but right now her lips were bitten-red and her eyes were dipping low, and Clem had a theory.

"*Liar.*"

She was still holding onto the cuffs of Mariel's sleeves; she let go, and Mariel swayed slightly on her feet, bringing her half a step closer. Clem had a laugh caught between her teeth and Mariel looked stuck somewhere between stern and lost, brow furrowed and mouth parted.

Clem was still looking at her lips when Mariel kissed her.

24

The kiss lasted for approximately three seconds. Clem just had time to go from wide-eyed disbelief that it was happening to immediate, enthusiastic acceptance of this new reality—her hand was halfway to Mariel's jaw when Mariel abruptly pulled away and made an odd, aborted noise that Clem *could* have argued, at a stretch, was something like desire.

It was probably more like visceral horror.

They stood staring at each other, Mariel's shirt half unbuttoned, the cuffs too long for her now they were untied, and then Clem broke the odd silence by laughing.

"You're welcome."

"What?" Mariel said, looking as if she'd recently been hit very hard over the head. There were spots of pink scattered across her cheekbones like fingerprints.

"I assume you were trying to say thank you. To me. For helping you with your shirt. Not sure it warranted such enthusiasm, but I don't know the Merry Men customs."

"Um," said Mariel. "That's . . ."

There was a quiet rap at the door. When neither Mariel nor Clem said anything, it opened, and a middle-aged woman with deep brown skin and graying curls stopped in her tracks and glanced between them, obviously confused by the palpable tension in the room. It must have looked very odd; either like they were about to kill each other or were halfway to a ravishing. Which, to be honest . . .

"Clothes, Captain," the woman said, putting a folded stack onto the rickety chair by the door. "As requested."

"Thank you, Asha," Mariel said stiffly. "That's . . . You can just leave them there."

"Yes," said Asha. "I have."

"You have," said Mariel. "Exactly. Yes. And—that's all."

"It is." Asha backed from the room, still seeming unsure if she should be calling for backup or recommending that they hang a sock on the door to prevent further interruptions.

Another silence stretched between them. Clem felt a little bit hysterical.

"So . . ."

"That's all," Mariel repeated. "You can go."

It was possible that Clem should have been offended by this casual dismissal, but quite frankly, she was having too much fun watching Mariel squirm. After all, *Clem* hadn't been the one to initiate a kiss and then start acting as if she were concussed. Mariel busied herself with her next task immediately, face still aflame, and then froze when she seemed to realize that she was essentially undressing with an audience; Clem gave her a brilliant smile, open, no ill intent or sharp edges, and didn't stick around for her response.

Back by the bar, things were getting increasingly raucous.

The lute and fiddle players had been joined by a slightly tipsy singer, who was regaling everybody with drinking songs and encouraging the room to join in, which it did with gusto. Some of the songs were familiar to Clem; others seemed to be particular to the Merry Men. Those were the ones that provoked the loudest and most spirited response from the crowd—Clem could see Kit and Josey standing up, singing along, Baxter sitting next to them slamming his hand on the table mostly in time to the beat. She pushed her way to their table and Baxter cheered and pushed a drink toward her.

"You're my favorite kidnappee," he said fondly.

"How many people have you kidnapped?"

He thought about this. "One. But you'd probably still be my favorite if we'd had more. You're just so chipper about it."

"That's because you're my favorite kidnappers."

"Aww, you're just saying that."

"I'm not, I swear. Wouldn't trade you for anything."

"You remind me of my sister," said Baxter. "I mean, I don't have a sister. But if I had one, I think she'd be like you."

"That makes absolutely no sense. I love it."

Josey came to fetch her drink, face glossy with perspiration. "Don't wish for sisters," she said, pointing her cup at Baxter. "They're a curse."

"That's not true!" Baxter said, scandalized. He leaned toward Clem, his tone confidential. "Josey has three older sisters. Lovely. Lovely sisters."

"They set the bar too high," Josey said glumly. "I'll

always be the worst one. Slowest. Least experienced. Bested in combat."

"You're . . . the *worst* sister?" Clem said disbelievingly. "But you're . . . really good. At everything."

"Best in most rooms," Josey said, shaking her head. "Worst at my own campfire." Baxter patted her on the shoulder; the fact that he wasn't refuting her claim to the title of worst made Clem suddenly desperate to meet these three shining older sisters.

Kit sat down, flushed and sweaty, his hair sticking up at the front.

"What are we talking about?"

"Oh," said Baxter. "You know. Siblings. I was just saying . . . Clem is basically part of the family now."

"We are not a family," said Mariel. Clem hadn't noticed her arrival, and tried to pass her startled jump off as a little nod in time to the music. "We are barely colleagues."

"You *know* that's not true, Mariel," said Baxter. "Not least because we are . . . literally related. I think."

"Step-cousins by marriage," Clem supplied, glancing up at Mariel, who had changed into her usual muted greens and one long plait. Clem imagined her doing up her buttons and tightly weaving her hair, putting everything back into order after a brief and dangerous encounter with disarray, and almost wanted to laugh again.

"Baxter," Mariel said sternly.

"Oh my God," said Baxter. "You called me Baxter! Does that mean your meetings are done and we're officially off duty right now?"

"Oi, Captain—where's your lute?" This last was Big

John, calling to Mariel as he made for the musicians. "Wait, wait, doesn't matter. Harish has a spare."

Rescued almost immediately from his state of lutelessness, he bounded over to the musicians just as they finished playing and struck up his own little number. What he lacked in tuning he made up for in enthusiasm, and the song he'd chosen was far bawdier than anything that had come before. The room was soon in high spirits bordering on hysterics, Baxter wheezing as he clutched his own knees for support. Mariel had rolled her eyes and shaken her head, but Clem kept darting glances at her and finding her laughing quietly as she watched, thinking she was getting away with it.

The song concluded to earsplitting cheers, Big John giving a silly little bow that almost relieved him of his recently procured instrument.

"All right, all right," he shouted. "Who's going to do the ballad?"

There were a few volunteers, but Clem saw his eyes lock onto Mariel and watched as Mariel glowered back at him and shook her head.

"Come on, Captain Hartley-Hood! Fresh from victory, and she's got the voice of an angel, she used to sing this for us when she was only a scrap of a girl."

At that moment, Mariel seemed her age, or even younger—a child, being asked by a drunk friend of her father's to do a trick, and imagining all the ways in which she could murder him so that she might escape this fate.

People were looking at her expectantly now, calling out in her direction, and although Clem could tell she found it painful beyond belief, Mariel smiled tightly and got to her feet. There were more cheers; Josey looked ecstatic, and Kit pressed a hand to his mouth and started muttering, "Oh my God, oh my *God*."

Mariel made her way to the front of the room, and somebody dragged a stool into place next to Big John so that she'd have somewhere to sit. She settled herself down onto it with perfect posture, looking fixedly at the floor.

Whatever "the ballad" was, apparently it commanded a certain amount of respect, because a hush fell as Big John started to pluck out the first few notes. Clem didn't know anything about music, but felt this fell firmly in the realm of *sad*, skirting just past *haunting*.

Ere I die, to the wood will I,
When fair summer draws to an end;
And ere I return, 'fore the home fires burn,
I retreat from the field and the glen.

Ere I sleep, and the kind thicket keep,
I will find my way under again;
Ere I fall, I will drink to you all,
The greenwood, the rootwood, my friends.

Her voice was higher than Clem would have imagined—soft, with a bit of rasp underneath that gave it depth. It was all right that Clem was staring because everybody was, even the hardest and the drunkest Men—even Big John, who had orchestrated this entire thing and was accompanying her with increasingly erratic strumming.

Clem actually saw a well-scarred woman, with enormous muscles erupting out from her sleeveless jerkin, wipe a tear as Mariel finished, and the applause that followed was much more earnest than it had been after Big John's drinking song about a buxom lady from Strood. Mariel looked almost *shy*, and Clem felt so inexplicably thrilled by getting to witness that expression on her face that she realized her leg was jiggling slightly under the table as Mariel made her way back toward the group.

She'd kissed the mouth that had sung that song—albeit only for a few seconds, and she'd only realized she was being invited to a kiss halfway through.

"Never," said Josey reverently, "in a thousand million years—"

"I've seen it before," Baxter said. "Not since we were little though . . . You've still got excellent pipes on you, Cap'n Cousin."

"Morgan is going to spontaneously burst into flame when they find out they missed this," said Josey.

"Probably . . . best . . . if we don't speak of it at all," said Mariel, but there was absolutely no authority in her tone. In fact, when she sat down, she wavered for a second before letting her head pitch forward onto her folded arms so that she was slumped over on the table. Baxter let out a shout of laughter, and Josey patted Mariel on the arm in mock-consolation.

This was not a Mariel that Clem had *ever* been privy to, and it seemed like her Men felt the same way.

Clem's leg was practically dancing a jig all on its own.

She wasn't entirely sure where all this odd, jittery energy

had come from, but something hit her as she watched Josey squeeze and release Mariel's shoulder: tonight Mariel wasn't untouchable, and that was *very* interesting indeed.

Clem had touched her before, obviously, dressing wounds and holding on for dear life on the back of a horse, waking up uncomfortably close in that narrow bed back at the inn, but each time the contact had felt either entirely practical or like an overstep. She hadn't entertained anything more because Mariel didn't *invite* anything more, and she had absolutely no interest in any sort of chase. Clem made friends easily, flirted freely, had always been a pretty good judge of who might be angling for a quick kiss on the border of the woods after a feast—not that it happened often, in a village as small as Oak Vale. She didn't throw herself at people who weren't going to catch her, because that was how you got kneecapped, emotionally speaking.

Mariel was obsessed with rules and order and rank, and no part of her belief system seemed to allow for romancing a hostage. It was ludicrous. Like something from one of Big John's bawdy songs.

But *Mariel* had kissed *Clem*. And then she'd opened her mouth and sung for this entire room full of comrades and subordinates, clear and sweet, her eyes downcast and her pride set aside for a few minutes. She was still slumped on the table now, her hand reaching clumsily for her cup without looking.

Clearly, they weren't playing by the rules tonight. So . . . yes. *Interesting.*

"Is she drunk?" Clem asked Kit. He glanced over at Mariel and then shrugged.

"Nah, I don't think so. Maybe a little tipsy. Constitution of an ox, this one."

"I can hear you," Mariel said, as she raised her head to take a sip of ale.

"Are you drunk?" Clem asked her directly. Mariel rolled her eyes. It was, after all, her primary form of communication.

"No."

"Good."

"Why exactly is that good? I would have thought you'd be thrilled at the likelihood that I might be about to humiliate myself. Or"—she broke off, looking pained—"humiliate myself any more than I already have this evening."

"It wasn't humiliating," said Clem. "It was incredible. You were incredible."

Mariel looked wary, worried that she was being made fun of, but then she came up against Clem's smile and just looked confused again.

"Stop having so much fun," Josey said to Clem from across the table.

Clem lifted her drink in a sort of toast. "No!"

The rest of the evening was a patchwork of light and sound and spilled drinks; Baxter made them all dance, almost destroyed a table in the process, and threw everybody around to the music for a while before asking Kit to join him in a lively number that made the tree roots quiver ominously above them. Josey vanished, and then Clem spotted her standing by the fiddle player, whispering something in his ear; the next song was much slower, the sort that was trotted out at the end of dances to give lovers an excuse to indulge in excessive *lingering*, and Clem watched as Baxter looked briefly taken aback before Kit took him by the hand and started to lead.

"Really excellent work," Clem said to Josey when she returned. "Subtle. Nefarious. Necessary."

"I have absolutely no idea what you're talking about," said Josey. They both watched as Baxter, uncharacteristically red and shy, leaned down and pulled Kit so close that their noses almost brushed. "Aw," said Josey. "They're going to make a *baby*."

Clem choked on her drink, and then set it down on the nearest table. People were starting to drift off to bed, and Ralph the barman seemed to be decidedly off duty based on the fact that he was currently dancing with his head on Asha's shoulder. Mariel, who had sat out the dancing, was nowhere to be seen. Clem supposed she must have gone to her room, and felt a little squeeze of disappointment somewhere around her midriff before shaking it off.

"'M'going to check on Morgan," she told Josey, who just nodded.

Clem wasn't drunk, but she was tired and tipsy; she found herself halfway to Mariel's quarters before she realized that she was fixating on the wrong room number, and had to turn back in search of number sixteen. She ran a hand along the wall as she walked, feeling the earth crumble in places, wondering if she should be concerned that this entire establishment might collapse down on top of her if Baxter did any more excitable jumping. When she reached number sixteen, the door was slightly ajar. She pushed it open and saw Mariel sitting by the bed, talking quietly to Morgan, who had one arm thrown over their eyes and seemed either half or fully asleep.

As much as she wanted to stand silently and see what on earth Mariel could be whispering to Morgan in the dark, it felt rude, so Clem announced herself with a small clearing of her throat.

Mariel jumped.

"I was just . . . checking," she said, getting to her feet immediately. "On Morgan."

"And?"

"And what?"

"Morgan, you should be lying on your side so you don't choke on your own vomit in the night," Clem said, and Morgan made an exasperated grunting sound before turning over with all the grace of a beached seal. "Very good, thank you."

Clem gave Morgan a once-over, but all that was left for them to do was to sleep it off. Mariel stood by the door, clearly uncomfortable without a purpose, and then followed Clem out into the hallway.

"That was nice of you," Clem said. "To check on them, I mean."

"Well . . ." Mariel said, apparently running out of things to say immediately.

"Funny," said Clem. "That we were both thinking the same thing."

"We were?" said Mariel. Clem definitely did not imagine that she glanced down at Clem's lips before catching herself.

"Yeah. About Morgan," Clem said slowly. "Do I have a room?"

"Do you . . . ? Oh, yes. Twenty-six."

"Nice. Neighbors," said Clem. "Can you show me? I can't remember the way."

If Mariel suspected that this was a lie, she didn't let on; she just nodded and then took off into the dark.

25

Clem tasted like bread and honey.

That was all Mariel could think about at first as they walked in silence down the tunnel, footsteps almost inaudible on the soft wood and thickly packed dirt beneath them. She felt like she'd stumbled into one of those fairy circles her mother had warned her about as a child, and come out of it changed and stupid.

A lot of things had changed in the past few days. Too many. They'd really been packing it in; Mariel was sure that, usually, there were far fewer hours between dawn and sunset.

For one thing: Clem had been right about the prisoners. It was so obvious—easy, really, barely even an hour or two out of their day, and all those people now free. It was the sort of thing Robin would have done without thought or discussion, but somehow Mariel's understanding of what their priorities were had become ruled by strategy and efficiency in a way that left no room for people to be people. It had felt so *right* that it had stirred something uncomfortable in her, something she didn't really want to examine, because if that was *right* then . . . did it mean that everything else she'd been doing was wrong? And if her father wouldn't have approved . . . what did that say about him?

She tried to picture speaking to the Commander about it. Telling him what she'd done; asking him why it wasn't their number one priority, getting in on the ground and helping people in exactly the ways they needed rather than in the ways they thought might shift the tide in the long run. *Or*, some terrible voice in the back of Mariel's mind dared to say, *in all the ways it helped the Merry Men's* pride *in the long run.*

It was all too much. Too confusing. Because it had felt so good to free those prisoners—not just selfishly good, something to prop up her ego, but truly like they were doing it for the good of the wood, as the saying went—but almost as good was the feeling that kept catching Mariel unawares every time Clem smiled at her. It felt like brushing up against something a little dangerous, and winning; like stepping off a too-high ledge and somehow getting away with not twisting your ankle. Mariel wasn't used to a wealth of good, and it kept unbalancing her, but she wanted to earn more of those smiles. She wanted to be somebody who deserved them.

There was no rule against captains dallying with anybody they fancied. The rules that did exist were focused on secrecy protocol and respecting rank. Kissing your captives would obviously be met with swift retribution if it constituted an abuse of position, but Clem was no ordinary captive, and she'd hardly been at Mariel's mercy—it had felt quite the opposite, alone in the candlelight with Clem pulling her in by the cuffs of her sleeves.

This thought was enough for Mariel to almost miss

the correct door, so she had to stop very suddenly outside number twenty-six. Clem's hand came up to prevent a full-body collision, and then it stayed pressed to Mariel's back, gentle pressure right between her shoulder blades.

"This is your room," Mariel said. It came out almost like a question. She wasn't sure why she sounded so uncertain—she *knew* it was Clem's room, because she'd asked Asha to keep them close under the guise that Clem was still an escape risk.

"Lovely," said Clem, infuriatingly smug. "Are you going to give me a tour?"

"Fine," said Mariel. It made no sense. She knew Clem wasn't really asking for a tour. Clem knew that she knew. Mariel should have pointed this out instead of going along with the charade, but doing so might have broken this weird spell, and she wasn't ready for it to end. Tomorrow she had to be a captain again. Tomorrow she had to work out what the hell they were going to do about her father, a problem so enormous she couldn't see the edges of it.

But tonight . . . ?

Clem's room was identical to Mariel's. Somebody had unloaded Clem's meager things from the horses, so her satchel crammed full of her weird experimental salves and antidotes was sitting neatly on the rickety chair. The candle was burning low, as if somebody had lit it hours ago, expecting Clem to retire long before . . . well, Mariel didn't know what time it was. Time didn't really exist in the same way in Underwood. It was a kingdom unto itself.

"I feel like I'd lose it a bit if I spent too long down here," Clem said, as if she had read Mariel's mind. She went to her satchel and opened it, riffling through the contents, taking stock. "Is it day or night right now? Is it hot? Cold? Are we still technically in England?"

"It's just a bolt-hole," said Mariel. "Temporary lodgings."

"It's more than that," said Clem. "I can't imagine people throw parties like *that* in safe houses."

"People throw parties everywhere," said Mariel. "Safe houses. Battlefields. Funerals." This sounded very serious, and so she followed it up with: "If the dancing goes on too long, the worms start trying to break through. They think we're rain."

Clem looked over at her, lopsided and lazy. Her eyes were so warm and forgiving. Nobody looked at Mariel like that. "There are worms this deep?"

"They come from above. They think the ceiling is the ground. Or—no, I mean—they think Underwood is the real world."

"Right," said Clem. "But it's not quite the real world, is it? It's a subterranean dance hall for bunnies." She stopped messing with her bag and straightened up. It was almost too much for Mariel to look at; Clem smiling at her easily, in no rush, taking her time. Her hair was still partially braided, from her mission in Stoke Hanham in that ridiculous, beautiful dress. She didn't seem nervous or confused, worried that they might be about to do something stupid. She seemed like she trusted Mariel with this completely; like she was exactly where she wanted to be. It made Mariel want to run.

"So, um. This is your room," Mariel said. Clem looked like she was trying not to laugh.

"Would you feel better if I said you could just stop talking now and I'd still kiss you?"

All the moisture vacated Mariel's mouth at once. She had to swallow hard before she nodded.

Why was it so easy for Clem to step in close and put her hands on Mariel—one to the outside of her wrist, one to her waist, like they were about to dance—while Mariel just stood there, useless, with absolutely no idea how she was supposed to do any of this?

That brief mistake of a kiss a few hours earlier had *not* been her first, but it had been the first time she had initiated one rather than simply fielding advances from enthusiastic fellow preteens around campfires, and it had not exactly gone to plan, primarily because there had *been* no plan. She had acted first, thought second, and while her instincts usually did her credit in the heat of a fight, they had let her down spectacularly when it came to whatever was happening here.

Clem didn't seem to have a plan, but it wasn't slowing her down. She was crowding into Mariel's space now, still not kissing her, just drawing her in closer until their proximity was almost unbearable.

Just do it, Mariel found herself thinking. *Get on with it.*

"What were you saying to Morgan?" Clem said, so close that her breath disturbed the strands of Mariel's hair that had fallen loose from her plait.

"What does that have to do with anything?" said Mariel, her throat still dry.

"Probably nothing."

"I was . . . apologizing," Mariel said, her mind whirling

as she tried to get the words out. Clem had a *lot* of freckles. "I may have been too harsh when the situation would have benefited from some . . . leniency. I was telling them that perhaps I understood a little of how they felt, because I've been admonished for letting my feelings get the best of me when it comes to the Sheriff's son. And that I was . . . glad to have them here. On the team."

Clem's expression fell into something unreadable; brows at a soft slant, eyes wide. "Damn it, Mariel, that's got everything to do with *everything*."

Clem kissed with her hands. That thought didn't make sense, really, but that was what it felt like. First one hand slid from Mariel's wrist to her elbow, and then the one on Mariel's waist moved to cup her by the back of the neck, firm and steady; Mariel felt like she was being gathered up, embraced in a way nobody had touched her for years.

To her utter mortification, that thought stuck, and she felt prickly heat spark up somewhere behind her eyes. *Touching* would not be her undoing, especially in the middle of a kiss that was supposed to be a brief respite from everything real.

It was a bit clumsy, a bit messy, probably because Mariel was trying desperately to stay out of her own head; Clem took a step backward, taking Mariel with her, and sat down on the edge of the bed. They only broke apart because Mariel held back.

"Are you trying to—am I supposed to sit in your *lap*?" Mariel said. Clem's shirt was partially undone, and from where Mariel was standing she could see a glimpse of freckled collarbone that made her feel seasick and reckless.

"You're not *supposed* to do anything," said Clem. She leaned back and braced herself on her elbows, a springy curl falling over one eye as she tilted her head to look up at Mariel. "What's your face doing? You look broken."

"Why are you doing this?" Mariel blurted out. Clem frowned and pushed herself upright again.

"Because I want to?" she offered. "Because it's fun?"

"Okay," Mariel said. This was acceptable. "All right."

"Because I like you," Clem said.

This was not.

"You *like* me?" Mariel said. "You've been traveling with me for the past week, and . . . you've seen who I am, and what I'm willing to do, and you *like* me?"

"Yes."

"I kidnapped you."

"I adjust easily to new people and situations."

"A little *too* easily, don't you think? Where's your sense of . . . of self-preservation? Don't you care what happens to you at all?"

Clem laughed. "*You* kidnap *me,* and it's a reflection of *my* deeply damaged psyche? Sure, sure."

"Stop avoiding the subject."

"Stop trying to talk me out of something I want," Clem said. There was a bit of fire in it, more authority than Mariel had ever heard in her voice outside a dire medical emergency. Mariel wanted to test it a little, to see where the boundaries were, but she also felt more mortified standing in front of Clem having a *conversation* about kissing than she had done a few seconds ago when they had actually *been* kissing, so she gave in and took a step forward.

Clem gave her another one of those heart-stopping, sunshine-and-honey smiles and then pulled her the rest of the way.

Mariel was not made for soft things. She had been trained hard and honed into a weapon; had been maybe seven or eight when she'd started shrugging off her grandfather's offers of piggyback rides, her father's awkward attempts at embraces. It hadn't been a conscious decision to withdraw into herself, to only initiate contact when it was absolutely necessary, but it had been a practical one. Most Merry Men weren't like that—they indulged in soldierly camaraderie, arms around shoulders, friendly punches, bonding rituals—but she'd modeled herself on her father, who kept everybody at arm's length, and never had any reason to doubt that choice.

Now it was coming back to bite her, because she couldn't just lean into Clem and kiss her and act like it was something she did every day. When Clem pushed aside Mariel's hair and then left her hand there, fingertips along her jaw, Mariel *shivered.* When Clem kissed her, open-mouthed and slow, Mariel tasted honey again, and it was so good that she squeezed her eyes tightly shut and let out a steadying exhale through her nose that made Clem laugh into her mouth.

Clem leaned back, slowly collapsing onto the bed, and this time Mariel went with her; when Clem was underneath her, blinking up with her eyes dark and wide, Mariel discovered that she had no idea what to do with her.

"Hello," said Clem. "You good?"

"I'm . . ." Mariel said. She had no words for what she was.

"Your bed is just next door," Clem said carefully. Seriously. "If you're tired."

Mariel shook her head. "I'm not tired."

Was that true? She couldn't tell. She felt warm and half-melted, barely capable of coherent thoughts; Clem smiled up at her and then sat up and switched their positions, easing Mariel down on top of the blankets. It was almost like she was being taken care of.

"*I'm* tired," Clem said. "So don't judge me based on this, all right? This isn't my best work. It's my sleepy work."

"Okay," Mariel said, tilting her head to meet Clem's mouth too soon, knowing she was probably coming off a little desperate and willing herself not to care. Clem held back for a moment, her face a few inches away, her eyes roving over Mariel's face in a way that Mariel found excruciatingly intimate. "Just *do* it."

"Do what?" Clem said, affecting confusion.

"You know what."

"Mmm," said Clem, running a hand through Mariel's hair, looking unbearably fond when Mariel had to close her eyes for a second to cope. "I kind of want to hear you say it though. Just humor me, I haven't got any hobbies."

"You are insufferable."

"I am insufferable *and* . . . you, Mariel Hartley-Hood, want me to . . ."

"Kiss me," Mariel said, her voice cracking slightly at the end. Clem was not a gracious victor. She laughed in triumph and then kissed away Mariel's answering noise of frustration until Mariel forgot she'd had any reservations about this at all.

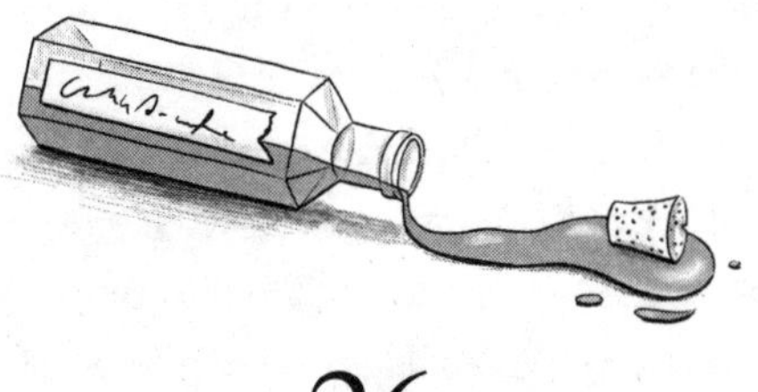

26

Clem woke up feeling like she'd had the best sleep of her life, and was somewhat confused to discover that she was cramped up against the wall, leaving the majority of the bed free for a curled-up, gently mussed Mariel. Her dark hair was loose—Clem had done that, pulled it free of its plait again so that she could properly run her hands through the length of it in a way that made Mariel go all kitteny and languid—and even though she seemed to be completely dead to the world, she had one hand on her hip, where her knife *would* have been if Clem hadn't insisted she remove it because it was digging into her pelvis.

Mariel disarmed and unconscious was still a strange and arresting thing to behold, but this time Clem could tighten an arm around her waist and pull her closer without a second thought.

Without a second thought, that was, until Mariel woke up with a start and immediately sprang up into a half-sitting position, hand clenching around her phantom weapon and coming up empty.

"Jesus," said Clem. "You nearly took my face off."

"What? Oh," Mariel said, relaxing very slightly. She had

the gentlest suggestion of a bruise on the lower slope of her neck, and Clem was assailed with the vivid memory of kissing her there until she made all manner of desperate, flattering noises while obviously trying not to. "What time is it?"

"Uh, I don't know. We're in a hole. It's hole o'clock."

Now upright, wary and with her hair sticking up on one side of her head, Mariel looked like a cat who'd half fallen in a pond and was convinced that Clem was trying to trick her into getting her feet wet again.

"The captains are coming," Mariel said, sliding out of bed and tucking her shirt into her trousers. "I'm supposed to be . . . We're meeting to discuss next steps. At daybreak. *Shit.* Where's my knife?"

Clem stretched, her back giving a few very satisfying cracks, and then sat up. "Slow down. Time isn't real here anyway. And you're catching up on sleep. Your knife is . . . hmm."

Clem had de-trousered and slept in just her shirt, and she saw Mariel look quickly away when she pushed the blanket off and got up to help look.

"They're just legs," Clem said. "No need to be offended. Actually, wait, scratch that—they're not *just* legs, they're very nice legs."

They *were* nice. Strong. Got her where she needed to be. Dependable legs.

Mariel allowed herself to look at Clem's knees.

"I know," she said, her expression all twisted up and mortified, and Clem laughed with surprise. "Clemence. Please. Knife. Help me."

Mariel had removed the knife, but Clem had been the

one to toss it aside; she followed the logical arc of travel and discovered it under the bed.

"Here. Don't stab me."

"Can you—my hair?"

Mariel turned around without waiting for an answer, and Clem rolled her eyes and started braiding it for her, favoring speed over tenderness and tugging quite hard to get it into the sort of military order that Mariel favored. Someone was knocking on one of the doors farther down the corridor, which only seemed to add to the urgency. Mariel had gone very still underneath her hands; when Clem finished, she still didn't move, although Clem noticed that she was breathing sort of weird.

"Turn around," she said, and Mariel did, her movements a little slow. Clem lifted Mariel's chin and kissed her lightly, and Mariel just closed her eyes, not a flicker of petulance on her face.

There was a loud, single knock on the door. They didn't even have half a breath to react before it was shoved—no, *kicked*—open. Josey was standing on the other side of it looking like she was having the best morning of her life.

"Morning, Captain," she said, not bothering to hide her smirk. "Healer."

"That wasn't a very fair amount of knocking," Clem said, as Mariel wrenched out of her grip.

"I knocked on the captain's door for at least a minute," Josey said, shrugging. "And then I grew concerned that our hostage may have taken a hostage in return, for purposes of negotiation."

"No you didn't," said Clem.

"Nah," said Josey. "I didn't. But it's plausible, isn't it? Captain, your comrades await you in the bar. Nice bruise on your neck, very subtle."

"I was in here checking on her wound," Clem offered, and Josey snorted. "What? I actually did!" She'd had a look last night, though it had been more of a cursory once-over. There had been a lot of distractions.

"Mmm. I bet you did."

Josey disappeared, and Mariel put her head in her hands and took a long, calming breath before straightening up and going after her.

"Your shirt isn't tucked in at the back," Clem called. "And I'm sorry, but that bruise really is—"

"Don't," Mariel said, holding up a hand. As she turned in to the corridor, Clem saw her hurriedly fixing her shirt with one hand and pulling her braid over one shoulder with the other.

The captains met in some sort of anteroom off the main chamber, and everybody else sat eating breakfast in various states of agony directly proportionate to how much fun they'd had the night before. Kit and Baxter were a bit hollow-eyed but absolutely holding hands under the table; Morgan could barely lift their head high enough to take in porridge; and Josey was so fresh she looked like she'd just been born into the world, excited to take on her very first day.

They couldn't hear what was happening next door, only that there was obviously some sort of enormous argument taking place. An hour later, Mariel came storming out, followed by a stream of Men who were talking in low voices. They distributed themselves out across the room or disappeared through doorways, and Mariel came to sit at the table and furiously eat a hunk of bread.

Unfortunately, it gave her hiccups, which she refused to acknowledge, rendering them even more ridiculous.

"They've told me to stay away," she said eventually, barely above a whisper, in response to Josey's questioning look. "They said well done for getting Big John back, good job, thanks for the intel, but it's time to let the *real* captains take over."

"They did not," Josey said, not bothering to lower her voice.

Mariel's hand clenched, the bread in it instantly pulverized back into dough.

"I am clearly not forgiven for what happened when we departed with Morgan. This is a punishment. It's classic Richard fucking Flores. They're sending us back to camp to take care of duties there." Mariel was almost shaking with rage. Clem thought about touching her arm, and then imagined life without the arm and thought better of it. "They told me it was important that I *reassure* people. Just like my mother wanted. She'll be thrilled."

It was spoken with immense vitriol; Josey's nose wrinkled, and Kit sucked in a sympathetic hiss of breath. Clem intuited, in all her genius, that Mariel's mother was just as much of a sore spot as her father.

"You told them what Colin said?" Morgan croaked bravely.

"Yes. I told them everything we know, I said that Deputy Commander Payne and my father are likely being held at Sherwood House, awaiting the Sheriff's return—but they won't even tell me what they're *planning*."

"Bit rough," Clem risked. "Seeing as he's your father."

"That's irrelevant," Mariel said, like the sound of a door slamming. "I'm a ranked captain. I have as much right to be let in on this plan as everybody else."

"So we're going back to camp?" said Baxter. "And the others are riding off to the rescue? And . . . none of us are getting tarred or pilloried for breaking Richard's nose?"

"Yes," Mariel said heavily, as if all of that were bad news.

Clem didn't know what to do with herself, so she just put some more bread into her mouth, which always seemed like a good idea.

Clem was sorry to leave Underwood. It had been nice to have a room to herself, even if she'd ended up sharing it—*especially* because she'd ended up sharing it. It had been reassuring to know nobody was about to attack them, and that there was always a supply of food and drink just down the hall. The luxuries of pillows and soup were not to be sniffed at.

They set off with supplies, changes of clothes, new horses that didn't hate them for all the running they'd been made to do over the past week. There was one for everyone except Clem; she dared hope, briefly, that Mariel might offer her a hand and pull her up onto her own dark gray mare, but when she very much didn't, Josey did instead.

"Don't take it personally," Josey said, as Mariel rode away out of earshot. "She's so angry she probably doesn't even know she's on a horse."

They traveled until the sky eased into a lavender dusk, and then dismounted in a clearing sheltered on one side by a sheer rock face and ribboned by a stream that opened up into a shallow pool just ten or twenty feet away.

It was a hot and sticky night, and they were sore from riding; Baxter was the first one to head for the water, already shedding his clothes as he walked, Josey not far behind.

"Be quiet," Mariel called after them in a loud whisper. Clem dismounted clumsily and offered a hand to Mariel, who ignored it and slid down with perfect poise to land lightly on the ground.

"I see," said Clem. "Spurned, m'lady, when I offered you a chivalrous hand."

"Don't talk to me," Mariel muttered. She was trying to open the saddlebag, but seemed to be having some trouble; Clem reached out to help, and Mariel shooed her away, and then yanked the strap so hard that it tore clean off.

She immediately lobbed it away and then turned back to the bag to wrench her waterskin out of it. The others were quietly disappearing away into the trees. It was probably the wisest thing to do.

"Mariel," Clem said, because nobody had ever mistaken her for wise. "Are you . . . ?"

"I'm fine."

"Really?" said Clem, crossing her arms and leaning against the horse, who didn't seem to mind. "Because I'm pretty pissed off. I've been doing some of my best work out here"—Mariel sniffed derisively—"some of my *best work*," Clem repeated, "healing left, right and center, somehow keeping everybody's wounds from festering against all odds, taking part in advanced and expertly executed espionage, and this is how they repay us."

Mariel took a drink from the skin, then wiped her mouth with her sleeve. "Us?"

"Yeah," Clem said. "Us."

Mariel replaced the water, and then removed her bow and quiver from her shoulder and dumped them on the ground with uncharacteristic carelessness. Clem watched as the brown-fletched arrows rolled, one of them half falling out of its pouch.

"It doesn't matter what I do," Mariel said suddenly. "It never matters. It's never enough."

Clem straightened up. "I think it matters quite a lot to your company."

"But it doesn't matter to the people who . . ."

The people who matter, Clem filled in. Which—ouch, on behalf of Mariel's company. But when your boss was *also* your dad, it really complicated things.

"You can't change how other people feel," she said. Mariel was half turned away from her, her breathing unsteady, looking at nothing in particular. "So you can't do any of this for them. You have to know that you might be the only person who ever truly sees everything you do, how hard you work, what you believe in—and just do it anyway."

"I didn't ask for a motivational speech," Mariel said dully.

"Well, you're getting one," Clem said, warming to it. "If you could just see yourself—"

Mariel kissed her. Clem rapidly recalibrated, her hands coming up to brush over Mariel's collarbones, but even as

Mariel pulled her closer by the back of the neck, it hurt her heart a little bit; she knew Mariel just wanted her to stop talking—for *everything* to stop for a second. She wasn't kissing Clem like this because Clem was just *so* irresistible, even if that would have been understandable. She was frustrated. She was angry.

Angry kissing was still better than no kissing. In fact, it had a certain appeal to it. Clem had to remind herself that it wasn't a good thing, and then keep reminding herself as Mariel crowded her back against the horse—who decided abruptly that it didn't want to be a surface to be kissed against and walked away.

This revealed that Morgan had come back to their bag for something and was currently standing looking mortified just two feet away.

"Oh," said Clem. "Hullo, Morgan. Feeling better?"

"No," Morgan said sullenly. "Because now I owe Josey *two* coins."

"Two?" said Clem.

"You and the captain," said Morgan. "Kit and Baxter. Ugh."

"Go," said Mariel, smoothing her hair back agitatedly. "Both of you."

Clem went. She followed the distant sounds of splashing until she came to the pond, where the others were already bathing. In the near-dark she could just see vague shapes; heads and shoulders, hands, the pale fabric of Kit's chest bindings. Clem stripped off her clothes and left them thrown over a tree branch before easing into the icy water. She let out a hiss from between her teeth as she went in up to her neck and then ducked under and shook her hair out like a dog, earning muted protests from Josey and Kit, who were within splashing range.

Now that she was in the water, the air above felt pleasantly warm instead of stuffy. The clouds had cleared, and Clem could see a generous sprinkling of stars glimmering through the gaps in the canopy above her.

Morgan stepped out of the trees and eyed them all suspiciously.

"You can't look while I get in," they said. "Okay? Close your eyes, all of you."

"They're closed," said Josey.

"But you're going to open them again," said Morgan, hesitating. "You can't open them again."

"How about this?" said Baxter. "We'll turn around *and* we'll keep our eyes closed."

There was the general sound of water in motion as they all turned away.

"Fine," said Morgan. "Good."

"Don't get that wound too wet," Clem warned, knowing she'd be ignored.

Once Morgan was submerged, they were all permitted to open their eyes again, and Clem filled her lungs with air so that she could float on her back and try to identify constellations that she could only half see.

"That's the Pernicious Rodent," she said to Morgan, pointing. "See?"

"No," Morgan said. "I can't see, and I think you're making this up."

"You can't see him? Those stars there are his little hands. He's rubbing them together, scheming."

"Liar."

"Fine, fine, you got me. What about the Amorous Whales? Can you see those? They're kissing. With tongues."

"No more kissing," Morgan said, sending a wave of water toward Clem and then snickering when she swallowed half of it and ended up choking. "I can't believe the captain let you *do that* to her."

"She did what with who now?" said Baxter, his head snapping up. Kit started laughing, tipping back and closing his eyes, almost drowning himself in the process.

"I wasn't going to say anything," said Josey. "But if you already know—pay up."

"I don't have any money on me," said Morgan. "In case you hadn't noticed, I am currently without pockets."

"Well, you can owe me," said Josey, grinning up at the stars. "I'm in no rush. I have the gift of prophecy *and* two coins coming. Business is booming."

They all hauled themselves out of the water and dressed in the trees, dripping and shivering slightly as the breeze chilled their damp skin. Morgan wanted a fire, but apparently this was out of the question right now, so instead they huddled together in a close circle as Josey took up the watch and Mariel took her turn to bathe.

They had parcels of cheese to eat, fresh apples, dried strips of gamey meat, and salty bread that had left its wrappings soaked through with oil. Morgan actually let Clem clean and dress their wound without complaining, and demonstrated to mimed applause that they were now capable of rotating the arm slightly in its socket.

"What will you do, back at camp?" Clem asked. "Just . . . sit and wait?"

"I don't know," said Baxter. "Wish I knew what the captain was thinking. To be honest, I'll be glad to stop for a bit. Rest. Eat at my parents' fire. Wish we could get there faster, but y'know . . . you can't make a horse go faster than a horse can go."

"Is that a proverb?"

"No. Maybe. It is now."

"Squirrel," Morgan said quietly, nodding toward a nearby tree. "Sixty-eight. You're still fifteen behind."

"I'm not worried. The wood is wide and full of squirrels," said Baxter. He looked at Clem. "Was that anything?"

"You might need to punch it up a little, to really make it sing."

They continued chattering softly, talking about nothing in particular. Mariel had taken her dismissal hard, but the others didn't seem to mind this sudden lightening of their load. Baxter started telling a story about his grandfather, and Clem leaned in eagerly to listen, still thrilled that she was able to hear Robin Hood lore straight from the mouths of those who actually knew him.

"This was after Robin and Marian split, but before she died," he said, between nibbles of cheese rind, "apparently everyone knew what was going on, Marian was always telling Robin to go for it, and he was trying . . . but apparently my grandad just was not getting the hint. Said he'd been in love with Robin from the get-go, but when Robin turned around and loved him back, he refused to see it."

"Runs in the family," Morgan muttered darkly, shooting a pointed look at Kit, who was leaning into Baxter's mountainous shoulder with easy familiarity.

"Anyway, there was some fight, some scrape they almost didn't get out of, and my grandad turns to Robin and says, 'I can't fight beside you anymore,' packs his things and goes to join some rebels pushing back farther south. And Robin was so angry he rode all through the night to find him, gets him at knifepoint and calls him a coward and a traitor, demands to know what it was that pushed him too far this time, and Will says, 'I was so distracted watching you flick your hair about and fire off arrows in that flirty little way of yours that I almost lost an eye,' and—"

"He did *not* say that," said Mariel, approaching from the trees. Her hair was wet and she was wearing something dark and sleeveless; even in the gloom Clem could see her tattoo, standing out against the pale skin of her biceps. Clem could see that bruise too, a smudge on her neck, and it made her feel warm and twitchy. Mariel came to sit down in their circle, only taking the spot next to Clem because it had been left conspicuously open. She looked a lot calmer than she had earlier, like she'd let some of that fire cool off in the pond.

"All right, go on then—what *did* he say?" said Baxter.

Mariel started combing her hair through with her hands, slow and deliberate, and Clem tried and failed not to stare openly at her fingers as they worked.

"He said . . ." Mariel hesitated, her face scrunching slightly with distaste. "He said he knew that Robin never lost, but he couldn't be so close, worrying that *this* might be the day he didn't beat the odds, because it was too distracting and because . . . because he loved him." Such earnest declarations of love were clearly difficult for Mariel, even if they were other people's. "And Robin said, 'You're right. I never lose,' and then . . ."

"Kissed him," Baxter said triumphantly. "Gave him a big wet one, right on the mouth."

"Vile," said Morgan, as the others laughed.

"Where are they now?" Clem asked. "That was the part nobody back home could ever agree on." Everybody looked at her.

"That's the sort of question one of the Sheriff's spies would ask," said Josey. "Although they wouldn't do such a shit job of it, so maybe that's a point in your favor."

"They're . . . retired," said Baxter carefully. "Sort of. I don't think Robin ever wanted to actually lead anybody. My dad always says that Robin and Will didn't think the Merry Men should *have* a leader."

"But they made Commander Hartley leader before they went?" Clem said, only realizing she'd messed up when everybody fell silent. Josey had appeared to grab some food, and she paused with a handful of cheese, waiting.

"No," said Mariel shortly. "He was raised to the position. Everybody wanted it to be him."

More silence. Clem wondered what terrible new thing was happening now. Baxter cleared his throat, and Mariel looked sharply over at him.

"What?"

He shrugged. "That's not . . . quite how I heard it."

"*What?*" Mariel repeated.

Nobody seemed to want to speak.

Josey finished her cheese and sighed, stretching her

arms out absent-mindedly like she was limbering up for a fight. Clem had never seen her look even the slightest bit nervous, but there was something off about her now.

"He took it," she said, breaking the silence with something that was potentially even worse. "There wasn't supposed to be a leader. Not how there was before anyway. But he wanted it, so he took it, and then he came up with all the ranks and rules and tried to rewrite the whole thing, which is why nobody tells that version of the story. But . . . Big John does."

"And . . . my parents," said Baxter. "Robin said no. So your father waited until he was gone. I'm sorry. I thought . . . you knew."

"That's not true," Mariel said, but there was hardly any weight behind it, like she'd already given in to the possibility that her father might be the worst. She had let her hands fall to her knees, and her fingertips were pressing hard into her legs, trying to ground herself in her own skin. Clem let her elbow brush against Mariel's very gently, and Mariel didn't even seem to notice.

"Sorry," Baxter said again, genuinely anguished. Kit looked at Josey, and then Josey moved to leave, patting Mariel on the shoulder on her way past. The others followed, going to fetch their things so that they could bed down for the night, none of them speaking.

Clem was the last to go, wishing as she did that she knew of anything at all to soothe a thoroughly broken heart.

27

Mariel took first watch because she always took first watch (and middle watch and last watch if she could, though someone usually made sure she couldn't). She paced small circles around their camp—stopped and stood completely still in the shadow of an alder, for long enough that all manner of nocturnal creatures felt safe to pick up their nighttime frolics again—then moved away so silently that they carried on rustling through the grass and calling out to each other, doing whatever it was animals did when they thought there was nobody around to watch.

The air had cooled, but Mariel hadn't put her cloak on. She didn't want to look at it right now: not the cloak, not the ornate bronze leaf pin that told most of the world she outranked them. She pressed her fingers into the tattoo on her arm and shivered.

She felt itchy. Restless. There was no sense in making these circles, but she did anyway, because if she stopped she thought she might explode. Her father was locked away in some nobleman's house and she was out in the wood—*their* wood, *his* wood—wondering if he'd been wrong about almost everything. It felt cowardly. Shameful. Like a betrayal, both of him and of the person she'd been just a week ago.

What was it, exactly, that he'd told her? Had he lied? Had she filled in the gaps herself, let herself believe that her father was the Commander everybody wanted? She couldn't remember, and she was desperate to hear it from his own mouth. She wished she'd had the presence of mind to pay attention, back when Robin left. She'd been a child, but that was no excuse.

Did it matter, really, how he'd come to be their leader, if her father was doing everything for the good of the people? *Was he* doing everything for the good of the people?

Eventually, Josey came to tap her on the shoulder and tell her to lie down before she wore her feet down to stumps from pacing, and Mariel did try for maybe two or three minutes to rest on the soft ground and close her eyes and think of absolutely nothing at all.

Then she got up and went to look for Clem.

Somebody—it could have been Kit or Baxter, they were both soft touches—had given Clem an extra cloak, so that she was curled up under one and had the other for a pillow. Familiar as she was with the ins and outs of injury and disease, Clem was clearly an indoors person, used to a roof and a mattress and bed linen. It must have been a hard week for her, but she had barely complained.

There was a leaf in her hair. Mariel ached to ease it out, but instead she just sat down on the ground a safe distance away, knowing that Clem was now awake without having to ask.

"You're just having a rough day," Clem said quietly, as if they'd been mid-conversation. "And night. And week. And maybe . . . life."

"My life is good," Mariel said, but it sounded so unconvincing even to her own ears that she wouldn't have blamed Clem for laughing. She didn't.

"Well, I'm cold, so come here and make my life a bit better, would you?"

There she went again, just asking for what she wanted, like it was the easiest thing in the world. Mariel was awed and appalled by it. She was also appalled that it worked; she shuffled closer and lay down, their shoulders touching. It was pathetic how nice it felt, to have somebody want to touch you like that, casually and without reservations. It was important that she didn't get used to it.

Clem leaned over and kissed her, a little blurry around the edges, and then stayed curled up and breathing gently in Mariel's personal space.

"I don't want to talk," Mariel said. "About anything."

"Right you are," said Clem. "Oh, I should warn you—everybody knows about this. Us. Morgan thinks it's *icky*."

"Morgan is correct," Mariel said, meaning it.

"All right," said Clem. "Want to do something disgusting with me?"

She reached for Mariel's face and then gently dragged her thumbs down her temples, mapping the shape, until she was cupping her chin with both hands. Mariel closed her eyes and let it wipe her mind entirely clean, focusing on the feeling of fingertips stroking along her jawline, tracing a path to the back of her neck. There was no danger of her getting used to this. This would *never* feel normal.

"I like your face," Clem said. Mariel could feel her cheeks burning. She couldn't have opened her eyes if she were at knifepoint. "It's a good face. Very frowny, but apparently I'm into that."

"I told you I didn't want to talk," Mariel said. "It's excruciating."

"Oh sorry, are my effusive compliments making you uncomfortable?"

"Yes," said Mariel. "Obviously. I don't understand why you can't just let it . . . be what it is."

A moment of madness. A distraction. A bit of fun for Clem, a bit of relief for Mariel.

"I should just kiss you and shut up, you mean."

". . . Yes."

"I'm just being honest," Clem said. "I'll lie, if that makes you feel better. Your face is rubbish and I am entirely unaffected by it. Same applies to your arms. Awful. Who'd want to be all lithe and muscular? Don't even get me started on your collarbones."

"Why would you have any particular feelings about my *collarbones*?"

"Purely a professional, medical interest," said Clem, as she dipped her head to kiss Mariel there, stalling Mariel's breathing on an inhale. "Extremely difficult to set these when they're broken. Very painful."

"Then maybe," Mariel said, her voice coming out all threadbare and husky, "you should stop *biting* them."

"No thank you," said Clem, but she did stop so that she could kiss Mariel properly on the mouth, deep and slow. No part of Clem was delicate really, not her gold-flecked arms or her strong, tree-trunk legs or her hair, which almost seemed to have a mind of its own, but her mouth was perilously soft, even when she was using it to tug Mariel's lip into her mouth so hard it almost felt like another bite. Mariel was on fire. She felt angry. She felt guilty. She felt like she wanted Clem to swallow her whole.

"My mother was always the liar," she said suddenly, and Clem pulled away to look at her, going very still. "Not my father. I just don't understand. If this is all true, then maybe I don't know any of the things I thought I did. I don't understand what I'm supposed to . . . what I'm . . ."

"I think you just have to do what you want," Clem said carefully. "And trust yourself. Your instincts."

"I don't know," Mariel said. "I don't know how to have purpose if it isn't given to you."

"Ah," said Clem. "Well. That's easy. You just become obsessed with something to the point of madness, forget to eat or sleep, and one day you look up and realize you've made something of yourself."

"Sounds very healthy."

"Oh, *very*. No doubt it's extending my lifespan years and years," said Clem.

"You made something of yourself?" Mariel asked, still reaching for distraction.

"I did," said Clem. "I mean, I do. I am. Whichever. My experiments in chemistry have proved surprisingly popular. Word spread. I actually thought, stupidly, when you first came to get Rosie . . . I thought you'd heard I was a genius, and needed my help."

"Hmm."

"All right, well, you don't come off particularly well in that story so let's not cast the first stone for the crime of overconfidence, shall we? We've had people come from all over to see if there's a better way to heal than with pus and God and leeches. I saved an actual *baby*, Mariel. A baby who might have died of fever. I've been experimenting with ways to clear the airways, for the people with hay fever and breathlessness. This woman down south heard about me and sent a messenger to ask for me specifically to help her son—I set a knee that was in about a thousand pieces, cleaned out that wound for weeks and weeks, got the guy back up on his feet, and got paid real coin to do it. I cauterized and splinted this old man's leg instead of amputating it, and kept treating him, and now he can walk with a stick. I'm *doing* things. I don't need anybody else to tell me it's right. I just know."

Mariel's throat felt like it was closing up. In a world without Regan and Jack, without expectations, maybe she could have been somebody who knew which way was north without having to be told. Maybe she'd have been able to spend her days how she liked, without looking over her shoulder to see who was watching her, and if they approved. But that wasn't her world, and it never had been.

It had been a mistake to get Clem talking. It almost always was. Clem looked surprised to be kissed, but she soon got over it, and Mariel tried to pull her closer, to urge her on, to force her own mind to go blank again—but it wasn't working.

Something about Clem's hot breath on her neck was not enough and too much all at once. It made Mariel feel weirdly naked, even though she was fully clothed. She couldn't remember ever wanting something—some*one*—like this, in a way that simultaneously demanded her presence and sent her brain skidding off somewhere unreachable. It wasn't practical.

In fact, it was irresponsible for her to do this—to chase this feeling, when there was so much at stake. Clem would be gone soon, back to Oak Vale. And Mariel was losing sight of what really mattered.

She dug her fingernails into her palms until she couldn't take it any longer.

"You're free to go," she gasped out.

"What?" Clem said, slightly muffled. She lifted her head and frowned.

"You're free to leave," Mariel said, able to enunciate far better now that Clem had stopped doing terrible and wonderful things to her neck. "You can go. Home."

"Right. Well—thanks. Right now?"

"No," said Mariel. "I mean, yes, if you want."

Clem's nose wrinkled. "I can't help but think this is damning feedback on my kissing abilities."

Mariel sat up, so that Clem was forced to move back.

"It's not personal."

"Mmm," Clem said. She was still flushed and glowing from the kissing, but now there was a frown on her face, and Mariel felt even more guilty for putting it there. "Feels a bit personal."

"You are no longer my captive," Mariel said, trying to keep her voice steady. "And after everything that's happened—it won't matter that I've let you go. You are not a priority."

"Not a priority," Clem repeated slowly. "Okay."

They weren't touching anymore. Mariel missed it already.

She was about to make muttered excuses and get up

when Josey appeared, with a stranger in tow and an urgent expression on her face. Mariel scrambled to her feet immediately.

"Who is this?"

The newcomer looked exhausted, and when he wobbled a little, Josey surreptitiously used her shoulder to nudge him upright.

"My brother," he said, breathless with effort, "was in that prison you broke into at Stoke Hanham. Half-dead, or maybe three-quarters, by the looks of him. We used to be in with . . . your lot"—he nodded toward Josey's cloak—"but we had some . . . ideological disagreements, a while back, and that turned into fisticuffs, and we decided to do our own thing. Never really trusted anyone claiming to be Merry after that, but . . . I got my brother home, and by the time he was well enough to talk, he told me I had to use the old ways to come and find you. Don't owe green cloaks any favors, but he—we—reckons we owe *you* a life debt, and if you're jailbreaking the lowly masses, you must be a better sort than some."

"What is it?" Mariel said, fighting her instinct to grab the man by the shoulders and shake him to get the story out faster.

"He was arrested at Clipstone. It was the last thing he saw before some guard beat the shit out of him, threw him on a wagon out of there and sent him off to die—they did it because he saw who they were unloading, the bastards. Your father's being held there. At Clipstone, at the King's Houses."

Just like that, Mariel was herself again.

28

Clem judged herself to be a pretty good judge of character. Of course, if her judgment was in fact poor, then the whole judging system was rotten. Rosie called her a "nightmare of an optimist." That was probably also true.

Mariel had taken a battering over the past week, and as a result, Clem thought she'd seen those walls of hers starting to crumble. It wasn't easy to admit that you'd been wrong, or to learn to lean on people, or to accept that your father might be a bit of a power-crazed despot with selfish intentions. It was a journey! But Clem was sure that Mariel had been taking the first steps.

From the moment the messenger opened his mouth, it was as if the last week hadn't happened.

Everybody was shaken awake and told to prepare to leave without any further information. Mariel wouldn't explain herself. She hadn't looked at Clem once. The only person she'd speak to was Josey, who looked graver than Clem had ever seen her. The atmosphere was pure poison, and it was doing something uncomfortable to Clem's insides.

When they were all packed back up and ready to go, Mariel slid her last knife up her sleeve and cleared her throat.

"We're going to the King's Houses. That's where my father is being held."

Clem had heard of the King's Houses. Confusingly, kings actually only visited; it was a massive country palace that was essentially a glorified hunting lodge, often left vacant, called into service when they wanted to do something stately and impressive.

"They execute people at the King's Houses," Morgan said, their brow furrowed.

Mariel didn't even flinch. "These people aren't as clever as they think they are. Getting Big John out was easy—"

"But we can't do the same thing again. They'll be looking out for us. And the King's Houses—that's not just an estate, it's a *castle.* I was there when the king visited, and—"

"You've been inside?" said Mariel, finally acknowledging that Morgan existed.

"Yes, but Mariel . . . It's not the *same.*"

"Morgan, you'll tell me everything you know, and we'll find a way in."

"Maybe we should slow down," Kit attempted, but Mariel shook her head.

"No time. If I know Captain Flores, the others will be mustering at Sherwood House for an all-out assault to retrieve my father. I don't know if we jumped to the wrong conclusions, or maybe they do have Deputy Commander Payne at Sherwood . . . but no matter. By the time they've realized the Commander isn't there and pulled together a new plan, it might be too late. It might . . . it could *already* be too late. We have to be the ones to do this, and we have to do it now."

In the quiet that followed, the only brave souls who dared speak were the crickets, accompanied by the shrill squeaks of an enthusiastic bat or shrew.

"Mariel," Clem said, because she was an optimist and a fool, and because she was the only person who didn't actually answer to Captain Hartley-Hood. "This is really dangerous. There are only six of us. We're good value for six, but still. Everyone's tired. You and Morgan are still injured. I think you're being rash, and I know that if you took a step back from this, you'd agree."

Mariel levelled a look at Clem that was so cold it felt like she was trying to strip the flesh from Clem's bones. "You are not a part of this company. Whether you come with us or go home is your business."

"Whoa," said Baxter, raising a large hand like it was a white flag. "Hold on. Mariel. Captain . . ."

Mariel relented ever so slightly. "Look. I need you to trust me. *This* is our chance to do something great, to take action like Robin would have. Whatever my father may have done . . . it doesn't matter now, with this much at stake. Nobody in this wood will ever doubt us again when we bring him home. And . . . it's his life on the line. I have to do this."

Josey nodded. The others followed. Nobody argued with her after that.

Clem wasn't entirely surprised. At the end of the day, they were a company. A band of outlaws. If they couldn't trust each other, what did that leave? Clem was new to all of this, and maybe that was why she couldn't possibly comprehend how this plan would work, but still—a rotten heaviness had settled in the pit of her stomach from the moment Mariel had told her that she was free to go, and as she mounted up behind Josey to ride, it only got heavier.

"Can we do this?" she said quietly in Josey's ear.

She felt Josey shrug.

This did not particularly lift Clem's spirits. "Getting Big John *was* easy."

"Yeah," Josey said under her breath. "I'm starting to think it was a little *too* easy."

The rock in Clem's stomach became a boulder. She had that feeling that always floored her after a shock and left her shaking, and on occasion, vomiting—that something bad was coming, and there was nothing she could do to stop it. Except that this time, it didn't feel absurd and illogical, a bodily response that made no sense.

How on earth was she supposed to tell the difference?

They rode on, not speaking. No games, laughter, not even humming or snatches of song. Mariel was soon so far ahead of them that all Clem could see was the movement of her horse's hoofs, flashing in the distant dark.

When they stopped for supplies outside a small village, Mariel disappeared without telling anyone where she was going, and Clem was finally able to voice something that had occurred to her while clinging to Josey's back.

"If I die . . . will somebody go and tell Old Rosie? I reckon she's probably been looking for me."

"Shit," said Morgan. "Don't say stuff like that. Why would you die? You're not going to die. You're always the one who looks on the bright side. You can't start talking about dying now."

"Well, I think dying is probably all right," said Clem.

"Crap while it's happening, sure, but fine after. Rubbish for the people left behind. I'm just trying to be practical."

"Well, don't," said Morgan. They said it with such force that Clem wanted to grab them by the shoulders and give them a little affectionate squeeze, like Baxter was always doing. She knew better, and kept her hands to herself. "If I die," they said, with a resolute lift of their chin, "just drop me at Lord Hanham's gate to rot."

"If you die we're throwing you a lovely funeral," said Baxter. "Flowers. Offerings. And it'll be extremely embarrassing. We'll all say really nice stuff about you, how friendly and kind you were, how much we loved you. And there won't be a thing you can do about it. So it's probably best if you don't. Stay alive. Avoid the humiliation."

"If you dare say something nice about me at my funeral," said Morgan, "I'll kill you."

"That's the spirit," said Josey, giving Morgan a friendly elbow to the ribs that actually jolted them sideways a few inches.

"We listen to Mariel," said Kit. "We follow her lead. But if it starts going wrong—we get out."

"Kit," Josey said, in a warning tone.

"Look, I'm not running away and putting anybody at risk. You know I'm no coward. But if the best chance of getting us all out of there is to run? I'm gone."

"Do you think she knows what she's doing?" Morgan said. They all looked in roughly the direction Mariel had gone; they'd last seen her deathly pale, fists clenched, silently working through the problem in her head, refusing to let anybody in.

"Usually, yes," said Kit. "On the whole. But things feel off to me. So if you need to? Run."

"And if anybody can't run," Baxter said seriously, "I'll carry you."

Morgan gave a hollow little huff of laughter.

"I mean it," said Baxter. "I can probably manage three, at a push. But I'd rather not push. So take care of yourselves, but don't be afraid to ask me, because I'll just put you on my back and we can make a dash for it, tortoise-style."

"Tortoise-style?" Kit said faintly. "As in . . . *slowly*?"

"No, like I'm the meat bit of the tortoise and whoever is on my back is the shell," said Baxter. "Maybe tortoise wasn't the best analogy. It's like . . ."

Kit leaned up and kissed him, a fist in Baxter's jerkin and desperation in the lines of his face, like he just couldn't help it. Morgan groaned and turned away, and Josey just raised her eyebrows at Clem and smirked half-heartedly.

"And if anybody's bleeding," Clem said amiably, "wave your Blood Hand in the air and I'll come and try to put the plug back in."

"Ugh," said Morgan.

"Ugh," Clem agreed.

Mariel's hands were shaking. It was all Clem could think about. She'd never seen Mariel's hands shake before.

They had dressed in plain clothes, left their horses at the edge of the wood and then approached from the village, brazen as anything, with baskets of linen and crates of apples. Each instruction from Mariel had been relayed only once before it was carried out. At one point Clem had noticed Mariel looking at her confusedly, as if she were about to ask what Clem was still doing there—but then it had been on to the next thing, and Clem knew that she must have ultimately been assessed as an asset rather than a liability. She'd tucked a few things into her pockets, anything that could fit without making an obvious bulge, hoping that she wouldn't need them.

The fact that the King's Houses were often left empty, until a noble (or royal) household descended to fill their grand halls, was to their advantage. When she'd finally bothered to let everyone in on her plan, Mariel had been certain that the serving staff would be a mixture of those who'd traveled with the household taking up residence and some supplementary locals. They were to hide among the locals, rely on the fact that there would be lots of unfamiliar faces. They would follow the real servants as far as they could. After that, they'd be splitting up to search the castle, with only their wits and their acting skills to get them to Jack Hartley's door.

That was it—the entire plan, as far as Clem could make out.

Morgan had told Mariel, in a small and toneless voice, that high-profile prisoners would likely be kept in a bedroom rather than a cell, as a "guest" of the house. The newer wing was used for actual guests, so the older wing was their best bet.

From the way they said it, it didn't seem like they were very convinced by the odds.

"Keep your heads down," Mariel said, as they crossed the ditch by the smaller bridge, a cart ahead of them and a group of men carrying a boar carcass behind them. "Don't let them see your blades until you have to. Once we have my father . . . that's when we fight. We're fast, we're smart. Robin did more, with even fewer Men. We can do this."

The knife in Clem's pocket was purely for cauterizing wounds and cutting away foreign objects. She had never wielded it to hurt someone before, and she didn't plan on doing so now.

They made it past the guards at the gate, who did stop for a cursory look through their baskets, but sent them on without comment. It immediately became clear why this was: all the servants were milling about in the courtyard and outbuildings, which seemed entirely separate from the rest of the castle. Mariel glanced sharply at Morgan, who shrugged, looking stricken.

"Guests don't come to this part," they whispered, strained. "I didn't know."

Clem felt light-headed as she watched Mariel's eyes dart around, looking for entrances and exits. She realized, as she did so, what was bothering her so much: she'd never had a reason to doubt Mariel's certainty before. Her absolute and unshakeable confidence in herself had felt real. Now it was a performance. She was pretending that she was still that person—the stubborn, arrogant captain Clem had met back in Oak Vale—but something had shifted, and now the mask didn't quite fit.

"We're looking for a gate without many guards," Mariel said, out of the side of her mouth. "*Anywhere* we won't have witnesses. If anybody asks—you're new, and you're lost."

Baxter, Morgan, and Kit, who were carrying apples, shouldered the crates and went off toward what seemed to be the kitchens. Mariel, Josey, and Clem followed puffs of hot steam and laundresses hefting their own baskets, but swerved at the last moment, skirting the edge of the courtyard until it narrowed and bent around a corner.

The gate there only had two guards, who relaxed slightly when they saw three young ladies approaching.

"Excuse me," Josey said, eyelashes armed. "We're new, and we need directions—would you be so kind as to . . . ?"

Clem was just glad that Mariel and Josey knocked them out instead of killing them. The look in Mariel's eyes hadn't inspired much hope for mercy. Clem had to help them drag the guards' inert bodies through the door so that when it shut behind them, it wasn't so obvious that something was amiss, and she felt nausea rise in her throat as they left the two men crumpled in a heap like discarded boots.

"Just keep going," Mariel said. She shoved a basket into Clem's hands and picked up her own again. "Don't look back."

Clem wasn't sure who exactly she was talking to, but they pressed on. The next courtyard was far less busy. They stood out horribly, incongruous in the middle of all that empty space, but she supposed the belief that guards were posted at every door and that anybody who'd made it through must have been thoroughly vetted was saving them. On the outside, you were a potential threat; once you were in, nobody asked questions.

The real trouble came at the next door. It was a gatehouse, perhaps dividing the older and newer parts of the castle from each other; when the two men standing there saw them approaching, they broke off their conversation and stared.

"Good morning," Mariel said. Clem wanted to wince at the telltale shake in her voice. "We were just—"

"Wait," said the guard on the left. He was pale and clean-shaven under his helm, and he looked a little nervous. He took a step toward Mariel. "Wait. Aren't you . . . ?"

Mariel hit him hard in the side of the head with the handle of her knife, and he dropped like a rock, unconscious. Josey already had her hands on the other guard when he said, "Josey, *stop*."

Josey stopped. The still-conscious and upright guard, who was bearded and brown-skinned, removed his own helm, revealing an expression of abject horror.

"Wait," Josey said, her own voice faltering. "*Harry?*"

"Captain Hartley-Hood," the man—Harry—said, in barely more than a whisper. "What are you *doing* here?"

"Captain Hassan? We're . . . What are *you* doing here?"

"Retrieving Commander Hartley! *Fuck*, Mariel. That man you just knocked out was a sympathizer. I've been working on him for months—we *needed* him. This is not good."

"I don't—I don't understand."

Harry glanced over their heads, panic in his eyes. "We were supposed to be the ones to escort the Commander from this wing to the great hall. The Sheriff is coming right now to speak to him, and we . . . There's a back entrance, a ghost door, there was a bridge there once, but now it's just an enormous ditch with only one way out. I have a rope. We were supposed to divert him that way, be gone before they realized he hadn't made it to the hall. I sent word as soon as I knew he was here, but it's been hard to make contact. Shit." He dropped to his knees and gave his fallen comrade a hopeful, frantic shake, before looking up at Mariel. "Captain . . . I can't do it by myself. They don't know me. He's been here for years—he was going to be my seal of approval, they wouldn't even ask questions. *We needed him*."

Clem watched this hit Mariel like a backhand to the face. Not good. Very not good. She went to kneel too, hands already reaching for what she'd stuffed in her pockets, but Mariel caught her by the elbow and yanked her up.

"Stop. Both of you stop, we're making a scene." The man on the ground groaned a little and turned over, his face very white. He didn't look like he'd be ready for duty anytime soon. Captain Hassan glanced around and scrambled to his feet. "How—how long has this been going on?" Mariel stammered. "Sympathizers? *Undercover*, at noble houses? My father hates sneaking around, he's always made that very clear. He didn't tell me, I—I had no idea."

"He only told a select, trusted few," Harry said, before seeming to realize his mistake. "Sorry. But it's true. The way things have been going, too many near misses, he wanted to make sure he had a way out if he ended up on the wrong side of this gate. So that was the plan. What the hell is the plan now?"

"I can fix this," Mariel said. Her hands were shaking even more than they had been before, and even though she'd stowed her knives she kept reaching for her hip reflexively with the kind of motion that anybody well-versed in combat would recognize from twenty feet away. Clem tried to calm her telepathically with sheer force of will. Weirdly, it didn't work.

Somebody walked across the courtyard behind them, and Josey had the good sense to push the inert body of the sympathetic guard into the shadows beneath the gatehouse.

"I can fix it," Mariel repeated, "I can. Tell me exactly where my father is, and where I can find the ghost door. We'll do it. We'll just do it anyway."

Harry did not look pleased. In fact he looked about as thrilled by this plan as Clem felt, which was not at all. But he nodded anyway because they had no choice, and opened the gate behind him, and they marched across the final courtyard and into the house as if they were headed to the gallows and didn't see any point drawing it out for another minute. Which, Clem thought slightly hysterically, they probably were.

They really did get a lot farther than she expected. Having somebody guard-shaped with them helped, even if he wouldn't stand up to closer inspection. They made it down three long corridors, across a short hall, Clem's heart pounding in her ears. She didn't dare look up. She focused on Mariel's feet in front of her, the only proof that any of this was really happening.

When the fighting started, it was so abrupt that it took Clem a moment to realize that they were under attack. One moment she was turning a corner, and the next she was throwing herself back against the wall, narrowly avoiding the tip of a sword as the others leaped into action and two guards went down hard and bleeding.

"That's it," Harry said. "We've got maybe . . . minutes."

"Then let's go," said Mariel.

They made it up the stairs to the old guest wing. Clem

had accepted that she had to look where she was going, but could barely take in her surroundings; it was all just flashes of stone wall, iron sconce, elaborate tapestry, oak door. The next guards they encountered were standing outside the room at the very end of the hallway, and she didn't have to look closely to know that Mariel, Harry, and Josey hadn't risked leaving them alive.

"If someone comes, yell," Josey told Clem, and then the three of them disappeared inside.

Clem didn't think she'd need the instruction. She sort of wanted to scream just standing there, avoiding looking at the guards, listening to the voices inside the room that surely meant they had found Jack Hartley.

Clem counted her breaths. It didn't help. She pinched the skin between her thumb and forefinger on her left hand. All it did was hurt. When somebody rounded the corner, despite the fact that her nerves were pulled bowstring-taut, she completely forgot she was supposed to call out to Josey.

"Clemence?" said the young man. He was tall and blond, muscular but somehow still soft around the edges. He looked completely nonplussed. "But—*what?* What on earth are you doing here?"

"Hello, Fred," Clem said faintly. "How's that knee?"

When Mariel stepped out into the hall, her sword raised, Clem knew from the look of stupefied fury on her face that she'd heard every word.

29

Fred?

Fred?

How's that knee?

Mariel had quite a lot on her plate. She had just untied her father from a chair. They were in the middle of a heavily guarded castle with a trail of bodies behind them and no plan of escape except to run like hell. Her nemesis was standing in front of her, caught off guard, with the sort of slow reaction times that Mariel could usually only dream of.

But all that was clanging around in her head was: *Hello, Fred. How's that knee?*

Clem at least had the grace to look mortified, but it wasn't anything approaching enough.

She was the healer who'd been crossing the line.

She was a liar. A turncoat. A coward.

She hadn't just been treating one of the Sheriff's men; she'd been treating the Sheriff's *only son*. Patching him up and sending him back out to make the world worse, one bastard thing at a time.

Mariel was so angry she could hardly see.

"Oh, Christ . . . *Guards!*" Frederic shouted, just as Mariel flew at him, sword first, only realizing when somebody else struck her that there had been a guard behind him.

Two guards. They were getting in the way, keeping Frederic covered. She was struck again, and she went down hard; when she grabbed for her sword, her hand slipped. She felt it cut, white-hot, into her palm. It didn't matter. She needed to get to Frederic. Where was all his chivalry and valor now? There were more Merry Men than there were guards. Morgan and Josey behind her, her father at her shoulder. It would be over soon, and then she'd have him.

"*Mariel!*" Jack shouted. "There's no time. Go."

Mariel didn't understand until she heard the distant sound of footsteps, of plate metal rattling. Reinforcements were on their way.

Her father was telling her to run. Not to stand and fight, to prove themselves a force to be reckoned with; to flee with their tails between their legs. First he'd put spies in the grand houses, and now this?

Mariel had clung so hard to the rules he'd given her, believing that if she followed them to the letter, he'd be proud. Now they were disintegrating into nothing, completely meaningless. There were no simple steps to follow to become worthy. Her father's word was law, and if he changed his mind—or if he felt differently, when his own neck was on the line—that was his prerogative. Mariel was the stupid one, forever believing in anything different.

They ran. The Merry Men, sprinting for the exits. Perhaps it should have been a clear enough sign of danger to make Mariel realize how much trouble they were really in. Instead, she felt like they were going in the wrong direction.

It only struck her when they had thundered down the stairs to the ground floor that Clem was still with them, keeping pace with Morgan, her face red and her hair flying.

Mariel wanted to tell her father that they should leave the healer behind. She wanted to tell Josey to stop glancing back to check on her. Let her stay here, with her true friends, and deal with whatever punishment Frederic de Rainault deemed fit for consorting with the Merry Men.

Perhaps she'd say she'd been a captive all along and tell them everything she knew. It seemed laughable, but what did Mariel know? Clearly, she'd been wrong about practically everything.

This is what happens when you let people in.

A company of four guards came clattering around the corner ahead of them, and Mariel's father raised the sword he'd taken from one of the fallen and showed them all exactly why he'd been made their Commander.

Except, of course—that wasn't how it had happened.

He fought like a demon. Teeth bared, never faltering. Mariel supposed that being tied to a chair for the best part of a week was very good motivation to take revenge. With Captain Hassan at his side, it was over in moments. Moments were all they had—behind them, she could hear more soldiers catching up.

Harry took an abrupt left and then a right—they were now catapulting through smaller service corridors, accompanied by the surprised shouts of serving men and women, who had to keep leaping out of their way. Blessedly, nobody tried to stop them.

"*Mariel!*" somebody—Baxter—shouted, and suddenly the two parties were reunited, Baxter slamming so hard into Clem that she was almost pulverized against the wall. She watched Baxter waste precious seconds pulling Clem upright, and felt her heart harden.

Leaving her behind was no good. She wanted to deal with this herself.

Baxter heaved an enormous decorative cabinet away from the wall, shouting at Mariel and the others to keep going; Mariel looked back over her shoulder and watched as he and the healer knocked it sideways, blocking the way behind them just in time. Mariel had to duck as she ran, to avoid the smattering of arrows that came after, ricocheting off walls and furniture, but then the hallway twisted and they were granted a brief reprieve.

A very brief reprieve.

It felt inevitable that someone would fall. Captain Hassan was leading them—it was just bad luck when a guard came unexpectedly out of a side room, took his chance, and stabbed Harry cleanly through the gut. The guard was dead before he could retrieve his sword, but the damage was done.

Jack stooped over Hassan, gentler than Mariel had ever seen him be as he checked the captain over, before straightening up and shaking his head at Mariel and the others.

It was like a gong had been struck somewhere, reverberating through her. He was dying. It was all her fault.

Everyone else was accounted for. They had to keep moving.

The door was there, just as Harry had said, not twenty feet from where he lay bleeding. It was only when Baxter and Jack had forced it open and revealed the enormous drop beyond that Mariel remembered the rope.

She doubled back without a word, sprinting around the corner and back down the hall. When she reached Harry, Clem was there.

Mariel had miscounted her Men. Except that of course . . . Clem had never really been one of hers after all.

In the near-distance, the soldiers were trying to break through the makeshift barrier. Mariel could hear the rhythmic *slam-slam-slam* of some kind of battering ram, the wood splintering, the cries to heave.

Every time they struck, Clem's entire body jumped, and her hands faltered on Captain Hassan's wound.

"*Move*," Mariel snarled. She pushed Clem away, lifted Harry's cloak, found the rope where it had been neatly coiled and tucked away, and relieved him of it. Clem had started removing his armor for him. He was still breathing, his chest rapidly rising and falling, his gambeson soaked through with blood. "Leave that. Go."

Clem didn't say anything. She just went back to her work, her hands moving automatically, even though they were shaking. She was putting pressure on the wound. She was trying to stop the bleeding.

Idiot. Lost cause. Liar.

"Move or die, Causey," Mariel shouted. "It's over."

Just out of sight, there was an almighty bang, the

splintering sound of a small explosion—and Mariel saw the moment that Clem's eyes went blank, her hands frozen, her breathing stopping completely before it was torn out of her in an enormous, shuddering gasp.

She didn't even seem to know where she was anymore, and they had all run out of time.

Baxter came barreling back around the corner to fetch them and stopped short when he saw Clem hunched over the body on the floor.

"Go," he said to Mariel. "The rope! Go. I'll get her out, I'll hold them off." When Mariel didn't move, he gave her a shove. "I'm right behind you."

Mariel ran. Back at the doorway, she tossed the coil of rope to Josey and her father, and Josey immediately set to work tying it around a wooden beam, wrapping it again and again, as fast as she could but still painfully slow. When it was secured, Jack went over first in case of waiting assailants, and then they sent Josey, and Morgan. Kit lingered, watching the wall where the corridor turned. They could hear shouts in the distance, the sounds of sword on sword.

Mariel gave Kit a rough shove in the direction of the doorway, and he went. Mariel couldn't bear that he looked so afraid.

It was Clem who came around the corner, not Baxter, and Mariel hated her for it. She was white as a sheet and stumbling, covered in blood that could have been anyone's, and when she reached the rope, Mariel had to put it in her hands. She didn't know if Clem could climb. Especially not like this. If she slipped, with Kit and Morgan still on the rope below her, she could doom them all.

"If you fall, you'll kill Morgan." Mariel had absolutely no hope that she'd attempt to preserve her *own* life, but if she knew the others were at stake, she'd cling to that rope until her hands were raw.

Still no Baxter. But he'd come, and they'd need to move fast, so she had to go.

Mariel could see her father and Josey below, boots on the ground, the others descending rapidly. On the other side of the ditch, hope: Harry's message must have finally made it, just in time. The first of the Merry Men waiting to receive her father had broken cover. She put her knife between her teeth and went backward over the threshold.

She was slipping down the rope, staining it with more blood as it burned her palms, still a good way from the ground when she heard shouts from above. Baxter. It was Baxter. It sounded like a cry of distress.

Against all reason, she immediately started trying to climb back up, the muscles in her arms screaming; below her, the weight had shifted, the rope jumping against the wall.

She was climbing too slowly. There was hot panic in her throat, pain screaming in her lungs. The hand that was cut kept failing her, no matter how hard she tried to ignore it.

There was a sound like something very big hitting something very hard from the doorway above, and Mariel let out a wordless shout of frustration, blinking the sweat from her eyes as she grabbed again and again at the rope and felt it rip through her palms, biting into her wound, white fire all the way up to her wrists.

Baxter appeared in the doorway above, bloodied and enormous and alive, and Mariel's spirits soared—but with a sickening lurch, she followed his horrified gaze to the window that was level with her own head.

An archer had realized where their escape route led and had come to put a stop to it. She found herself staring at the sharp point of an arrow as the bowman took careful, almost leisurely aim directly at her.

There was nowhere to go. No time to get out of his way. He drew back, ready to loose.

Mariel looked up at Baxter, and their gazes caught for a fraction of a second, both of them steady and resigned. It meant that she was watching when his expression changed, eyes wide with shock, as the point of a sword drove through his chest.

And then his arm came down in an arc, his knife flashing sunrise-pink as he severed the rope.

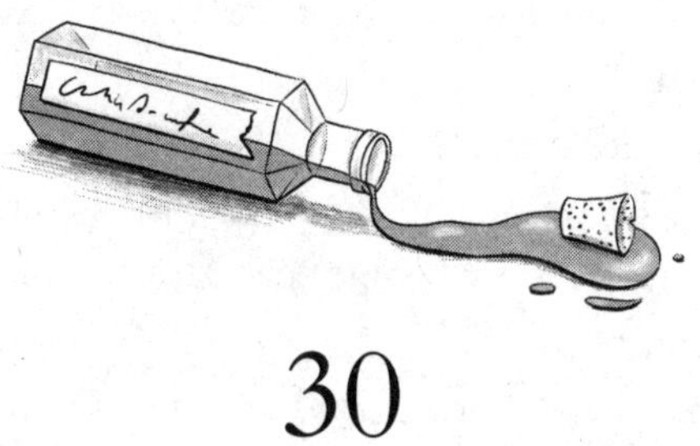

30

The panicking hadn't started right away.

Little Clem had already been at Oak Vale for a few months, eating endless bowls of lumpy stew and watching Rosie at work with her patients, when it happened for the first time. There had been a fight in the village, some visiting trader trying to rip somebody off, and almost everybody had come out of their houses to weigh in. It had turned into a cacophony of shouting and tussling, the front door rattling in the frame, so much noise so close that Clem had fallen to her knees, pressed her hands to her ears, and begged Rosie to make it stop.

Luckily, Oak Vale was a quiet corner of the wood, and it wasn't often that something got under Clem's skin by day—but after dark, there were the nightmares. They were near constant for that first year, leaving her red-eyed and dull every morning, and even as they ebbed, sleep continued to be a problem. She'd told herself that she'd grow out of it eventually, but almost a decade later, she found that stretch between laying down her head and finally succumbing to exhaustion to be the worst part of her day. She'd stopped bothering to tell Rosie about it, even though the old healer had been the one to give her warm milk and sit with her until she fell asleep again, back when she'd been small.

Sleeping among the Merry Men had felt easier. Their days were so hard that she barely had time to think about drifting off before it overtook her. Besides, somebody was always keeping watch.

The panicking, however, had only been getting worse.

Now, in the aftermath of the King's Houses, Clem sat safe in the clutch of the wood still drenched in sweat, feeling hollow right down to her roots.

The Merry Men who'd been waiting outside the castle had leaped into action to get them out of that ditch—archers covering them, Men dropping ropes and climbing down to fetch them, a perimeter around them to keep the guards away when they reached the trees. Then they'd all been hustled away, pulled up onto horseback and spirited into the wood.

Clem's mind had still been in free fall. When they finally came to a stop, she'd simply sat down where she'd been left and stayed there, her chest feeling like it was cleaving apart, even though she knew that, medically speaking, there wasn't much wrong with her.

Footsteps approached. Clem watched a tiny, iridescent beetle climb up and over the indent of her own footprint in the soil, and then keep going on its merry way. She was expecting Mariel, or Jack Hartley, or some anonymous jailer come to tie her up again for her crimes. She couldn't bring herself to care.

"Clem?"

It was Josey. She had a head wound, the blood still wet on her brow. She sat down next to Clem in the dirt and then stayed there, silent, a calming and solid presence, as Clem's breathing finally started to slow.

"Your head," Clem said eventually, when it stopped feeling like the ground had a heartbeat. She fumbled in her pocket, looking for her supplies, wondering if she'd left them on the floor next to Harry Hassan. "Let me—"

"Stop." Josey put an arm around Clem and pulled her close, squeezing with all her considerable strength, and then released her.

"It's my fault," Clem said, feeling hot tears spill over as the truth of it overwhelmed her. "If I hadn't—"

"Don't. There's going to be a lot of that," said Josey, her voice tight. "I think everybody's going to want to claim this one's their fault. Maybe we all made some mistakes. I could have been faster. We could have been smarter. I don't know. But we've got enough to cry about without playing the blame game. Why add to the list?"

Clem leaned against Josey, giving her all of her weight. Josey patted her on the arm.

"You should really let me look at that wound," Clem said thickly. "You're still bleeding."

Josey shrugged. "It'll stop when it stops." A single tear dripped down her cheek, and Clem knew she was right.

When Kit approached, he looked distraught. Clem wondered, very briefly, if he might be feeling somewhat less forgiving than Josey. But instead he knelt in front of Clem to check her over with unsteady hands, gently investigating where the blood was thickest. She had a gash on her arm and bruised ribs—she could feel them every time she tried to breathe—but otherwise, she was physically whole.

"I'm sorry," she said. Kit had been crying the entire time he'd been looking her over without any fuss or fanfare, not even bothering to wipe the tears away, as if he'd realized they weren't going to slow down anytime soon and that he'd have to get on with things regardless.

"I know," he said. "Me too."

Josey was looking at her oddly. "You sure you're not bleeding out in secret? You're shaking."

"I'm fine," Clem said automatically, trying to smile, and then she paused and shook her head. "Actually, I had a . . . I panicked. It happens sometimes. My brain stops working. It doesn't even make sense, but it's . . . it's like I'm not safe, even if I know I am. Although obviously this time . . . the reaction was . . . appropriate."

Kit nodded. "My father has those. He saw his brother die."

Clem stared at him.

Her entire life, she hadn't been able to make sense of this, and—just like that, she wasn't the only one. Her mind was not uniquely, monstrously broken. In all the time she'd spent trying to unlock the secrets of the body, she'd never found anyone with a complaint quite like hers. But now, a gift: *My father has those.* Like he'd been talking about nearsightedness or double-jointed elbows.

Her researcher's mind perked up a little, muffled as it was by the circumstances. Kit's father had seen his brother die. A shock. A loss. It all lined up. It made sense.

It didn't solve anything. But it was a door cracked open, letting some light in.

"Where's Morgan?" Josey said sharply, and Clem looked up, searching the gathered crowds.

Kit grimaced. "Debriefing."

"With who?"

"Commander Hartley and Captain Hartley-Hood."

"No. *Now?*"

"I told Mariel to be quick," Kit said, with more than a little danger in his tone. "Or I'd come back and drag Morgan out of there myself."

When Morgan didn't come back, not even when Jack Hartley had been spotted striding off to talk to somebody else, they had to launch a small search party.

It wasn't that hard to find them in the end. They just had to follow the sound of crying, until they found Morgan alone, sitting on a tree stump a short distance from everybody else.

Kit went to them immediately, arms open, and Clem almost expected Morgan to push him away—but instead they folded into his embrace, sobbing painfully into his shirt.

Clem didn't see any point in stopping her own tears from falling. She couldn't pretend to know how much it hurt the others, having only known Baxter so briefly, but even so—it was as urgent and disarming as a stab wound. She felt lucky that for her it was a clean, uncomplicated sadness; she had met somebody great, and now they were gone.

"Let Clem look at your leg," Kit said to Morgan in a low voice. "All right?"

Clem had already been eyeing up the leg in question. Morgan was holding it stiffly, like a dog trying to disguise a pricked paw.

"No," Morgan said, half choking on the word. "I don't want her to, I don't want to do anything. I don't want anything to happen now, I don't—"

"They hit the ground pretty hard," Kit said to Clem. "Twisted ankle, maybe. It doesn't seem too swollen."

"I can check it," Clem offered quietly. "I won't do anything to it. I'll just have a look."

"No," Morgan said again. The sound of their crying was almost unbearable, but Clem let herself feel it, like a blow to the sternum each time. "There's no *point.* Why are we doing any of this? I don't want to be here—I don't want to be *anywhere.* Why is everybody just standing around like . . . like . . ."

Kit closed his eyes, and fresh tears made tracks down his cheeks. He had blood on his chest, a dark bruise just visible under the neck of his shirt. Josey bent to offer Morgan a flask of something from her pocket, her movements slow, looking tired to her bones. All this love had made such a mess of them.

"It's sweet wine. For the shock."

"I don't want anything for the shock," Morgan shouted, making Clem jump. "I don't want to calm down, I want . . . It's *my fault.*"

At this, everybody went very still, listening to the sound of Morgan's labored, ragged breathing.

"It's not your fault," Kit said eventually, tightening his grip on Morgan. "What would make you say that?"

"I knew it wouldn't be okay," Morgan wept. "I was the only one who'd been inside that castle, and I should have said—I should have *told* her not to go."

"Morgan," Josey said. "That's not . . ."

"He always looks out for me," Morgan said. "Always. He's my friend. And I never should have let him—"

"Morgan, listen to me," Kit said quietly, sounding about a hundred years old. "It wasn't your fault. We all went along with the plan. We *all* could have said no, including Baxter. We went knowing it'd be dangerous, that we'd be in for a fight. He went . . ." Kit broke off to gather himself. "He knew what he was doing. He decided to come. And *he* decided to stay behind and guard that doorway to keep us safe. The last thing he'd want is for you, or for any of us, to feel guilty. You know that."

He was talking to Morgan, but his eyes flicked over to Clem. Clem blinked back at him in quiet thanks.

Morgan's heaving sobs subsided into gentle shudders, quiet little gasps of pain into Kit's neck.

"I can't believe this is real," they said eventually, their voice thick.

"I know," said Kit, giving Morgan the saddest smile Clem had ever seen and then wincing. "Oof. God. This is going to hurt like hell."

"Yeah," said Josey tearfully. "It is. So have a sip of wine. We're in it for the long haul."

31

Mariel's hand hurt.

It was silly, really. She'd had wounds far worse than this. She'd fallen heavily on her side when Baxter had cut the rope, from such a height that it was a miracle she was only bruised, the thick grasses at the bottom of the ditch saving her from worse breakage. She was still recovering from being gut-stabbed after all. But her hand was in constant use, and each time she so much as twitched a finger, it sent a bolt of pain lancing across her palm.

She found herself twitching her fingers on purpose as her father talked, letting it distract her from everything else that hurt.

". . . two dead, because you couldn't follow simple orders. You were sent back to camp, Captain, and you must have known it was *exactly* what I'd have told you to do under the circumstances. You should never have absconded in the first place. It's not for you to decide what to do about a mole in the ranks, or to launch your own ill-advised rescue attempts. In fact, if I didn't already have serious doubts about your abilities—what the hell was that healer doing running around the castle freely? She's your *captive*. She should be under guard at camp, working, until the time comes to send her home. You have shown a serious lack of judgment, and I have no choice but to . . ."

He had paused for a reason, it turned out, but it took Mariel too long to snap to attention, and her father seemed, if possible, even more disappointed. No, not disappointed—*withering.* Had he always been so gray at his temples, in his beard? It had grown out from just its usual goatee, and it made him look older. At least he was back in his blacks now, a cloak, a new pin—the others must have been taken as trophies, because he hadn't been wearing them at the King's Houses. Black had always made him look very powerful.

It wasn't exactly practical though, was it? The first tenet of the Merry Men: not to risk being seen, unless you meant to be. Or unless you thought you looked good in black, perhaps.

He'd stopped talking because he was holding out his hand expectantly. Mariel stared at his calloused palm for a long time before she realized what he was doing.

She unpinned the bronze oak leaf from her cloak and handed it over, feeling gutted down to her bones.

"You can tell the Scarlets how you lost their son, Mariel, and that is your last duty as captain. After that . . . you need to think seriously about whether this is the right path for you, because you'll have to earn it back, and it won't be easy. Nothing I've seen so far has given me any faith in you as a leader, and I'll be damned if people think I'm going to be soft on you because we're blood."

He was right about everything. She'd lost Baxter and Harry. She'd been single-minded and pigheaded and so desperate to prove her father wrong that she'd achieved the exact opposite, and done something unforgivable into the bargain. How was she going to tell the Scarlets? How could she ever look the members of her company in the eye? At least she didn't have to be their captain anymore. They'd probably never speak to her again, and Mariel couldn't blame them.

Her father had stopped shouting at her, and in the ringing silence, all she could think was *Baxter, Baxter, Baxter*—Baxter insisting she come to build dens with him when her parents were arguing, Baxter defending her when the other children called her snooty and weird, the long gap of early teenagerhood when they'd drifted apart, and the tentative, genuine smile on his face when, reunited, he'd been assigned to her captaincy. He'd said, "I'm right behind you," and then he hadn't been, and Mariel wished her father would scream and rage at her to drown out all the Baxter in her head. She clenched her hand into a fist and let the pain overwhelm her for a moment.

"I'm sorry," she said, her mouth feeling dry and cottony with grief. "I didn't know. I thought we could get you out. I had no idea—you didn't tell me you'd put Men inside the houses—"

"That was told to very few Men, in confidence. It was a safeguard, in case I ever needed it. I don't expect you to understand this, but Commander is a coveted position, and as recent events have demonstrated . . . you cannot be overgenerous with trust."

"You don't trust your own Men? You don't trust me?"

"Don't be a child," Jack said curtly, and Mariel took a shaky breath. "We'll discuss this later."

"Where are you going?" Mariel said, sounding just as childish as he thought her. Normally he'd have told her, or perhaps brought her with him.

"We're trying to fetch back the bodies," Jack said grimly. "I have to speak to Captain Flores."

The bodies. Three bodies. Two at the King's Houses and one at Sherwood House; Deputy Commander Payne had been the one held there, succumbing to his wounds, and now he was dead.

Richard Flores, whose nose had still been satisfyingly black and purple, had been the one to haul Mariel out of that ditch, although he'd done it with wordless reluctance; he was being promoted to fill Payne's place, and Mariel felt sick about it.

She took a risk, with the little time and grace she had left.

"When my grandfather stepped down," she said, making him pause, "when did you know that you'd become Commander? Before? Or after?"

Jack shook his head; his eyes narrowed in confusion, as if he had no idea why this could be of interest.

"Before," he said shortly.

"Because he asked you to take his place? Because people had . . . voted for you?"

"Because the Merry Men needed a leader, Mariel, and I stepped up," her father said, with a hint of disbelief. "You *know* this. You've always known this."

"I . . . wasn't sure," Mariel said. "I couldn't remember."

"Sometimes, if you want things done right, you have to take matters into your own hands. The voice of many is not always the voice of reason. But not everybody has what it takes."

His meaning was clear. Mariel ducked her head and stayed silent as he walked away.

She wasn't sure how long she sat there before the voices in her head became too loud, and the numbness that had encased her broke open, bringing forth a hot spring of anger.

When she found Clem, the healer was sitting in a huddle with the rest of Mariel's company. *Ex*-company. Her inclusion hurt more than it should have. She was an outsider, a traitor—and they had put their arms around her, shared their grief with her, while Mariel weathered the responsibility and the consequences alone.

"You lied," she spat, unable to restrain herself. Clem flinched.

Morgan was squinting at Mariel through bloodshot eyes, openly hostile. Mariel had known that they weren't in any fit state to be grilled by her father about the inner workings of noble estates, but she hadn't said anything, and now Morgan had even more reasons to hate her.

"I didn't lie," Clem said. She looked . . . gray. Drained. At least she wasn't trying to crack jokes. Mariel would have drawn her sword, just then, if Clem had tried to be funny about any of this. "I told you that very first day. I said that it was me. I said it was our business who we treated, and I meant it."

"He's the *Sheriff's son.*"

"Well, I didn't know that," Clem said, infuriatingly calm.

"You called him *Fred*!"

"That's just what I call him. I knew he was wealthy and had connections to the Sheriff. I didn't ask for his last name. I didn't even know the Sheriff had a son, specifically. I've been meeting him in his outbuildings mostly, I thought he might be some minor—"

"You've been to the Sheriff's *house*?" Mariel hissed. "And you didn't think that was worth mentioning?"

Josey cleared her throat. Mariel ignored her.

"If we'd gone to Sherwood House, I'd have mentioned it," said Clem. "But we didn't. So I didn't."

"He's the Sheriff's son!"

"He's not to blame for who his father is."

"You betrayed the wood! Aren't you ashamed of yourself?"

Clem let out a humorless huff of laughter. "Ashamed of myself? No. He was injured, so I treated him. Someone in the household had heard about me, and they sent for me specifically. I was testing my salve on him. Seeing if I could keep the wound clean enough to stay free of inflammation. He paid well, and I intend to set Rosie up with enough coin to keep her going when she can't heal anymore."

"But you know who they are," said Mariel, feeling dizzy with horror in the face of all this placidity. "You know exactly what they think of people like you, and you helped him anyway."

"I do know who they are," Clem said. She took a deep, steadying breath. "Look, I need to say something, and I need you to stop trying to kill me with your eyes while I do it. It won't make you forgive me, but I don't expect you're going to do that anyway."

Mariel wanted to tell her to shut up, but Kit had put a comforting hand on Clem's arm and shot Mariel a warning glare, and that was upsetting enough for the rebuke to die on her tongue.

"When I was nine," Clem said slowly, "my parents got whitecap fever. We didn't have a healer in our village, but I knew where I could find one, and I thought they could be saved. It's not contagious if you're careful and you keep your distance, if you wash everything and don't share things like food, but . . . it *can* get into food. Even contaminate crops, if you work with them. We lived near one of the big houses, a guy called Lord Whitworth's estate, and my parents grew fruit for them. When the Sheriff's men got word that they were sick, they didn't listen to reason. They didn't care that there was a healer coming, and that we'd been careful, and that nothing had come in or out of that house without being checked. They barred the door and they burned it, with my parents inside." Morgan made a small sound, and Clem winced. "That's what I found when I came back. I can't even—I don't know how to explain it, but—they set my entire life on fire. I tried to get the doors open, but I couldn't, because it was too late, and the roof collapsed, and I was nine, and . . . what I'm trying to say is, I have just as much reason to want to hurt the Sheriff's men as anyone. But Rosie taught me that when people come to her door, they're just patients. It's not up to us to judge who lives or dies, just as it shouldn't have been up to the Sheriff. Somebody came to me in need of a healer, and I helped him. That's what I do. I don't have Merry Men and oak pins and tattoos and secret bird calls. That's my creed."

There was quiet, before Josey spoke. "I forgive you."

Mariel's mouth fell open. It took her a second to remember how to speak.

"She helped *Frederic de Rainault*—"

"Yeah, and I hate the guy. He's a twat. But I don't hate Clem. And I get it. That's how she does her business, this is how we do ours. Although—I have to be honest, Mariel, I'm not entirely sure we've been doing good business lately. Something's . . . missing. I don't know. Maybe it's us. Maybe we've lost our way."

It was sort of like being stabbed again. Especially when Kit nodded.

"I'm here to help people," he said firmly. Mariel couldn't meet his eye. "That's why I joined. I have a family outside the Merry Men, and I love them, and I came here anyway because I thought this was where I could make a difference. My parents came from Nihon when they were children with early trade envoys, and they stayed in London where the work is. I see them, maybe . . . once a year now? Twice? My little sister was a baby when I left, and now she can say everybody's names but mine because she doesn't really know who I am. I know I'm lucky to have somewhere else to go, food on the table, a family who welcome me home as their son—I know that's not the case for everyone. But I don't want to fight for *territory* anymore, to move lines around on a map while people starve. That's not why I'm here, and it's not what Baxter . . . I know he felt the same."

Mariel wanted to throw this back in his face—say, *What would you know, we're practically blood, I knew him first, I knew him longest*—but what good would that do now?

"I want to make the Sheriff's men pay," said Morgan. "And I don't really care how we do it. But . . . I forgive Clem, and . . . and I forgive you."

Mariel didn't want to be forgiven, and she didn't want to be lumped in with Clem, and she didn't want to be standing here having this conversation anymore. She'd tried going her own way, following in Robin's footsteps, she'd dared to question how her father had always done things, and this is where it had left her—Baxter dead, and Mariel abandoned by her own company, who'd rather take a traitor's side over hers. She'd made the wrong choices, and trusted the wrong people. She was completely adrift.

Winning her father back was all that mattered now. She'd prove to him that she could keep her head down, follow orders. It was the only path forward that made any sense.

She knew what she had to do.

"I'm taking you back into custody," she said to Clem. The reaction from the others was immediate, but Mariel couldn't care about that now. "You are still Commander Hartley's captive until he decides to release you. You will go where you're told and work as a healer where you're needed."

"Mariel," said Kit. "*No.*"

Clem got unsteadily to her feet, but she didn't run. She just nodded, resigned. Morgan was crying. Mariel wasn't looking.

"You can take it up with my father," Mariel said to Kit, still not able to look at him. "I'm not your captain anymore."

32

It wasn't as if Clem had *wanted* to do something nice for someone like Frederic de Rainault.

She knew exactly what Mariel was thinking, because she'd thought it herself: screw the Sheriff, and the Sheriff's men, and anybody the least bit associated with them. When she was first called to Sherwood House, she'd thought about how badly set bones never properly healed, sometimes putting people out of action forever. She'd thought about how easy it would be to sit back, do nothing and let rot unfold. She'd thought of slow poisons, administered gently over time, until the body ground to a halt looking like it had finally fallen prey to an illness that couldn't be beaten.

But she'd watched Old Rosie treat the angry, podagra-ridden man from the next village who swore at her for being too slow and paid a pittance, and the children who threw stones at the house and called her *witch*, and she had understood that it didn't matter to Rosie who these people were or what they did when they weren't coming to her hut for aid. Rosie had sworn an oath, never spoken aloud and witnessed by nobody but herself, to help anybody in need. Clem had inherited that oath without really noticing it had taken hold, cleaning the hunting wounds of the sobbing, vomiting boy who'd called her ugly when she was twelve, and then helping to wash and bury him when they proved too deep to close.

Every time she helped someone, she imagined the approving nods of her parents, their hands steadying her whenever she faltered. She couldn't change what had happened, no matter how many times she'd imagined herself returning to the house earlier—being stronger, better, smarter—but she could try to make up for it, to save enough lives to try to tip the balance, to make them proud.

She'd had to steel herself and stay almost completely mute every time she treated the boy she now knew was Frederic de Rainault, with rings on his fingers that could have fed her village for a year, but she'd seen other things too—how eager he was to make polite, stilted conversation with her, sounding like a knight in a poem, and how his gaze always shifted to the door as she treated him, as if he were expecting somebody else to check on him and always being left disappointed—and it had dampened the flames of her anger into something manageable.

She didn't hold out much hope that Mariel would be able or willing to do the same. She seemed completely lost to them. Just as she'd been that first day. Stiff; remote. Trying desperately hard to reach for something that was always being snatched away from her. Clem couldn't even really feel angry. It was all just too sad.

She had been handed over into the custody of some anonymous Men who didn't bother introducing themselves, and then put on the back of another cart—which almost felt soothing in its familiarity—as they relocated. Once they'd arrived at their new camp, she had been left in a small tent next to Commander Hartley's, tied to a stake and blindfolded once more, with nothing for company but the sounds of people murmuring on the other side of the canvas.

She slept somehow, and woke up aching at dawn to the sight of Josey removing her blindfold with disgust, looking ashen and exhausted.

"They got him back."

"Baxter?" Clem said, feeling very awake very fast.

"Yeah. And his family are here. So we're going say goodbye now."

"And I'm allowed to—?"

Josey put up a hand to stop her. "Nobody said anything about allowed. But nobody said anything about *not* being allowed either, and Morgan was about ready to start punching."

"Noted," said Clem. Josey untied her from the pole, not pausing to let her stretch out her limbs and try to regain a bit of feeling in her legs, just leading her by the roped wrists out into the first tentative stirrings of dawn.

The birds were singing a wild chorus, a discordant little choir accompanying them from every branch as they walked through the deserted camp. Clem smelled the fire long before she saw it, her throat tightening as it always did, but this time no matter how hard she tried to breathe evenly she couldn't loosen that thrumming panic in her chest.

It was impossible to tell herself that the smell of smoke didn't mean there was disaster on the horizon, because this time it had already happened. This was the aftermath; the wreckage that had been left behind.

They eventually reached a clearing packed with people. Barely anybody looked at Clem as Josey moved them through the crowd. They were all looking at the pyre that had been built carefully in the middle. Clem could see a short, stout, blond man and a much taller, mousy-haired woman of around forty standing by, their mouths tight and backs bent with grief. Baxter's parents. Mariel was there with her father, Jack dressed in his black cloak and glossy pin, Mariel like his shadow behind him.

Baxter was already on the pyre, wrapped in his own cloak, almost entirely obscured by bright heaps of blossoms. Somebody had washed him and put flowers in his hair. Somebody had baked fresh bread, scored with intricate webs of leaves and dotted with herbs, and left it within reach. As Clem watched, Kit stepped forward with fistfuls of white wood anemones, waxy wild roses and daisies; her breath caught painfully as he leaned down to say something in Baxter's ear and then pressed the flowers into his folded hands.

Josey finally pulled them to a stop at the front of the crowd. Clem didn't realize who they were standing next to until Kit walked back toward them and was greeted by Morgan, who stepped forward, slipped their hand into his and gave it a fierce squeeze, face glittering with tears.

Clem didn't want to look at Baxter, beautiful as he was, wreathed in love and flowers; she looked at Mariel instead, and that was almost as hard. She had braided her hair severely back from her face, leaving her nowhere to hide, and she was rising to this occasion magnificently, somber and military in her bearing. Clem was sure her father would be—well, not *proud*, but not openly disappointed. A little win for Mariel on the worst of days.

Clem wished she didn't still want to touch her. To comfort her. But it was impossible to look at her like this and not want to offer her an arm, knowing that nobody else would.

A man stepped forward, holding a burning torch. He offered it to Baxter's parents; Baxter's father looked as if he were about to reach for it but then faltered, shaking his head, so his mother took it instead with devastating resolve.

Jack Hartley raised a cupped hand to his mouth and Clem tensed, waiting for some speech full of platitudes, an obligation rather than an act of love, but instead he did something entirely unexpected: it was the bird call, the one Clem had heard the Merry Men use to signal to each other. It came from all around her, from Josey on her left and Morgan on her right, ringing out in shambolic harmony with the dawn chorus.

There was no answering call, but the birds in the trees kept on singing, and at the horizon the sky was turning a brilliant pink. Baxter's mother nodded, more to herself than to anybody else, and then stepped toward the pyre.

There was a sudden movement at Clem's side, and she realized that Kit had grabbed urgently at Morgan's wrist.

"I don't want them to . . ." he said, panicked.

Clem knew what he meant. She had seen it before many times in her line of work; how hard it was to say goodbye, that final time. She thought she understood. If she'd been able to hold on to her parents, she didn't know how she would have ever let them go.

The pyre was lit. The flames took hold. Kit turned away but didn't leave. Clem's eyes blurred with tears and, next to her, Morgan was sobbing again. It was unbearable, but they bore it, because there was no alternative.

Mariel had taken her place a respectful distance away with her father, hands clasped behind her back. The firelight illuminated the tear track on her cheek, the only one she had let fall.

"Come on," Josey said eventually, her voice croaky. It could have been minutes, or hours. "Let's go. You've got a date with a pole."

It wasn't funny, but she was crying when she said it, so Clem let it slide.

When somebody entered the tent a few hours later, Clem expected it to be Mariel. She was ready for round two—for Mariel to vent all her grief and her frustration in Clem's direction, for Mariel to cry or to very obviously be trying not to, perhaps even for her to pause in the middle of that mess and to actually *listen*—but when she looked up, she discovered that it wasn't Mariel at all.

"Right," said the stranger. "Up you get. Time to go."

33

After the funeral, Mariel couldn't bring herself to care about much of anything.

Telling the Scarlets had been worse than watching them say their goodbyes, but only just; Mariel had fought very hard to keep from crying on both occasions, and it was like something in her chest had calcified now, become solid and immoveable.

When Captain Flores told her to go and walk the perimeter on first patrol, clearly enjoying giving her orders, she didn't even have it in her to be annoyed. This was how it would be from now on: she would carry out directives to the letter, for however long it took, until her father believed in her again. He might not be perfect, but Mariel was clearly in no position to judge; he might have demoted her, but he was the only one who hadn't cast her aside completely. He believed she could earn back his trust. That had to count for something.

She checked the trees for their guard posts. She counted the Men. She walked long circles, her focus never faltering as she scanned the trees, on high alert for anything out of the ordinary. When a squirrel broke cover and dashed across the forest floor in front of her, her heartbeat spiked, and once her breathing had returned to normal she had to swallow the cannonball-sized lump in her throat before she could continue.

The next time the trees rustled, she had an arrow nocked in her bow and ready to fly. Kit walked toward her with his hands raised, and she was so blindsided that she didn't lower her arms for a good few seconds.

"Thank you for deciding not to shoot me, I guess," he said. There was a weird expression on his face. Mariel realized that he was trying to smile.

"What is this?" Mariel said, as Josey and Morgan also made themselves known.

"Intervention," said Josey. "And also a news bulletin."

"I don't need . . . I'm busy." Mariel tried to keep walking, but Morgan stubbornly blocked her path. "Don't interfere. I have a job to do."

"The thing is, we're very interfering by nature," said Josey. "And also, you'll want to hear this."

"They've taken Clem," said Kit.

"Taken her where?" Mariel said sharply, before she remembered she wasn't supposed to care anymore.

Josey's nose wrinkled. "Right, well, this is the thing. Your father's just left on a secret rescue mission. A secret rescue mission we definitely aren't supposed to know about, because Big John told us, and if Big John tells you something . . . it's definitely confidential. I admire that man."

"They've taken Clem as their healer," said Kit. "Well—as their *prisoner.* But it's dangerous. And I don't think she should be theirs for the taking."

"She is a prisoner," Mariel said automatically. "She's in my father's custody until such time as he decides to release her. This is nothing to do with any of us. Go back to camp."

"The Sheriff has your mother at Sherwood House," Morgan said in a rush. Both Kit and Josey looked at them disapprovingly, as if this were not how they had agreed this conversation would go.

Mariel had frozen. *Regan?* Why would the Sheriff bother with *Regan*? This wasn't some grand love story, a damsel in distress captured by the dastardly villain—Robin and Marian in their heyday, or even Robin and Will. Her father barely ever talked about her mother, unless it was to relay that Mariel was expected to receive a visit from her.

Except . . . Jack would never be able to let a slight like this slide. Ex-wife or not, it would be an utter humiliation for him and the Merry Men if they couldn't retrieve the mother of his child. It would look weak. The one thing her father couldn't abide.

"He's using her as bait," Mariel said slowly, and the others nodded in unison.

"Obviously," said Josey. "And I'm sure Commander Hartley knows it. But the Sheriff just suffered an enormous embarrassment, losing the leader of the Merry Men from right under his nose. He wants Jack back now. And he knows that the Commander would never back down from this fight."

Mariel could picture it all, as if it had already happened. Her father would be marching south already, with as many Men as he could muster. Perhaps they'd have a man on the inside, like they had at the King's Houses, but most likely it would be a show of force. Sherwood House wasn't a castle. It wasn't even properly fortified. He'd throw as many Men as he needed at it to get the job done, and the Sheriff would do the same, to no avail. After would come the funerals. Then all they would need to do was wait for the cycle to repeat itself.

That's just how it goes, she reminded herself. It was not for her to question why. Not with instincts as dangerous as hers.

"I've been told to stay here on patrol," Mariel said eventually, shouldering her bow and replacing the arrow in her quiver, "and that's what I plan to do. I'm staying here. Unless you've been told to go, I suggest you do the same."

Morgan shrugged. "They didn't invite us. We were thinking we might . . . do our own thing. Together."

"No, Parry. We're not a company anymore. I'm not your captain."

"Well, yeah, I guess. But you're still our *friend*," said Morgan.

This was perhaps the last thing Mariel had expected to come out of Morgan's mouth, and it stopped her in her tracks.

It didn't make sense. They all hated her, didn't they? She'd led them into danger instead of protecting them from it. Failed as their captain. They'd sided with the healer. Even Josey, whom she'd known since childhood.

Mariel didn't have friends. Being a captain had superseded everything else—she hadn't had *time* for friends, or the luxury to let her guard down, not when it might be used against her at a later date.

But now, this. In spite of everything. An extended hand. She didn't deserve it.

"Mariel," Josey said slowly. "Are you *crying*?"

Mariel wiped her eyes on the back of her cloaked arm. "No. I'm just . . . I'm tired. I think I'm really, really tired."

"Yeah," said Kit too kindly. "That'll be it."

Morgan was suddenly coming straight at her, and Mariel didn't have time to react—and then she was being *hugged*. By *Morgan*. And it was making her eyes leak and her chest feel like it was cracking open, revealing a terrifying well of feeling that would never be empty no matter how hard she tried to be rid of it.

When Morgan finally released her, Josey grabbed her by the shoulder, which was just as terrifying in a different way.

"Mariel," she said fiercely. "There's no right time to tell someone that their father is a dick, so here it is: your father is being a dick. You're a good soldier and a good captain. You've made some mistakes, but we all have. You're allowed. And you're at your best when you're following your gut, not when you're trying to impress Commander Hartley."

Kit threw his hands up in the air, like they'd also talked about how to broach *this* subject, and now everybody was deviating from the plan again.

"We're still your company," he said. "We still want to ride out with you, whether you're our captain or not. We aren't going anywhere."

"Well, hopefully we're going *somewhere*," said Morgan. "Or this has all been for nothing."

Josey let go of Mariel's shoulder. "We can't abandon

Clem to almost certain death. Nobody's going to be looking out for her in there, and you know she's useless with a weapon. No matter how you feel about Frederic de fucking Rainault, you know she was just keeping to her code, like you'd keep to yours. She's one of ours. So let's go and get her, yeah?"

Her father would never forgive her. Mariel knew that. But some part of her also knew, standing there in the dark of the wood encircled by her friends, that he'd decided she was unforgivable from the very beginning. She didn't know what her sin had been. Perhaps it was just enough to be Regan's daughter. But no matter how much she wanted it, that moment of perfect acceptance, of being drawn into the glow of the home fire with no fear of being cast out, had never come. Would never come.

These were the people who always found her at the end of the night, who'd come to her without her even having to ask, and thought she was worth coming back for, even when she'd fallen so far she couldn't see a way out.

Mariel looked around at them, their faces expectant and intent in the moonlight, and then nodded.

"Let's ride."

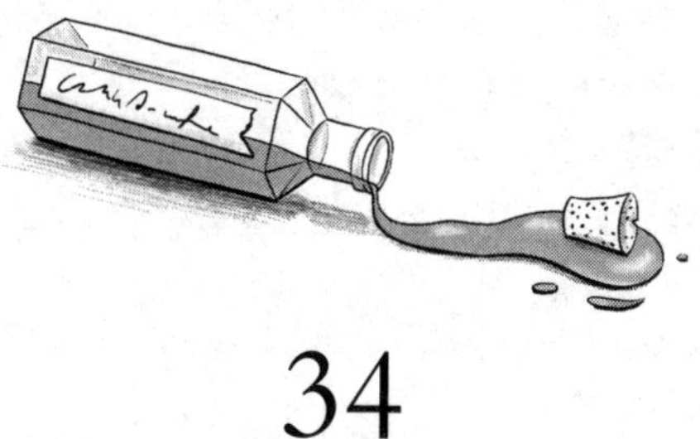

34

Clem was beginning to feel like being kidnapped was her natural state of being.

Granted, her previous captors had allowed her more liberties—freedom of movement, japes, even a little bit of kissing—than her current ones. These new faces were very serious; they didn't talk directly to her, and weren't particularly forthcoming when she asked questions of her own or tried to make small talk about the weather.

In all honesty, she was flagging slightly. Mariel had clearly informed her father that Clem had been inside Sherwood House, because one of Jack Hartley's men had questioned her relentlessly about it for two hours, after which Jack himself had come to repeat those questions with sinister cordiality; she had answered most of them to the best of her knowledge and kept a few pieces of information stubbornly close to her chest. Jack Hartley was very difficult to predict. She had actually half expected a little bit of violence, maybe some shouting for a treat, but when he reached the end of his questions he had simply given her a very penetrating look and left the tent.

It had felt like she'd got off lightly until it became clear that this was not her final destination. Blindfolded and restrained, she had found herself in the back of a cart again. She'd taken a nasty blow to the cheek while she was being loaded—she'd distinctly heard a muttered *Oops*, so hadn't taken it too personally—and was getting a pretty severe rope burn.

These new Merry Men didn't even seem to be playing the squirrel game.

Morale was low.

And that was before she realized where they were going.

"You're to stay close in case you're needed," said Captain Flores, when they stopped and she was relieved of her blindfold. "But *any* funny business, and I won't hesitate to put a knife in you."

"Who set your nose?" Clem asked conversationally. "I can break it again for you if you like, and put it back properly."

Captain Flores laughed hollowly. "Are you threatening me, healer?"

"Actually not. That's how you fix a nose. I'm being quite friendly."

Captain Flores touched his nose, obviously slightly confused. "Your hands will stay tied until you're needed."

"Great," Clem said, with a heavy sigh. "Just say when."

This did not bode well. She'd seen the aftermath of one of Commander Hartley's dramatic attacks. She'd visited the mass grave. She could only hope that she was deemed useful enough to be worth protecting, when push came to shove.

She was loaded onto the back of a stranger's horse, which felt very weird, and secured to the stranger, which felt not only weird but actually quite poor from a health-and-safety point of view.

Sherwood House was a very frilly structure, with a small gatehouse that looked more ornamental than anything, and some dramatic balconies, probably for the Sheriff to strut about on in his morning gown while he drank his breakfast wine and thought about all the peasants he'd step on that day.

It looked like a very fancy, slightly grubby cake, of the sort that Clem had never seen in real life, because nobody wasted time icing cakes in the greenwood.

It seemed that the only way in was through that gate, and Clem wasted a few minutes worrying about it before remembering that as a non-consensual participant in this heist, how they planned to get in wasn't any of her business.

She had wondered if they might be approaching by stealth; when the first explosion momentarily stopped her heart and almost sent the horse she was on fleeing for the trees, she realized the answer was decidedly not.

Incendiary projectiles. Just what she needed to make this day better.

When the horse set off in the right direction, all she could do was cling to the man in front of her and hope he was good at evasive maneuvers.

Inside the courtyard was hell. They succeeded in pushing through that far, and came to an abrupt stop against a wall of the Sheriff's men, who did not seem particularly enthusiastic about their plans to enter the house itself.

Everybody was yelling. They were in the middle of a seething mass of green, blue, scarlet, and steel. There was no room to turn the horse, and it immediately felt like a mistake to even have a horse within the walls; Clem heard the whistle of an arrow and ducked, and when she dared open her eyes, she realized that the man she was tied to had taken it through the chest. It had come so close to piercing her too that the point was pressed lovingly against her sternum.

"Oh shit," she said faintly, as his weight sagged against her. Was he alive? Was there any hope that she'd be able to get him out of here? Perhaps if she gave the horse a gentle kick, it might go running for the exit—but there was every chance that he might go toppling from the saddle, taking her with him.

No. She had to be sensible. What was it that Mariel was always sighing about? Her lack of self-preservation.

Clem spent precious seconds taking a breath and gradually releasing it, letting it slow her mind.

She had to save herself before she could save anybody else.

The rope that bound her to the man in front was within scratching distance of the arrowhead, and she muttered a genuine apology to him before she started using it to saw through her bindings. It only took a moment, even if she did such a poor job that it left a deep scratch across the inside of her wrist. It turned out that the threat of imminent stabbing did wonders for her time-management skills.

The horse was shying backward now, trying to move away from the worst of the fighting. Clem pulled herself free and dismounted clumsily, before it could decide to bolt, leaving the man draped over the saddle. Her hands were still tied to each other—now that she was on the ground, she wasn't sure what exactly to do about it.

Horse and arrowhead were already backing out of reach.

Clem was just frantically trying to map her exits when

something odd happened: a booming voice emanated from one of the balconies, and it was so surprising, everybody actually stopped to listen.

"Hartley!" the Sheriff of Nottingham shouted. "I have your wife. Lay down your weapons, and no harm shall come to her."

He was standing with his ornate sword pressed across the throat of a bound woman who must have been Mariel's mother. She was tall and pale like her daughter, her dark hair streaked with gray. It was loose right now, and she was wearing a scarlet gown, which made for a very dramatic effect; she was holding her head high, her hair lifting in the breeze, her eyes bright and steady.

The Sheriff was head to toe in midnight-black velvet, with so many silver buckles he must have jangled like a horse when he moved. He gave a little wave of his sword in a manner that he might have thought was threatening, but really just revealed his lack of expertise; it might as well have been a sharp baguette for all the damage he'd do if he tried to use it. Even *Clem* could hold a sword better than that.

The pause in the fighting only lasted as long as it took for heads to turn to see how this threat would be received. Then somebody fired an arrow directly at the Sheriff; he had to duck to avoid it and then he scrambled back inside out of danger, to shouts and jeers from the Merry Men, leaving his captive behind.

The fight was back on at once, but Clem was still staring at the woman up on that balcony.

It only took a second before she realized exactly where she'd seen Regan before.

35

Mariel enjoyed fighting. It was one of the few times she could turn her mind off completely and rely on the instinct of her muscles, letting them get on with things while thinking took a backseat. During her childhood, the Merry Men had trained to disarm or injure as first ports of call; anything fatal was a last resort. This was a hangover from the days when they did not spend half of their time engaged in open warfare, and as the years had gone by, the training had become deadlier.

Mariel had never warmed to it. Even if some of the other Men were a little more stab-happy these days, she avoided a body count if she could help it. Of course, sometimes she really *couldn't* help it, and the first few times she'd done it she had been left nauseated and reeling for days afterward. It got slightly easier, as most things did with repetition, but not so easy that she was ever in a hurry to do it again.

It was all right for Josey; she was so fast, so nimble, that anyone she came up against spent most of their time trying to work out where the hell she'd gone. She rarely needed to kill anybody. One moment they were upright, and the next they were unconscious.

Kit was a *marvel* to watch with his swords. He fought beautifully, with the kind of flourishes that would have got a lesser man killed. Morgan, on the other hand, fought like a goblin. It involved a lot of growling and stamping on feet.

Mariel had always tried to emulate her father. To stand her ground. Be solid, movements kept to a minimum, holding fast when her attackers might expect her to dodge. It had never quite worked for her in the way it did for Jack.

She tried to remember if he'd ever complimented her on her form, her hard work, all the hours she'd spent training, the way she mirrored his movements and gave them right back to him when they sparred. *No.* It had always been about what she hadn't done. What was next.

She was ready for this fight.

They had ridden hard and fast to get to Sherwood House, just half an hour behind the Commander and his Men, and as soon as they arrived, an archer tried to shoot her from a window—that was all it took to get her blood up and her mind focused, and then it was *on.*

The courtyard she entered on foot with the others by her side was already so packed full of tussling combatants that it was impossible to consider a next step before being thrown into it: engage, fight, disarm, incapacitate, turn around, and begin again. It was like dancing, if dancing involved punching people in the solar plexus with a fistful of sword hilt, which, based on Mariel's limited understanding, was relatively unusual. She could barely draw breath, let alone her bow. It was all blades and knuckles, and the hope that you would be fast enough with either to live another minute.

They had come in search of Clem, but it was next to impossible to spot one person in a sea of blades and heads, and blades connecting with heads. Mariel *did* see her father, struggling toward the steps that led to an upper balcony and finding himself the target of every soldier in the vicinity; when she followed his gaze, she realized what he was looking at.

Her mother. Tied to a pillar, with nowhere to hide, in a courtyard full of sharp weapons and ill intentions.

Regan might not have been a great mother, or even a good one—she might have disappeared at the first sign of trouble and left Mariel behind, giving up the Merry Men for a life of home comforts and soft beds—but Mariel wasn't going to let her die as a pawn in the hands of the Sheriff of Nottingham. She didn't deserve much, but certainly not that.

"I'm going to get Regan," Mariel shouted to Josey.

Josey, who was on the ground with her arm pressed to an unfortunate man's throat, nodded and jumped to her feet.

"We'll find— Wait, Mariel, look!"

She was looking over Mariel's shoulder; when Mariel turned, she saw that Clem was right there on the other side of the courtyard. She was injured, unarmed, and her hands were tied together.

Behind her, there was an open doorway that probably led to freedom.

But as soon as Clem locked eyes with Mariel, she started moving through the crowd toward her without looking back.

Mariel had kidnapped her—three times, if anybody was

counting—sent her away, shouted at her, handed her over to her father, and still she was pushing her way toward Mariel determinedly like she was trying to part the sea.

"Idiot," Mariel snarled. She threw herself bodily into the crowd and started fighting her way across, using her elbows, her sword, her knife in her off hand. A spray of blood splattered across her face, and she didn't stop to check if it was hers. Clem's mop of hair kept disappearing and reappearing from her sightline; every time it vanished, Mariel feared the worst—until she saw the tops of those ridiculous curls again.

When they finally met, Clem held out her hands and Mariel brought her knife down hard to sever the rope that was keeping them bound.

"We need to—"

"Mariel, I have to tell you—"

"*What?*" Mariel said, grabbing Clem by the shoulder and practically throwing her to the floor to avoid the flail of a sword. Clem's answer was delayed by the fact that the sword's owner turned and started trying to hack them both to pieces; Mariel hit back, but then the pain from the wounds on her wrist and palm flared into life and she fumbled her blade, allowing her opponent to press his advantage.

It happened so fast, it was like a nightmare: Mariel couldn't raise her arm high enough to push him away, and he managed to shove her off-balance, without enough time for her to repair her guard.

He raised his sword and then made a strange "*Oof!*" sound. When Mariel looked down, she realized that Clem was holding one of Mariel's knives, and that she'd driven the sharp end into the man's thigh.

He staggered backward and was swallowed by the crowd. Mariel's hand went to her boot, and came back empty.

"You stole my knife," she said. "You *stabbed* someone."

"Borrowed it," Clem grunted, as Mariel helped her to her feet. "You've got loads. And he'll be okay, unless somebody else finishes him off, which . . . isn't my business. I didn't hit any of the important bits."

"You need to go," Mariel said—but Clem was shaking her head.

"Mariel, your *mother*."

Somebody stepped between them, his armor askew, and Mariel took the opportunity to punch him right in the lungs.

"I know—I'm going to get her," Mariel managed to shoot back, over the shoulder of the man she'd just winded. When he fell, she stepped over him, back to Clem. She looked awful—dead-lipped and drained—and when Mariel touched her she sagged a little against her hand.

"No, you don't understand. When I came to the house—I didn't know, I wasn't . . ."

Mariel had to pull away to stop an overenthusiastic boy with a shortsword for an off hand from windmilling at them with both of his blades.

"*What?*" Mariel said, when she could. "Clem, just *go*."

"No, listen—I saw your mother."

"You saw my mother?" Mariel said, trying to make sense of this.

Clem took a shaky breath. "When I came here before, to

treat Fred . . . your mother was the one who'd requested my services. She was here. And this was *months* ago, Mariel, back in the spring. She wasn't a prisoner. She was ordering people about. I thought Frederic—de Rainault—was her *son*. Mariel, something's really wrong here. I think . . ."

Mariel couldn't hear her anymore, thanks to the ringing in her ears. She had turned to look up at her mother, the very picture of righteous, wronged innocence, still standing like the figurehead of a ship on the balcony, as the smell of blood filled the air.

36

Mariel needed answers, and she'd be damned if she was leaving this courtyard without them.

The one good thing about the fact that her father was currently under attack from just about everybody in the vicinity was that it made it a lot easier for Mariel to slip past the fray, around to the side of the building, where she risked sheathing her weapons so that she could grab on to the wall and climb. Clem had been with her, under the protection of Mariel's sword arm, for as long as it took to get them out of the thick of the fighting, but now, if she'd had the good sense to actually listen to Mariel's instruction, she'd gone to hide.

If the Sheriff hadn't insisted on a house with so many *frills*, Mariel wouldn't have been able to climb it at all, but as it was, there were plenty of handholds and footholds—even with her hand throbbing, she made it to the balcony before the first arrow was fired in her direction.

Her mother was still tied, not making any attempt to escape; when she saw that it was Mariel climbing over the balustrade to reach her, she had the gall to look *concerned*.

"Mariel," said Regan, once her daughter had removed the gag from her mouth. "What are you *doing* here?"

Not exactly the words one hoped to hear after scaling a building to rescue someone from the clutches of a velveteen madman.

"Where else would I be?" Mariel snarled, cutting her other bindings.

"I heard . . . I thought your father had relieved you of your duties—"

"You heard wrong," said Mariel, unsure how she'd heard at all. "We need to talk."

She used her sword to bar the only door, hoping that anyone inside was too preoccupied keeping intruders from the lower levels to think to check out here, and then yanked her mother behind the pillar, out of direct range of enemy fire.

"Are you the mole?" Mariel said, raising her voice to be heard over the sounds of battle, knowing she was more choked up than she had intended. Her mother's face fell. Mariel hadn't believed it was possible to be any *more* disappointed by her, but life had a way of surprising you like that.

"What do you mean?"

"The *mole*. Don't lie to me. I know you've been staying here at the house, I know you're not really a prisoner."

Mariel felt her heart pound three, four, five times before her mother answered, punctuated by the sound of arrows clattering against the balcony, too close for comfort.

"All right," she said, slowly, like she was calming a horse. "All right. Just promise me you'll actually listen." Mariel made a noise of derision. "I mean it, Mariel. This isn't going to be easy to hear, darling, but I think it's time you understood what's really been going on. Jack—your father—he's not a good man."

She paused, as if waiting for Mariel to argue with her. Mariel said nothing. "He didn't want to make the wood a better place, he just wanted to play at silly soldiers. We knew my dad planned to leave, and he saw it as an opportunity for change—and I knew we had to keep things the way Robin liked them. Simple. Easy. He didn't have Commanders and Captains, he just had a dream that inspired people, and a knack for getting himself out of trouble. Your father and I didn't see eye to eye, and . . . I never wanted to be a leader, but sometimes you're forced to step up—to *say* something. After my dad left, your father was headed down a bad path, and I wanted to cut him off before it got worse."

Mariel's entire childhood seemed to waver before her eyes, fragile and ready to collapse.

"He was convinced he needed to take command. We argued and argued until I was worn down to the bone, but there were people who agreed with me, and when I told him that—when I told him I was finished, and that I'd be calling a meeting, so that people could hear what I had to say and then decide for themselves who they wanted to lead—he didn't like that one bit. He gathered his little troops and sent me away. Exiled me. Said I'd wanted feather beds and silks, and that I'd turned my back on the wood. Announced himself leader, Commander, whatever it is he calls himself. Made it official. Eventually he told me I could visit on *his* terms, but he made it clear that we would always be supervised, and that if I caused any trouble . . . told you what he'd done . . . he'd tell you I was lying, and you'd believe him, and I wouldn't be welcome back at all."

Mariel had been ready to hear that her mother was a traitor; this she hadn't seen coming at all. She took a step back, unsteady on her feet, and then had to take another step forward again sharpish when somebody seized the opportunity to try to shoot her.

Regan tried to speak again. Mariel waved her away with the slightest lift of her hand, and then closed her eyes to breathe in and out, and try to quiet the roaring in her ears.

If this were true, and her mother hadn't left her . . . then Mariel's father was lying to her. Had been lying to her for a long time. Had stoked the fire of her resentment with things both said and unsaid. Had shaped Mariel in his own image, molded her into who he wanted her to be, and then somehow still found her wanting. She could have had a mother. An imperfect mother, yes—but still, Mariel remembered the way that Regan would always be the one to take her bow from her hands and insist that it was time to have some *fun* instead, and felt a stab of grief for her younger self, and for the person she might have been.

It was all too much. Because if her mother hadn't left her—had tried to come back to her, and been kept at arm's length—Mariel couldn't hate her for it anymore. After all these years, she didn't know how to stop.

"Let's just say that's true," she said slowly. "That doesn't answer my question, or explain what you're doing *here*."

Her mother sighed. Her eyes roved over Mariel's face. They were standing so close together in the cover of that pillar, it was almost familial. "Mariel—this is the part where I need you to have a little faith. What your father has been doing is wrong. He sends people all across the wood to fight these vanity battles, because he wants to make a name for *himself*, to be the man who won back the wood—he's forgotten what the Merry Men are *for.* I know that we can be great again, but not under him."

"We?" Mariel repeated.

"Yes. I spent a long time very angry, and then eventually I thought I'd better do something about it. So at the beginning of this year . . . I paid a visit to the de Rainaults."

Mariel's eyes narrowed. Regan made a fluttery little motion with her hand, like she was trying to cool the flames of her daughter's anger. "I know, I know—a means to an end. He has men, resources. I put on a little play for him. The spurned woman, the exiled mother, out for revenge . . . And you know what these people are like; he was all too willing to believe it. Sweetheart, you must understand—I just needed someone with the power to take your father out of the picture."

Mariel had always thought her to be a dreamy idealist, a whim-prone child who floated off after the latest idea humming a little song. Such cutthroat scheming from a woman who'd wandered the camp with flowers in her hair came as an enormous shock.

"You went to the Sheriff," Mariel said slowly, "so that you could launch an attack? On the Merry Men? On *us*?"

"I had a *plan*, Mariel, and we made an agreement. Nobody was going to get hurt. We'd just pop in, grab your father and his Deputy Commanders, and then ship them off somewhere far away where they wouldn't be a nuisance anymore."

She sounded like she wholeheartedly believed it could ever have been that simple. It was delusional.

"People *died* when he attacked that convoy."

"Yes," Regan said gravely. "I think Roland got a bit carried away."

"*Roland?*" Mariel said, voice thick with disgust. "A member of my company nearly died in that attack. We lost Baxter Scarlet getting my father back."

"I know," said Regan, sounding genuinely remorseful. "I know, and I'm sorry. But it was easy enough getting Big John out, wasn't it? I always liked him. He agreed with me at least half of the time. I put the idea of Hanham Hall in the Sheriff's head—they never quite mastered their security. Your father had to go, and that dreadful Deputy Commander Payne, who just parroted whatever Jack said—but John I wanted to keep. It would have eased the transition. Sometimes, for the greater good—"

"Was it for the greater good?" Mariel spat. "Or are you just as bad as each other? You think you're rescuing the wood, but maybe you're just tussling over it like spoiled children."

"Mariel, we don't know each other as well as we should. You can thank your father for that. But we can fix this. We just have to go back . . . back to when things were simple, and easy, and *fun*. We used to sing songs as we robbed people! Can you imagine! It's been dreadful for me staying here, living a lie, under the de Rainaults' roof . . . Good God, if my father could see me now! But I did it because I knew, in my heart, that I could make this right. Will you make it right with me?"

Mariel wanted to believe her. She wanted to come stumbling from the revelation that her father wasn't who he'd said he was right into the embrace of a loving mother who had a plan, who could take things from here, so that Mariel could lay her arms down and rest. It was so tempting just to say yes, to get her hopes up one more time.

But her mother had stood and watched the plumes of smoke from those funeral pyres after the ambush, knowing it was all her doing, and the callousness of it frightened her. Her flightiness, her idealistic nature—her father hadn't invented *those*, and they put Mariel on edge. She just didn't have it in her to believe that it could all really be okay.

"This was all a trap, yes?" she said, ignoring her mother's question. "You're not really a prisoner right now."

"Well, that's the thing," Regan said, her eyes darting about, genuine nerves peeking through. "I wasn't supposed to be. We were meant to be drawing your father out, and this seemed like the quickest way. But unfortunately . . . I think the Sheriff has rather changed his mind. Once he has Jack, I'm of no further use to him, and I believe he's decided to betray me. There might be honor among thieves, but my goodness—*lords* have never heard of the concept."

"So if I leave you here . . ."

Regan gave her a grim smile. "I'm afraid it'll be curtains for Mummy."

"Ugh," said Mariel. Regan really was committed to choosing the worst possible way to phrase *everything*. Below them, the violence seemed to be kicking up a notch.

Mariel had to act right now. "Look, I'm not saying I agree with you. But I'm also not going to leave you here to die."

A hint more apprehension. "You're going to deliver me to your father then?"

"No," Mariel said, the word coming out of her mouth before she realized she'd decided. "As shit as you've been . . . I can't stand behind him either. I'm just going to get you out. Don't do anything stupid on the way."

"Jack was always the stupid one," Regan said brightly. "Go on then. Lead the way."

They couldn't follow the Sheriff inside without risking being stabbed the second they walked through that door. On the ground, Mariel could see that there was a little pocket of safe passage; nobody had come around to the side of the house, and the fighting was keeping them all preoccupied in the main part of the courtyard, near the front entrance.

"We're going to have to climb."

To Regan's credit—and Mariel went out of her way *never* to give her mother more than she deserved—she immediately hiked up her ridiculous skirt, tied it in a knot, and followed Mariel over the edge of the balcony without hesitation.

They had made it to the ground, Mariel helping her mother with the last jump from a sill, when the Sheriff spoke.

"Regan Hood, you duplicitous wench."

He was standing not twenty feet away on the path that encircled the building, flanked by absurd topiaries, and he was holding a bow strung with an arrow that was barely staying nocked. Mariel would have laughed, but he was far too close. Even a child with a weapon was a danger to those within easy killing distance.

He barely even drew back—he just let the arrow fly.

It was going to hit her mother. Mariel could map its path, the impact that would take her mother from her the moment she'd managed to get her back, and there wasn't anything she could do to stop it.

Time stood still.

Then Clem came out of nowhere, arms wide, holding nothing but Mariel's knife, and took the arrow into her chest like an embrace.

37

Was it disingenuous of Clem to describe herself as a pacifist if the sight of Mariel running full-tilt toward the Sheriff of Nottingham in her defense was really doing it for her?

From where she lay on the ground, Clem could see that he had thrown down his bow and drawn his very un-serious sword instead. If it weren't for the two guards behind him backing him up as he advanced, he would have been as good as dead.

"Oh dear," Mariel's mother said, bending over Clem with a frown. "You're that healer, aren't you? The witchy one, with all the salves."

"Not a witch," Clem wheezed. The pain was so widespread in her abdomen that she couldn't tell where the arrow had entered, and she wasn't feeling quite brave enough to probe with her fingers. "Just a genius. People get the two . . . confused."

"And you've been shot," Regan said with a little tut, as if Clem were experiencing a mild inconvenience, like ants in her mutton. "That's a shame."

Clem was starting to feel a bit cold around the edges. Very not good. "Can you just . . . could you put pressure . . . just press your hands . . . don't touch the arrow."

"I'm afraid I've rather outstayed my welcome," Regan said. She was straightening up, glancing around. Clem would have grabbed her by the skirts, if she were capable of such a thing, and dragged her back to the ground where she could make herself useful. "It's not going quite as I'd planned. I do hope you feel better though."

With that, she left. Clem was left gaping up at where she'd been, now an empty frame full of mottled gray clouds.

She'd taken an *arrow* for that woman, and in return, she'd just . . . wandered off?

This really was the last straw. If she lived through this, no more doing other people favors. Probably. Maybe. She'd take weekends off, at least.

She urgently needed Mariel to come back, but from what she could see by craning her head—which was *not* a good idea at all, as it brought on the urgent need to vomit—Mariel was still otherwise engaged. In fact, she seemed to be getting farther away. Or maybe Clem's mind was starting to drift.

"Nope," she told herself firmly, trying to slow her breathing. "I'm here, I'm alive, I've just got a bit of arrow in me."

She knew that moving was a bad idea, but lying here right in the middle of the path so close to the courtyard didn't seem wise either. At an excruciatingly slow pace, she started shuffling toward the topiaries, careful to keep her abdomen as still as possible and experiencing gut-wrenching agony regardless.

"Okay," she told herself, on an out-breath. It helped if she imagined she was soothing a frightened child. She supposed she sort of was. "You're all right. Just breathe. I think maybe it's time to have a little look."

The little look was fruitful, in that she got a general idea of the problem, but also troubling, as she then had to turn to the side to throw up. Swings and roundabouts. She could do this.

She *might* have actually been very lucky. From the placement and angle, there was a good chance that the arrow had lodged in that tiny strip of real estate between lung and liver that was the ideal location for a penetrative wound. She wouldn't know for sure until somebody pulled it out—and then she'd probably know quite quickly, for better or worse.

"I need an apprentice," Clem said suddenly. It wasn't the best time to come to professional realizations, but these things happened when they happened. If it turned out that *she* was the only person who could save *herself* from this injury, she'd be very annoyed.

She couldn't even hear Mariel anymore. She did hear somebody approaching from the other side, and she used the very last of her strength to raise her head to have a look. Commander Jack Hartley was standing in front of her, looking down the side of the house where his daughter had last been seen, covered in quite a lot of blood.

He glanced at her, barely seeming to register who she was, and then he was gone.

Wonderful.

A pox on both of Mariel's miserable parents.

She tried a gentle exploratory probe with her fingertips, but they were shaking so much that it was impossible to be delicate, and even the slightest touch felt like lighting kindling in her chest. The pain was overwhelming now, obliterating all rational thoughts, until all she could think was *fire fire fire fire fire.*

She couldn't tell how long her eyes had been closed when somebody took her hand.

Was she dead? Had somebody come to take her to heaven?

She opened her eyes and saw Frederic de Rainault. So: okay. No.

She closed them again, but his hand didn't retreat, and when she squinted up at him, neither had he.

"Wha'th'hell," she said, in one blurred rasp.

"Mistress Clemence," he said, looking concerned. "You are hurt."

"Big arrow," Clem said. "In me."

"Yes. Indeed there is. Is there anything I might do to help?"

"Press on it," said Clem. "Don't touch it. Just some pressure. For the bleeding."

To his credit, he took off his gauntlets and did so.

"Are you . . . hiding?" Clem said, still trying to work out what Frederic de Rainault was doing tucked half behind a bush, pressing on her wound.

"No," he said. "Well. Yes. A little. You toiled hard over my knee, I know, but sometimes it still lets me down."

"Sorry," said Clem.

"Not at all. I was very grateful to you. Who . . . shot you, good lady, if you don't mind my asking?"

"Your dad," said Clem, wincing as it made his fingers jump on her side.

"My father? Shot *you*? A healer? Were you trying to do him harm?"

"No," said Clem. "Wasn't personal. He was trying to shoot Regan."

"*Regan?*" said Frederic, looking even more horrified. "But she was always so kind to me." It would have been funny if Clem weren't possibly bleeding out. It seemed to be news to this young man that his father was considered, without much contest, the main villain of the wood.

"He's not very nice, Fred," Clem said faintly. "Has it ever occurred to you that . . . you might be the bad guys?" Frederic looked uncomfortable and then sympathetic.

"I think you're confused," he said kindly, and Clem laughed. It hurt. A lot. It occurred to her to be frightened, and suddenly it was all she was. She grasped for Frederic's arm and held it as tightly as she could without rupturing something.

"Don't leave me. I don't want to be here alone."

"All right," said Frederic. "I can tell you a story, if you like. About a noble knight, on a daring mission to rescue a fair maiden in—"

"No thank you," Clem said, closing her eyes. "If it's . . . all the same to you. I'd rather you didn't."

38

There was still a battle taking place around her, but all Mariel could see was the Sheriff.

At first, her only thought had been to keep him and his men away from Clem. All she'd had time to process was that the healer was still alive—sitting up slightly, even, plenty of light left in those pale brown eyes—and she was clinging to that image now, as if it would ensure that she was still exactly how Mariel had left her by the time she came back.

Unfortunately, while she was busy taking care of his guards, the Sheriff had run—and in her fury, Mariel had no choice but to chase him. When the fight had moved to the back of the house, they were no longer alone—she was surrounded by guards and Merry Men alike—but she kept her gaze pinned to the idiot in velvet.

He was easy to spot, because he didn't move like a fighter. He moved like a man who'd only ever aimed for haste so that he could get the best seat at dinner, or slap a serving boy for making eye contact. Fleeing was unfamiliar to him. He could temporarily vanish behind some of his men and put some distance between them, but that didn't mean that he was safe—Mariel was blazing a path through anyone in her way like a righteous comet.

She wasn't the only one trying to take a stab at him, but she was the only one pursuing him with single-minded purpose.

Everything else in her life might be a mess too thorny to hack her way out of, but this was simple. The Sheriff of Nottingham had to die.

Not just for what he'd done to Clem, or the Merry Men. Not just for giving the order to burn Clem's parents in their beds, and torch the village that couldn't pad his coffers. For every corner of the wood he'd touched and left tainted and rotten; for every family he'd bled dry and left to die without a second thought. For his smug carelessness, his extravagances at the cost of the people, the position of office he had abused so thoroughly to serve his own ends.

For wearing velvet to a battle. The list went on and on.

She wasn't paying attention to where she was going, only that it was in the Sheriff's direction, and Mariel found herself quite unexpectedly in a rose garden. It was absurd to be surrounded by pink blooms and butterflies and happy bees as she ran full sprint with death in her heart. Like a dream. Except that, in a dream, the Sheriff would always stay just out of reach. Here, she knew she could catch him. She *would* catch him. That was how this was going to end.

Somebody whistled, and Mariel realized with a spike of exhilaration that someone on her side was waiting just around the corner. All she had to do was force the Sheriff to turn, and then . . .

Morgan leaped out from behind the bush, and Mariel's heart sank.

It wasn't that they weren't capable of fighting. They were. But Mariel had been counting on the element of surprise, and the Sheriff was about twice their height, and his sword was already up when Morgan went barreling into him.

It was very brave of them to do so alone. Brave *and* stupid. But that was becoming something of a motto for Mariel's particular band of Merry Men.

They struggled on the ground, Morgan raising their sword to try to deal a killing blow, but the Sheriff knocked it from their hand and seized Morgan by the collar.

"*No*," said Mariel. She only realized that her knife had left her hand when she saw where it had landed.

It was buried deep in the Sheriff's neck. It was so plain, incongruous with the rest of his outfit, it looked a little ridiculous. He let go of Morgan, and Mariel came to a halt standing over him, her sword drawn.

He wasn't dead yet. He was bleeding plenty, but his eyes were still roving, looking for her face.

"What do you want?" he spluttered. "You can have it. We'll strike a deal. I—I'll call my men back, and we can come to an arrangement . . ."

"No arrangements," said Mariel, a strange calm settling over her like a heavy cloak. "No deals. You are a coward and a blight. You have caused nothing but death and misery for the citizens you were sworn to protect. You have committed crimes against the people of Sherwood in the belief that they could not touch you, so your reckoning would never come."

The Sheriff didn't even seem to be listening. He was probably still expecting that there'd be some last-minute loophole that could save him, if he just handed over enough gold. Mariel bent over, to ensure she had his full attention. "You were wrong. I am your reckoning."

It didn't feel good when she ran him through, but it didn't need to.

It just needed to be done.

When she found Frederic de Rainault crouched over Clem's body, she almost killed him at once—but he raised his hands, palms covered in blood, and Mariel realized that Clem was still alive. Gray, shaking, bleeding, yes—but alive.

"What the *hell* are you doing?"

"She didn't want to be alone," Frederic said. Mariel still felt like she was dreaming.

"Move," Mariel hissed. She kept her knife to his throat as she knelt by Clem's side. "Clem?"

"Still here," Clem said, through chattering teeth. "For now."

The fighting seemed to be waning. Morgan had gone to fetch the others—they arrived now in a filthy, bloody rush, and all stopped dead at the sight of the tableau before them.

Mariel straightened up with great effort and turned to the Sheriff's son.

"Your father did this," she said. "And now he's dead."

Frederic let slip a gasping breath, like it had been punched out of him. He squeezed his eyes shut and then opened them again, his gaze pinned to the tip of Mariel's blade. He was *right there*, without a weapon in his hand. It was everything she'd ever thought she wanted. They stared at each other. The only children of supposedly great men.

"I should probably kill you now," she said heavily. "Your line would be broken. No more de Rainaults to burn through the wood." He swallowed hard. "I don't forgive you for anything you've done, and I don't expect you'll forgive me. But we aren't the ones who really matter in all of this. And I want to do better by the people who do." Frederic's gaze wandered back to Clem, and Mariel let her knife press gently into the hollow of his throat. "*Tell me you understand.*"

"I—I understand," said Frederic.

"I am sparing your life right now to give you a chance to be something greater. You owe me a debt. If you break faith with me I will find you, and I will kill you. I won't hesitate for even a moment."

Frederic nodded, a tiny movement, wincing at the slide of the knife. A single drop of blood welled and trickled down his neck.

Despite herself, Mariel believed him. He lived by his own code after all. Even if it was a deluded one.

"Good," said Mariel. She removed her knife, watching Frederic's hand, Frederic's sword on the ground. He made no attempt to raise either.

The adrenaline that had been keeping her going was snuffed out like a candle.

"Everyone's pulling back," said Josey. "I heard them give the order. It's over."

"All right," Mariel said. With the absolute last ounce of her strength, she bent to pick up Clem; Josey had to support her as she straightened up, but once Mariel had her in her arms, she knew she wouldn't let her go.

"Oh wow," Clem said, in a very small voice, laced with pain. "In any other circumstances . . . this might be considered quite romantic."

"Don't talk," said Mariel. She looked to the others. "Cover me."

"On it," said Morgan. Mariel had no doubt about that either.

The courtyard was a mess. The only people who weren't on their way out were the ones too dead to think of it. Mariel clutched Clem to her chest and kept walking steadily toward the wood.

"Captain," somebody shouted from over by the gate. It took Mariel a second to realize that they were talking to her. Didn't they know she wasn't a captain anymore?

"Come, quickly. It's the Commander."

Three sets of hands received Clem and lifted her weight so that Mariel could run.

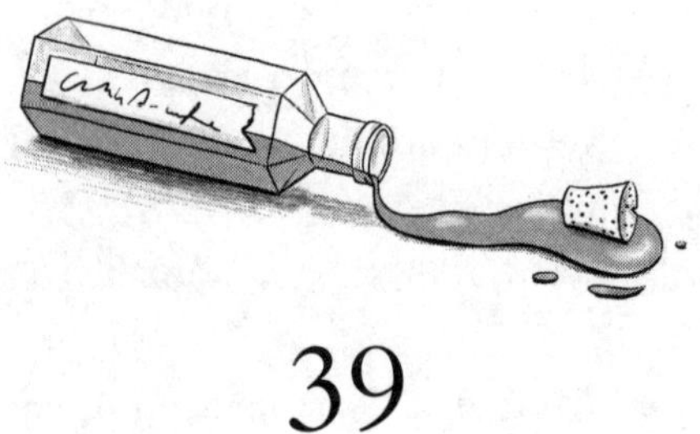

39

Jack Hartley had his own healer, and Clem knew this. He had a few of them, actually, each of them more into bloodletting than the last. No matter that he'd lost vast quantities of blood already—they'd spent the past day since the return from battle arguing about the fact that taking just a little bit more might realign his humors, heal all his ills, water his crops, et cetera.

"Stop," Josey said warningly when Clem tried to get up.

She had a point. Clem was not well. She'd barely felt up to offering pointers when one of the aforementioned healers had removed the arrow from her person; luckily they'd been too busy with more important injuries to try to steal any of *her* blood. If someone else had come to her with a gut wound like this, she'd have called them a fool and prescribed them at least a week's rest.

It was very hard to prescribe herself a week's rest though, because unlike everybody else in the world, she was very important and had a lot to get on with that didn't allow for wound healing.

"I can see you thinking you're just going to get up as soon as I'm not paying attention," Josey said. "And I'm telling you right now that if you do that, I am going to punch you right in your gut-hole."

"You wouldn't," Clem said, but she was pretty convinced. Josey just raised her eyebrows.

This camp was unlike any iteration Clem had ever seen before. It was more like a makeshift hospital without the monks, hammocks strung hastily between trees to give the wounded places to rest. It was almost impossible to stay lying down when she knew so many people needed her—it went against everything Clem believed in—but although she was fundamentally opposed to learning from her mistakes as a key facet of her personality, she had to admit that everybody had a point.

She couldn't help anyone like this. She'd just work herself back into her hammock and be even more useless for much longer. She had to put herself first, and then see to everybody else.

Although . . .

"Josey?" Clem said, trying to sound both winsome and pitiably sickly. "When he gets a second, could you tell Kit to send over a few people he trusts so I can talk to them? Good heads on their shoulders, not into leeches, that sort of thing."

Josey gave her a very hard look. "And if I do this," she said, "you won't move?"

"I won't move," Clem agreed. "I just want to give a . . . a brief crash course in basic healing, so Kit isn't the only one with sense out there patching people up."

"Fine," Josey said. "I'll tell him. Stay there and try not to have any more *ideas*."

"Couldn't even if I tried," said Clem, closing her eyes. "Thanks, Jose."

Somehow, she slept. She suspected that Kit might have added quite a lot of alcohol to the tincture he'd had her drink for the pain. She hadn't even checked what it was before knocking it back. If that wasn't trust, she didn't know what was.

When she awoke, Mariel was leaning against one of the trees Clem was strung between, her arms crossed, watching silently.

Clem meant to say hi, but she sat up slightly, and so it came out as "Ow."

"Stop," Mariel said immediately, pressing Clem gently back into a prone position. "Don't be an idiot."

"Like asking the sun not to shine," Clem said. Mariel didn't laugh. "How's your father?"

"Not good. He's in a lot of pain. I have a lot to talk to him about, but it didn't feel appropriate to pick a fight with a dying man."

"He's dying?"

"I don't know," Mariel said, pinching the bridge of her nose and then releasing it with a sigh. "The only person I'd trust to tell me for sure is . . . you."

Clem gave her a faint smile. Mariel couldn't return it.

"There were some . . . revelations," she said. "About Regan. And Jack."

Clem tried not to interrupt as she listened, although it was very difficult—there was a *lot* to be horrified about—and when Mariel had finished, they just looked at each other, Mariel tired and numb, Clem full to the brim with outrage on her behalf.

"Where is she?" she said. "Your mother, I mean?"

"Gone," Mariel said. "She ran. Maybe she realized that she was never going to get everybody on her side after this much death. Maybe it didn't play out how she imagined it in her dream journal. She so badly wanted me to know that she *hadn't* run away when I was a child, and then at the first opportunity . . ."

"Scarpered," said Clem. "Mariel, I'm so sorry."

"Unless things improve, I suppose I'll be fatherless soon too."

"You can't claim orphan benefits until you're actually an orphan, sorry."

Mariel pushed her hair back from her face and sighed. "It's strange—I'm so angry at him for so many reasons, but I really, really don't want him to die. He's done so many awful things, he's not the person I thought he was at all, but . . . I don't know. I don't think he should be leading the Merry Men, but I don't want him *gone*."

"I don't think that's strange," said Clem. "It's rarely . . . black and white, hero or villain. That would be far too easy. And he's your father. Love muddies the water."

"Yes," said Mariel. She was looking at Clem thoughtfully, too tired to mask it. "It does."

Somebody nearby let out a cry—a quiet, animal sound. Perhaps they were wounded, or just tired, or perhaps they were taking their first steps up what felt like an unassailable mountain of grief. Perhaps it was all of the above.

"I'm sorry," Mariel said suddenly. "I think I owe you . . . about a thousand apologies. For pushing you away. For not trusting you."

"For kidnappings one through three."

"Yes," said Mariel, suddenly a little tearful, although clearly trying to hide it. "For those too. I was so desperate to be right, but I suppose I just wanted my *father* to think I was right. And I couldn't make sense of you. You kept giving so much, and I couldn't understand why. I'm not accustomed to . . . generosity."

"I know. God, you're killing me standing there looking so sad—come here," Clem said, wincing as she shuffled over, trying to make room.

"Josey told me to shoot you on sight if you moved even an inch," said Mariel, but she hoisted herself up anyway, the makeshift bed forcing such an abundance of proximity that it was easy for Clem to put her arm around Mariel and pull her close. She wasn't sure Mariel would let her—if any of this was still allowed—but she didn't move away. They lay like that, just breathing, the hammock rocking them gently.

"I don't know what to do," Mariel said. Clem held her a little tighter. "I don't know how we start again. And I don't know how to do this without Baxter."

"I don't know either," Clem said honestly. "But you just will. It'll probably be really shit and hard. But . . . you've got a lot of people in your corner, so I hope that's something."

Mariel let out a shaky breath, pressed herself closer. "It's something."

Clem kissed her on the forehead, and when Mariel raised her tear-stained face to meet her, she cupped Mariel's jaw and kissed her gently on the mouth too. It was soft and wet and sad, but it was Mariel, so it didn't matter, and this time she wasn't sending Clem away. They pulled apart, Clem still holding her, Mariel looking at her with a gold-shot intensity that made Clem feel bright with purpose.

"I'm not sorry I killed him," Mariel said suddenly.

Clem understood. They had to see each other clearly. "I'm not sorry I helped Frederic," she said. "Even if he is a fop and an asshole."

Mariel nodded. She tucked her face into the crook of Clem's shoulder and let Clem stroke her hair as daylight dwindled around them. They stayed curled up around each other, saying everything and nothing, Clem almost drifting off with her hands and her head and her heart full of Mariel, until somebody cleared their throat nearby and startled her eyes open.

"Um," said a young man Clem had never seen before, flanked by more strangers. "Kit sent us? To . . . receive instruction?"

"What is this, Causey?" Mariel said flatly, not getting up.

"You'll have to excuse Hartley-Hood, she's had a long day," Clem said, easing herself up on to her elbows with a wince. "All right, are you good at memorizing things? If not, maybe go and beg someone who isn't bleeding for some parchment and a pen. Kit thinks you're all smart, capable geniuses, so don't let him down. You're going to be my *apprentices*. Ready? Right, let's start with sword wounds, that's as good a place as any . . ."

40

It wasn't hard, once the funerals were over, for Mariel to pitch *No More Mass Funerals* to the Merry Men as one of their new goals. Everybody was tired, stretched too thin—the camp was small enough that they had all lost someone recently, whether it was a close loved one or a passing fire-side acquaintance—and the grief piled up and slowed them all down. It helped to be in it together, but it also meant that life ground to a halt somewhat, everybody fully pre-occupied with the basic tasks required to keep people fed and watered and healing.

Mariel's father had started trying to dictate orders from his bed almost at the moment he'd been lucid, but to Mariel's overwhelming relief, people had been too tired to hear them. Word of how he and Regan had really parted had spread since the battle at Sherwood House—Morgan's fault, definitely, aided by a newly emboldened Big John—and while things were somewhat muddled by the (true) rumors that Regan had been working with the Sheriff, enough goodwill remained toward Robin Hood's daughter that people weren't so quick to jump to attention when Jack called for them.

Mariel hadn't gone to see him for a long time. Only when she was ready, and on her terms. There had been more important things to do. People to take care of. Richard Flores had died of his wounds after the battle at Sherwood House—Mariel was surprised to find herself sorry to hear it—and inexplicably, now that she was known as the girl who'd killed the Sheriff, people had started looking to her automatically during her father's absence. She had redirected them to Big John, who had broken his arm and sustained a nasty gouge to the forehead during the fight but was more than happy to take the reins. Despite her insistence that the decisions were his and his alone—that she trusted him, and would follow whatever orders he issued to her—he kept insisting on seeking out her counsel. It was very suspicious.

When she remarked on this to Clem, she just shrugged and said, "Well, you're very easy on the eyes—that's important, in a politician," which was no help at all.

Two weeks into this new, slower pace of life, her father requested her presence in his tent, and she went. She kept a fair amount of distance between them, standing by the door. She didn't owe him anything more.

"I can't fight," he said bluntly. "Damaged too much, this time. Your healer says I'll be fine, but I need to . . . accept my limitations."

Mariel could only imagine how that conversation might have gone.

"If I can't fight, I can't lead the Merry Men," he said, shocking Mariel back into the room.

"There's no requirement to—"

"I know that," he said tetchily, before taking a moment to compose himself. "I know, but that's not how we do it here. A leader shouldn't send people to do things he's not willing to do himself. That was one of Robin's tenets, and he was right."

"Okay," said Mariel. "So what are you saying?"

Jack sighed. He adjusted slightly in his seat, easing the weight off his left leg. "I'm saying . . . the Merry Men are yours. It's not what I would have chosen, but as you killed de Rainault, it makes the most sense. It's better you take control now, before somebody else tries to stake a claim—"

"No," Mariel said immediately. "That's not how this is going to go."

"What?" said Jack, frowning. "Mariel, listen to me. You have to strike while the—"

"No," Mariel said again. "No striking. I'm going to . . . to take some time to think about this, and then I'll get back to you."

Her father obviously had more to say, but Mariel was done listening. She left the tent and did a few laps of the camp. She sat down to eat with Clem, Kit, Josey, and Morgan, just listening to the gentle back-and-forth of their dinner talk, warming her hands above the flames and watching as, all around her, people did the same. Despite everything, they broke bread and laughed and sang together, ensconced in halos of gold from their fires. Mariel rested her head on Clem's shoulder, ignored Morgan's groan of protest, closed her eyes, and focused on the feeling of Clem tracing steady patterns into her arm. She'd invited Old Rosie to come and live with the Merry Men the week before, and they'd both laughed until it hurt when Clem had been handed her reply: *Looked for you, you cheeky whelp. Not like I have a bad knee or anything. No to the invite, thanks. Please send back my good paring knife.* Clem would be returning to Oak Vale soon, to her patients and to Rosie, with a plan to split her time and visit home as often as she liked. She wanted Mariel to come; Mariel wasn't sure she'd be welcome.

Clem had laughed when Mariel voiced this. "She can never stay mad at a pretty face. How'd you think I lived there for so long, messing with all her stuff, without her killing me?"

"I know what we should do," Mariel said now, in the soft darkness of their tent.

"Hmm?" Clem said blearily, lifting her head and blowing away a curl stuck to her mouth. She still moved too quickly for her wound, constantly forgetting it was there and then having to readjust. She was very terrible at taking her own advice. "I mean, I'm basically asleep, but . . . I could be convinced."

"No," Mariel said. "I mean—about the Merry Men."

"Oh," said Clem. "That's good. The other thing was better for me personally, but I'm not a monster . . . I can see the bigger picture."

Mariel kissed her just to stop her from talking and laughed when Clem pulled the blanket over them both, a mess of elbows and knees and sleepy indulgence.

When Mariel finally returned to her father, she took Big John with her too, and every captain she could find still living.

"We put it to a vote," she said. "That's the only way to do this. Anybody who wants to stand can get up and explain how they think things should be, and they decide."

Captain Hughes expressed long, boring arguments to the contrary, and her father sat silently and listened, worrying at his thumb with his teeth—a new habit, and one that seemed very unlike him—until he was finished, and then simply turned to Mariel and said, "Fine."

When the day of the vote finally came, Mariel awoke to hear some sort of disturbance taking place in camp. She reached for her sword, went outside to investigate, and discovered that Robin Hood and Will Scarlet had ridden into camp at dawn.

They were far older than they had been the last time Mariel had seen them—gray-haired and shrunken—and they looked tired too, as if they'd ridden hard for weeks on end. She watched as Baxter's father went to Will and embraced him, both of them crying, and saw Robin squinting through the crowd, searching for something.

She felt almost shy as she approached him, but he hugged her hard and then held her by the shoulders and said, "Tell me."

She did. They walked down to the stream and followed it for what must have been at least three miles, Mariel telling him haltingly of everything that had happened since he'd left for France.

"I'm sorry I wasn't here," he said eventually, when she'd tapered off into silence. He sighed, scrubbing a hand across his face. "Bloody hell. *Regan.* I only wish she'd written, but I suppose I can understand why she didn't commit *Hello, Father, I have decided to throw my lot in with the son of your sworn enemy* to parchment."

"Did you know?" Mariel said. "That my father had sent her away?"

"No," said Robin. "Your father and I never saw eye to eye. I'll be having words with him, and I won't be mincing them. But your mother is . . . She's very independent. Doesn't like to need people. There's not a chance in hell she'd have asked me back to fight her battles for her. Terrible at asking for help. I seem to remember you inherited a little of that."

Mariel winced. "I did. But I'm trying to do better."

"Good," said Robin, patting her on the shoulder. "That's all we *can* do. Fuck the fascists, and introspect."

That afternoon, a piece of parchment containing three names was pinned carefully to an ancient oak, and for hours people lined up to make their mark. It filled Mariel with some inexplicably immense emotion; she stood and watched from afar, listening to Morgan argue with Kit about the best way to mend a fletching, leaning back against Clem and letting her pretend to be the taller of the two of them for a while until her spine ached too much to carry on.

Robin cast the last vote, in the middle of the night. Mariel had expected people to drift away to bed, but there was a surprisingly big crowd gathered to watch him do it. It was *supposed* to be anonymous, but he winked at her on his way out, and Mariel rolled her eyes and tried to suppress a grin.

They announced the results the next day. The people voted in favor of dissolving official Merry Men territory. They voted against fighting for the sake of fighting. They voted for going back to their roots, to helping the community, albeit with a little more planning and order than had existed in Robin's day. They voted, overwhelmingly, for Mariel.

She had to give a speech of sorts, and it was awkward and stilted and couldn't have gone worse, but afterward, when everybody was feasting and talking, energized by the promise of change, she caught the eyes of her closest and most trusted companions and they sneaked away from the firelight and mounted their horses. They rode fast through the trees, laughing, chased by the first cold breeze that signaled the end of summer. When they slowed down to an amble, Mariel closed her eyes and allowed herself to imagine a future that existed wholeheartedly for the good of the wood, with her gently guiding the helm. It was absolutely petrifying. She couldn't wait.

"*Robin Hood* gave me his last potato tonight," Clem said, awestruck. Mariel opened her eyes so that she could give her a withering look.

"You're being extremely embarrassing," she said. "Just call him Robin."

"I can't call Robin Hood *Robin*," Clem said, sounding scandalized. "It'd be like calling Chaucer *Geoff*."

"Are *you* ever going to stop looking like you've been poisoned when people call you *Mariel*?" Morgan said, from one horse behind them. Mariel winced. She knew the last names had to go, along with the rank of captain, but it was one of her more painful concessions.

"The only name you should be concerning yourselves with is what we're going to be called instead of the *Merry Men*," said Mariel. "I expect everyone to present ideas to me by the end of the week."

Robin had been surprisingly vocal about getting rid of that one. Outdated, he said. Sort of ridiculous, when you thought about it.

"We shouldn't have a name," Josey said immediately. "It's passé."

"Not practical," said Mariel.

"The Woodspeople," Clem said in a rush, as if she'd been waiting hours for someone to ask her. "The Mighty Acorns. The Cloaked Crusaders."

Mariel looked at her. She had cut her hair shorter, curls on top and sheared on the sides—entirely practical, or so she'd claimed, but Mariel had caught her smirking at her reflection like a freckled Narcissus one too many times for that to be entirely plausible. The bird tattooed on Clem's arm was fresh, still a little red and raw, probably the best-cared-for tattoo in England after all the complaining she'd done during its application about the stupidity of willingly obtaining an open wound. She was currently grinning at Mariel, halfway to laughing at her own jokes.

The future was a lot less terrifying, somehow, as Mariel smiled back.

"Squirrel," Kit said quietly. "That's five-three to me."

"Damn it," Morgan grouched. There was a pause, and then they let out a long breath and said, with a spirited attempt at bravado, "I miss Baxter. He was so much worse at this game."

"Yeah," said Kit. "I know. Oh my God, look—*squirrel.* Six-three."

Morgan swore so loudly that birds exploded out of the trees. Clem laughed and leaned dangerously far out of her saddle to kiss Mariel, presumably aiming for her mouth and getting her chin instead.

They kept going until the moon rose above the tree line, and then without announcement or discussion, they all turned their horses in unison and headed back home to camp.

Acknowledgments

This book was the hardest I've ever written. It was wildly outside my comfort zone and easily had the most BPC (breakdowns per chapter) of my short career, but I set out to write the gay forest adventure of my childhood dreams and I hope it will encourage you to stomp out into the woods to touch a tree and/or make plans to overthrow the bourgeoisie.

A huge thank-you is owed to Chloe Seager, my tall and handsome agent, for championing me always and putting up with my deranged WhatsApp messages. Thank you also to Valentina Paulmichl, Maddy Belton, and the brilliant team at Madeleine Milburn.

Thank you to my editors, Hannah Sandford and Catherine Liney, and to Ellen Holgate, Beatrice Cross, Alesha Bonser, Fliss Stevens, Mike Young, Isi Tucker, Ben Schlanker, Nick de Somogyi, Jessica White, and everybody else at Bloomsbury who does such amazing work on my books. On the other side of the pond, thank you to Vicki Lame and the team at Wednesday: Vanessa Aguirre, Meghan Harrington, Kelly South, Rivka Holler, and everyone beavering away behind the scenes to make magic.

Thank you to Olga Grlic, Laura Bird, Nicole Deal, and Thy Bui for making my books look so delicious.

Thanks also to Photine for all the medical expertise I completely butchered, to Zoe for helping me come up with rhymes for "boobs," to Freya Marske and Hope Anna for invaluable feedback when I was freaking out, and to my other early readers: El, Hannah, Donna, Alice, Crystal, and Fox.

Thank you to my family, and to our beloved cat Maizie, who left us a few days before Christmas to remind us that she's the main character. Thank you Nick for pretty much everything, but especially for running up the road to buy me sandwiches.

I have been completely blown away by the support of booksellers, librarians, and readers, especially as I entered the world of YA. Thank you from the bottom of my heart for reading, recommending, and hand-selling my books, for showing up to events and signings, for preordering and sharing and making this job and life possible for me.

Thank you to Nana Sato-Rossberg, Professor of Translation Studies at SOAS University of London, for your generosity of knowledge. The name de Rainault was borrowed from Evelyn Charles Henry Vivian, and I used Andy Gaunt's 3-D reconstruction of the medieval romantic landscape of Clipstone to envisage the King's Houses. Thank you also to Toni Mount's *Medieval Medicine*, Mercian Archaeological Services, and the Sherwood Forest Archaeology Project.

***New York Times* bestseller and winner of the Books Are My Bag Readers Award for Young Adult Fiction**

"Exactly what I needed right now—a delightful, heart-warming, hilarious historical romp, overflowing with queer panic and terrible jokes. I loved it."
—**Alice Oseman**, bestselling author of *Heartstopper*

"A total rollicking delight . . . Lex Croucher is one of my favorite rom-com authors, and they should be yours too."
—**Casey McQuiston**, #1 *New York Times* bestselling author of *I Kissed Shara Wheeler* and *Red, White & Royal Blue*

Turn the page for a sneak peek . . .

His royal highness King Allmot of England hereby declares that the royal tournament at Camelot will commence on the first day of Whitsuntide.

(Please disregard dates announced in previous declarations. Construction will be completed by Whitsun.)

Knights of daring and valor who embody the chivalric spirit are encouraged to fight for their king in the lists, at archery, in single combat and the melee, until a victor is proclaimed on the nineteenth day of August.

Please bring your own swords, maces, and morning-stars, as none will be provided.

When Gwen woke up, she knew she'd had the dream again—and that she'd been *loud.* She knew she'd had the dream because she was feeling exhilarated, loose-limbed, and a little flushed in the face; she knew she'd been vocal about it because Agnes, the dark-haired lady-in-waiting who slept in the adjoining chamber, kept biting her lip to keep from laughing and wouldn't look her in the eye.

"Agnes," Gwen said, sitting up in bed and fixing her with a well-practiced and rather imperious look. "Don't you have water to fetch, or something?"

"Yes, your highness," said Agnes, giving a little curtsy and then rushing from the room. Gwen sighed as she stared up at the bed hangings, lush velvet heavy with embroidery. It was probably a mistake to send her away so soon—she was young and flighty, and would likely be off gossiping with anybody she encountered. At least Gwen's nocturnal exploits wouldn't stay top billing for long. Today was no ordinary day; tournament season was finally upon them. Any mortifying morsels Agnes slipped the other ladies-in-waiting would be forgotten in all the excitement by noon.

When Agnes came back with a pitcher of water Gwen

stepped out of bed, raised her arms above her head so that Agnes could remove the thin tunic she slept in, and then stood yawning and blinking in the early morning light as she was scrubbed and oiled to within an inch of her life. Agnes was just easing a new shift over Gwen's shoulders when the door was nudged open and a tall, pale, copper-haired young man walked in, his head buried in a stack of parchment.

"Have you seen this?" he said, not lifting his eyes from the page.

"Er. Gabriel," Gwen said, looking at him incredulously. "I'm not dressed."

"Aren't you?" Gabriel looked up and frowned at her briefly, as if she had removed her clothes just to inconvenience him. "Oh. Sorry."

"The Greeks wrote a lot of plays about this sort of thing," Gwen said, as Agnes rushed over with a dress to cover her, her fair skin flushing a delicate pink. Her blushes were probably less to do with the impropriety of the situation and more to do with the fact that almost every woman at court harbored a persistent crush on her brother. Many had tried to catch his eye, and so far, all had failed. He wasn't really one for talking at all, unless it was to Gwen. She had always held this as a point of pride.

"The Greeks wrote a lot of plays about putting on dresses?" he asked now, brow still furrowed, as Agnes yanked the dress inelegantly over Gwen's head.

"No," Gwen said, emerging with quite a lot of her hair stuck to her mouth. "You're missing the . . . Are you even listening to me? You walked into *my* room, you know." He turned over the piece of parchment he was reading to peruse the other side, not acknowledging that he'd heard a word. "Gabriel. *Gabe.* Can you hear something? The sound of a spectral voice upon the air? It almost sounds like I'm talking."

"Hang on, G," he said, raising a hand to indicate that he needed a moment. Gwen considered this, and decided he hadn't earned it. "*Ow.*"

Gwen had taken one of the brocade slippers Agnes had offered to her and thrown it at him with considerable force.

"Please arrive at the point with haste."

"Ah—fine," Gabriel said, still rubbing his head. "Father is having me look at the accounts with Lord Stafford—costs for the tournament season mostly, but I also saw *this* and I thought . . ." He trailed off, handing her the parchment so she could read it for herself.

Agnes started expertly weaving Gwen's long red hair into braids as Gwen's eyes skimmed quickly down the page, taking in an extensive list of assets. Chests full of silks and damask, an ancient jeweled dining set, endless porcelain vases; all marked to be leaving the crown's coffers in the coming months. Comprehension dawned as she reached the end of the page and the entry denoting the enormous Biblical tapestry of Ruth and Naomi that currently hung in her chambers.

"This is my dowry," she said slowly. "Gabe. My *dowry.*"

"I suppose it's that time already," Gabriel said, with a sympathetic grimace.

"Shit," said Gwen, sitting down heavily on the end of the bed.

"Shit," Gabriel agreed.

★

In theory, being betrothed since birth could have been a comfort to Gwen, especially as it was to somebody so close to her own age. It meant there would be no nasty surprises; no new political alliances to forge with elderly, ornery nobility through marriage. Better the devil she knew, et cetera.

Unfortunately, this was encapsulated far too literally in the man she had been sworn to marry. Arthur Delacey, heir to the title Lord of Maidvale, was—in Gwen's opinion—the devil incarnate.

They had met for the first time on the day she was born, barely more than a shrimp and already promised to him; he'd been two years old, shuffled into Camelot along with his parents and hundreds of other families courting favor with the crown. She could just picture Arthur's affronted little face, scowling down at her in her cradle, disappointed already. She had often wondered if her parents had considered committing wholly to the bit and calling her *Guinevere* to match him, but had chickened out just in time and chosen *Gwendoline* instead, the uncomfortable legacy of the former's extramarital affairs with roguish knights staying their hands.

Her first true memory was of Gabriel giving her a piece of warm, fragrant honey cake, sneaking it to her outside the kitchens before dinner to calm a tantrum.

Her second memory was of Arthur taking it from her. It had been sixteen years, and she was still angry about that honey cake.

Among other things.

He had pulled her hair at mass. Mocked her relentlessly at feasts. Tripped her in the courtyard in front of every petty lord and lady of the realm, and then stepped smugly over her as she lay sprawled on the cobblestones with a skinned knee. The first stirrings of summer meant that a visit from Arthur was nigh, and so she learned to dread brighter mornings and hawthorns in bloom. On her ninth birthday, she had tried to get ahead of him by setting a trap outside his chamber, enlisting Gabriel's help to stretch a thin length of twine across the doorway; he had stumbled spectacularly over it and broken his wrist in two places. The guards had apprehended him a week later trying to push a feral cat through her bedroom window one-handed.

That September, the queen had politely suggested that it might be best if they were separated for the time being. Gwen had been so happy when she heard the news that she had skipped around the castle all day, buoyed by the prospect of Arthur-free summers. Her skipping had ended abruptly that evening when she heard her father refer to Arthur as her "betrothed."

"Gabe," she had said, seeking him out in his favorite corner of the library. "What's a *betrothed*?"

"It's the person you're going to marry," Gabriel replied, looking up from his book.

"I was afraid of that," she said glumly. "Who's your betrothed?"

"I don't have one."

"That's not fair."

"No," Gabriel had sighed. "I don't suppose it is."

About the Author

© Hannah Croucher

Lex Croucher is the *New York Times* bestselling author of *Reputation, Infamous,* and the young adult novel *Gwen & Art Are Not in Love.* Lex grew up in Surrey reading a lot of books and making friends with strangers on the internet, and now lives in London.